Diamond Playgirls

Diamond Playgirls

Daaimah S. Poole

Miasha

Deja King

T. Styles

Conceived and Edited
by Karen E. Quinones Miller

KENSINGTON PUBLISHING CORP.

http://www.kensingtonbooks.com

DAFINA BOOKS are published by

Kensington Publishing Corp.
850 Third Avenue
New York, NY 10022

All Kensington titles, imprints and distributed lines are available at special quantity discounts for bulk purchases for sales promotion, premiums, fund-raising, educational or institutional use.

Special book excerpts or customized printings can also be created to fit specific needs. For details, write or phone the office of the Kensington Special Sales Manager: Kensington Publishing Corp., 850 Third Avenue, New York, NY 10022. Attn. Special Sales Department. Phone: 1-800-221-2647.

Dafina Books and the Dafina logo Reg. U.S. Pat. & TM Off.

ISBN-13: 978-0-7582-2356-2
ISBN-10: 0-7582-2356-0

First Kensington Trade Paperback Printing: January 2008
10 9 8 7 6 5 4 3 2 1

Printed in the United States of America

CONTENTS

DIOR EMERSON

by Miasha

January 3, 2008

"Here you are, miss."

"This is the place? Is this 119th Street? Oooh, this *is* the place. It's beautiful," Dior Emerson said as she peered out of the cab window. "It's just like the pictures."

"The pictures?" The cabdriver turned in his seat and looked at her.

"Yes," Dior said excitedly, wiggling her shoulders as she spoke. "I just got a new job here in the city, so I had to find a place fast, so I contacted a broker and they sent me pictures and I picked this house. I've always heard of brownstones, but I'd never seen one before. I can't believe—"

"Yeah, well, this is the place," the driver said, obviously no longer interested in Dior's story. "That'll be twenty-two fifty."

"Oh! Okay." Dior pulled some bills from her Gucci bag and handed the cabbie three ten-dollar bills. "Keep the change," she said grandly.

The driver looked at the money, then back at Dior and stuffed the bills into his pocket.

"So, you just got a new job, huh?" he said, suddenly interested as he flipped a switch to unlock the car doors. "What are you going to be doing?"

"A copywriter for an advertising agency," Dior said excitedly. "Senior copywriter, to be exact. And guess what? They found me through a headhunter. That's really a big deal because that means they were looking for someone like me. And it pays so much more than my old job in Montreal."

She joined the driver outside as he took her bags from the trunk. "This is like my dream job, in my dream city. I always wanted to visit New York, and especially Harlem, and now I'm living here! I'm telling you, I was destined to live in New York. I mean, you can't walk down the streets in Toronto and just bump into celebrities like you do in New York. Or go into restaurants and run into Robert De Niro or Woody Allen or Spike Lee or Beyoncé."

"Well, you're probably not going to run into them in Harlem too much, maybe Spike Lee. Most of the others hang out downtown." The driver looked at her hopefully.

"And shopping! I can't wait to go shopping in the Big Apple," Dior gushed. "I want to get all of the latest fashions."

"The best shopping is downtown, too, miss. You want me to take you downtown now?"

Dior shook her head as she looked at her luggage. "No, I should go ahead into my apartment and start getting unpacked."

The driver shrugged, then got in his car, leaving the luggage on the sidewalk.

Goodness, Dior thought. He could have at least carried it to the building. She sighed and grabbed the handle of one bag and threw the strap of another over her shoulder and lugged them over to the brownstone. January in New York, it seemed, was as cold as in Montreal. Even though her thigh-length mink was warm, she wanted to get inside as soon as possible.

"You must be Dior Emerson."

Dior looked up and saw a middle-aged woman with a blue wool coat, a blue felt hat pulled low over her graying dreads, and a cigarette dangling out of her mouth.

"I sure am. And you must be my new landlady! Mrs. Graham, right?" Dior stuck out her hand to shake the woman's hand.

"I am, but you can call me Margie. I've been looking out the window for the last hour waiting for you to arrive. This house I'm renting out, I call it Margie's Diamond Palace." She pointed to the building they were standing in front of. "And that one"—she pointed to the brownstone two buildings down—"I live in."

"They're both very nice," Dior said politely.

"Yeah." Margie looked at her very strangely. "Very nice. What kind of accent is that?"

"French."

"I thought you were from Canada."

"I am, but we speak French in Montreal. All of my family also speaks English, though. I've been speaking it since childhood."

"Is that right? Not that it's any of my business. None of my business at all. Well, come on, I'll give you a quick walk through the palace and then give you your keys. I wanna get to bingo before it gets too crowded."

The woman dropped her cigarette on the sidewalk and stamped it out with her foot. "Let me help you with your bags. Youse a little bitty thing, aren't you? What are you, a size three?" She picked up the smallest of the bags and walked down three steps to a private entrance.

"Size zero," Dior said as she picked up two of the bags and followed her new landlady.

"I don't even understand a size zero. Doesn't compute. How can someone be a size zero? Makes it sounds like they don't even exist, if you ask me." The woman pulled out a large ring of keys and fiddled around until she found the proper one and inserted it into the steel-gated door. "Still, it looks good on you. You so petite. I hope you don't have one of them eating disorders they be talking about on *Oprah*. Not that it's none of my business if you do. None of my business at all."

"How you ladies doing?"

Dior looked up to see a tall scruffy-looking brown-skinned man wearing an army jacket smiling down at them. Even from twenty feet away Dior could see the plaque on his yellow and brown teeth. "This your new tenant, Miss Margie?"

"Yes, she is, and don't you be harassing her, Jerome."

"I was just trying to be nice," the man said in a hurt voice as he shuffled his feet.

"Carry your ass down the street and be nice to someone else," Margie barked as she pushed open the door and shooed Dior inside.

"Not one of your favorite people, I gather?" Dior said as they entered the building.

Margie grunted. "Most of the people on this block are nice. But that damn Jerome is a pain in the ass. Whatever—you don't be nice to him, because if you do he'll be in your face all the time and trying to get into your panties, too. Damn shame. That man's pushing thirty years old and still living off his mother. Trifling is what I call him."

"Oh my God, this place is just beautiful," Dior gasped as they entered the apartment. "It looks even better than the pictures the broker sent me!"

"It should look good. I spent a bunch of money on the renovations. They just finished sanding down the floor, so make sure the moving men don't scratch them up when they move your furniture in."

"The floors are gorgeous. I've never lived in a place with hardwood floors before. And look how high the ceilings are. It makes it look like a ballroom. Oh my God, does that fireplace work?" She rushed over and ran her hand over the wooden mantelpiece. "I can just see myself drinking champagne in front of a roaring fire! Oh, I'm going to love it here!"

Margie chuckled. "Look at you getting all excited. Yeah, the fireplace works. Come on, let me show you the rest of the place."

"And oh my God, look at the shutters! The windows actually have shutters!" Dior ran over to the window and started flipping the shutters open and shut. "It's just like in the movies."

"Uh-huh, just like in the movies. Listen, are you mixed with something? You look like you might have some Chinese in you with them small slanted eyes and that long black hair.

Your mother was Asian? Not that it's none of my business. Not my business at all. But I'm just curious."

Dior smiled. "No, I'm all black. Both of my parents were light-skinned, too, though."

"Okay, just asking. It looks good on you, anyway. Now, you wanna see the rest of the apartment? Like I said, I don't wanna be late for bingo."

The walk through only lasted another fifteen minutes, but Dior enjoyed every moment. The kitchen was spacious and had all new cabinets. The bathroom, on the other hand, was quaint and old-fashioned, with a large tub that looked as if three people could fit comfortably. And because she had what Margie called the garden apartment, she also had use of the small backyard.

"Now, here's your keys. This one is for the front door, and this is for the apartment," Margie said when they were through. "You don't have a key to the upstairs front door because you're not going to be using it. I rented out the three upper floors, and the new tenants are going to be moving in soon, but you're the only one with a private entrance. That's why you're paying twelve fifty a month instead of eleven hundred like everyone else. And believe me, that's still cheap. But that's enough for now, 'cause I gotta go. And remember, I just live two doors down if you need me."

Dior waited until her new landlady left, then pulled out her cell phone.

"Auntie Claudia, I'm here! I'm at my new place! And it is sooo beautiful! It's just like the pictures! The hardwood floors are amazing and the fireplace, Auntie, it's marble!" Dior exclaimed, rubbing her delicate hands across the mantel. "Oh, and the ceilings, they reach up to the heavens, Auntie, I swear to you!"

Dior walked into the bedroom and opened the closet. She thrust herself inside and leaned her back against the wall. She closed her eyes and smiled. "Auntie, the closets are to die for!

They're huge! And there are quite a few. I can use one just for my pocketbooks!"

"Hard to believe with as many pocketbooks as you have," Aunt Claudia joked. "I would think you'd need two or three closets."

"Well," Dior giggled, "we all have our vices."

"Honey, I just want to let you know how proud I am of you, landing this new job and moving to a new city on your own. You're really proving yourself to be quite a young lady."

Dior smiled. That meant a lot to her. Aunt Claudia had been the guardian of her and her two younger brothers since their parents died in an automobile accident ten years before when she was only sixteen.

"Thanks, Auntie," Dior said sincerely.

"The only thing is, Dior, I want to remind you that you have to be more responsible about your finances. You spend way too much money on clothes and pocketbooks. I don't want you getting in over your head, okay?"

Dior sighed. "I won't, Aunt Claudia. I promise. But listen, I'm going to get off the phone because I want to do some sightseeing while it's still light out. I love you!"

"I love you, too, baby. Be good now!"

Dior hung up and went into the living room and laid her suitcase down to open it and realized that it was locked. She dug through her duffel looking for the key and then her pocketbook. She couldn't find it. She began to rack her brain trying to figure out where she had put the key to her suitcase. All of her clothes and shoes were in that bag. All she had in the duffel were pajamas, underclothes, and toiletries. She started to panic thinking about what she would have to wear for the next few days if she didn't find the key to her luggage.

She snapped her phone open again.

"Auntie Claudia," Dior said frantically. "I cannot find my key to my suitcase and all of my clothes are in there."

"Well, did you look in your pocketbook?"

"Yes. It's not in there. And it's not in my duffel bag, either."

"Well, what about your jeans and your coat? Check all of your pockets."

"I have. I can't find it anywhere! Auntie, it's lost. I don't believe this. I'm going to have to go out and buy some new outfits."

"Dior," her aunt all but shouted. "Didn't we just talk about your spending habits? Girl, just take a bobby pin or something and pick the lock."

"You're right," Dior said quickly. "I'll do just that. Love you!"

Now, Auntie knows me well enough to know that any excuse I have to buy new clothes is a good one in my book, and come on, no one can deny that this is a very good one, Dior thought as she checked her pocketbook to make sure that she had everything she needed—her credit card, her cash, her cell phone, her keys, and her lip gloss.

The walk to 125th Street only took a few minutes; the shopping took almost two hours. Despite the wintry cold weather, the streets were packed with shoppers and drivers. Dior was enthralled with not only the stores, but the dozens of street vendors who lined the streets hawking their wares. There was eye-catching activity everywhere. On one corner there were two guys break-dancing. On another, a man was playing the saxophone. Dior hadn't seen a city like it, especially in the dead of winter. Even the advertisements seemed to have life. Big and bold, they appeared as a backdrop, adding their own exciting element to the scene. The streets were packed with herds of people, various kinds of people, from old to young, white to black, short to tall, and everything in between. *If you don't fit in here, you don't fit in anywhere,* Dior thought. And she felt right at home.

She picked up a couple of pairs of jeans and tops from a boutique, but couldn't find anything she thought suitable for work. She did find a wonderful Louis Vuitton garment bag, and had the salesclerk put her new clothes in it rather than shopping bags. Then, remembering what the taxi driver had said about downtown shopping, she quickly waved down a cab and asked him to take her to the famous Fifth Avenue.

Dior bounced around in the backseat as the taxi driver zipped in and out of traffic like a bat out of hell. Clutching the passenger seat's headrest, she stared out the window, taking in the sights.

Stores lined the sidewalks for miles and there was indeed something for everyone. You had your small wholesale shops, your high-end boutiques, your big chain stores, and a host of independent retailers selling merchandise right on the streets.

Everything seemed to be fast-forwarding—the people, the sounds, and especially the traffic. There were hundreds of cars sharing the street, 90 percent of which were other taxis. Cars were double parked and other cars were weaving around them swiftly. Horns and screeching brakes acted as a sound track to the motion picture of Dior's new hometown—New York City.

Suddenly, traffic was brought to a standstill, causing the taxi driver to slam on the brakes.

"Oh, good grief," the taxi driver sighed.

After being jerked forward and then back, Dior sat up in her seat to get a glimpse out of the front window.

"What's going on?" she asked, staring at the crowds of people standing on the corner up ahead.

"It must be someone famous," the driver responded, pointing to the double-parked Maybach about four cars in front of him.

Dior's eyes widened as she anticipated seeing which celebrity would hop out of the much respected, luxury vehicle.

The taxi driver tried to maneuver the cab into another lane, but it was no use. People were holding up traffic waiting to see who was causing such a parade.

"I wonder what's going on," Dior mumbled as she watched photographers and news cameras emerge from the crowd.

Then Dior's question was answered when she saw an older man holding up a Scarface poster that read HEY, AL, SAY HELLO TO MY LITTLE FRIEND.

"Oh my God," Dior blurted out. "I think it's Al Pacino! He must be going into that restaurant!"

"Ohhh, today is the day that he is opening his new restaurant, that's right," the driver said. "I read it in the newspaper this morning."

"How much do I owe you?" Dior asked in a hurry. "I have to see Al Pacino! He is my favorite actor! And I'm not just saying that because he's out there, either! I'm serious. Since I was little, I've loved Al Pacino. I never thought I would meet him, and now that I have the chance to, I can't let it pass! I would kill myself first!" Dior exclaimed.

"Oh my. Well, just give me eight dollars. Don't worry about—"

"Here, keep the change." Dior cut the driver off, shoving a ten-dollar bill in his palm. She quickly got out of the cab.

"Thank you," she called out, speed-walking toward the crowd, lugging the garment bag with her new clothes over her shoulder.

"Excuse me, wardrobe. Excuse me, wardrobe," she said repeatedly until she found herself at the front of the red rope.

As if it were planned, the minute Dior got into position, a middle-aged white man wearing a tuxedo opened the back door of the Maybach. First an unknown female got out and then Al Pacino followed. Unable to help herself, Dior screamed. Her idol was just a couple of feet away from her in arm's reach. It was unreal. She didn't have a camera, but she figured she could get a few pictures with her phone. While he stopped to sign autographs, she took her phone out of her purse and started snapping. As he started to walk her way, she realized she didn't have anything for him to sign. Other people in the crowd had posters of him or memorabilia. She had nothing—nothing she could get to easily and quickly. Her nerves were out of control as he signed an autograph right next to her. She could have reached out and rubbed his face he was so close. As he finished up and started to walk past her to the next person with something he could sign, Dior quickly lifted up her shirt and asked him to sign her chest. He chuckled, but he didn't say no.

"I love you so much!" Dior shouted out as Al Pacino signed his name right above her bra.

"I love you, too," he said, moving on to the next fan.

Dior was in heaven. She had just gotten to New York and already had one of her lifelong fantasies fulfilled. She was sure that she would love every ounce of her new life and was more eager than ever to get it started. The flashes from the various cameras, the screaming fans, the news reporters, and the presence of Al Pacino made her feel like she was in Hollywood at the premiere of a blockbuster. But she was just on a regular corner in New York City. This was what she had to look forward to, getting that kind of action on a regular day on a regular street.

She threw her garment bag over her shoulder and walked back through the crowd.

Three hours swiftly passed by and Dior felt like a million bucks, perusing Manhattan's most luxurious strip carrying countless shopping bags and sipping a Starbucks latte. She had spent just about up to her limit when she decided to run across the street to Gucci just to see what new things they had. She promised herself that she wouldn't buy impulsively, but then she spotted the most beautiful handbag she'd seen since in Vegas two years earlier. The oversized signature brown and gold leather hobo seemed to be calling out to her. She tried to ignore it, but to no avail. It screamed *classic,* and if there was one thing in the world Dior could never pass up, it was a classic purse. Pocketbooks were her weakness, but a classic pocketbook would be the death of her.

After trying the bag on and talking to the sales rep about its material, its style, and its price-to-use ratio, Dior convinced herself that the bag was worth its eleven-hundred-dollar retail value. She counted out seven hundred dollars in cash and then put the balance on her Visa.

Dior flagged down a cab and gave the driver her address.

As he pulled away from the curb, she peeked down her shirt just to see that the autograph was still in place. She got a warm feeling just looking at it. Sitting back in the seat, Dior smiled. *New York, New York*, she thought. *Imagine what the summer's going to be like. I need to go bra shopping.* She had wanted to shop for a few household items, but that was out of the question as Dior had spent all of her money on attire and accessories. She had about one hundred dollars left on her Visa, but she would need that for food to last her until her first weeks of pay ahead. She was a little doubtful that she had made the right decision by buying the Gucci bag over the important things on her list, but what the hell, you only live once, she thought. She got comfortable in the backseat of the cab and zoned out for the rest of the ride home.

Twenty minutes later the taxi driver pulled up to Dior's house and double-parked. Dior dug in her wallet to collect the $16.22 that she owed for cab fare. To her surprise, she only had two dollars and forty cents to her name. She looked up at the cab driver, who was eyeing her suspiciously in the rearview mirror. Then she looked down at her bags that were laid out beside her on the backseat. She looked back at the driver and in a single moment she gripped her bags, opened the door, and jumped out of the cab.

"Hey, what are you doing?" the driver asked as he jumped out after her.

"Here," Dior said, handing him the two dollars. "I have to go inside and get the rest of the money."

The driver reached out and took the money with one hand and then gripped Dior's bags with the other.

"Well, leave your bags out here, then," he said.

Dior was alarmed. She knew she didn't have the rest of the money in her house and even if she did, she was not leaving her bags with a complete stranger. She tugged on the bags to try to get the driver to release them and instead he tugged back. The next thing Dior knew, she was having a tug-of-war with the taxi driver.

"Let go of my bags! What is wrong with you?" Dior shouted.

"What is wrong with me?" the driver shouted back. "What is wrong with you? You're the one trying to stiff me for the fare!"

Cars riding down the street were slowing up as the people inside them were trying to see what was going on. Neighbors started to come to their doors. Everybody was wondering what the fuss was about. Dior was embarrassed and wanted so badly to diffuse the scene, but she'd be damned if she was letting go of her thousands of dollars in merchandise over a petty fourteen dollars.

"Yo, what's the problem, B?" the smarmy guy from the day before said as he approached them.

The driver looked at the guy and maintained his grip on Dior's bags.

"This lady owes me sixteen dollars and she's trying to give me two and run. I'm not having that," the taxi driver said.

"I said I would get the rest of the money out of my house!" Dior rebutted.

"Well, if that's true, then why won't you leave your bags out here until you get back?"

Dior was so mad she could have exploded. "Do you know how much I paid for this stuff?"

The taxi driver responded sarcastically, "Let me guess, too much that you can't pay for your cab?"

"Oh my God, how dare you insult me like that!" she snapped at him.

The guy looked at Dior and at the driver. He chuckled at the two of them, then pulled three crumpled five-dollar bills from his pocket. He handed the money to the driver, who finally let go of Dior's bags but not before he sneered at her. The driver got in his cab and angrily took off.

"Thank you. I will give you the money back," Dior told the guy as she walked toward her door.

The guy walked beside her. "We haven't been formally introduced, but my name's Jerome. I live right up the street, so we're neighbors."

"It's nice to meet you, Jerome," Dior said as she put her key in the door.

"Do you know that I have a fetish for small, light-skinned women with Chinese eyes and straight black hair and foreign accents?" he asked while flashing his yellow toothy grin. "It's a coincidence that you fit that description, isn't it?"

"Yes, it is. I'm flattered. Listen, how about you come by in two weeks and get the money I owe you?" Dior suggested, trying to brush Jerome off.

"I'll do you one better," Jerome began. "How about you give me your number and we call it even?"

"No, that won't be necessary. I can pay you the money back. It's just that I don't have any cash on me at the moment."

"Oh, so I can't have your number?"

Dior shook her head no, told Jerome good-bye, and attempted to close her door.

Jerome put his hand up on the door, keeping it open.

"Well, you're going to have to give me the money now. I'll stand right here and wait," he said.

Dior was irritated beyond words. She had already gone through a mess with the cabdriver and now Jerome was pestering her with nonsense. She couldn't believe how he had gone from a charming gentleman to an ignorant jerk in seconds. She wanted to tell him to go to hell, but she was in his debt, so she played nice.

"I can't give you a number that I don't have," she explained. "I just moved in, remember?"

"Oh, well, let's try this," Jerome said. "I'll leave you alone if you promise to give me your number when you get a phone or the money when you get the cash, whichever one comes first."

"Deal," Dior agreed. *Anything to get you off my doorstep,* she thought.

The minute Jerome walked away and Dior retreated to her air mattress in relief, her doorbell rang. Annoyed, she got up and walked to the door to see who it was and what they wanted. It was Margie, standing with one hand on her hip and the other bringing a cigarette to her mouth. Dior opened the door and forced a smile. Before she could say hello, Margie started talking.

"Hey. Listen, I just thought I'd tell you a few things that will help you out in the future. Number one, if you can buy Gucci, but can't afford a cab ride, walk or take the bus. Number two, I warned you about Jerome yesterday. Give him more than a minute of your time and he'll be at your door every day. And number three, Margie doesn't play when it comes to collecting rent, so you better not think about trying to get over on me like you did that cabbie. Okay?"

"Okay," Dior said wearily before Margie cued her to close the door.

Exhausted and confused about how she had overspent, Dior went back in her bedroom and plopped down on the floor. Her shopping bags were scattered about before her, but she didn't even have the desire to go through them and try on all her new stuff like she normally would. Not even her new pocketbook made her feel better about what had just happened.

The sun burst through the windowpane, disturbing Dior's sleep. Squinting, she stretched her arms above her head and let out a yawn. She felt around on the floor for her cell phone and picked it up. Despite the bright sunrays, she was able to make out the time. It was 7:15. She couldn't believe that she had woken so early on her first weekday off in months. She lifted the quilt off her and stood up from the air mattress.

She went into the kitchen and grabbed the half-drunk twenty-ounce bottle of orange juice that she had bought the day before in the airport. She finished it off and placed the empty bottle on the counter. *Maybe I should have bought a trash can instead of that Gucci bag,* she thought.

She grabbed her laptop computer and set it up on the kitchen counter. Since she was up so early she decided to spend some time on the Internet. While she only had that hundred dollars on her Visa, she still had her American Express card. She hated using it, because the balance had to be paid in full every month, but she did need something to sit on, after all. Besides, by the time the bill came in she'd have received her first paycheck, so everything would be all right. She found a quaint leather sectional that would go perfect in her living room. She also ordered a glass coffee table and two leather chairs to complete the modern look she was going for. For her bedroom, she came across a low-to-the-ground bed and the dresser and nightstands to match. It was all black/brown wood and sleek. She couldn't wait for it to be delivered.

After making her purchases and checking her e-mail, she Googled nightspots in New York to see which Harlem club she should check out that weekend. A spot called MoBay Uptown seemed interesting, she decided. It was right on 125th Street and had jazz on Thursdays, Fridays, and Saturdays. Usually she liked going to dance clubs, but she'd always heard that the jazz spots in Harlem were something else, and this was her chance to find out firsthand. Besides, it probably wasn't as expensive as the downtown clubs, and she was going to be cash poor for a while.

She scrolled down the page to check out more links about the club and in the process a link for a MySpace profile appeared. Dior clicked on it to see what the MySpacer thought of the nightspot.

According to Mr. Good Black Man 2008, it was a hip spot for African-American professionals and a perfect place for meeting attractive singles. She chuckled at the thought of going in and seeing wall-to-wall cute men in suits. That would be heavenly, she thought. She started to close the profile page but decided to read more about the person giving this bit of networking advice. She was disappointed to see there was no picture, and no description except that he was "a single black entrepreneur who lived in Harlem."

Hmmm, she thought, *he lives in Harlem, I live in Harlem. Might be worth checking him out.*

She clicked on the link that said *Send Message,* but a blurb came up saying *You must be logged in to do that.* She'd always toyed with the idea of becoming a MySpace member, and since it was free, and she wasn't doing anything else, she figured this would be as good a time as any. Twenty minutes later she had put up her own profile page. It was only barebones, but she could hook it up later, she decided. Right now she was on a mission. She clicked back on to Mr. Good Black Man 2008's profile page again.

> *Hi. I'm new to Harlem and new to MySpace. I came across your page when I was looking for advice about MoBay's. Do you really think it's worth checking out?*

Kind of lame, but it would do as an icebreaker. She hit the Send button, then retrieved another bottle of juice from the refrigerator. She had gone back to the computer to turn it off when she saw that she already had a MySpace message. She smiled when she saw it was from Mr. Good Black Man 2008. That was fast. She noticed his *online now* cursor was blinking.

> *Hey, Newcomer, welcome to the neighborhood. Yes, MoBay's is a great place. You should really try it on a Thursday night. The saxophonist is off the hook.*

She took a sip from her juice, then typed:

> *I didn't expect to hear back so soon. Thanks. How do you like living in Harlem? I just moved here from Montreal.*

A few minutes later she received another message:

*I've traveled almost all over the world, and I can tell
you that there's no place like Harlem. You'll love it here.*

They went back and forth with polite niceties for a while
before Dior finally typed:

*I notice that most people have their pictures on their
profile page. Why don't you?*

Ten minutes later:

*I used to have my picture up here but I kept getting
messages from women telling me how cute I was, and
how they wanted to meet me. I'm not into superficial
people who only care about what someone looks like,
so I decided to take it down.*

Wow, Dior thought. *He must really be good looking if
women were on him like that. Wish I knew what he looked
like, though.*

Mr. Good Black Man 2008 must have been reading her
mind, because just a few minutes later came another message:

*You sound like a nice person, so just between you and
me, I'm tall, chocolate-colored, and have been told I
look like Blair Underwood.*

The scene from the movie *Set It Off* where a shirtless Blair
Underwood came out of his house to say good-bye to Jada
Pinkett popped into Dior's head. She started salivating.

So what do you look like? was the next message Mr.
Good Black Man 2008 wrote.

Dior smiled to herself as she wrote *I would tell you, but I like your original philosophy.*

Touché, was his reply. *So what do you do for a living? Or would that be too personal?*

Actually, I start my new job on Monday, she wrote him.

She told him her job title and a brief description of her upcoming duties. He wrote back that her job seemed interesting and that he might have to hire her agency one day to advertise his business. Dior lit up like a Christmas tree and in her next message she asked him what kind of business he owned. He told her that his primary business was an investment firm, but that he also owned lots of real estate around Manhattan. Dior didn't know how to act. Dollar signs were floating all through her head and she started seeing doubles of her Gucci bag.

They went back and forth for another hour before Dior said she had to go, but asked if they could stay in touch.

We certainly can, came back the reply. *I'd love to be your Harlem tour guide. Just message me when you're ready to see the sights.*

Dior was tempted to message him back to say she was ready at that moment but decided against it. She turned off the computer, stretched, and went back to bed.

Dior was excited about starting her new job. She stepped out her door with pride. Being senior copywriter, she had to dress the part and she did, in a black Nicole Miller skirt suit and some black and white Chanel pumps. Her thigh-length mink shielded her from the January cold and with her black crocodile briefcase in tote, she looked like she meant business. She walked over to 116th Street and Malcolm X Boulevard to take her first rush-hour subway ride, feeling like a true New Yorker. Luckily, she was able to find a seat and immediately realized most of the people who had seats also had reading material. Duly noted, she thought, she'd bring a book or magazine along to pass the time on her next ride. She nonchalantly glanced over at the newspaper the woman next to her was reading. Her eyes widened as she saw pictures of Al Pacino in front of his new restaurant signing autographs.

"Do you mind if I look at your paper?" Dior asked eagerly.

The woman looked at her like she was crazy, but said, "You can have it. I get off at the next stop."

Dior quickly scanned through the photos on Page Six of the *New York Post*. No, she wasn't in any of the pictures. Damn the luck.

When she arrived at her office in the heart of Times Square, Dior was in awe. *This is what I'm talking about*, she thought. She went in the revolving doors and was greeted by a security guard. She told the guard where she needed to go and he pointed her in the right direction. She took the elevator up to the fifteenth floor and immediately after getting off she walked to the glass door that read KACEY AND PATNICK and introduced herself to the receptionist.

A few minutes later a short redheaded girl came into the lobby to meet her.

"Hi, I'm Larissa, Barbara's assistant," the girl said. "Follow me."

"Dior Emerson, hello," Barbara said with a warm smile. She shook Dior's hand and waved her to a seat. "So, we finally meet."

"Yes, and it's my pleasure," Dior said.

"Well, here's the thing." Barbara took a sip of her coffee. "Normally your first day would be pretty laid-back, but something's come up. If you don't mind, we'd like to put your orientation off for a while. We're trying to land a new major account, and we want all of our best people on it. And although you're new, we're all familiar with your work and we're confident we want you to be in on this."

Dior eagerly leaned forward in her chair.

"Al Pacino opened a restaurant here in the city a couple of days ago. We heard word that he's about to fire the advertising company he hired because he was dissatisfied with the coverage he got for the grand opening. He wants a major campaign in place immediately, and we've already reached out to him and told him we have one ready for him to look at. Of course we don't. The meeting with him is scheduled for this time next week, so by then we have to have a presentation that will blow him away and land us the account. So we want you to get to work immediately trying to come up with some ideas. We don't have much time, so we'll screen the ideas that the copywriters come up with, pick one, and have them ready to present it to Mr. Pacino personally when he comes into the office."

Dior's head was spinning. *What is the likelihood of this?* she thought. *What do I look like presenting business to this man after I lifted up my shirt and asked him to sign my chest in public? He's going to laugh at me, then tell my boss how I acted a fool. Then he's going to tell her no thanks and go over to the competition for a campaign proposal that was actually done by a professional. Then my boss is going to fire me on the spot because she can't have such poor representation of her agency roaming the streets of New York. How do I get out of this?*

"Like I said, normally we wouldn't immediately throw you into the fire so quickly, but this is major, and we're familiar with your work and we think you can handle it. And between you and me, in the next couple of years we'll be looking for a new partner. Landing a major account like this in your first week at work will look very impressive." Barbara folded her hands on her desk. "No pressure, of course."

As she walked out of her new boss's office, Dior quickly thought of things she could say to Al Pacino to excuse her raunchy behavior; then she figured the best thing to do would be simply to deny it. It wasn't her. He must be mistaken. There were so many people there that day he couldn't possibly remember just one face. That was it. That would be her defense. *It wasn't me,* she thought.

"Uhhh!" Dior moaned as she pulled off her knee boots. She had just gotten in from work and her feet were killing her. She couldn't figure out why, though. She had worn those boots a hundred times in Montreal and this was the third time she had worn them in New York. And the two times before that, she did lots of walking in them—her first day at the airport and her second day walking up and down Fifth Avenue. She wondered if her feet were growing from all the walking she had been doing lately. That was all New Yorkers did, walk.

She sat down on her pile-it and leaned her back against the wall. Suddenly she felt a sharp pain in her behind. It came and went so fast that she dismissed it and just repositioned herself. She started to pick through the mail, coming across her electric bill. As she opened it, the pain in her behind returned. It felt like something had stuck her, and she thought maybe she had gotten a splinter from the floor. She stood up and scanned the bill, directing her eyes straight to the balance and due date. She couldn't figure out if the amount of the bill said $341 or if the pain in her butt was causing her to hallucinate. She figured she would take care of one problem at a time, and her ass came before the bill.

She put the mail up on the mantel and came out of her mink. Then she began to rub her butt as it was so sore. She started to feel around on her back pockets to see if there was something in them poking her. She felt nothing. Wanting to find out what was sticking her, she sat back down and sure enough the pain returned, this time causing her to jump to her feet as if she had gotten the Holy Ghost. She immediately unbuttoned her jeans and pulled them off. She went into the bathroom and tried looking at her butt in the mirror, but it was too high, and even sitting on the sink she couldn't turn herself around enough to see her backside. She started to feel around on her bare butt, trying to locate a splinter or a cut or something. But there was nothing but a pimple. And that had been there for days and hadn't given her any problems before, so she was sure it wasn't the culprit.

Confused, Dior went back into the living room and picked up her jeans off the floor. She examined them. Then she decided to turn them upside own and shake them, thinking that if it was a splinter or a pin sticking her it had to be in her back pocket. After a few shakes, a tiny gold key fell out of her jeans and onto her hardwood floor.

"Ohhh!" Dior squealed. "This is where you were hiding!"

She picked up the key and kissed it. "I was looking all over for you!"

She crawled over to her Louis Vuitton luggage that had been sitting in her living room since she moved in and turned it on its back. She put the key in the lock and opened it. She then unzipped the suitcase. A rush came over her. You would have thought she was taking the lid off a pot of gold. Her eyes lit up and she was overwhelmed with joy, looking at all her clothes and purses. She felt like she had gone shopping all over again as most of the things were new items that she had bought just before she left Canada.

"Hum," she huffed, closing the suitcase. Finding the key had almost made her forget the drama of the workday, but not quite. She decided to get online for a little while.

So how was your first day at work? was the one-line message Dior read from Mr. Good Black Man 2008 when she logged on to MySpace. Once again she saw that his *online now* icon was blinking.

It sucked, she typed back.

Sorry to hear that. What happened?

Dior sighed. *Long story.*

I guess we've all had those kind of days. Hope things get better.

You spend a lot of time on the computer, Dior typed. *Must be nice to have all this free time.*

I do most of my work on the computer. Believe me, I have very little free time. But what little time I do have I've already discovered I like spending with you.

Dior smiled. *How can someone as sweet as you still be single?*

His response was that he had a fiancée whom he was supposed to marry a year and a half ago, but she ended up cheating on him and so he called off their wedding. After that heartbreak, he wrote, he chose to be single for a while.

I'm so sorry to hear that, Dior typed.

That's life, came the reply.

Dior and Mr. Good Black Man 2008 went back and forth sending each other messages for the whole of the night. In between ordering food, going to the bathroom, taking phone calls, and even running to the store, they wrote each other. They got to know a lot about one another and realized they had much in common, the funniest and most significant being they both were Al Pacino fans. She impressed him by telling him that she was working on a campaign for their idol's new restaurant.

The two of them sent LOLs constantly as they both laughed aloud in their homes. They found out that they were both into zodiac signs and their signs were good together. They were in the same age bracket and they both liked jazz even though they were fairly young.

It was after midnight when Dior finally turned off her computer, clicked off her living room light, and retreated to her air mattress. She pulled back the quilt and the sheet and lay down, resting her head on her makeshift pillow. *Good black men aren't hard to find,* she thought. *Shit, they come with profiles and everything now. I like this.*

She closed her eyes and immediately began imagining Mr. Good Black Man 2008 in bed with her, and found herself getting aroused. *Damn,* she thought, right before drifting herself to sleep. *This online thing is nice, but I could use a noncyber man right about now.*

"I'm Gordon Jacobs."

Dior looked up from her desk and the presentation she was trying to prepare to see a short light-skinned man with freckles and spectacles standing in front of her, with one hand on his hip and the other holding a manila folder. It was Friday, and her presentation to Barbara and the other company bigwigs was scheduled for Monday, so she was mildly irritated by the interruption.

"Hi, I'm Dior. Dior Emerson."

"Uh-huh, believe me, I know who you are," the man said in an effeminate voice. "How's it going? You going to nail that Al Pacino campaign?"

"How'd you know about that?"

"Girl, please," he said, waving his hand. "I work for Human Resources. We hear everything down there. So, you going to nail that account or what?"

Dior smiled. "I'm going to do my best."

"Well, just so that damn Candace doesn't get it. I can't stand that witch."

"Candace Waller?"

"Uh-huh. She thinks she's hot shit, and word around the office is she sees you as the main competition for the account, so you must be the one that's really hot shit because she sure the hell ain't."

Dior paused, not sure what to say. Why would this person she'd never met before be telling her all of this?

"Well, anyway, I gotta go. You can thank me for the tip another time. And believe me you will," Gordon said as he sashayed off.

That evening Dior excitedly let the air out of her air mattress. She folded it up and put it in her hall closet. She swept and mopped all her floors and wiped down the woodwork, mantel and window seals. She was good and ready by the time the deliverymen came with her furniture.

She opened the door and before her stood a chocolate god. He was at least six feet tall, 220 pounds of nothing but muscle. His skin was so smooth it looked like silk. His bald head glistened against the sunrays. He had the whitest teeth and sexiest smile. He was not to be taken lightly. Mr. Good Black Man 2008 might be nice, but the man standing in front of her was real. Everything about him yelled *fuck me*. Dior was turned on instantly. Her womanhood started to thump in her pants and her breasts felt like they were waking up from a long nap. She couldn't control the feelings she was getting just looking at the guy, so there was no telling what she would do once he started moving her furniture in.

"Hello, Mrs. Emerson?" He broke the silence.

"Ms.," Dior clarified. "I'm not married."

"Oh, okay," he said with a smile. "But you are the person we're supposed to be delivering this furniture to, right?"

"Oh yes, of course," Dior said, gazing into his deep dark eyes.

"Okay, well, I'll just have you sign this paper and my guys will start bringing your stuff in," he said, holding a clipboard out in front of Dior.

Dior signed her name as fast as she could so that she could get another look at him before he went back inside his truck. He took the clipboard back and ripped off the back portion of the paper. He handed it to Dior and walked away.

Dior was in a trance watching his every move. She particularly concentrated on his butt cheeks and his back. She felt herself getting so moist that she was concerned she might have an orgasm. She tried to shun the sexual feelings she was experiencing, but they were too overpowering. She stepped outside without a coat on, hoping the cold air would straighten her out, and all that did was make her nipples harder. She couldn't believe what she was feeling for a perfect stranger. But she liked it.

She had turned to go back into her apartment when she noticed a voluptuous young woman heading up the stairs to the brownstone's front door.

"Hi," Dior called out. "You must be my new neighbor. You just moved in a couple of days ago, right? I saw the moving men bring in your furniture."

The woman stopped and slowly walked back down the stairs. "Hi," she said in a sweet southern accent. "Yes, I have the first-floor apartment. My name's Tamara."

"I'm Dior."

The two women eyed each other warily. "Well, I gotta go. I've got of lot of work to do," Tamara said finally. "It was nice meeting you." She headed back up the stairs.

"All right, Ms. Emerson, do you know where you want everything to go?" Dior's fantasy asked. She looked at him and wondered if he had noticed the curve of those shapely hips trotting up the steps, but his attention seemed devoted entirely on Dior. Good, she thought, as they went back into the apartment.

"This is the bed frame," one guy said.

"That goes in here," Dior said, leading them into her bedroom.

The guys laid the boxes out on the floor and went back to the truck for more. Dior just stood around watching as the guys took several trips to the truck and back to her apartment. Every so often, the chocolate god would bring something from the truck inside, but for the most part he was directing the two other guys. Once all the boxes for the bedroom were inside, the two guys got to work putting the bed, nightstands, and dresser together. Meanwhile, Dior's dream man looked around in the living room.

"This is a nice place. How long have you been living here?" he asked, his deep voice sending shock waves through Dior's body.

"Thanks. Just a week," she answered. "Can I get you or your guys anything to drink?"

"No. We're fine, thanks."

"Speak for yourself!" one of the other guys yelled from the bedroom.

Dior and the guy who appeared to be the boss chuckled and then Dior asked the worker, "What would you like? I have water and iced tea and a couple sodas."

"A soda is fine," he shouted out. "Thank you."

Dior took a soda out of her refrigerator and walked it into the bedroom to the guy. The bed and nightstands were already together and they were working on the dresser. Dior was surprised to see how fast they had worked and she went back into the living room to tell their boss how impressed she was.

"They're getting it done so fast," she said. "I wish I had cash on hand to tip them."

The boss guy flagged her playfully and said, "Oh, that's all right. These guys get paid to do this."

"Yeah, and what do you get paid to do?" the same guy who asked for the soda shouted out. "Stand around and talk to the customers?"

"Exactly. It's my job to satisfy the customer and your job to satisfy me," he retaliated. Then he turned to Dior and explained, "That's my little brother. He's always talkin' trash."

Dior chuckled again and then asked flirtatiously, "What size shoe do you wear?"

"Thirteen," he said, licking his lips.

Dior blushed as they stared at each other. She figured that she wasn't doing a good job keeping her feelings for him a secret. He clearly knew that she found him attractive and it was obvious he knew how to handle it. He flirted right back.

"All right, the bedroom is done," one of the guys said as he entered the living room.

The other guy followed, drinking from the soda can.

"We're going to get the living room stuff now, okay?" he said to Dior.

"Okay," she said, rushing into her room to see the end result.

"It looks nice," she thought aloud, looking around her room. She was happy at her choice in furniture and with the deliverymen's work ethic.

She went over to the bed and sat down on the pillow-top mattress. She bounced up and down on it, testing the firmness.

"It feels good, doesn't it?" the boss asked as he appeared in the bedroom.

"Yes, it does," she said with dreamy eyes. Then she toned down her desperation and got up off the bed. She walked into the living room and the boss followed.

"Listen," the boss began, "what are you doing tomorrow night?"

Dior paused and turned around to face him. "Nothing," she responded, grinning.

"Well, I'm free, and I would love to show you around. You are new here, right?"

"Yes, as a matter of fact I am," Dior said. "You know I would love that. Now, I guess, is a great time for you to tell me your name."

The boss extended his hand and in gentleman form, he said, "I'm Chris."

Dior placed her hand in his and said, "It's a pleasure to meet you, Chris. And from now on, just call me Dior."

"Dior, huh?" he said. "Is that short for high maintenance?" He chuckled.

"It all depends," Dior said, chuckling along with him.

Dior and Chris exchanged numbers just as the other two guys reentered her home. They had smirks on their faces as they knew what was going on. They quickly unwrapped all the furniture and put it in its place. Then the boss handed them a twenty-dollar bill from his pocket.

"This is a tip from Ms. Emerson," he said, winking back at Dior.

The two guys took the money and thanked Dior. She smiled at Chris and told them no problem. They gathered their belongings, Dior signed off on the delivery, and the three men left.

"I'll call you," Chris said with his lips only.

Dior nodded as she stood at her door watching the three of them get back in their truck. Just as she turned to walk back into her apartment, she heard one of the guys say, "You really satisfy the customers, don't you?"

She stood outside, watching the furniture delivery truck drive down the street, then turned to walk back into her apartment when suddenly someone grabbed her by the arm.

"Hi, lovely lady. Remember me?"

If I didn't remember your face I'd remember those yellow teeth, and that horrid breath, Dior thought. Out loud she said, "Sure, I remember you. Jerome, right?"

"Right. Your knight in shining armor. You gonna give me your number?"

"I thought we agreed that I'd pay you back in two weeks," Dior said desperately. How the hell could she let her spending habits put her in a situation like this? Of all people, she sure didn't want to be in Jerome's debt.

"Yeah, but I decided I'd rather have your number so we can get to know each other better. I know you got a phone by now. If you don't, just give me your cell number."

"Look, I'd much prefer to—"

"Jerome, youse one trifling bastard!" Margie called out her window. "Leave that girl alone. Dior, don't give him nothing. I done paid him that money for you already and he knows it."

Dior looked from Margie to Jerome. "You did?"

"Yeah. He came around here the other day crying about that was part of the money his mother gave him to go pay the electric bill, and I like his mother and didn't want her in the dark. Just add the twenty dollars to your rent, baby."

Dior snatched her arm away from Jerome and glared at him. "It was only fifteen dollars."

Jerome's eyes darted from side to side. "Well, you know. Interest."

"Yeah, I got your interest right here," Margie shouted as she waved a baseball bat in the window with one hand while flicking the ash from her cigarette out the window with the other. "Now get your trifling ass down the street."

"Man, forget you," Jerome said as he backed away. "I was just trying to be nice because you're new in the neighborhood and I thought you might need a friend."

"Hmph. With friends like you I certainly wouldn't need any enemies," Dior said angrily. "Miss Margie," she said, turning to the woman in the window, "I'm sorry. I'll give you the twenty back in the rent check like you said."

"Okay, dear. And don't worry about Jerome. He's stupid but he's harmless. Just don't give him any more of your time and he'll soon be leaving you alone. And just put him in his place one good time and you won't have any problems. That girl in unit three chewed him out so bad you can bet he won't ever say another word to her again. You just need to get a little more spunk in you. Not that's it none of my business. Not my business at all."

That fool has some nerve, Dior thought when she walked back into the house. Angry as she was, though, she couldn't stay mad long as she looked at her new furniture. Her new apartment was looking more and more like home. She sat down on her new bed and smiled. It sure would be good to break this in right. This was possibly her time and Chris was possibly her match.

When she powered up her laptop later to check her bank account balance online, she noticed that she had a couple of messages from Mr. Good Black Man 2008, and that his *online now* icon was blinking. She turned off the computer without reading the messages and went to bed.

Chris arrived at Dior's door at seven o'clock on the nose. Looking quite debonair in a tasteful pair of Rock & Republic jeans, a black sweater, and a pair of black and white Gucci sneakers, plus bearing a box of chocolates, he definitely got the date started off on the right foot. Dior greeted Chris with a kiss on the cheek as she took the chocolates off his hands. She invited him in just so that he wouldn't have to stand in the cold while she touched up her makeup and put on her coat. He sat on her new sofa and waited patiently for her, commenting, from time to time, on how nice she had decorated since he had been there the day before.

Chris opened the door for Dior and escorted her inside his 2008 Cadillac Escalade. He then walked around the back of the car and got in the driver's seat. He was being a perfect gentleman. Dior was pleased. The two drove through the busy Saturday night Manhattan traffic, making stops, at Nobu's for dinner, the Belasco Theatre to preview a play, and Serendipity's for dessert, finally ending their night on the town at Pacha Nightclub for a drink and a dance.

Choosing to go to various spots was Chris's way of showing Dior several parts of the city and entertaining her at the same time, and Dior was more than satisfied as that was the most fun she'd had in a long time. At one point she almost suggested that they go to MoBay's since she still hadn't made it to the jazz club, but quickly decided against it. Stupid as it sounded she felt like that would be cheating on Mr. Good Black Man 2008 since that was the club he recommended.

Throughout the evening Chris and Dior laughed and conversed and learned a lot about one another. As the time wound down, neither of them wanted the date to end, especially not Dior, who, instead of kissing Chris good-bye once they arrived at her apartment, invited him inside.

Dior was tipsy and still up for a good time, so she figured it wouldn't hurt to have him come in for an hour or two. Unbelievably attractive, well groomed, well mannered, well rounded, and apparently well off, Chris was everything she could want in a man.

Dior took off her coat, with Chris's assistance, and hung it in her closet. She took Chris's leather blazer and hung it up, too. The two sat on the sofa and stared into each other's eyes for a moment.

"You are so beautiful," Chris said, eyes glassy from the numerous Grey Goose martinis he'd had at the club.

"It's funny, I hear that a lot from guys, but hearing it from you, I got all tingly inside just now," Dior responded with a blush, playfully hitting Chris on his knee.

Just then, Chris leaned in and kissed Dior on her lips. She returned the kiss and the next thing Dior knew, her hand was rubbing Chris's thigh and his hands were rubbing hers. They were kissing and feeling each other's body parts and before long, they had made their way into Dior's bedroom and were breaking in her new bed.

Dior was in fairyland as she hadn't had any in a long time and Chris lived up to his massive sex appeal. He was as great in bed as he was to look at, maybe greater. When they were done, Dior was wide open. She helped him put on his boots and everything. She even flushed the condom down the toilet for him.

After about a half hour, Chris and Dior parted ways. It was close to five in the morning when she walked him outside. He bent down and kissed her once more, then walked to his car, which was parked up the block. Dior went back inside her apartment and closed her door. She leaned up against it, folding her arms over her chest, and exhaling with a huge smile on her face as if she were in love.

She glanced around at her furnished apartment and thought back on the amazing sex she had just had with the equally amazing man and she patted herself on the back. *This was a good week*, she thought to herself. *The furniture and Chris were both a perfect fit.*

Dior was both exhilarated and scared witless as she sat in the conference room. She and two other senior copywriters had made their presentations in front of the company brass the day before, and it was her campaign that the company had decided to go with. Now her insides were doing jumping jacks as she waited to make the presentation in front of her movie idol.

Just deny it was me, she reminded herself over and over again. *And maybe he won't even remember me. I'm sure I'm not the only girl whose chest he's signed.*

Larissa brought a pitcher of ice water and several cups into the room. She also made sure the coffee- and teapots were filled.

"Dior, this is quite impressive. I knew you had it in you," Barbara said, skimming over the last of the six pages. "And you came up with this in a little over a week, that's great. And I love this catchphrase, *when you only have money left for food, do you pay the driver?* That's funny. I think he'll go for it. You ready?"

Dior's mouth was too dry to speak, so she simply nodded. Just then the intercom buzzed.

"Mrs. Roman, we've just been notified your guests are on their way up the elevator."

Barbara stood up quickly. "Dior, you wait here. I'll meet them at the elevator and bring them in here. Are you sure you're okay? You look a little queasy."

"I'm fine," Dior managed to croak.

Just deny it, just deny it, Dior said to herself over and over again. She stood up as the conference room door swung open.

"Ms. Barker, this is Dior Emerson, one of the bright young stars at Kacey and Patnick. She's the one who came up with the campaign and will be making the presentation today. Dior, this is Kit Barker. Mr. Pacino's publicist."

Dior's eyes widened. "His publicist? I'm sorry. I was under the impression Mr. Pacino would be here himself."

Kit Barker chuckled. "No, dear. Mr. Pacino would need stunt doubles to go to every business meeting of his. I'll be the one you have to convince. Then I'll present it to Mr. Pacino, and of course he'll have the final say."

God, you're the bomb, Dior said in her head as a feeling of relief came over her. She could do her job now without the fear of being found out and having her reputation scrutinized. She proceeded to give her presentation as if it were a walk in the park. Afterward she walked out of the conference room head held high, and with a huge grin on her face.

"I take it that it went well, then?" Candace Waller asked as she passed her in the hall. "Congrats. I hope they go for it."

"Thanks," Dior said airily. Candace had been shooting dagger looks her way since the day before when the company had chosen Dior's presentation over hers, but even the woman's attitude couldn't bring her down at the moment.

"I heard you nailed it, girl!" Gordon said when he stopped by her desk later that afternoon. "Um-hm, you know you're going to be the new company golden girl if you did."

Dior beamed up at the man. "Gordon, I really think I did."

"Uh-huh. And you know Miss Candace is hating on you right now." The man laughed. "Serves her ass right. She thinks just because she's a copywriter she can treat everyone else like shit. You know if her presentation had been picked they would have automatically promoted her to senior copywriter, right? I sure would have held up her pay raise, though. We do have some power in Human Resources, you know."

Now that the presentation was over, Dior had extra time on her hands, so she decided to surf the Net for a while checking out the latest Gucci and Versace fashions, though promising herself she wouldn't buy anything. After a half hour or so she logged on to MySpace and found seven messages from Mr. Good Black Man 2008 logged in over the last forty-eight hours. Most were simply wondering where she was, and how she was doing, and how the Pacino presentation went. She was getting ready to log off when she saw his *online now* icon suddenly start blinking.

Hey, I'm sorry I haven't been in contact for a while. I've just been so busy at work, she quickly typed.

Good to hear from you. I was worried.

No need to. I'm fine.

How's work?

Work is great! I think I have landed the Pacino account!

Get out! Congratulations! I'm so proud of you.

Wasn't that sweet? Dior thought. *He doesn't even know me but he's proud of my successes. He's a real gem.*

I almost blew it, though, she typed.

What makes you say that?

Dior grinned as she typed a message telling him about her first day in New York City and her chance meeting with Al Pacino.

LOL. You are crazy! I knew I liked you for some reason. When will you find out for sure if they're going to go with your campaign?

Probably in another week or so.

Well, let me know if you get it because I'd love to take you to celebrate.

Dior hesitated. The temptation was too much to bear. She started typing.

How about we just go ahead and celebrate now? I'm free tonight.

But before she could hit the Send button her cell phone began vibrating.

"Hello. This is Dior."

"Hello, beautiful lady," Chris's cheery voice said.

Reality check, Dior thought as she erased the message without sending it to Mr. Good Black Man 2008. *A real man in my bed is better than a cyber one I've never met.*

"I'm fine," Dior said as she logged off the Internet. "In fact, I'm psyched! I think I might have landed a major account. Congratulate me!"

Chris chuckled. "Okay, congratulations."

"In fact, you should take me out tonight to celebrate." Dior leaned back in her chair and crossed her legs. She could feel herself getting moist as she remembered the passion they had shared just three nights before.

"Funny you should say that. I was just calling to see if you were free. I can't get you out of my mind."

"Now, that's what I like to hear. See you at seven?"

"It's a date."

Ding-dong! Ding-dong! Dior's doorbell rang repeatedly. She glanced at the clock on the mantelpiece as she rushed out of the shower. It was only six. She hoped Chris wasn't coming over early. Throwing on her bathrobe and sliding into her slippers, she ran to the intercom.

"Who is it?" she asked, a little frazzled.

"It's your knight in shining armor," the voice responded.

Dior frowned. "Who?"

"It's Jerome," the voice sounded.

"What do you want?"

"I just wanted to apologize for the other day. I gave Miss Margie her money back so you can just go ahead and pay me now so we can keep the peace."

Dior suddenly got so angry she stormed out of the door in her robe and slippers. "Jerome, I don't believe you."

"What? I thought I was being nice. . . ."

"Go to hell! Before I smash you in the face, you lousy bastard."

"Yo, you know you don't have to be so—"

"Jerome! What I tell you about harassing my tenants? Boy, don't make me go get my baseball bat and swat the shit outta you," Margie's voice rang out behind them.

"Miss Margie," Jerome started stammering. "I was just—"

"Boy, I know just what you was trying to do," Margie said as she walked up behind him and swatted him upside the head. "Now get outta here before I call your mother and tell her you're still out here trying to hit on young girls with your trifling ass."

"Man, forget you and her," Jerome said as he backed away from the door. "I got me a real nice girl. A professional girl with a good job, too. I don't need to be messing with you."

"Yeah? Well, then don't," Margie shouted at his back. The woman then giggled and turned back to Dior. "Actually, this time it looked like I was saving him from you rather than saving you from him. I thought for sure you were going to knock him out with your little bitty self. Bet he won't be bothering you anymore."

"He'd just better not," Dior said as she stomped back into her apartment.

Later on that evening, Dior relaxed in Chris's arms. "You know what? You really grow on a girl."

"Talk about growing . . ." Chris smiled and moved Dior's hand to his manhood.

A wicked smiled appeared on Dior's face. "Better yet, let's not talk about it. Let's get to doing something about it."

"Dior! You did it! You landed the account! I just heard back from Pacino's people. Congratulations!"

Dior looked up at Barbara in disbelief. "Really?"

"What do you mean, really? Yes, *really*! And I'm really taking you to lunch to celebrate. In fact," Barbara said grandly, "I'm taking the whole team out to lunch! No, scratch that. We're going out for cocktails. I'm feeling good today!"

"Congratulations," Candace said with the most insincere smile Dior had ever seen. "I guess you've cemented your position here, haven't you? But then maybe I could have landed the account if . . ." Candace's eyes narrowed. "Oh, never mind," she muttered as she walked away.

Dior wondered what the girl was going to say, but didn't wonder long. She had phone calls to make. First to her aunt Claudia, then to Gordon in Human Resources, who said he'd already heard and told her that the powers-that-be had already arranged for her to get a five-thousand-dollar bonus, and then to Chris, who heartily congratulated her.

After Dior finished her calls she turned on her computer to do some shopping. She hadn't been at her new job a month and already she landed a prestigious account. *I owe myself a new purse for this one.* She gasped when she saw that Gucci had a new clutch bag priced at $980 with matching sunglasses for an additional $550.

She felt only the slightest pang of guilt as she ordered two of each. True, she did need to pay off the coming American Express bill, but after all, a bonus was supposed to be spent on luxuries, not necessities. At least that was her philosophy.

She felt a stronger pang of guilt when she logged on to My-Space and saw that there were eight messages from Mr. Good Black Man 2008. She'd been almost totally ignoring him for the past week because of the time she'd been spending with Chris.

But that's life, she thought as she deleted the messages without reading them. *And Chris is real life. And real good.*

"Are you ready?" Larissa interrupted Dior's leisure.

Dior looked up a bit startled and asked, "What time is it?"

"Four thirty."

"Oh, I didn't realize it was so late. Let me just shut down my computer."

"Okay. Just meet us in the lobby," Larissa said, leaving Dior's cubicle.

Dior logged off MySpace and shut down her computer. She gathered her belongings and went into the bathroom to fix her hair and makeup. She made sure she looked as cute as she did when she first left her house that morning. From what she read, there were going to be lots of prospective companions at the lounge she was on her way to.

Dior, Barbara, Larissa, and three other ladies from the agency took the elevator to the parking garage. Half of the group, which included Dior, got into Barbara's Mercedes S550 and the other half drove in Larissa's Infiniti M45. Larissa followed Barbara to Chill Lounge in Midtown. They valet-parked and went inside the lively after-work spot. The music was a mix between hip-hop and R&B and pop. The atmosphere was laid-back but sophisticated. Couches for seating and lit candles and fireplaces gave the place a warm, cozy feel. The attendees were businessmen and -women, still in their work clothes, munching on hors d'oeuvres and sipping fine wines. Dior followed her party to a private room with a large rounded booth just for their group.

"This is a nice place, Barbara," Dior complimented her boss's taste. "Thanks for inviting me."

"Don't mention it," Barbara replied, opening the menu. "This is where all the professionals meet. You can enjoy happy hour, network, and even close deals here."

"It beats the golf course, that's for sure," Larissa butted in.

The ladies chuckled, all except one, Candace, who sat sullenly silent.

"So," Candace said after they ordered their drinks, "what's it like in Canada?"

"Well, Montreal is like any regular city."

"Oh yeah? Well, did you ever run into any celebrities in the streets in Montreal like you did here in New York?" she asked.

Dior wasn't sure where Candace was taking their conversation, but she went along. "No, not at all."

"So I guess seeing someone famous overly excites you, or is this how you land all your clients?" Candace sneered, as she pulled a weekly tabloid magazine out of her pocketbook and threw it on the table.

Dior's mouth dropped open when she looked at the picture staring at her. There she was in front of Pacino's restaurant with her breasts cupped in his hands while he kneaded her nipples. Beneath the picture was the caption PACINO GETS A HANDFUL AT HIS RESTAURANT'S GRAND OPENING IN JANUARY.

"Oh my God, this is so fake!" Dior protested. The gasp that escaped from the other women at the table caused her to furiously blush.

"So you weren't at the grand opening?" Candace began interrogating.

"Yeah, I was there, but—"

"But you didn't lift your shirt?"

"I lifted my shirt, but—"

"But what?"

Dior looked around the table and the women were all looking at her waiting for her response. "I was just getting an autograph. I love Al Pacino and I never saw him up close before and, well, I didn't have anything for him to sign so I, you know . . . "

"So you had him autograph your breasts?" Barbara asked in an incredulous voice.

"No! Not my breasts, just my chest. My breasts were covered. It wasn't like I flashed him. For God's sake, I was wearing a bra!"

Candace picked up the article and laughed. "Not in this photo you're not. If you ask me, it was more than an idea that made them give you the account."

"Well, who's asking you?" Dior grew furious. "First of all, I didn't even know that Al Pacino's restaurant would be my first account! Second, I am very professional! I get clients based on my ideas, my presentation, and overall my results! I have a proven track record! That's why I was hired here in the first place! And third, that photo was doctored. I never showed him my breasts!"

Embarrassed and angry, Dior excused herself from the table. But before she could walk away, Barbara placed her hand on her arm and told her to sit back down.

Dior did so, while grimacing at Candace.

Then Barbara said, "You have a point, Dior. The opening was before I told you about the possibility of our getting that account, so there's no way you could have done that to land it. And"—she coolly picked up her apple martini and took a sip—"to tell you the truth, when I first moved here twenty years ago I was a huge Bruce Willis fan. I'm not going to tell you what piece of my anatomy I had him sign."

All of the women at the table, except Candace, exchanged stares, then burst out into laughter.

"Of course I was a college sophomore at the time, and you're supposed to be a professional woman, but we all have our little misjudgments in behavior," Barbara said, glancing over at Candace, who was now beet red. "So, how about we just get rid of this?" She picked the article up off the table and began to crumble it.

Dior stopped her and asked, "Can I have it?"

"For what?" Barbara quizzed.

Dior blushed and shyly responded, "For a keepsake."

Barbara laughed and Dior and the other ladies followed, except, of course, Candace.

Barbara gave Dior the article and Dior thanked her. She then folded the paper neatly and placed it in her pocketbook. She felt relief as she picked up her menu and continued on with her evening. Deep inside, she was glowing. She hadn't been living in New York for but a second, and already she was being harassed by a hater and a tabloid. She felt like a star. *Now all I need is a teacup yorkie*, she thought.

* * *

"Hey, Dior, did Barbara tell you your campaign is starting in a couple of days?" Larissa appeared at Dior's cubicle a few weeks later, cheerful as usual even on a Monday morning.

Dior lifted her eyes off her computer screen and landed them on Larissa. "Yeah, I know," she said. "I can't wait to see it."

"Well, the account execs have a list of the time slots. I'll grab you one when I go down there later."

"That'll be great. Thanks, Larissa," Dior said, returning her eyes to the numerous unread messages in her MySpace inbox.

Dior read and replied to several of the messages that were pretty general from people she didn't know. Then she came across four messages from Mr. Good Black Man and she kind of froze up. He was asking how she had been and he wanted to make sure she was all right since he hadn't heard from her in a while. She looked at the date of the last message. It was more than a week ago. He must have finally given up on her.

She wanted to reply to him, but she had grown such feelings for Chris that she didn't feel that it was necessary to continue going back and forth with Mr. Good Black Man. Plus, realistically, Chris was her better bet. He did exist and every quality was proven, whereas Mr. Good Black Man was still a mystery, nothing more than a person who could type. On the other hand, Mr. Good Black Man had piqued Dior's curiosity. She did get to know and like him and if she didn't go further with him, she knew she would always wonder if he really did look like Blair Underwood.

As she was contemplating what to write back to Mr. Good Black Man, her cell phone vibrated on her desk. She took her hands off the computer keyboard and picked up her phone. Mandingo appeared in her caller ID. She pressed the Talk button instantly to avoid missing the call from Chris.

"Hey," she said, using her soft *I'm at work* tone.

"What's up? Are you busy?" Chris asked, considerate of her time as usual.

"No. Just sitting here on the computer at work."

"Oh, is that what your eight hours is used for?" Chris joked.

Dior checked him. "Actually, I am on lunch. I just decided to stay in today. It's so cold outside."

"Yeah, I know," Chris agreed before getting to the point of his call. "Listen, I was wondering. I mean, this is probably short notice, and I should have asked you before, but I was wondering if you'd like to go out Thursday . . ." He paused. "For Valentine's Day."

Dior leaned forward, placing her elbows on her desk. She smiled and said, "I have to check my calendar, but I can tell you right now, it's looking like a yes."

"Well, I hope so. I have somewhere I want to take you. So check your calendar and call me with the results. In the meantime, I'll be keeping my fingers crossed," Chris said.

"Who are you talking to?" a deep voice sounded in the background of Chris's phone.

"Hold on," Chris told Dior. "Matter fact, let me call you back."

Dior was slightly confused, but she didn't think much of Chris's sudden need to hang up with her until seconds after ending their call, he called her right back. She pressed TALK and put her ear to the phone anticipating Chris's explanation. But instead, she heard the male's voice again.

"I heard you, Chris!" he said. "You sounded like you were damn near having phone sex!"

"Cut it out," Chris's voice returned. "I was talkin' to a customer!"

"A customer? So do you ask all your customers to spend Valentine's Day with you? Is that some kind of special you're giving out?"

There was a brief silence.

Then the male's voice said, "Uh-huh! See, Chris, I caught ya ass this time! I was standin' right outside that door! You really did it with this one! You hear me?"

Chris finally broke his silence. "Baby, it wasn't like that at all. I'm tellin' you. You caught the conversation wrong."

Dior's mouth dropped open as she realized what was going on at the other end of her phone. She felt like she had to throw up. She ended the call and hurried to the bathroom. Inside a stall, she sat down on a toilet seat and held her hands over her face. She was trying to gather her thoughts and calm her stomach. She was disgusted. Thank God she hadn't violated her golden rule of never doing it without a condom. But even still. She stood up quickly and leaned over the toilet, retching until it felt like the lining of her stomach was going to make an appearance in the commode.

After a while, she left the stall and went up to the sink to rinse out her mouth and wash her hands. She looked at herself in the mirror, and the feeling of her having to throw up returned. She leaned over the sink waiting for something to come out, but nothing happened. She patted her face with warm water and wiped it afterward with a paper towel. She finally got herself together and went back to her desk.

She picked up her phone to call Chris and curse him out and she noticed she had a missed call from him. She opted to check her voice mail first before calling him back.

"Dior, I'm sorry about that. My roommate and his friend were arguing. Call me back when you can. Bye."

Dior pressed 9 to save the message, then hung up and dialed Chris. *Who did he think he was fooling?*

"Chris, hi, it's Dior."

"Yeah, my bad about that," Chris started off.

"Chris, there's no need to drag this on," Dior said. "You called me back by accident and I heard your whole conversation and I know it was you arguing and not your roommate and his friend."

Chris didn't say anything so Dior took it upon herself to go on.

She rested her head in her palm and said, "I should have known you were gay."

"No, no. See, you're wrong! I'm not gay!" Chris all but shouted.

"Yeah? Well, is it called something else in New York?"

There was a long pause before Chris finally said, "Dior, I am bisexual. But—"

"There are no buts, Chris," Dior said.

"Listen," Chris pleaded, "I know I should have told you up front, but it wasn't like I was planning on messing with you while I was messing with a man. I'm very considerate when it comes to that. If I'm dating a woman, then I'm straight and monogamous at that time. And when I'm dating a man, I'm gay, but still monogamous at that time."

"Even if that was acceptable, and it's not, but even it was, I don't trust that it's the truth," Dior said.

"I'm telling you—" Chris started to beg.

"What you're telling me and what I heard are two different things and I prefer to go with what I heard. Good-bye, Chris."

Dior hung up her phone and put it on her desk. She rested her head beside it. She couldn't believe how wrong she was about Chris. She had misread men before, plenty of times actually, but good grief, this topped them all. She was hurt, but more confused. A million questions twirled in her head and she didn't have an answer for one of them.

She felt so shitty she actually wanted to call out sick the next day, but she managed to drag herself into the office two hours late. But try as she might she couldn't concentrate on her work. Everybody who walked by her desk asked her what was wrong, even Candace. She told them that she was just a little tired, but that was it. She wasn't one to tell her business, especially to coworkers. It would be all over the office if she did. She shuffled papers around for about an hour or so, then gave up on even trying to put on a pretense.

She logged on to the Internet and immediately went to My-Space to see if there were any new messages from Mr. Good

Black Man 2008. She was so disgusted and disappointed with Chris that she needed somebody to talk to immediately.

Hey, she started her message, *I've been a little busy with work. My campaign is being run and a lot of finishing touches had to take place in the past few days. Anyhow, I'm freed up again so you have my undivided attention. What's been up?*

She waited anxiously for Mr. Good Black Man to reply, but he wasn't online so she didn't expect it to be soon. Dior was restless, looking for things to do to take her mind off Chris. She walked to the front lobby to see if Larissa had gone and got the time slots that indicated when her commercials would run. It turned out that Larissa was at lunch. She started walking back to her desk, deciding to hell with it, she'd just go home after all.

"Okay. What's wrong with you?"

"I'm fine, just a little tired." Dior stuck to her story.

Gordon crossed his arms and gave Dior a full up-and-down look before continuing in a more gentle tone.

"Tired of what?" he asked. "What did he do? You can tell me, I won't say anything."

Dior was suspicious of Gordon's persistence, but for some reason she felt comfortable talking to Gordon more so than any of her female counterparts. Plus Gordon was gay and maybe he would have some advice for her pertaining to Chris.

"You have to swear to me you won't say anything to anybody," Dior said.

Gordon touched his forehead, his chest, his left shoulder, then his right shoulder, making a cross with his finger. Dior trusted in his gesture and gave him the spill. His lips were tight and his eyes were intense as he hung on to Dior's every word. When Dior finally got to the punch line, Gordon fell back into his chair and put his hand over his mouth as if he had heard the most shocking story in his life.

"Girl, no!" he gasped.

"I am in shock, Gordon," Dior said, shaking her head despondently. "I was really feeling something for him. I didn't see that one coming at all."

Gordon sat back up and leaned forward on his desk. "Well, let's take it back some. You said when he first came to your house to deliver the furniture, he looked real nice?"

"Yeah, you know, put together nicely."

"Okay, I can understand him being all dolled up when y'all went on your date. But coming to deliver sofas and stuff, I don't see a man getting shitty sharp for that. So that there, Ms. Dior, should have told you one of two things about Mr. Chris— either he was a playboy whose sole purpose of being a delivery boy was to entice his lady customers and see how many of them he could end up in bed with, or he was gay."

Dior smirked at Gordon's snap analysis, but then shrugged. Hell, who was she to disagree with him? She was the one who had just been played for the fool. "You might be right."

"Damn right, I'm right."

Dior sighed. "I wish I had this talk with you much sooner."

Gordon grinned. "Well, you got me now, so put me to use. What else you need to know, girlfriend?"

Dior chuckled and then she had an idea. "Well, I do have one other prospect. I should let you read his profile and see if there are any warning signs I should look out for."

"Profile? You met him on one of them online thingees?"

Dior nodded her head reluctantly. "On MySpace."

"Girl, please. Don't be embarrassed about that. I've met many men on MySpace who checked out. I love it!"

Dior grew excited. "Really? Well, let me pull up my page real quick and read these messages of his that I saved. Tell me what you think and tell me what I should write back."

Gordon walked behind Dior's chair while she logged on to her MySpace page on her computer. The two of them read all of the messages between Dior and Mr. Good Black Man from the first to the last.

"Um, um, um, he sounds spicy!" Gordon said.

"Does that mean gay?" Dior worried.

"No! Oh, God no. I would have said tangy if I meant that. He's straight—definitely straight. Now, everything else, like how white his teeth are and the size of his penis, those are all up for grabs, you know what I mean. But it's worth a chat and chew," Gordon instructed.

"So you think I should pursue him?" Dior asked.

"Uh-huh. If you don't, I will," Gordon teased.

Dior gave Gordon the look. "You know that's a sensitive subject."

"I'm just playing." Gordon laughed. "Okay, back to business," he said, getting serious again. "When he writes you back, no matter what he says, you reply by asking him out tomorrow for Valentine's Day. Now, don't say Valentine's Day in the message. Just say Thursday. You don't wanna sound too mushy asking him to be your Valentine. Plus, this will be a clear sign of whether or not he's taken. Because if he says I have something to do and asks to make it for another day, then the truth of the matter is, he is spending V-day with his primary. And I'm not talkin' 'bout a doctor. You keepin' up?" he asked, looking up at Dior.

Dior nodded her head.

"Now, if he accepts the date for Thursday, then you propose to meet him at MoBay—"

"You know about MoBay?" Dior cut in. "That's one of his favorite clubs."

"I know, I just read all his info, remember?" Gordon began writing something on a Post-it note. "It's a nice little spot in Harlem and they have jazz musicians play there on Thursdays, Fridays, and Saturdays. But you don't want to go on Friday or Saturday, why?" He turned to Dior.

"Because I specifically want to spend Valentine's Day with him."

"Because why?" Gordon further tested.

"Because that'll tell me that he's single."

"Right! Ooh, Ms. Dior, you learn so quickly. I can do this with you all the time."

Dior hugged him enthusiastically. "You know, you're my first real friend here in New York. And I've been here over a month."

"Really? You haven't made any girlfriends yet?" Gordon asked in surprise.

Dior shook her head. "I've got three women my age who live in my building, but they all seem very busy and maybe not too friendly."

Gordon waved his hand. "Well, child, don't even worry about it. Every girl needs a male gay friend and now you got one. Now go ahead and handle your business."

Dior grinned and took the neon-pink Post-it note that Gordon had given her. She glanced over it and saw that it had the name and address of MoBay on it. It also had *Good Luck* written on it with a smiley face beside it.

Gordon gave Dior a hug and headed back to his office. "Don't let one monkey stop ya show, girl!"

Dior glanced down when her cell started vibrating. When she saw it was Chris's number she turned the phone off without hesitation.

After that, she went on Gucci.com. She knew she had work to do and she had every intention on getting to it, but first she had to clear her head. And even though Gordon's talk did her some good, a new Gucci pocketbook would top it off. That would make her forget all about Chris. And in order for her to get back into her work, that was exactly what she needed. Besides, if everything went according to Gordon's plan, she would have a hot date the next day for which she would need something new to wear, and every woman knew that the pocketbook was the staple to any wardrobe. *So let's start there,* she thought.

After work Dior went inside a quaint boutique that had caught her attention a few weeks before. There were two women in there, one behind the counter and the other greeted her at the door.

"Hello, welcome to Chell-C's. If you need help with anything please let me know," the medium-height, skinny, pale woman said.

"I'd like to see that dress in the window," Dior told the woman.

"Oh, let me get it for you. Would you like to try it on?"

"What size is it?"

"It's a zero," the woman responded.

"Yes, please."

The woman took the dress off the mannequin and carried it to the dressing room in the back of the store. She neatly laid it across the plush lounge chair inside the dressing room and held the curtain up allowing Dior inside.

"Let me know if you need help putting it on," the woman said as she exited the dressing room.

Dior stripped down to her stockings, panties, and bra. She slowly stepped into the knee-length long-sleeved dress that seemed to sit perfectly on every inch of her body. The fabric felt good against Dior's skin and the deep floral print looked rich and made a statement. The dress was surely a one-of-a-kind. It was just right for Valentine's Day at MoBay, sexy and bold, yet classy and sophisticated. Dior looked at herself in the mirror, turning to see her back and each side to make sure the dress looked good from every angle. Then she looked at the tag to see just how much it would set her back. Five hundred and fifty dollars, she read. Then her thinking cap went on as she rationalized spending that kind of money on a dress when she had a world of other priorities.

This is the dress that I could be meeting my future husband in. It has to be something that stands out from the rest and it has to say all the right words. Now, I could easily go to Bebe or BCBG and get a cute dress for half the money, but I'd be risking walking into MoBay dressed like somebody else or two other people for that matter. Everybody shops at those stores. This is a first impression and it must be a lasting one, Dior thought.

She gave herself one last look and one last justification before she decided to take the dress. Before paying for it, though, she asked what the store's return policy was. She wanted to make sure she could get a refund if Mr. Good Black Man didn't accept her invitation. Everything worked in her favor and she paid for the dress with her American Express card and left the store. *I'll pay the bill off as soon as it comes in,* she thought as she took a deep breath. Outside the boutique, she raised her new dress slightly in the air, in part because it was her only means of getting the attention of a cab driver, but more so as a salute to her efforts. *Here's to giving love one more chance,* she thought as she stepped up to a taxi and got inside.

Dior couldn't wait to get home to see if Mr. Good Black Man would say yes to meeting her in person at MoBay. And it wasn't really about going on a date, either. She was more eager to read through his response. It became about the challenge at that point. She wanted to see if he would fall through or if he really was what he cracked himself up to be. Lord knew she didn't need any more impersonators. She wanted the real deal, and if a man was not that he need not apply. Her time was too valuable for pretenders.

"Mr. Good Black Man said yes," Dior boasted.

"Goodie!" Gordon cheered, clapping his hands. "So that's one worry down."

"Yeah, one down and one hundred to go," Dior replied.

Gordon flagged Dior playfully and jumped right into the interrogation. "Are you excited? What are you going to wear? What time did you tell him to be there? You are going to arrive later than him, aren't you? You're not going straight from work, are you?"

"Yes. A really cute dress. Seven. I don't know. And no, to answer all your questions."

"Okay, let me get this straight," Gordon said, holding up a finger. "Yes, you are excited. Okay, good. You're wearing a really cute dress, not so good."

"Why not? You think I should wear jeans?"

"No, a dress is appropriate. But when you say really cute dress, it makes me think of a fifth-grade graduation dress, you know, something your grandmother makes for you," he explained, frowning.

"Oh no, not at all. When we Canadians say really cute we mean like . . ."

"Hot?"

"Yeah! Hot! It's a hot dress!"

"Okay, okay, now we're talking. And you want him to be there at seven, but you're not sure if you should arrive before or after him?"

"I don't know," Dior said, leaning against Gordon's desk.

"I would say get there early. Not too early, just like five, ten minutes before him. This way you get to play what I call sneak peeks. Once I had a blind date and we were to meet at this club. And this is a club that's known for fine men, so I was like if this guy turns out to be a monster, then I need to be able to diss him and get with somebody else in the club. The only way I figured I could do that was by showing up early and scoping out the guy first. See, we had planned to each bring a white rose so we could point out each other. Well, I hid my white rose in my man bag. I was sitting at the bar looking at everybody walk through the door. Finally he came in with that white rose and I almost fainted. Girl, he looked like King Kong and Shaba's gay son."

Dior laughed.

"You know who Shaba Ranks is, right?"

"Yeah. I'm from Canada, not Mars, Gordon."

"I'm just checkin'," Gordon said. "But anyway, that white rose stayed in my bag the whole time while I danced the night away with some other guy."

Dior and Gordon talked some more, Gordon giving Dior tips on what she should and should not do on her date. At the end of their lunch break, Dior retreated to her office and finally used her time to do some work.

* * *

"Happy Valentine's Day, Dior," Larissa said, placing a wrapped gift on Dior's desk.

"Thank you, Larissa," Dior said, picking it up. Dior handed Larissa a box of candy hearts and wished her a happy Valentine's Day also.

"It's an office survival kit," Larissa volunteered, smiling.

"Aw, this is so cute," Dior said. "You would be the one to find a gift like this."

"I got Barbara a coffee mug that says 'Boss's Coffee, I am the Boss. Come and talk to me before you decide to piss in my coffee,'" Larissa excitedly told Dior.

Dior chuckled. "That's cute. Where do you find stuff like that? All I got her was a bottle of vintage wine."

"Well, she likes wine."

Dior shrugged her shoulders. "Next year I'll be more creative."

"Well, I'm not going to keep you. I see you're pretty busy," Larissa said as she gestured at all the papers scattered across Dior's desk.

"Well, thanks again, Larissa."

"You're welcome. Thank you," Larissa said, leaving Dior's cubicle.

Dior took a brief break to look through her gift from Larissa. She laughed at the comments that each candy referred to, particularly at the peppermint that read *you pretend to work, we'll pretend to pay you*. "Imagine that," she mumbled as she thought back on all the on-the-clock hours she spent surfing the Web. She put the candy back down and looked at her watch. It was ten thirty—six more hours before she would be able to go home, and two and a half hours after that she would be seeing Mr. Good Black Man for the first time. She couldn't wait. The day couldn't move fast enough.

Dior worked constantly throughout the day, trying to make the time fly. She didn't get online once, unless it was for research, and she only took a twenty-minute lunch. When four thirty rolled around, she was already on the elevator when normally she would just be shutting down her computer.

Outside was pleasant, although brisk. But the winds were calm and there was no precipitation or signs of any, so for winter weather in New York that was considered pleasant. First, Dior walked a couple of blocks to the bank so that she could get some money from the ATM. She wanted to have cash on hand to pay her drivers throughout the evening and in case for some odd reason she would have to buy her own drinks.

On the subway ride home she leaned her head against the seat and drifted off; organizing what she would do when she got home in her mind. She would run herself a bath and while waiting for the tub to fill she would lay her dress out across her bed. She would get the nude bra and panty set she had bought specifically for the dress out of the Victoria's Secret bag and take the tags off. Then she would take her Donna Karan nude stockings out of the pack and lay them across the dress. She would wrap her hair up neatly and get in the tub. She would put on her Michael lotion by Michael Kors and the matching perfume. She then would put on her undergarments, do her makeup, and let her hair down. Last, she would slip into her dress and put on her pumps. She would check herself out in the mirror. Then she would transfer all her important items such as her license, lip gloss, cell phone, money, and condoms into her new Gucci purse. Once all that was complete, she would put on her mink and walk outside to hail a taxi.

Everything went according to plan when Dior got home. She was dressed to kill and ready to meet the man behind the MySpace messages. Her purse in one hand and a single white rose in the other, she got into a cab she hastily hailed at the corner. As soon as she sat down on the seat and gave him the address for MoBay, the driver turned around so fast you would have thought he had whiplash.

"Oh no. Not you!" he said with a scowl.

Dior looked startled as she tried to figure out why the driver was mad at her.

"You're the one who tried to run without paying me," he reminded her.

She put her hand on her forehead in frustration. "Oh God, it's you. Listen, I'm so sorry. I really am. I didn't mean any harm," she said.

"Sorry doesn't pay the cab fare," the driver snapped. "You want me to drive you to MoBay on 125th Street? That will be six dollars."

Dior nodded. "That's fine."

The driver glared at her in the rearview mirror. "Show me the money."

"What?"

"Show me the money," he repeated stubbornly.

Dior was ready to say to hell with the driver and try to hail another cab, but it was getting close to seven o'clock and she didn't want to be late. And the fact remained that if the driver was acting shitty he had every right to do so. After all, she *did* try to stiff him for the fare. She blushed at the memory.

She opened her purse and pulled out a twenty-dollar bill.

"See!" she said, showing it to the driver.

"Good. Now pay in advance."

"You're kidding!"

The driver shook his head. "How do I know you're not going to stick that money back in your pocketbook and then jump out without paying me?"

Dior sighed and handed him the twenty. "You can keep the change," she said wearily.

The driver looked at her queerly. "You sure? You gave me a twenty, you know. I said the fare would be six dollars."

"I know. This is just my way of saying I'm really sorry about what happened last month. And believe me, I've never even done anything like that before. Please, forgive me. But can you start driving now? I'm going to be late."

"Sure, and thanks." He put the cab in gear and prepared to pull off but all of a sudden stopped.

"Now what's wrong?"

"This money isn't counterfeit, is it?" he asked suspiciously.

"Oh, for God's sake!" Dior reached for the car door.

"Calm down, calm down. I was just kidding," he said as he started down the street. "So, you have a hot date for Valentine's Day? You look real nice. I noticed that when you got in the cab."

I know this man isn't trying to push up on me. Dior grimaced and rolled her eyes, then noticed the driver looking at her in the rearview mirror again.

"Listen," he said in an annoyed voice, "I was just trying to be nice. You don't need to make a face like I'm trying to pick you up. You're nothing but a fare to me. And shoot. I don't even like women. I'm gay."

Dior blinked her eyes in surprise, then burst out in laughter.

"What's so funny? You have something against gay men?" the driver asked with a growl in his voice.

"No, no," Dior hurriedly assured him. "Listen, you're not going to believe this, but . . ."

As they drove down Malcolm X Boulevard, Dior spilled her guts about her tragic encounter with Chris, the encouragement she'd been given by Gordon, and her plan to meet a blind date that evening.

By the time he pulled up next to MoBay they were chatting like old buddies.

"Can you move up just a little so you're not right in front of the club? I'm following Gordon's advice and scoping him out before I find myself jumping from the fire into the frying pan. Don't worry. I'll pay you extra."

"Don't worry about it. Besides, now that I've heard your story I almost feel obligated to wait for you." He turned in the driver's seat to face her. "No offense, but you don't seem to have any kind of Gay-dar going for you. I want to stick around and make sure you get a straight guy this time."

Dior giggled. "I can't even get mad. Thanks."

Patrons went in and out of the chic lounge, but none carrying the white rose Dior and Mr. Good Black Man agreed to bring with them. Butterflies started to dance in Dior's stomach as she embraced the idea that she might have gotten stood up. She opened her purse and took out her mirror to touch up her makeup, and in that moment Mr. Good Black Man jumped out of a cab in front of MoBay and headed for the door.

"There he goes!" the driver said. "That guy has a white rose."

Dior sat up in her seat and peered out the windshield. The only visual she and the driver could get of Mr. Good Black Man was his profile. But when he reached out and put his hand on the door to open it, he turned around and the two of them got a good look at his face.

"Oh no! It can't be!" Dior groaned and fell back onto the seat.

"Isn't that the guy who took care of your tab that day?" the driver said, oblivious of her reaction. "Naw, he ain't gay. But no offense, because he was nice to you and all, but he seemed like he had the making of a real jerk if you ask me."

Dior was sick to her stomach. Mr. Good Black Man was pesky Jerome from her block. She was too through, wanting to go back home and cry herself to sleep. How could she have been so stupid? she thought. She should have seen through his "I don't post my picture because I'm not superficial" routine. A Blair Underwood look-alike? Jerome was butt ugly, no matter what he was wearing, and he didn't even bother to dress up for the blind date. He was actually walking into the club wearing that same old dingy army jacket. And a business owner who owned real estate? Jerome didn't even have a job and he lived with his mother! She should have known better than to go out on a blind date with a guy she met on the Internet. She got just what she deserved.

"So, what are you waiting for?" the driver asked, interrupting Dior's pissed-off thoughts.

Dior shook her head in disgust. Here she was all dolled up to meet the man of her dreams and the whole night was a bust. The thought of going back home and spending the night alone in her apartment contemplating her series of bad decisions brought tears to her eyes. *No*, she decided as she tried to blink back her tears. *I'm out, and I'm going to make the best of it.* She wasn't going to go home and waste her stunning and costly outfit. Besides, she could use a drink, so she decided that she wouldn't abandon an evening at MoBay. Instead, she paid the driver and right before she stepped out of the cab, she handed him the white rose. "Happy Valentine's Day."

"Huh? What's this for?"

"You don't really think I'm going to waste a perfectly good rose on that fool, do you?" she said with a smile. "And I'm certainly not going to let one monkey stop my show. I'm going to go in and have a good time by myself."

The driver grinned. "Good girl. But you don't think he'll recognize you?"

Dior shook her head. "We never exchanged pictures, and I never even gave him a description of myself. He'll recognize me from the block, but I don't think he'll have the nerve to come over and say anything to me." She smiled when she remembered what Margie had told her about him not bothering people once they stood up to him.

She walked inside MoBay and took a seat at the bar. "What would you suggest I have?" she asked the bartender when he came to take her drink order.

"Harlem mojitos are the house specialty. Can't go wrong with that," the man answered politely.

"Hey, that's what I'm having. You'll love it."

Dior turned and faced Jerome, who had come up behind her. The man seemed stunned. "Oh, it's you."

"Well, look what the cat dragged in," Dior said with a sneer.

"Forget you. I'm here meeting my girlfriend," Jerome said angrily.

Dior snorted. "Judging by the way you look I can just imagine what she looks like."

"I'll have you know she's a professional woman with a job. And she looks better than you," Jerome retorted.

Dior snorted and turned back to the bartender, who was putting her drink on the bar. "Who's that playing?" she asked him, pointing to a light-skinned man with long dreads blowing the sweetest sounds from his tenor sax.

"Julian Meyers. He's pretty good, isn't he?"

Dior nodded, then noticed a couple getting up from their table. She hurriedly paid the bartender, grabbed her drink, and rushed over before someone else could claim the spot. Her mood still lousy, she placed her jacket over the back of the vacant chair at the table to make it look as if she had a companion who had perhaps gone to the restroom.

Thirty minutes and two Harlem mojitos later, Dior's mood finally began to mellow. She started swaying her shoulders to the soulful jazz and looked around the bar. *This place really is nice*, she thought. *I really am glad I stayed.* She looked over at the bar, then did a double take. Was that the girl who lived above her squeezed in at the bar? What was her name again? Tamara?

Things are looking up, after all, Dior thought happily. *Who needs a man? Sometimes sisterhood is all it takes.*

TAMARA MURPHY

by Daaimah S. Poole

January 3, 2008

Tamara Murphy profiled in the mirror, striking pose after pose before finally settling down and squinting closely to apply just the perfect amount of black eyeliner to her beautiful brown eyes. Once she was satisfied with her eyes, she started to touch up her cheeks with a rose-color blush that accented beautifully her golden wheat skin. She then went back to striking poses. Yes, she decided, she looked good. The brown wrap dress clung tightly to her voluptuous body.

At twenty-eight she had no complaints about her extra proportions that were passed on from her mother, Beverly, and grandmother Joan. She was a bit on the thick side, but she was far from fat, and she knew how to work what she had and she worked it well. She pulled as many men with her size 14 as any of her size 3 friends. She spun around, letting the hem of the dress twirl around her as she surveyed her body and sprayed her signature cologne True Star.

The ringing of the cordless phone interrupted her daily morning routine.

"Hello," Tamara answered.

"You better get your butt up. You're going to miss your flight," Tamara's mother yelled in her ear loudly, hurting the inside of her ears.

"Mama, I'm getting ready now," she said as she stepped away from the mirror.

"What time does your flight leave?"

"I have to be at Hartsfield by ten. My flight leaves at eleven thirty."

"Girl, you need more time than an hour and a half at the airport. You have to go through security and all of that."

"Mama, nobody flies out on Wednesday. I'll be just fine," Tamara said, trying to keep the annoyance out of her voice. She loved her mom, but sometimes she could be such a mother!

"You know your grandmother's still upset you're leaving," her mother whined.

Tamara smiled. It was her mother who was having fits about her only daughter moving hundreds of miles away, but like always, she put the blame on Tamara's grandmother.

"I'm sure she'll get over it."

"I don't know, Tammy," her mother said with a sigh. "Oh, Tamara, how could you do this? Why would you take a position all the way in New York City? And taking an apartment in Harlem of all places!"

"Mom, this is a great opportunity for me."

"I know but it is just so far, and you didn't even see your apartment yet. How about if it doesn't look like the pictures and it is rat infested? You know what they say about Harlem."

"Mom, you watch too much television. The broker assured me that it's a beautiful place and she sent me dozens of pictures of it."

Just as she expected, her mother changed tactics. "But if you go to New York, how will you meet your husband and get married?"

"There are plenty of men in New York. And besides, I'm not ready for marriage."

"You should be ready for marriage, you're twenty-eight and tapping on thirty," her mother said with authority.

"Mama, I'll talk to you later. I have to finish packing."

"Tamara, you're not finished packing?" her mother exploded.

"I'm just about finished," Tamara said as she looked at the last of the empty suitcases laid out on the bed.

"Well, do you want me to take you to the airport at least? I can drop you off on the way into the city."

"No, Nicole is taking me. I'll be fine. I'll call you once I get settled. Okay?"

"Okay, please be careful," her mother said.

Tamara sighed into the phone. She couldn't understand why her mother was acting like she just had decided to move. Like she didn't know for the last three months that she had accepted a job offer in New York City. Like she didn't just have a going-away breakfast a few days ago New Year's morning.

"So I have to get ready. Okay?"

"I can bring you some breakfast," her mother said hopefully. "You should have taken one of these pies with you. They probably won't have any good food up there."

Tamara rolled her eyes. She loved her mother's cooking and she would miss it, but she was not about to carry a whole apple pie on the plane with her.

"Mom, please stop. I will be okay!"

"Okay, okay. Call me as soon as you get off the plane."

"I will," Tamara promised before pressing the Off button on her cordless phone. She looked around her empty tenth-floor condo. She couldn't believe all her furniture was gone and that she was actually moving. She was excited, yet part of her was a little scared. But it was too late to change her mind. The movers had already come and were on their way up north. Even if she wanted to, there was no turning back now. Atlanta was her home. However, she was leaving home to go and conquer the unknown.

The unknown being New York City, a dream town for anyone in her line of work. Her mother and grandmother insisted on calling her a party girl, but she was actually a prominent club and party promoter.

New York would be refreshing because Atlanta's scene was becoming saturated. There was somewhere to go seven days a week and every well-known guy on his campus called himself a party promoter. They all thought they were CEOs of their own record label and they were always name-dropping, saying, "Tyler Perry is my man." "Usher came to my last party." Or "Me and Jermaine Dupri be hanging out together." It had taken Tamara almost six years, but she had finally broken away from the pack and made a name for herself as the most successful promoter in the ATL. Her big break came when she managed to talk herself into a job promoting a big event for the Atlanta Falcons' season opener.

Over the years she had learned the right amount of kiss-butt tactics to get the right people at her parties, and she went all out for this one. She lured her athletes, rap artists, models, and film stars in with the promise of VIP treatment, complimentary bottles of champagne, and pretty girls. She paid radio hosts to slip up on air and talk about her *exclusive* party. Tamara knew when people heard the word exclusive they automatically wanted to be included. She invited all Atlanta's elite, and they all showed up. So many, in fact, that some pretty prominent people had to be turned away. That one party made her the official "It Girl." After the big write-up the event got in the *Atlanta Constitution* she was booked for two years and began getting corporate accounts and doing album release parties. People were begging her to work for them because they knew if she promoted a club it was sure to be packed with every celebrity living in the city, as well as any who might be visiting at the time. Tamara was living high as the star of Atlanta's nightlife.

Then, just three months ago, she was offered the job of a lifetime by no less than the famous Harold brothers.

Everyone in the country knew the duo, thanks to the big write-ups they'd gotten in *Black Enterprise*, *Ebony*, and *Jet* magazines.

Maurice Harold was the older brother; he was thirty-six, married, with one son. Then there was Kendall Harold, who was thirty-three, single, with no children. They were raised by their father and stepmother in Newark and worked for their father's grocery store as boys. Maurice was the hardworking one, and had a master's degree in business from the prestigious Wharton School. Kendall was the party boy. Still, they made a powerful combination. After finishing school they had struck out on their own, with their father's blessings, and were now successful real estate investors and owned several restaurants and bars in Chicago, Detroit, and Baltimore. Now they were opening a new nightclub in New York, and when they started asking around for someone to promote their latest enterprise, Tamara's name was one that came up time and time again. So they contacted her and asked her to promote the new club, which was called Onyx Lounge and was opening in six weeks on February 13, 2008.

Having already conquered Atlanta, Tamara was ready for a change, and she couldn't wait.

Tamara looked out the window and reflected on the success she'd received since graduating from Clark Atlanta University five years before. Still, with all her achievements, she hadn't been able to impress her mother or grandmother. They could never get past the fact that at twenty-eight she was still single, and were constantly trying to hook her up.

But Tamara didn't trust her mother's or grandmother's selection of men. They both had been married multiple times. If they couldn't get it right for themselves, how could they get it right for her?

Tamara's mother was Mrs. Beverly Murphy Johnson Halston Matthew. She had walked down the aisle three times and also been divorced three times. Then there was her grandmother Joan. She was the first-generation serial *marryer*. She has been married four times. She was sixty-four when she married her fourth husband, James, in November. He was twenty years her junior and looked like he could be a distant cousin of Denzel Washington. Tamara loved her mother and grandmother, but did not want to end up like them. Both women desperately always needed a man. They needed men to escort them to all the social events that they attended. They needed a man to hang a picture on the wall or just to take out the trash. Tamara wanted to one day marry, but she would not make it her life goal or the center of her universe.

Besides, too many men were very intimidated by her work. Seeing a man groupie is not pretty. Have you ever seen a guy scream and jump up and down like a teenage girl when she meets her idol? Tamara knew this firsthand; she'd seen it way too many times, and always dropped the guy immediately afterward. Then she met Donovan, a successful thirty-year-old attorney, at a charity auction. He worked for a law firm downtown and he lived in Buckhead and drove a Lexus SC430 convertible. He seemed supportive of her work, but not overly interested. He made it clear from the beginning that he was into her, not what she did for a living. They became kind of serious immediately. But the more involved they became, the less work Tamara did. Donovan would even tell her she didn't have to work her little job because he could take care of her. He even began complaining about her hours and said that he didn't like her going out every weekend. Although Tamara was in love she wasn't going to stop her life for him. Donovan wanted someone waiting for him at home. When she wasn't always available, there was an argument. They were together six months before eventually falling apart.

He didn't understand why she left him, because her mother and grandmother loved him and had already begun calling him son. If she would have let them have it their way they would have planned a summer wedding at the Piedmont Room in a garden tent. And after the fabulous wedding they would have planned a beautiful honeymoon in Barbados. They would even have named her daughter and even picked out what the baby girl would wear home from the hospital. Then two years into Tamara's perfect marriage they would call and tell her that she needed to leave him. Their reason would be that he was not spending enough time at home. They would tell her what divorce attorney to use to make sure she got hefty alimony payments. Then they would invite her to get-togethers to complain how men ain't shit. She'd seen the cycle so many times she knew it by heart, and was glad she escaped it.

Donovan was a year ago and since then she hadn't dated anyone seriously. She didn't have the time. The last thing Tamara was trying to do was settle down with one man. Her goal in NYC was to date like a man and not get caught up on one.

She suddenly glanced at her watch. Time was moving quickly; it was already 9:15. She had about forty-five minutes to finish packing. She scurried around her place picking up what was left of her belongings and throwing them into her suitcase. Nicole would be on time—she always was.

Forty minutes later Tamara looked down at her ringing phone and its flashing red screen. Nicole's number was blinking. Tamara picked up. Without saying hello she answered, "I'll be right down."

"Hurry up," Nicole yelled in Tamara's ear.

Tamara took one last look around her place and closed the door. She walked to the elevator, dragging her two large black suitcases behind her. Nicole waved at Tamara to hurry up while talking on her cell phone. Nicole had on dark blue skinny jeans with flat-soled brown boots and matching scarf and hat. Her curly dark brown hair stuck out a little. Tamara dragged her luggage as fast as she could, which wasn't fast enough for Nicole. She momentarily took the phone away from her ear and finally yelled, "Come on."

Once Tamara reached Nicole's Nissan Sentra she popped the trunk for her and helped her load the heavy bags in the car. She gave her a fast sideways hug and ran to the front seat. Tamara opened the door and entered the car and put on her seat belt. Nicole was on the phone arguing with someone. Tamara sat back and looked one last time at her building. She then tuned into Nicole's heated conversation.

"What do you mean?" Nicole screamed. "I don't know about all that. What are you talking about? . . . Yeah, well, if that's the way you want it, fine. Well, Rahsan, you know I wasn't like that when I met you. Well, I can't change who I am. No, I won't. Listen, I'll talk to you later," she said as she turned on the radio and snapped the phone shut. The Frank Ski Morning Show was blasting.

"Forget him," Nicole said aloud.

"Forget who? Who got you all worked up this morning?" Tamara asked as Nicole's window wipers swayed, cleaning the light rain off the windshield.

"Nothing, it's just that guy Rahsan."

"Rahsan?"

"That guy from my grad class. Rahsan."

"Okay, okay, I remember who he is. So what's the problem?"

"Well, I've been dating him three weeks and already he's talking that mess."

"What mess?" Tamara asked.

"He said that I should stop perming my hair."

Tamara laughed and managed to get out a "What?" between giggles.

"Yeah, isn't he crazy? He is trying to turn me into an Afronconic or something."

"You mean Afrocentric."

"Yeah, Afrocentric, Afroconic, whatever, same thing. So I told him I like weave and I get a touch-up every six weeks. This is how you met me and I'm not changing. He's a vegetarian, too! I tried those soy burgers. I stopped eating meat in front of him, but my hair, that's where I draw the line."

Tamara shook her head at Nicole's latest rant, but knew it was only a matter of time before Nicole flipped the script on her. She was always amazed how Nicole would switch her style of dress and attitude for whatever man she was dating at the moment.

Changing the subject, Nicole said, "So, what's up with you? How do you feel about leaving? You are going so far away."

"I'm a little scared, but I'm ready. I still have all my contacts here and if I ever want to come home I can. But how many times will I get a chance to go to New York and take over?" Tamara said to Nicole while still convincing herself that she was making the right decision.

"That's true, but I'm still going to miss you."

"You'll be okay."

"Yeah, maybe I'll move north after grad school!"

As they approached the airport, Tamara's stomach began to turn and she became a little dizzy. However, she took a long, deep breath and closed her eyes and said a little silent prayer. When she opened her eyes the car had stopped and she had arrived at the airport. She gathered her luggage and gave Nicole a firm hug. Tamara then took a five out of her wallet and handed it to the skycap who assisted her to baggage check. She checked her luggage, grabbed a coffee, then sat down and sipped her coffee until her flight was announced.

The first thing that greeted Tamara as she exited the airplane in La Guardia International Airport was the cold weather. She was not dressed appropriately for the weather at all. The cold wind was blowing through her dress. She would have to wear the big coat she packed. She had no idea where baggage claim was, so she followed the other passengers off her plane. They all seemed to know where they were going. They were walking fast and she tried to keep up with them. There were people everywhere, all shades and colors, walking by speaking different languages. Some with slanted eyes; others with wide eyes. Some of the people were looking like they ran the world and others just as lost as she was. She continued to follow the passengers from her plane to baggage claim. Tamara claimed her bag and then went and stood in the taxi line. Ten minutes later an older brown gentleman pulled up. He grabbed her luggage and asked her if she had any more bags. He opened her door and she took a seat. There was jazz playing lightly on his radio. He opened his cab partition window and asked her where she was going.

"One hundred and nineteenth Street and Malcolm X Boulevard," she said to the driver.

"You are going to Harlem, huh?"

"Yes," she said.

"Are you visiting?" he asked

"No, I just moved here."

"From where?" he asked.

"Atlanta," she said.

"Atlanta? I have family in Savannah."

"Really?"

"Did you go to Spellman down there?"

"No, Clark Atlanta," Tamara responded as she stared out the window looking at her surroundings. She didn't want to be rude, but she didn't have time to make small talk with him. She had calls to make. She looked in her planner in search of her new landlady's name and telephone number.

After a twenty-minute ride Tamara raised her head and noticed the rows of houses and apartment buildings on each block that she passed by. The houses were very large and so close together. She had arrived in Harlem. There was a lot to see. They rode down 125th Street, and it was just like she'd always heard. Even though it was in the middle of the afternoon and most folks should be at work, the street was crowded with people walking around, heads held high and looking neither left nor right as they strode down the block. Street vendors stood in front of tables filled with books, CDs, jewelry, socks, gloves, just about anything, and yelled for people to stop and take a look. Huge billboards hung over the top of buildings, with pictures of celebrities endorsing sneakers or announcing a new CD. On the corner was a young girl with pants so tight they looked like they were painted on, screaming on a guy with pants that hung so low on his hips they looked like they were going to fall off. The couple looked like they were getting ready to come to blows, but no one even stopped to look.

Yeah, Tamara, thought. *I'm really in Harlem. And I love it already.*

As the driver continued to talk, she ignored his ramblings and dialed Marjorie Graham, her new landlady.

"Hello."

"Good afternoon, Mrs. Graham, this is Tamara Murphy. I was just confirming that I will be arriving shortly."

"That's fine, dear," the woman said nonchalantly. "I'll be here when you get here."

Tamara hung up her phone and the man continued to talk. He didn't get the picture yet that she was not listening to him. She was too busy typing in her BlackBerry phone.

"Over there is a nice place, MoBay," he said, pointing to a small club in the middle of the block. "They have a really good jazz band and my wife loves the Harlem mojitos. You should check it out sometime."

"Yeah," she said.

Moments later he said, "Well, we are here." She looked up at the tall three-story brownstone. Four stories really, if you counted the garden apartment, which was just four steps down from street level. Margie's Diamond Palace, the landlady had called it. Looking at it now, she could see why it was called a palace. It was huge, as were the fifty or so brownstones that lined the block. She handed the taxi driver his $22.50 fare and waited for him to get out and open her door for her. It took her a few minutes to realize that wasn't happening. She jumped out of the car and walked around to the trunk and waited for the driver to slowly get out and pop it open. Now that he had his money he wasn't as talkative or courteous as he had been in the beginning of the ride. He did reach in and took out her two bags and deposited them on the curb before hopping back in his cab and pulling off. It was up to her to haul the luggage up the steep stairs to the brownstone's front door.

She dialed the landlady again, who said she would be right there to meet her. While Tamara waited for her, she noticed a tall scruffy-looking man with penitentiary eyes staring at her bags. Taking no chances, she picked them up and climbed the stairs. He probably was about to rob her in broad daylight. He began walking toward her smiling very hard, like they were old friends. Something about his smile frightened her, but she didn't turn away. She had to keep her eye on him to see what he was doing. As he approached the steps he looked up and said, "How you doin'?"

Tamara just looked down at him without blinking. She tried her best to look as mean as possible. She knew that men were like dogs; if they detected fear they would attack. But if you showed them no fear they would walk past. So she mean-mugged him directly in the eye. And just like a dog he slinked away, but she knew unlike a dog the man would likely be back again. Her thoughts were interrupted by a short heavy woman who was climbing the stairs.

"Are you Tamara? I'm Marjorie Graham. You can call me Margie. Everyone else does." The woman was panting by the time she reached the top of the steps. She obviously didn't care too much about her appearance. She had on a blue wool coat, and a brown felt hat was pulled down low over her graying dreadlocks, and she was wearing purple socks with white slippers. And she reeked of cigarette smoke.

"Welcome to Margie's Diamond Palace. Come on in," Margie said as she unlocked the door. "That's all you have?"

"No, the movers will be delivering the rest of my things tomorrow."

"Well, when they come make sure they don't scratch my walls up, okay?"

"I'll make sure they won't," Tamara said.

"Where are you from again?" she asked.

"Atlanta."

"Yeah, that's right. How was your flight?"

"Okay."

"Well, that's good. Here's your apartment right here. You've got the first-floor apartment. There's one apartment below you. That's the garden apartment. Just had another young girl move in last week. Probably same age as you." Margie cocked her head. "How old are you, anyway?"

"Twenty-eight."

"Twenty-eight, huh? You look younger, and you got that little girl voice going for you, too. Bet it drives men crazy, huh?" The woman shrugged. "None of my business if it does. None of my business. I'm guessing the girl downstairs might be a little younger than you, but maybe not by much. You'll get to meet her, I guess, being you all living in the same building. Maybe not. None of my business if you don't. None of my business. Come on, let me show you the apartment."

For someone who keeps claiming things are none of her business she sure seems to be all up in mine, Tamara thought, though she managed to keep a smile on her face as she followed the woman around.

The bathroom had one of those old-fashioned tubs, the kind with the curved legs, and the kitchen was totally renovated with new cabinets and woodwork. The living room, dining room, and bedroom all had their original hardwood floors and gigantic bay windows. The ceilings were high, and all sported white ceiling fans.

"This is really impressive," Tamara said as she looked around.

Margie shrugged. "Should be. I spent a fortune in renovations," she said as she handed Tamara the keys. "Listen, if you need anything, I live in the brownstone two doors down. Just ring my bell. Or call me out the window. Hope you like it here." And with that she was gone.

Tamara closed her door, then went to the window to see if that strange man was there, but he was gone. She felt a little reassured and began imagining where and how she was going to set up everything in her apartment. There was a big mirror attached to the closet door in the bedroom. She looked into it.

She was still impressed with herself. She had really moved to New York City all on her own. She smiled and fluffed her hair and said, "New York, I'm here and I'm about to take over."

Tamara was awake for thirty minutes before finally getting out of her bed. She was still so tired from the day before. She had been directing the movers and moving and unpacking boxes all day long. Tamara told herself she would get up early and finish unpacking, but she didn't feel like moving yet. She lay in the bed and stared at the ceiling. Then she closed her eyes for ten more minutes. She was on her way back to sleep when the phone rang.

"Good morning, little girl," her mother sang in her ear.

"Hi, Mama."

"I'm on! I'm on here, too!" her grandmother said.

"Hi, Nana."

"How are you? How is New York so far? Did you get mugged yet? Did you see a bunch of graffiti?" her mother and grandmother questioned simultaneously.

"No, Grandma, everything is great," she lied. Tamara dared not tell them about the strange man hanging around her building.

"Well, I'm glad you like it. Because we were thinking about coming to help you get settled in."

"No, you can't come up," Tamara said quickly.

"And why not?" her grandmother Joan asked.

"Nana, well, because I'm going to be very busy and, well, I won't have time."

"That's okay, we can take in a show and do some sightseeing," her mother, Beverly, added.

"No! Y'all can't come and I have to go. I'm going to be busy. Let me do a few things and then I'll call you back."

"We can buy things for your new place. And help you set everything up. I bet you didn't even set up your bed yet," Tamara's mother said.

Tamara looked at all the brown boxes still stacked all around her. And sure enough, her bed was still on the floor. Her mother knew her very well and that angered her. Tamara decided to end the double team and said, "Another call is coming in, Mom. It's my boss. Love you both, good-bye."

Tamara was going to let them visit eventually, but just not right now. She sat up and thought about what she was going to do for the day. She didn't have to start her new job until Monday. She had a few days to learn her neighborhood, unpack, and decorate her place. She decided to write a list out and get started on it, right after she showered.

After a long hot shower, Tamara dressed in pink and gray sweats and Nike running shoes. She began to pace in her new home. She couldn't decide which task to complete first. Tamara was going to first go to the grocery store and then start setting up everything in her apartment when she got back.

She couldn't believe it. As soon as she closed the front door behind her and climbed down the steps the weird-looking guy from the day before was in her face.

"Hey. You just moved in, huh? I saw them bringing your stuff in yesterday." He flashed a smile that showed yellow teeth pasted with an inch of plaque. "Welcome to the neighborhood. Where you from?"

Tamara threw her head up high and moved past him without saying anything, hoping he'd take the hint. Like the dog she already knew he was, he didn't.

"Girl, you ain't gotta be so mean," he said, trying to stay in step with her. "I'm just trying to be friendly. You want me to show you around or something? I got some time on my hands."

"Jerome!"

Tamara swung around to see who was shouting and saw her landlady leaning out the window of the brownstone two houses down from her own.

"Jerome," the woman shouted again. "Leave that girl alone. Didn't I tell you to stop bothering my tenants? The girl ain't even move in good and you harassing her."

"Oh, shut up, you old bag. You just mad I'm not talking to you," Jerome grumbled.

"I heard that. Ain't nothing wrong with my ears, you know." A cigarette dangled from the woman's lips as she spoke. "Why don't you go get a job with your trifling self 'stead of trying to talk to every girl you see?"

Tamara couldn't help but smile as she walked away while they bickered. Living in Harlem was going to be a far cry from Atlanta. But hell, she could handle it.

When Tamara returned from the market she began preparing breakfast. Though Tamara didn't do it often, she loved to cook. All the women in her family did. She could remember at four blending yellow batter and helping her mother bake cakes. She cracked an egg in the pan and put on a cup of coffee. She then looked at her watch and decided she would check in with her new boss. It was eleven in the morning on a Thursday. He should be available. She dialed his number and his phone rang five times. She was prepared to leave a message when he picked up.

"Good morning. Mr. Harold? This is Tamara Murphy."

"Hey. Um, good morning, hold on," he said. Tamara heard him ordering breakfast. He then came back to the line and said, "Are you in town yet?"

"Yes, I arrived yesterday."

"Are you settled in?"

"Just about."

"Good. I'm glad to hear that. If you're available I would like for you to meet with me tomorrow. Scratch that. Actually, I'm about to have breakfast. Why don't you join me at Touver Café now?"

"Okay," Tamara said reluctantly. Her breakfast was halfway cooked, but she couldn't tell him no. It wouldn't make a good impression. She felt like kicking herself for even calling him.

"How soon can you get here?" he asked, all pushy.

"I'll be right there," she said as she jotted down the address. Tamara sighed as she began taking her gray sweats off.

She rummaged through her boxes and tried to find something presentable to wear. She changed her clothes several times, but nothing looked right. She settled on pointy-toe brown riding boots, black slacks, an olive-green button-down blouse with a black puffy-waist jacket, and a black hat that she tilted to the side. She grabbed her briefcase and planner and took a cab to the restaurant.

Café Touver was busy and congested. Tamara stood in the front and scanned each table to see where he was sitting. She located him and began to walk his way. He stood up and she admired how tall and beautiful he was. Maurice Harold was a warm walnut brown, with a closely shaven head. He had near perfect white teeth and salmon-pink gums. His legs appeared strong even through his dark blue slacks.

"Thanks for meeting up with me on such short notice. I just wanted to go over everything with you," he said as she sat down. He pulled out a notepad with a list of things written down. "Oh. And go ahead and order something."

"No, I'm okay," Tamara said as she took a quick glance at the menu and placed it back on the table. She was hungry but a loudspeaker with her grandmother's voice rang in her head saying "No eating in front of men. And if you have to eat in front of them, just have something light. Nothing messy."

"You sure?" he asked.

"Um, I'll just have toast and coffee," Tamara said.

"No, you have to try their blueberry waffles. They are delicious," he said as he wiped his mouth with a white napkin. He offered again and she declined. As the waitress came over to the table Maurice smiled and said, "Please bring the lady toast and coffee."

"Sure, sir. Would you like me to refill your coffee?" the waitress offered. Maurice said he was good and then the waitress left the table. Tamara noticed the extra attention the waitress gave him. Somehow women can detect success on a man. She had to admit she was impressed herself. Maybe it was the way he was dressed. Or maybe it was the way he was not coming on to her. Either way there was something special about him. It might have been the way his words came out of his mouth or the way he stood. He was a man of wealth, but he didn't flaunt it. You could just feel his confidence. Most men she encountered wanted her to know that they were wealthy the moment she met them. It was something simple like giving her their business card with doctor such and such on it or rolling up their sleeve to reveal their expensive watch. Maurice was at least a five-hundred-thousand-dollarnaire and moved through life like the average Joe. There was something sexy and intriguing about that. But he was married, and her boss and she could never mix business with pleasure.

The waitress came back within minutes with the toast and coffee. "If you need anything please don't hesitate to ask," she said as she bent down and smiled. She was directly in front of him and ignoring Tamara. Maurice smiled and said thank you.

"So, how do you like everything so far?" Maurice asked.

"It's good."

"New York is a hard place to get used to. I'm not from here. I'm originally from Newark. But the city has grown on me."

"That's in the northern part of New Jersey, right?"

"Yeah, the brick city. I still live in Jersey. I'm right across the bridge. I wanted to stay close to my son."

Tamara's heart skipped a beat. "I thought you were married."

"No, I'm divorced. I've been divorced about two months now. But I still have to be close to him to teach him how to be a man. My father made me and Kendall work since we were ten. I want my son to have the same work ethic. I bagged bags at the market and had a paper route by twelve."

"You were a little entrepreneur, huh?"

"Yeah, but enough about me," Maurice said as he pulled some documents out of his briefcase. "Here are some pictures of the club. You should probably get down there in the next day or so to get the feel of the place. The club holds seven hundred. I have a contact list from previous events we held in Miami and Detroit. But I want you to make some new contacts as well. If necessary we will pay for hotel and flight to get them here. Offer everyone a bottle of champagne and a table. Also, here is a list of things that still haven't been done yet."

Tamara looked over the contacts, noticing big names in film, music, and television.

"Call and confirm the address and then send the invitation. Yeah, do that immediately. We have less than six weeks. So you need to get started ASAP." He talked fast, but she already noticed that most of the people in New York did so.

Tamara nodded and said, "I will." She then exhaled as she scrolled through the things that still needed to be done on the list. She thought about all the work she had ahead of her.

"My brother wanted to hire this young white kid who thought he knew everything. I didn't like him. He was well connected, but I didn't like his vision. He seemed like he didn't really care about our business."

Hmph. He's putting me on notice that I can be replaced. Not likely. Then she asked with a slight attitude, "So, what have you done so far? Have you contacted any media? Do you have any sponsors in mind?"

"No, we don't have any sponsors and to be honest we haven't had an opportunity to take care of anything yet. But that's where you come in. I'm confident that you will handle everything. You were handpicked."

Tamara looked down at Maurice's list and tried to keep her composure. As together as the brothers were supposed to be, they weren't together at all. Sure, they were smart enough to hire her, but they should have at least started some of the groundwork before now. Six weeks was a long time, but it wasn't that long.

"Are you aware of the success rates of nightclubs?" Maurice asked Tamara.

"Yes, most clubs close in their first year," Tamara said, looking Maurice in the eye.

"Exactly. But we are not closing. We are here to stay. I want everyone in this city to know that Onyx Lounge is the only place to go. I don't want it to be the hot club for the moment. We're trying to be a staple in New York nightlife. We have to be different. This town is a different animal than Atlanta, Tamara. These people are used to the biggest, the flashiest, and the brightest. They are not impressed easily. People see celebrities walking down the street every day like so what. So once we get this club up and going, we want to open more clubs in Vegas and then Los Angeles. Do you see where I'm going with this?"

Tamara nodded her head and continued to take notes as Maurice rambled on. He kept saying how great and dynamic Onyx Lounge was going to be. Maurice Harold was talking a lot of shit. Tamara had met men like him in the past. He was a fast talker. He was a man who could get you hyped and ready to go out and sell anything. He had that same type of charisma that a television evangelist had or the late-night commercial get-rich-overnight sellers. You don't know why you believe, but you do. And she had to give him credit. Tamara was already somewhat believing in the dream.

Now that Maurice had finally stopped talking, it was Tamara's turn to start asking questions.

"Is there a kitchen at this location?" she asked.

"Yeah and no. It's still getting worked on and we are only doing light appetizers for the grand opening."

"Did you have any color schemes, or themes in mind for the grand opening?" Tamara asked.

"No, I just wanted something very chic. I was thinking about making it a winter white event, or since we are opening the day before Valentine's Day, maybe something all red."

Tamara thought both of his ideas were horrible. "Maurice, you said you want a chic event. So why not make it an all black event and call it the Blackout? I mean, the club is called Onyx, and an onyx is black."

Maurice smiled at Tamara and said, "That's a good idea. Let's go with it."

"Is my office inside the club?" Tamara asked.

"Yeah, I wanted to talk to you about that, too! They're not finished with that yet, either. Won't be for another two weeks. So for right now you're going to have to work out of your apartment? Is that okay?"

Tamara was beginning to wonder what the hell she had gotten herself into. The Harold brothers didn't have a solid guest list, theme, or menu for an event that was only weeks away. Maurice must have noticed the displeased look on her face. "Of course I'll reimburse you for any expenses while you're working out of your place."

"Of course," Tamara said as she took a sip of her coffee. *Damn right, you will,* she thought.

The meeting was over a half hour later. Tamara tucked the list inside her briefcase and exited the restaurant. She would deal with it later. She just wanted to enjoy her new city. She headed to Central Park to take in the sights. There were nannies pushing expensive big-wheeled carriages with babies bundled up like little caterpillars. Joggers with spandex were running around with not enough clothes on. A man was handing out a free newspaper call the *New Democracy.* Tamara walked past a curbside vendor selling hot peanuts. The aroma was enticing. She didn't think she could trust eating food from the street, but she grabbed a bag anyway.

It was three hours later before Tamara was home and laying all her notes on her kitchen table. She looked over his contact list and huffed. She had to take advantage of every moment she had. She decided to write her own list. She needed a host, a radio station to promote the event, and she had to contact local and national media, photographers, a caterer, and sponsors. Then she still had to get her guest list together and figure out how she would decorate the event without getting into the club for another two weeks. Tamara was beginning to feel overwhelmed. However, she knew no matter what happened she had to get it done and the outcome had to be great.

Tamara thought working from home would be easy. All she had to do was roll out of bed, get her coffee, shower, and get on the telephone. However, she was having difficulties getting herself and things together. She had not made any progress in days. She spent the weekend watching VH-1 and told herself she would get to everything on Monday. When Monday came, instead of starting on her list she spent the day catching up with her grandmother and mother on the phone. Then she read her favorite online blogs and browsed her favorite gossip Web sites.

Tamara knew she was behind and the only way she would be able to get everything accomplished was by hiring an assistant. Ideally she was looking for a young college student who could help her a few hours a day. She went to Craig's List and posted a help-wanted ad. Hopefully someone would respond as soon as possible.

Tamara began to check her e-mail. She saw one from Nicole with *Call me. Important* in the subject line. She opened the e-mail. It read for her to call Nicole at work.

"Nicole Gilham," Nicole answered.

"What happened with Rahsan?"

"Okay, listen, I need your opinion on something. I told Rahsan I would try the whole natural thing out, right? But he said I have to start from scratch and cut all my hair off. So do you think I should cut my hair?"

"No."

"Why not?"

"Because it is your hair and if he can't appreciate the woman you are, then forget him. How about if it doesn't work out and you cut off all your hair for nothing?"

"Yeah, you're right. Well, how are things working out for you?"

"It's okay. I have a lot of work to do but I can handle it. You know how I do."

"I looked your bosses up. They are cuties."

"Yeah, they are. They're just unorganized as hell. I still have to do all this work. They don't even have a host or a radio station to promote the club."

"Really? Well, you know one of my sorors, Shaunell, works on the radio up there in New York. I don't know which station, but I can find out for you."

"That would be so good. See what you can find out. Your sorors work everywhere."

"They do. That's why you should have pledged pink and green," Nicole sang out.

"I wasn't with all that skiwee stuff. Back then I didn't have time," Tamara said, laughing.

"Don't say stuff like that or I won't call," Nicole said seriously.

"Stop getting bent out of shape and just get the info for me. I'll call you later. Bye."

Truth be told, Tamara did wish she would have pledged something. She wished she was part of a sorority, a Delta or an AKA. But back then she was more into trying just to graduate and get out of college. But now she regretted that she missed out on all the connections.

Tamara thought she would get started with her work after lunch, but then she decided she needed to call her mother again.

"Mom, what are you doing?"

"Getting things together for the Evans wedding next week. You know Latia Evans met her husband in college? Smart girl, right?"

Tamara ignored her mother's comment. "Yes, smart girl, Mom."

"How about the men out there? Any hopefuls yet?"

"No, not yet, Ma. I only been out here a couple of days."

"Something will come through for you. And I'm glad you called. Do you think you will be able to take a week off in

May? I want to take Nana on a cruise for her sixty-fifth birthday."

"Tell me the dates. They probably have cheaper tickets online."

"I'm not putting my credit card number in the air so somebody can go in my account and steal all my money."

"Okay, Mom. I'll talk to you later."

After Tamara hung up with her mother she went online to price cruises and e-mailed her mother the results. She turned on the television as she started unpacking, and turned to *Oprah*. After *Oprah* went off, there was a song that needed to be downloaded. Tamara had toes that needed the polish removed and hair that should be washed. By five o'clock she had retired for the day. It was too late to make phone calls and she was plain ol' tired, although she hadn't done anything work related.

The next morning Tamara began calling names from the list that Maurice had given her. Half the numbers were disconnected and the others no longer worked for the person anymore. Only about a fourth of the list was good. She decided to compile her own list of rappers, athletes, and entertainment elite. She dubbed it her must-haves wish list. If she got a third of them to show up, that would be great. She got their contact info and began calling. Her first ten calls she got three yeses, and one maybe, and six flat-out nos. She was a little discouraged, but she kept trying. She decided to get the hot new model everyone was talking about, Natalia. She dialed her publicist, Adriana.

"Hi, this is Tamara Murphy. I'm calling to invite your client Natalia to the grand opening of Club Onyx, a premier VIP club owned by the Harold brothers."

"Yes, I've heard of them. What's the date?"

"February thirteenth."

"Sorry, she's going to be out of town. Good luck, though," she said shallowly as she ended the call. Tamara crossed her name off the list of hopeful guests. The next three publicists said they had to check schedules and call her back.

Tamara took a walk around her apartment and then decided to stop calling publicists. She would finish her list later. She began making press kits to send to newspapers, television stations, and magazines. She left a message for the *Fox Morning Show* and the *New York Post*. She then looked in the *New York City Globe* and called the entertainment editor. She got another voice mail and once again introduced herself and stated the reason for her call. Two minutes later she got a call back.

"Hi. Tamara Murphy please."

"This is she."

"Hi, this is Stephanie Meadows. I received your message. I would love to cover the grand opening of the Onyx Lounge, but more importantly can you get me an interview with the Harold brothers?"

"I'm pretty sure I can do that."

"Thanks so much. I'll try to get them as much coverage as possible. Let me know what their availability is."

Damn, she thought as she hung up the telephone, *why couldn't all of my calls go like that?* Tamara was so excited about the Globe being secured she began to relax a little until she got a reality check call from Maurice Harold. "Tamara, how are things going?" he asked.

"Oh, things are going great. I got you an interview with the *Globe*."

"The *Globe*? Okay. What about the *Daily News* and the *Post*?"

"I'm still working on them."

"Still working on them? You've been at it a week now, haven't you?"

"Not quite. And like I said, I'm still working on them." Tamara struggled to keep the attitude out of her voice.

"Well, if it's okay I would like to meet up with you. You

don't have to come out. I can come to your place. Maybe about noon?"

"Noon? That's fine," Tamara said as she jumped out of bed and tried to figure out how to make her apartment look livable in three hours. She pushed all of her boxes into her room. She set up her kitchen, then her bathroom. Her place was coming together. She jumped in the shower and then put on a black skirt and a purple shirt with a collar.

She looked out the window just as Maurice was getting out of his car, and saw that the girl from the garden apartment was walking out her door as Maurice was starting up the stairs to the front door. Tamara rushed out to meet Maurice instead of waiting for him to ring the bell. She saw how her neighbor was eyeing him, and she didn't know why, but she was a little jealous. She'd met Dior, a small china-doll-looking chick, a few days before, and she seemed nice, but still, she didn't have any business making eyes at her boss.

"Hi, Maurice, come on in," she said as she opened the door. "Oh, hi, Dior. I didn't notice you there." The woman smiled. Tamara smiled back.

Maurice followed her into the apartment. Tamara had paperwork lying around like she had been working very hard.

"This is a great place. I love these hardwood floors. How did you find it?"

"Through a broker."

"You're lucky. It's really hard finding something this spacious and this nice. These hardwood floors are beautiful."

"Thanks," Tamara said.

"Did you find a host yet?" Maurice asked as he took a seat on the couch.

"No, but I'm working on it. I just about have Shaunell."

"From WKAZ? I really like her. Make that happen. She is good. Also, I want you to call Daron Pearson's publicist. I want him there. He's in town shooting a movie. If we get him to come, that would be great."

Tamara made a mental note of that. Daron Pearson was the

next Eddie Murphy, Jamie Foxx, Chris Tucker, etc. "So, what else?"

"What are your plans after this?"

"I don't know. I'm going to make some more phone calls and I'm hiring an assistant."

"Okay, well, I want you to go with me to pick out office furniture."

"When?"

"Can you go now?" he asked.

He really was pushy, but then again he was also fine, and there was nothing wrong with taking time to go out shopping with a handsome man. "Sure," she heard herself saying. "Let me grab my coat."

They went to the Furniture Warehouse, where she picked out a glass table, silver filing cabinets, and a big black leather office chair. Then they went to Staples to purchase office supplies. He took care of the charges, on his platinum American Express. She glanced over at him and noticed him staring at her legs. As soon as she caught him, he turned away. Then she caught him again. For a moment she imagined how his strong hands would feel going up her legs and then he caught her staring at him.

"Are you okay?" Maurice asked as he came up to her and began scrunching her shoulder. His simple touch excited her even if it was only her shoulder.

"I'm fine," she said, pulling away from him. *Keep everything in check*, she reminded herself. He might be nice, good looking, and newly single, but he was also her boss. The last thing she needed was to get caught up on him. "You ready to leave?"

He paid for the items and arranged to have them delivered to the club, then dropped her back off at her brownstone.

"You're doing a great job. Keep at it," he said before pulling off.

Tamara was officially on a roll. She had secured the *Fox Morning Show* and had two sponsors, Genaurd Cognac and

Maziane Jeans. She decided to do a few more follow-up calls and send a few e-mails, right after she watched an episode of *Maury* to see who the baby's father was. She couldn't turn the television off yet. Her eyes were fixed to the screen. Even as she brushed her teeth she came out of the bathroom to make sure the volume was up to the maximum. Maury took out the envelope and said, "You are the baby's father." The woman on the show jumped up and then began to yell at her proven baby's father. Tamara turned off the television and began to get back to work. She checked her messages; there were five. One from Nicole, one from her mother, and three were calls in reference to the assistant position she had listed online.

"Nicole, what's up?"

"I have all my soror Shaunell's information. She hosts the afternoon drive at WKAZ. I can call her."

"No, just give me her number and I'll call her," Tamara said. She called the radio station and asked to speak to Shaunell and was sent directly to her voice mail. She didn't want to come across too eager, so she left her name and information and asked her to call her back.

The next day Tamara met with candidates who had responded to her ad for an assistant. She scheduled all of the appointments thirty minutes apart. The first person who came was a joke. Before he sat down she wanted to scream. He was a young nerdy Asian guy with an engineering degree. He didn't have any experience in publicity or office work. He began to tell her how he didn't have any money and at this point he was willing to take anything. Tamara felt sorry for him so she bought him lunch, told him to go to Monster.com, and wished him luck. The next person she interviewed was Amira Smalls. She was about twenty-two and had interned at her hometown radio station in Ohio. Tamara was really impressed initially, but after speaking with her she realized the girl was not very polished. Her hands were ashy and she kept using slang. She spoke to Tamara like they were homegirls. Although she really liked Amira she didn't like her "round the way" approach. She tore up her resume as soon as she left. She waited around for her next interview, but he never showed up so she went home to take care of the rest of her business.

The popping and whistling noise from the radiator interrupted Tamara's thoughts. She had just over a month to get everything together. She still needed an assistant desperately. She had interviewed seven people and didn't find anyone she liked. Tamara walked to her window and glanced out of it. She dreaded going outside. It was too cold out and it was supposed to snow. Tamara didn't want to leave her warm apartment, but she had to meet up with Shaunell. She had returned her phone call earlier and asked her to meet her at the comedy show that she hosted every Wednesday. She needed Shaunell to host the event. She did a little research on her and found that she was a hot commodity. Shaunell was number one in New York City for the afternoon drive slot. With Shaunell on board as her host, other doors would open, or so Tamara hoped. But at this point she was getting desperate. NYC wasn't as easy a nut to crack as she had thought it'd be. Initially everything was coming together for her. But now she had problems getting a caterer, and more sponsors. The last couple of publicists she had spoken to were very rude. It was becoming somewhat frustrating. In Atlanta Tamara had everything on lock because she knew everyone, and people who she didn't know knew someone who she did. But this was new for her. Being rejected and people telling her no. She was becoming more than a little discouraged. She was beginning to think maybe she had made the wrong decision. Maybe she should go home before she got embarrassed. She was in over her head and she knew it. She missed her mother and Nana. She was lonely in New York City.

Despondent, Tamara decided to check her messages to see who else called back to turn her down.

"Tamara, this is your mother. I just wanted to say I was

proud of you. It takes a lot to get up and move to a new city. I wish I had half of your determination, daughter. I love you! And eventually you will get that husband, so don't give up, 'cause I need some grandbabies."

She played the message twice. Her mother actually said she was proud of her? Maybe things weren't so bad after all.

Tamara walked into the small dark comedy club. There were little circle tables with black tablecloths and red candles flickering on each table. There was a small stage where a comedian was telling jokes with props, throwing them everywhere. People were clapping and stomping their feet at his jokes. Tamara saw a man wearing a WKAZ T-shirt. He was six feet, and he was very handsome with jet-black naturally wavy short hair and a rich peanut butter complexion. She walked up to him. "Hi, excuse me, I'm looking for Shaunell."

"She's over there at the bar. She'll be right back," he said.

"Okay, thank you," Tamara said as she took a seat at the bar.

"Is there anything I can help you with?" the man asked.

"No, that's okay. I'll wait for her." The man was attractive and being sweet, but she didn't have time to be nice. She was there on a mission. A few moments later Tamara spotted someone who looked like she could be Shaunell walking toward the bar. She had tanned brown skin, a long auburn weave, and fake eyelashes. Tamara walked over to her and said, "Shaunell?" The woman turned around and said "Hello" like Tamara was her fan and kept walking.

Tamara followed her and said, "Shaunell, I'm Tamara. Nicole's friend. You told me to meet you here."

The woman's attitude did a complete 180. "Hey, girl, sorry, I thought you were a listener. Give me two seconds. I'll be right back."

Tamara took a seat at a table and a bartender came over and asked if she needed anything to drink. She ordered a cosmo as Shaunell told the audience to give it up for the last comedienne who left the stage. Shaunell then ran back over to the table and thanked Tamara for waiting. As soon as she was seated Tamara began telling her about the club.

"I wanted to meet with you, to see if you would be interested in hosting an event at Onyx Lounge, a new club. It is a mostly VIP club opening next month on the thirteenth. You will receive complimentary tickets for three guests, a bottle of champagne, a table, and a hosting fee." Tamara told her about the invited guests and a little history on the Harold brothers.

"Oh, so this is major, huh? I'm so glad you thought of me. I'm there. What's the dress code?" Shaunell asked.

"It's an all-black affair."

"I have a nice black dress already. Maybe I might meet me a Valentine's Day date," Shaunell said, laughing between sips of her drink.

"Yeah, there will be plenty of men. I'm working on ways now to let everyone know about it. "

"Well, I'll do my part. I'll tell everyone I know. You should probably speak with my promotion director. He can definitely help you. He's right over there," she said as she pointed to the man who had been trying to make conversation with Tamara earlier.

"I'll have him come over to meet you," Shaunell said as she waved for the man to join them at their table.

"Hey, Aaron, I want you to meet Tamara. She's a friend of my soror Nicole."

"Nice to meet you," he said like he had forgotten Tamara was rude to him less than a half hour ago. Although Tamara was embarrassed she was not going to suddenly get nice and change her position. Shaunell began to speak again and said, "Aaron, she and the Harold brothers are opening a new club, Onyx Lounge, in a few weeks. She needs some help getting exposure, so take care of her. I'm hosting. So see what you can do."

"I'll take care of her."

Shaunell walked back to the stage to introduce the next comedian.

Tamara asked for Aaron's business card and she stood up to leave. Aaron reached in his pocket and handed her his card and suggested that she stay for a while. Tamara took him up on his offer and stayed for the rest of the show. They made small talk between the comics' jokes.

"I heard about the Onyx Lounge. Do your need our station to broadcast live?" Aaron asked after the show was over.

"No, we just want to do some promotional stuff and give away some tickets."

"I'll try to help you out as much as I can. But I do have to discuss it with my sales manager. We'll see what we can come up with. I'll give you a call tomorrow."

"That would be great," Tamara said as she left and told the man it was nice meeting him.

The sun was beaming into Tamara's room. It was morning again. She looked over at her alarm clock. It read seven. She decided to get an early start on her day. Tamara began her morning routine. She started a pot of coffee and showered. She then put on her clothes, poured her coffee, and sat on the sofa to begin checking her e-mail. There were six more responses for her assistant position. She knew it was too early to contact them, but she printed them out and looked over the resumes. One woman was too experienced, the other not enough. Out of the six she was only interested in meeting three. She circled their strengths and weaknesses and placed notes on their resumes. She then e-mailed the candidates her cell phone number and told them she would like to meet up with them as soon as possible. Tamara had decided hopefully they would check their e-mail and get back to her. After that she continued to go over her agenda for the day. She had to meet with two caterers and call a few more publicists. So far she had Amerie, Mya, and Gabrielle Union as yeses. She was still working on a rapper named Calcutta and an R&B singer, Debonair. Tamara heard her phone rang and hoped it was good news at the other end.

"Hello."

"Are you busy? What is your schedule looking like today?" Maurice asked.

"I'm a little busy. Why?" Tamara said.

"Can you squeeze in a lunch meeting? My brother's in town and I would like for you to meet him."

"Um, let me call you back," Tamara said. She was getting more than a little irritated the way he kept calling and pretty much demanding she drop whatever she was doing so she could meet with him.

"Tamara."

"Yes."

"Make it happen. This is important," Maurice said in an authoritative voice that did something to Tamara.

Right after he hung up, another call came in. Tamara answered and a woman's voice said, "Hi, yes, I need to speak to Ms. Murphy."

"This is she."

"Hello, this is Kyra Daniels. I'm responding to your ad for the assistant position."

"May I place you on hold?" Tamara said as she got her thoughts together. She then grabbed the resumes on her sofa and came back to the phone and said, "Hi, Miss Daniels. I was looking over your resume and I was interested in setting up an interview with you. Can you meet me this morning?"

"Yes."

Tamara was going to meet Kyra Daniels at ten at a restaurant a few blocks away. She had just enough time to interview her, then go straight to lunch with Maurice. Tamara showered, dressed, and went to the interview. She was rushing and still a little behind. Kyra had already called to let Tamara know she was there waiting for her. She told her to grab a table and she would be right there. Kyra was a young woman, about twenty, with long braids gathered up into a ponytail. She was dressed appropriately, in a burgundy pantsuit. Tamara was impressed. She walked over to Kyra and shook her hand. She pulled out

Kyra's resume and began quizzing her about her work history. Tamara was satisfied with all her answers. She wanted to hire her on the spot until she mentioned her child. Tamara knew she was wrong and out of line, but she began to ask her questions about her baby. She wanted to know if she would be able to make it to work if she hired her. Tamara liked her but could not have someone calling out because her baby was sick.

"You have a child? Who watches your baby?" Tamara asked.

"My husband does. He works at night and I'm working in the daytime so we won't have to pay for day care."

"Wow, you married young," Tamara said, surprised.

"Yes, right out of high school."

"If you don't mind me asking, how old are you?" Tamara felt uncomfortable asking the questions, but Kyra continued to answer.

"I'll be twenty-one next week. My baby is six months. I'm going to start back to school as soon as he is one and I save some money."

Tamara was impressed; Kyra was young, polished, professional, and determined. Tamara scanned her resume to see if there was anything she had missed. There wasn't. She was confident that she could work with Kyra and offered her the job and told her she needed her immediately. Kyra accepted and thanked her.

Tamara had just enough time to meet Maurice and Kendall for lunch. When she arrived Maurice complimented her as soon as she entered the restaurant. His brother, Kendall, got up and shook her hand. He was very handsome, but didn't look anything like Maurice. They were polar opposites. Kendall was standing a few inches shorter than his brother and he had a golden brown complexion with no facial hair. He looked fifteen years younger than his actual age.

"I wanted you to get a chance to meet my brother and he had questions and things he wanted to go over with you,"

Maurice said as Tamara sat down. "Would you like to order lunch before we begin?"

"No, I'll just take a coffee."

Maurice waved down their waiter and ordered Tamara's coffee. Kendall coughed and cleared his throat and said, "Tamara, I wanted to meet you because my brother said you are doing a great job. However, I have some concerns."

"What concerns do you have?"

He looked at his brother, then back at Tamara and said, "Tamara, let me be honest with you. I have spoken to several people and they have not heard of my club yet. This is very disappointing to me."

"Really? You must be talking to the wrong people, because there is a buzz about Onyx Lounge," Tamara said.

"Are you sure? Because my club needs to be the most talked about, sexiest club ever. How are you going to make that happen? I want sexy women, I want a sexy wait staff. I want everything that will attract men. What is your plan to have the sexiest women in New York at our club?"

Tamara thought about her answer before she answered the two men staring at her. "Well, I was going to bring in dancers and have cigar girls," she said as the waiter placed her coffee and cream in front of her.

"Cigar girls? I like that, but every club has those. How do you feel about caged dancers with body paint?"

Tamara wanted to say the right thing. But the right thing didn't come out of her mouth.

"I don't like the idea," she said as she took a sip of her coffee. "I think there are better ways to show off beautiful women without demeaning them."

"Like what?" Kendall demanded.

"I'm sure I can come up with a number of ideas," Tamara said. She wanted to slap him. The idiot. She was kind of dumbfounded she couldn't think of any ideas, but she didn't like body paint. She didn't like the idea of women walking around with their asses and breasts exposed.

"Kendall, I trust Tamara's decision-making skills," Maurice interrupted the interrogation. "She has media coverage lined up and she's been keeping me updated with her progress."

"Getting us coverage in a local newspaper and morning show is not real exposure. I mean, our name is on the line if she messes up. It is not just on you. It is on me, too! And I don't feel like she is capable," Kendall said as his voice began to elevate and he looked his brother directly in the eye.

Tamara felt like she had to defend herself. He was questioning her capability. "Kendall, I have been working very hard. Under the circumstances I think I have been doing a great job. I've only been on the job two weeks and I have Shaunell from WKAZ to host the event, and that in itself is going to bring in a bunch of the type of people we want. I also have been speaking with the promotions department and they are going to do giveaways. Plus, I have calls in to almost every celebrity in the city. I had to actually hire an assistant because I have been so busy. And I have two major sponsors and am working on getting more."

"Well, I don't think you're busy enough. Because right now I'm not impressed. I didn't want to hire you, my brother did. I'm not really sure you are cut out for the job."

Tamara's mouth dropped open, and she knew what was getting ready to come out of her mouth wasn't going to be pretty, but before she could say anything Maurice practically jumped up from the table.

"Excuse me, Tamara. I'll be right back," he said before pulling Kendall over to the back of the restaurant. Tamara didn't know what to think. She didn't like Kendall. She sat and waited for them to come back, trying to figure out how to turn this meeting so she didn't get fired. But she also knew that if Kendall came back with that same attitude she'd probably throw her coffee in his face and tell him to kiss her ass. She thought her best bet would be to leave, so she got up and walked out. On the way home she questioned her future with the Harold brothers. She wanted to cry, but refused.

* * *

Maurice started blowing up her cell phone before she even walked in her door. "Listen, I have to apologize for my brother. He was totally out of line."

"Please, don't worry about it," she said, trying to play it off.

"I think it's important we talk, okay? I can meet wherever you want."

Tamara hesitated, wondering if he wanted to meet simply because he wanted to fire her. "Well, I really have a lot of things I need to get done by this evening, and I—"

He cut her off. "Tamara," he said in a pleading tone. "Please?"

Tamara was taken by surprise. She was much more used to his demands, though she wasn't necessarily sure she liked them, than to this new subdued Maurice.

She agreed to meet him at Sushi Bar that evening, and she arrived not knowing what to expect.

"First of all, let me apologize again for Kendall's behavior. He tends to fly off the handle and speak without thinking," Maurice said after she was seated in the booth with him and he'd ordered her a drink. "And second, I want you to know that I'm extremely pleased with your progress. I know we didn't give you much notice, but you came into town and took off immediately, and I appreciate that. In fact, I'd like to offer you a bonus."

Tamara let out a sigh of relief. "Thanks, Maurice. It's good to know that my work is being recognized." She was so relieved she wasn't getting fired that she began to giggle as she took a sip of her drink.

"What are you laughing at?" Maurice asked with a smile.

"Nothing," she said. "I'm just enjoying my drink. I'm glad you convinced me to come out, after all. I needed a little unwinding."

He reached over and put his hand over hers. "I'm glad to help you unwind." Maybe it was the drink, which was kind of strong, but she didn't pull her hand back, even though she knew she should. They ordered sushi and more cocktails.

As the night went on they kept laughing at each other's jokes. Maurice was rubbing Tamara's arm. Was it appropriate? No. But his hands felt so good, so she didn't make him stop. Then they began holding hands. Then there was a simple hand rub that led to Maurice's fingers tapping and scratching her palm. His touch shot pulses of waves into her feminine V. Then his hands moved from hers to gently massaging her shoulders. Maurice then whispered in her ear how good she looked in her dress. She was turned on. Before Tamara knew it they were kissing and hugging and cuddling up in the booth.

"Is something wrong?" he whispered as his hand slid from her shoulder to her hip.

"I'm not sure yet," she said breathlessly. She was a professional and she had to tell him to stop rubbing her leg under the table. She was going to tell him right after he stopped massaging her ass.

When the server came to the table with the final bill, Maurice pulled out several twenties and placed them in the server's book. Tamara slid out of the booth and he helped her put her coat on. She was full of giggles. Maurice then grabbed her hand and said, "Come with me." They never addressed exactly what they were doing; they both were just going with the moment. He walked a few buildings down to a hotel.

"Who are you meeting in here?" Tamara asked

"You."

"Me?" Tamara said, as he led her into the hotel and she tried to understand why he already had a room. He walked past the front desk and onto the elevator. They stopped on the sixth floor. He slid in a room key and opened the door. He wasted no time, and pushed Tamara onto the floral comforter on the bed. She didn't know what to do or how to feel. She knew getting personal with her employer was a sure way to either be part owner of the company or get fired and have a one-way ticket home. But she was so light-headed, and he felt so good.

"Hold up, let me get up for a minute. I have to go to the restroom," Tamara said as she stumbled to the bathroom. He kissed her and walked her to the door. She looked at herself in the mirror and then sat on the closed toilet seat. What was she doing? What was going on? First she thought she was meeting Maurice to get fired, and now she was about to sleep with him in a hotel room.

A hotel room. It hit her. Why did he have a hotel room? Did he plan on coming here already? Was he tired? When did he get the room? She knew Maurice was used to getting what he wanted and it suddenly became obvious that he thought because he wanted her she was just going to go along with it. But she wasn't going to give in to him. She stood up and turned the water on and splashed some on her face just as he knocked on the door and asked if she was okay.

"Yes, I'm fine." She opened the bathroom door, prepared to tell him that she had to go, but before she could say a word he grabbed her in his arms and suckled on her neck. Her whole body went limp.

"Maurice, please stop!" she said faintly as he stuck his tongue in her mouth, wildly licking sideways. He noticed her weak protest and began trying to calm her down by whispering, "Listen, nobody has to know we are seeing each other" in her ear.

"But I work for you," she mumbled.

"It doesn't matter. You know you want this just as much as I do," he said while licking her earlobe. And he was right. Tamara did want Maurice. She wanted his body close to hers. So she allowed him to kiss on her neck and take her panties down. She let him hold her tightly and kiss her all over her body. She was in a daze until Maurice pulled out a condom and began tearing the wrapper. That's when Tamara snapped out of it. She couldn't sleep with her boss. How would she be able to work with him after they had sex?

"Maurice, I have to go."

"Go where?" he asked.

"Home."

"Are you serious?" He looked at her like she was crazy.

"Very." She grabbed her coat and headed for the door.

"Hold on, hold on," he said finally. "Let me help you catch a cab. I am a gentleman, you know."

"No, that's okay. I'll be fine. I'm sure we'll talk tomorrow."

Once the cold air hit Tamara she was relieved that she left Maurice. She then realized she wanted her job more than she wanted him.

"Hello," Tamara said groggily into the intercom.

"Hi, it's me. Kyra," a cheerful, vibrant voice answered.

Tamara glanced over at the clock as she buzzed Kyra in. The girl was twenty minutes early, just as she had been since her first day.

Kyra was really a godsend. Initially, Tamara thought it would be strange to have someone in her apartment, but it wasn't. Tamara treated Kyra like a little project that she wanted to mold. She wanted to dress and teach her like a big sister. And even though they were cool, Kyra didn't take Tamara for granted. She was very respectful and professional.

Kyra walked in and handed her a cup of Dunkin' Donuts coffee. "Want me to get started with the follow-up calls? I know exactly where I left off yesterday."

Tamara nodded as she gratefully took a sip of the hot brew. "I'm going to be making some calls, too. Hopefully between the two of us we can work some magic today." She smiled. "We've got to earn our pay, you know."

Actually, things were going much smoother. She had yet to meet up with Maurice again, though they had spoken several times over the telephone. He had never mentioned what happened, but she hoped that they could face each other in person without it being too uncomfortable.

"Hi, yes, this is Tamara Murphy. May I speak to Elizabeth Shoemaker?"

"Yes, this is she. You've called me four times in the last two days. How may I help you?"

"Hi, I wanted to invite your client Ayinde to the grand opening of the Onyx Lounge nightclub."

"Well—"

Before the woman could finish, Tamara hurried on. "We're so looking forward to her attending. We have a hotel room for her, and we'll be glad to make the travel arrangements. First class, of course."

"Oh, well, what did you say the date was?"

"February thirteenth. The day before Valentine's Day, so of course we'll make sure to have a complimentary bottle of Moët and large box of chocolates," Tamara said quickly. "I think I read that she's partial to strawberry-dipped chocolates, right? And of course everything she wants at the club will be comped."

She was laying it on thick, but after all, Maurice did say money wouldn't be an object, and Ayinde was the hottest new actress on the scene. There was even talk about her getting a Golden Globe award for her latest movie, and she was scheduled to start a new film with Spike Lee.

"Well, her schedule just happens to be free that day, so yes, I'm sure she'll be glad to come," the publicist said finally. "And she will, of course, be in the VIP section?"

"But of course!" Tamara patted herself on the shoulder as she hung up and put a checkmark by Ayinde's name.

Tamara looked at the next item on her to-do list and smiled. She wasn't sure why, but this was a call she was really looking forward to making. She put on her flirtatious voice and said, "Hello. Hi, Aaron, this is Tamara Murphy. Shaunell introduced us at the comedy club a couple of nights ago, remember? I was calling to see if you were able to talk to your sales manager."

"You know what? I have. I've been meaning to contact you. How are things going for you so far?"

"It's okay. Not what I expected."

"Really? What are you having problems with?"

"I'm not used to people saying no to me. I've been calling people and some are not even returning my calls."

"Who hasn't called you back?" he asked.

"Well, I called Debonair, Calcutta, and Jay Lands, to name a few. And I still have to get a deejay and a caterer."

"Really? Maybe you need some help."

"Maybe I do." Tamara smiled. Yeah, this guy was nice.

"Well, I can help you, but . . ."

"What's the but?"

"We'll talk about the but later. However, I do know Deb is on tour. Calcutta, I got his number and I'll call his manager. He owes me a favor. And Jay Lands is a good friend of mine. I'll call her right now." Tamara heard him call on another phone. "Jay, what's up? This is Aaron. Yeah, a friend of mine is opening a nightclub. I need you there. It's the thirteenth next month. Yeah, I'm going. Well, I'm going to give her your number. Come through, all right?" He then came back to the line.

"See, I made that happen for you. So now you owe me."

"I owe you?"

"Yeah, are you free this evening?"

"It's short notice, but maybe I could be."

"I know it is last minute, but I have two tickets to the Knicks game. It's a station event. And we can discuss the package then."

"What time?"

"Like seven. You could meet me there."

"Where should I meet you?"

"The box office at Madison Square Garden."

Tamara repeated what he said and hung up the phone.

Tamara took the number 3 subway train to the Thirty-fourth Street station and walked upstairs to the Garden. She hoped she remembered what he looked like. He was wearing dark blue jeans and a rust-brown corduroy jacket with a brown button-down shirt underneath it. She was surprised how cute he was dressed. He had light brown skin with waved and curled dark black hair going into a short 'fro. He greeted her with a big hug and led her inside the arena. They stopped at the concession stand and got popcorn and sodas and walked to their seats, which were four rows from the court.

"These are really good seats," Tamara said.

"That's one of the perks of working at the station."

Must be nice, Tamara thought. She wasn't really into sports and had no idea what was going on. She tried to get conversation going during the game, but Aaron was really into the competition. After the game she rode with him to a live WKAZ broadcast event at a nearby club. She took a seat with him at a booth. It was a nice place. Not as nice as the Onyx Lounge, but it had the type of crowd they were going after— young, professional, and with extra money to spend. Tamara made a lot of contacts and gave out exclusive invites she'd brought with her to anyone who looked nice.

"I see you working the room. Okay, I like that," Aaron said.

"Always. Thanks for bringing me out," Tamara said.

"You welcome, ma'am," he said, mocking Tamara's southern accent.

"My accent came out," Tamara laughed.

"It sure did."

"I try to hide it."

"Where are you from again?"

"Atlanta. What about you? Are you from here?"

"No, I'm not, I'm from Connecticut. Are you dating anyone?"

"No."

"Why not?"

"I just got to town and I'm focusing on my business, that's all."

"We are going to have to put an end to that and take you off the market," Aaron said with a flirtatious smile. "Excuse me for a minute," he said when someone began pulling on his arm. Everyone was coming up to him and needing something from him. He was very nice about it and she knew he was working and trying to have a good time at the same time, but after a few hours she was tired and told him she needed to get home. He walked her outside to her cab, and then before she opened her apartment door her phone was ringing.

"Just making sure you got in okay."

"I'm fine, thanks. The club still packed?"

"Yes, sorry I got caught up."

"No problem. I understand you were working."

"So, can we get together again?"

"Maybe."

He laughed. "Okay, I'll let you get some rest. Call me when you wake up."

"Okay," she sighed as she sleepily set her phone on the nightstand.

The next morning Tamara was back at work. She went and met with a florist and picked out a red velvet cake covered with silver icing. The cake was going to read in black writing *The Blackout*. She got a call on the way home. It was Aaron.

"Miss Tamara, I secured you our deejay, Problem Child. And I know this caterer who does a lot of our events and I gave him your number."

"You did? Thank you." He was so sweet! And he was helping her make up for lost time.

"Yeah, and the promotion packages with the giveaways I got for you for five thousand. They wanted ten."

"He's really gaining points with me," Tamara said after he hung up.

Kyra was still in the apartment when she got here, and so was a large bouquet of pink roses.

"Those are for you." Kyra smiled as she covered the phone

receiver. Tamara walked over to the flowers and read the note attached. *Enjoyed spending time with you. We have to do it again. Aaron.*

He was *really* gaining points!

Kyra handed Tamara all her messages and told her that she had found a place to hire the dancers for the party.

"Here are head shots and measurements of the girls. The woman said all you have to do is pick out the girls you want."

"Really? Well, I'll let the men handle this. E-mail the information to the Harolds."

Three weeks to go and the club was almost completed, which was a good thing, but also a bad thing. Tamara now had to get up and go to an office every morning. She didn't have the luxury of rolling from bed and going right to the office. Tamara walked in and saw that a lot of the work was still not completed. There was the sound of banging hammers and of drills. It was driving her crazy, but it was worth it because they were doing a helluva job. The club was beautiful. She just hoped she could pull off getting it filled to capacity.

She went back into the office and turned the heat on. It was a big empty room, even with the office furniture, and there was a draft coming in from somewhere. They brought in a heater, but she and Kyra were still cold. In fact, Kyra had her coat on and was coughing. "I'm going to find out what's going on with this heat. Then I'm going to get you something to eat," Tamara said after making the girl sit closer to the heater.

When Tamara came back into the office, Kyra handed her five or six messages. One read *Maurice's girlfriend. She just wanted to check out the club.* And yet another read *Maurice's wife. She wants him to call her when he gets in.*

Tamara felt like she'd been punched in the stomach. "Maurice's girlfriend *and* his wife?"

"Yeah, they called back to back. I'm sorry, Tamara, because I might have gotten him in trouble because when his wife called I said he hasn't come in since when you first called. Then she started asking me all these questions."

"Don't worry, I'll tell him," Tamara said, throwing the messages back on the desk. "And next time tell them to call him on his cell."

Tamara couldn't believe her ears. She was upset with Maurice, but couldn't let Kyra know. She was mad because the women got smart with Kyra, but even more upset that she'd almost had sex with her married boss who also had a girlfriend. Even though she didn't have feelings for him it was just the fact that he tried to play her.

About an hour later Maurice came into the club, looking around and yelling at the construction workers.

Tamara went up to him. "Oh, your wife and your girlfriend called."

It looked like the blood drained out of his face. "Yeah, I'll talk to you about both situations later."

"So, let me understand this. You are not exactly divorced and you have a girlfriend? And you want me to date you?"

"No, let me explain."

"There is nothing to explain. I'm not your woman," Tamara said, stopping him.

"You could be," he said as he walked up closer to her.

"I doubt it. I work for you, remember? What happened the other night was a mistake."

"Tamara." He came closer and tried to kiss her.

"Look, I can leave now or I can stay and finish your event. Plus, I don't go on dates with married men or with other people's boyfriends."

He backed away. "Well, maybe after this event we can talk about establishing an us."

Maybe? Puleeze, she thought.

Two days later the heat was finally on and the club looked ten times better. Kyra and Tamara sat around talking and going over everything that needed to be done.

Maurice came to the club with a young white guy about thirty years old with jet-black hair, fitted blue jeans, and a blue shirt with black shoes.

"Hi, Tamara, I want you to meet Seth. He's the club manager. I want you guys to work as a team."

"Hey, Tamara. Good to meet you." The man stuck out his hand for Tamara to shake. She did so reluctantly, because with just one look at him she realized she did not like him at all. His smile was not genuine and he seemed shady.

After Seth started walking around to look at the club, Tamara's thoughts were confirmed when Maurice said, "Keep an eye on this guy. He is really good. We butted heads a couple of times already."

Great, she thought after Maurice left, *one more thing for me to worry about.*

Actually, things were going a lot smoother at this point. Return calls were finally beginning to trickle in, six sponsors were in place, and thanks to Aaron she had her deejay and her caterer.

Thinking about Aaron made her feel guilty. He had been so sweet to her, yet she hadn't really spoken to him in almost three days. Not because he wasn't trying, but every time he called she was too busy to talk. And she always meant to call him back but never seemed to get a chance. Her thoughts were interrupted by Kyra telling her that she had a call.

"This is Tamara Murphy," she said, picking up the phone.

"When are you going to make time for me? I know you're Miss Busy, but do you think you might have to take a break this evening to go to a speed-dating event?"

Tamara smiled. "You're going to live very long. I was just thinking about you."

"Good thoughts?"

"Maybe."

"So does that mean you'll do the event with me tonight?"

"Possibly. Let me get back to you."

"You can spend time with me and give out some more invitations."

That sealed the deal. "I'll be there," Tamara said.

"I knew that would make you come," Aaron said with a laugh.

The speed-dating event was boring as far as Tamara was concerned, but at least she was able to give out dozens of invitations to the Onyx Lounge. The next night Tamara was sitting on Aaron's cream sofa in his apartment since he'd invited her over for dinner. He had a huge flat-screen television and black and cream end tables. It was a pretty nice place, but kind of small. A real bachelor's pad.

She'd been on a total of five dates with Aaron, and she had to admit he was really growing on her. He was always so sweet and helpful. The right kind of guy if she were looking for the right kind of guy. The problem was, she wasn't. Still, he was good company, so she had readily accepted when he invited her over for a home-cooked meal. She was sitting in his living room looking at his parents' wedding picture.

"My parents have been married for thirty-five years," Aaron said proudly when he noticed her looking at their wedding picture.

"That's nice. I never knew anyone that stayed married that long. It seems impossible. One person all those years," Tamara said.

"What do you mean? That's not impossible."

"I think so. I'm not sure if anyone in my family can stay married for five years. Men always want a different woman."

"Not me. I only want one woman. I want my one and only soul mate."

"Yeah, right. All men want more than one. Marriage is overrated. I know for sure that a woman can have everything going for herself, a body, house, and money, and a man will still find a flaw and cheat or leave her."

"Let me find out you have a pessimistic view on marriage," Aaron said, laughing.

"My mother has been married three times. It is a fact. And do you know my grandmother is on her fourth husband? Marry, get a divorce, marry again, get another divorce, what the fuck? I would never put my kids through that. It just isn't fun." Tamara stood up and walked to the window. "I had so many stepdads and families. My mom would tell me 'Go say hi to your aunt Beatrice,' some lady I didn't know, or 'That's your uncle Frank,' and they would only be around for a couple of months," Tamara said, laughing. Behind the laughter was a little pain. She really did resent her mother bringing different strangers into her life temporarily and labeling them family.

"So instead of getting a divorce do you think your mother should have stayed in bad marriages?" Aaron asked.

"No, but how about not get married at all and wait and get to know somebody? That's why I'm not getting married and having kids anyway."

"So you're going to let their mistakes and mishaps dictate how you live your life?"

"Of course not," Tamara said.

"Seems like you are."

"No, I'm not," Tamara said, getting upset.

Aaron walked over to her and held her from behind and said, "You know good people do still exist."

Tamara didn't answer him. She just thought about what he said.

Dinner was so good Tamara felt sleepy and full, and lay down on the couch, and Aaron cuddled up next to her. He had made green beans, corn on the cob, and fried chicken, and he had done too good a job at it. It reminded her of home.

"I think it's time for me to go," Tamara said.

"You know you can stay here," Aaron said in a soft voice.

"No, I better go home. I have calls to make in the morning." She turned to him. "I'm really enjoying spending time with you."

"Me too! So don't leave."

She wanted to leave him, but she couldn't so she stayed on the couch next to him. She kissed him and pulled him in closer by his collar. "I like you, you know."

"I like you, too. And I want to tell you right away, I want a woman."

"You want a woman," Tamara repeated and laughed at him. The thought of commenting to her after only knowing him for two weeks was extremely funny.

"I do, and I think you are her." He held her hand and looked at her lovingly. He was genuine. He then leaned over her and kissed her sloppily. Their tongues were moving in different directions. Both of their faces were turning side to side, not exactly getting it right. But it was still a perfect kiss. A kiss that made you want more. Tamara didn't move as they lay on the sofa in each other's arms. Aaron's body was soft and smooth. He had almost no body hair. She took off her shirt and got comfortable. He kissed her all over and pressed his body in and out of hers the entire night on the edge of his sofa.

Tamara opened her eyes and felt someone grabbing her hand. It was Aaron. She was lying in her bed next to his warm body. It felt so good. She didn't want to move; she felt protected. But at the same time, she wanted him out!

Tamara had been enjoying the past few days and nights she was spending with Aaron, but it was becoming too much. She couldn't do any work at home with him there. She was starting to feel like he was invading her space. Asking her what she wanted to do for the day he had been with her since their Friday date. It was now Sunday. It was obvious he wanted her to settle down, but she wasn't ready. She was going to date more than one man. She was going to do that so she wouldn't get caught up. But when she finally convinced him to go home, he left, grabbed some clothes, and came right back. She was confused. If she didn't know better she would think she had somehow unknowingly gotten herself a boyfriend by default. Somehow he had worked his way into her life when she was supposed to be remaining focused. She checked her messages and became increasingly mad when she heard all the messages and calls she hadn't returned because she was playing house. She was supposed to be on her hustle, on her grind with her New York state of mind. She hadn't done any work since Thursday. And she had only two weeks before the grand opening.

She took a deep breath. It would be okay. She had this when they were just friends, no attachment. She could just stop picking up when he called and allowing herself to be comforted in his big beautiful arms that felt like a headrest. She had to just stop laughing and enjoying his sense of humor and adoring his smile. Yes, all of that would have to stop today.

"Good morning."

"Hey," she said.

"Tamara."

"Yes."

"I think I might be about to fall in love with you," he said.

"You're what?" Tamara was in shock. *In love? We just met!* Then he asked what she hoped he would never ask. What he wasn't supposed to ask after only two weeks.

"What are we, Tamara?"

"We are two grown people enjoying each other's company," Tamara responded with no hesitation.

"So we are friends."

"Not exactly."

"So what would you call us?"

"I don't know."

"Because we are more than friends, right? I make love to you and you lie in my arms. Friends don't do that, right?"

Tamara was at a loss for words. She didn't know what to say, so she walked out of her room and into her kitchen. She couldn't believe he was getting soft. *Don't try to put a name on what we have,* she thought. That was the woman's job to start getting insecure about her position and rank in a man's life. Why was he acting like, for lack of a better word, a bitch? Getting all sappy and love-struck.

"Did you hear me, Tamara?" he said, coming out of her bedroom in his boxers.

"Yes, I heard you."

"So why didn't you answer my question?"

"I don't know what we are," she said, looking directly at him.

He stared at her with a puzzled look, then finally said, "I'm not going to hold you. You are everything I want my woman to be. You're sexy, beautiful, and intelligent. I've been in this city for years. I dated around and, yes, I had my fun, but now I want to settle down. At the end of my hectic day I want a woman I can trust and come home to."

"I think everybody wants that, Aaron," Tamara said, walking back into the bedroom.

"Everybody wants that, but what do you want?" he said, frustrated, as he followed her.

"I came here to this city for a job opportunity. I don't think I'm in a place in my life where I should make a commitment. I'm not looking for love right now. I don't even know how long I will be here."

"Yeah, but you have to have a personal life, too!" he said.

"I don't have time for a personal life. Do you realize since I've been with you I haven't done any work since Thursday?" she said adamantly.

Aaron took a deep breath. "Is that a no?"

"No, that's a let me see. Give me a moment. I am really stressed right now. I need some space."

"I'm going to give you space. But make me a promise."

"What's that?" Tamara asked.

"That you will think about us and while I'm giving you this space you won't date anyone else. At least until after the party."

"Okay, I promise." Tamara sat down on the bed.

"You're not going to date anyone?"

"No one."

"You promise?"

"I swear," she said.

He undressed her and began to give her body all the affection that it needed. Every time he entered her body she adored Aaron more. She just wasn't ready to settle down.

Seth had been getting on Tamara's nerves. He was a pain in Tamara's right and left ass cheeks. Seth wanted to be in charge of everything and Tamara wasn't having it. He even had the nerve to tell her what radio stations she should be using to promote the club, clearly not his job. They argued over everything. Tamara explained to Seth that although he was the club manager the club was not open yet. So therefore he didn't have anything to manage. The only major contribution Seth brought with him was a bar and restaurant kitchen staff.

"Seth, you can send your people home. The kitchen is not going to be ready, so we do not need a kitchen staff."

"I'll send them home after I talk to Maurice."

"I already spoke with him. He said to send them home." Tamara didn't want to go word for word with him, so she took a lunch. Kyra followed behind.

When they returned they noticed a woman going in the club door. Tamara ran up to the half-dressed model with thigh-high boots and said, "May I help you?"

"Yes. Is this where they are holding auditions for the models?"

"What models?"

The woman pulled out a piece of paper and said, "I'm looking for Seth."

Tamara marched into the club to find a bunch of women waiting. Seth was holding an exotic dancer audition in the middle of the club. There were about twenty girls. None of them were pretty but they were all siliconed up. They all had green and blue contact lenses in and bleached blond hair, all ranging in color from ebony to super tan. He was making the women dance provocatively and then give simulated lap dances. Tamara walked up to him and said quietly, "Seth, this is inappropriate."

"Listen, don't tell me what's inappropriate. Why don't you just shut up and sit your ass down?"

"What? Who the hell are you talking to?" Tamara said as she walked up into his face.

He paused momentarily, then said, "You fucking black bitch" under his breath.

"I know you didn't just call me a black bitch."

"Tamara, have a seat. I did not call you a bitch or a black bitch for that matter."

"You called me a bitch. That's it. This thing is over. Excuse me, this audition is over. Please leave."

The women began picking up their stuff and leaving.

Tamara called Maurice immediately and repeated the racial slur Seth had just used.

Maurice was on the premises within fifteen minutes. He came to the club and started yelling. Seth could not get one word in.

"Don't you ever disrespect this woman. She is in charge and if you can't handle it, then, oh well. And I know you didn't call her a bitch. I know she must have been hearing things."

"Listen, you know I have a certain way of doing things and if I don't have a say I can't have my name connected with this club," Seth shot back.

Maurice then looked directly in his eyes and said, "This is my damn club. If you don't want to be a part of this, walk out the door."

For a moment Seth stood still and twisted his lips as if he was thinking about it. Then he held his hand out to Maurice and said, "Brother, it was good working with you."

Seth tried to shake Maurice's hand on the way out, but Maurice left him hanging. Seth walked out the door, taking his bartenders and wait staff with him. Tamara didn't want to be the reason that they didn't have a club manager, but he was messing shit up. She started to walk away.

Tamara had realized that although she had hated Seth, now she had created more work for herself. Something inside her just went off. She felt sick and out of nowhere she began to start freaking out. The pressure was starting to get to her. Everything was starting to weigh on her shoulders and she could hardly breathe. She was having an anxiety attack, but she didn't want anyone to know. She went into the bathroom and Kyra followed her as she sagged against the wall. She felt like she was being weak. But she couldn't be weak. But Tamara needed rest and to relax.

"Are you okay, Tamara?" Kyra asked.

"Yeah? Why, do I look like I'm not okay?"

"You don't look so good." Kyra sat Tamara down and Maurice came into the women's bathroom and suggested that they all take the rest of the day off. As Tamara reluctantly left the building, her phone rang. It was Aaron. "I'm on my way home to get some rest. I'm having a bad day and feeling really out of it. I'll talk to you later," she said abruptly before hanging up. She just couldn't deal with one more thing today, not even Aaron.

Tamara went to her apartment and took a long, hot shower, but it did nothing to end her fatigue. She was so tired and didn't want to think about the work she had in front of her. Less than two weeks to go and now, thanks to her, they didn't even have a club manager. *Oh, God,* she thought, *this is going to be a disaster.* She wrapped a towel around her and exited the bathroom and headed straight for the bed. All thoughts could wait until tomorrow. Her head was pounding so hard she couldn't think anyway. She hadn't closed her eyes but five minutes before her telephone started ringing.

"Open up. I'm ringing your doorbell."

Tamara slipped on a robe and went to answer her front door. Maurice followed her into the apartment.

"What are you doing here?" she said as she leaned weakly against a wall.

"I just wanted to make sure you were okay," he said, standing in the doorway.

"I'm fine."

"You sure?" he said, looking into her eyes. He gave her a kiss and held her body right in her doorway. Tamara was so vulnerable and felt like she wanted to invite him in, but that would be wrong. He would never respect her. Just as she argued with herself about holding Maurice while she was half naked she heard the front door open. The lock must not have caught after she'd let Maurice in.

"Tamara," Aaron called out as he walked through the hallway toward her apartment. He stopped when he saw her and Maurice in the doorway. She pulled away from Maurice and looked over at Aaron. He stood there frozen for a moment, then ran back down the hallway and out the front door. Tamara tried to run after him, but Maurice grabbed her arm.

"Let him go. I'll stay with you."

Tamara's eyes narrowed as she looked at him. How the hell was it that she was about to be so weak? she wondered. She told him to leave, then pushed him out of the doorway to show she was serious. This was the second reality check she'd had with him.

She threw on her jeans and ran out in the street with just her robe covering her upper body to see if she could catch Aaron. She didn't have to go far. He was waiting on the corner trying to flag down a cab.

He looked up when he heard her. "So I guess that was your idea of going home and relaxing?"

"Listen, that was my boss checking up on me."

"Don't explain. It's my fault. You told me from the beginning that you weren't interested. I should have respected that."

"Aaron, listen." He began walking away. She wanted to run after him, but she didn't know what she could say, and besides, she felt too weak. She was so sorry he was upset, but come on. He had known her all of two weeks and he wanted to settle down. She told him that was not what she wanted and he didn't listen. It wasn't her fault he got hurt. She leaned on the concrete banister and started back up the steps.

"Hey, nice outfit you got there," Jerome said, walking up close to her.

She didn't feel up to turning around to fix Jerome with a mean mug. As it turned out, she didn't have to.

"Jerome, leave that damn girl alone," she heard Margie call out from her window. "You ain't got nothing better to do than harass my tenants?"

Aaron called her phone nonstop for the next week, but she let his calls go straight to voice mail. He would hang up, cuss her out, hang up, and then call again. So Tamara finally answered her telephone.

"So you finally decided to pick up the telephone?" he asked.

"I can't deal with this right now," Tamara said.

"Just answer one question. Maybe I'm tripping. But it seemed like we were on our way somewhere," Aaron said.

"We were on our way somewhere. Nothing has changed," Tamara said.

"I asked you if you could not date anyone else until we figure everything out."

"Yes, I told you I wouldn't date anyone else and I didn't. That was my boss."

"Well, your boss looked real comfortable with you. He was rubbing all up on your ass."

"Aaron, I am not having this conversation with you. It doesn't matter anyway."

"It doesn't matter? You're right. It just questions your character. You're having sex with one man and spending time with him and then you have another coming out of your apartment."

Aaron was taking it too far. Tamara wasn't going to sit still and let him tell her how wrong she was. "Don't disrespect me. You don't hardly know me."

"I know that. I really wanted to get to know you, but as soon as we became close you pushed me away."

"I didn't push you away and I don't have to explain. I have to go," Tamara said as she hung up on him.

He called her right back, and for some reason she decided to pick up even though she could see from the caller ID that it was him.

"So why did you lie to me? You said you weren't dating anyone."

"I wasn't. He is my boss and he is a married man. He was checking on me. I broke down earlier and he sent me home. I've been consumed with work. If you can't understand that, oh well. I know what it looked like but it wasn't."

"Wow! You are dating a married man."

Tamara couldn't believe the only thing he heard out of everything she just said was "married man." "No, he is separated, but I still don't deal with people unless they are one hundred percent honest."

"Like how you were honest with me, right?" Aaron said.

"I'm tired. If you're looking to argue with someone, you're not going to get it from me." She hung up on him again. She was tired and not in the damn mood for any bullshit. She had a long day ahead of her.

Still, it was hard for her to shake her guilt. Aaron had been so nice to her, and she was acting like a little bitch. "I'll send him some flowers, leave a voice mail and an e-mail," she said out loud. "And whatever he decides to do is on him. I can't let this effect me anymore. I've got a club opening. I have to make it a success."

It was time for Tamara to put her Superwoman cape on. There were only three days left before the big event. The club still didn't look like there was going to be a grand opening in a few days. There was still dust everywhere and plastic that needed to be taken off all the chairs. Even the glasses needed to be put up. She hired bartenders and drink waiters through an agency.

She began setting up the tables and chairs herself. Maurice had found a friend who used to own a club to promise to come in on opening night to help with the managing, but she knew most of the load would be on her.

She called Shaunell to confirm she was still going to be her host. But she couldn't get in touch with the deejay, Problem Child. She had been leaving messages for Aaron, but he hadn't returned her calls in four days. She was going to leave her last message.

"Aaron, this is Tamara. Please have Problem Child call me. I need to confirm that he will be here." Tamara hung up the phone.

After they had their little spat Tamara was concerned that Aaron might not help her. She didn't want to feel like she needed him. She didn't need him; she didn't need anyone. Uh-huh. And if she didn't have a deejay she would be ruined.

"Kyra, grab the Yellow Pages and find me three deejay companies."

Two hours later she hired a deejay, name Khali, and told him to report to the club at six. She then left a message on Problem Child's answering machine.

"Hi, Problem Child, this is Tamara from the Onyx Lounge. I won't be needing your services after all. Thank you, and hopefully we can work again in the future."

The next day Tamara was still getting things set up and ready. She had been practically living at the club. She had hardly seen the inside of her apartment.

"Hello, Tamara."

"What's up, Aaron?" She hoped he wasn't calling her to lecture her again. She didn't want to hear about how she wasn't a good person and wasn't acting like a decent woman. She wasn't trying to hear it. "What can I do for you Aaron?"

"My deejay just called me, he said that you didn't need him. What's up with that?"

"Well, I didn't know if I could depend on you. I have been calling you. And I didn't know if you were going to call me back. And I was calling him and he wasn't calling me back. So I hired somebody else."

"Listen, what me and you have going on has nothing to do with business. I said I was going to get it done and I meant it."

"Well, you didn't answer your phone and I couldn't take the chance."

"Why would you think I would ruin that for you? I'm not petty."

"You didn't call back so I didn't know what to think. So I didn't have a choice. I had to hire someone else. Thanks but no thanks."

"Well, you are going to have to come up with a solution or pay him, because he could have been somewhere else that night. I can't believe you were being that unprofessional."

"Me? Being unprofessional? Listen, I don't wait for anyone. I get shit done. So the first time you don't return my call, forget you."

"That's your problem, you're impatient and feel like no one is allowed to help you. You think men are out to hurt you," Aaron screamed in Tamara's ear.

Tamara hung up on him.

Today was the big day, February 13, 2008, the day of the big grand opening. Tamara had barely gotten any sleep in days and her eyes looked like someone had drawn black circles under them. She was trying to get rest but couldn't. She was nervous and scared. When she did manage to get a few minutes of sleep she kept having the same recurring dream: nobody was going to show up to the grand opening and she was going to have to go home to Atlanta on a Greyhound bus. So to ensure that didn't happen she was in overdrive. Tamara had even resorted to handing out flyers outside other nightclubs at three o'clock in the morning. She listed the celebrity guests who were scheduled to attend. She posted the event on every party Web site in the New York City metro area with pictures of the club and announced the first two hundred people could get in free. She knew that there wasn't going to be enough room for all the people she was hoping would show up, but that was the plan. The longer the line, and the more people who weren't able to get in, the more exclusive the club's reputation would be. And now, hours away from the opening, it looked like her plan was going to work. As petty as Aaron was acting, his radio station was coming through like a champ with the giveaways, and Shaunell had been doing her part blowing it up on the air. Celebrities whom she had been calling for weeks were now scrambling to get callbacks from her to make sure they could get in. Kyra was even bringing in her husband to help with miscellaneous things like security until the real security arrived.

Tamara was prepping to speak with the *FOX Morning Show*. The cameraperson and reporter were setting up inside and outside the club.

"Good morning, this is Tracey Daniels and I am reporting live from the Onyx Lounge in downtown with the owners the Harold brothers, Maurice and Kendall."

"Good morning, Tracey," Maurice said, smiling.

"So, tonight what can people expect?" Tracey asked.

"You can expect a great VIP atmosphere," Kendall said, looking very excitedly into the camera.

"Tell me, who are some of your invited guests?"

"Tracey, everyone will be here this evening from Gabrielle Union to P. Diddy to Queen Latifah," Kendall said proudly.

"And as you can see, it's not just the invited guests that are making the Onyx Lounge New York's premier nightspot, it's also the club itself," Maurice broke in. "We've spent almost a million dollars in renovations. And this is just the beginning.

In a few weeks we will be opening the restaurant," he said as he showed the cameras around the club.

After the interview was over, it was 10:00 a.m. Maurice and Kendall left and said that they would talk to Tamara later. All the important things were done. All she had to do was wait for everyone to show up. Tamara's phone kept ringing non-stop.

"Yes, I was hoping I could get one of my other clients to walk the red carpet."

"Hold on," Tamara said with attitude. This was the third person that this particular PR woman was trying to add. "Who's this person?"

"Um, he is a new up-and-coming singer. His brother plays for the Minnesota Timberwolves and his album is about to drop."

He sounded like a nondescript nobody to Tamara.

"Um, I'll have to get back to you. And for sure if somebody cancels I'll give you a call," she said with no intention whatever to call her back.

No sooner had she hung up than the phone started ringing again. She handed it to Kyra. "Tell whoever it is they cannot walk the red carpet and our guest list is closed." A few weeks ago no one was returning her calls. Now she was telling people no. Tamara felt so powerful and was impressed by the way things were turning out. The time was now three o'clock.

Everything was moving along perfectly, so Tamara went home and put on her black suit. At first she was going to wear a black dress, but she knew every woman with half a decent body would have the same look. Tamara wanted to be different. Her suit pants were supertight and hugged her legs just right. Tamara's jacket was short-waisted and was pleated in the back and she was wearing a chunky cluster diamond necklace and her makeup was flawless. She was dressed with time to spare and headed out to the club. But when she got there, she found that things had turned to chaos. And there was only three hours before the doors opened.

Tamara walked into the club and to her surprise everybody seemed like they were having a good old time doing nothing. Maurice's club owner friend who had promised to come early to make sure everything was tight hadn't shown up. The floor was still covered with dust. Kyra was on her cell phone with a frantic look on her face, and the press releases she had asked her to fax were still sitting on the table.

"I was trying to send the releases, but the fax machines aren't working and I couldn't e-mail them because the Internet server is down for some reason."

"You should have taken matters into your own hands. Go fax them at Kinko's if you have to. I don't care! No excuses. Get it done!"

Tamara felt the bitch coming out of her. She was trying not to be that bitchy lady, but she had to. She didn't care how she came off. She was about to be that bitch who makes employees suddenly start working extra hard.

"Excuse me, what's your name? Can you come and mop and wax this floor?" Tamara said as she looked around the club in disgust.

"I'll clean it right now. The lady told me to wait until she's done."

"She is done, now get started," Tamara yelled at the worker. She looked down at her phone. It was Maurice.

"How's everything going? Are you ready for this evening?"

"Yes, everything is fine," she said confidently, walking away from the commotion.

"That's good to hear. I'll see you shortly," Maurice said to Tamara.

Tamara was walking back into the middle of the club when she felt her legs going into different directions. The next thing she knew she was doing an unintentional split in the middle of the dance floor. She heard her pants rip open at the seam and she tried to get up, but she was sore. Kyra rushed to assist her. She knew everyone wanted to laugh. Tamara didn't care, she just got up and took her suit jacket and tied it around her waist. That was a temporary solution for the bigger problem: what the hell was she going to wear? Her outfit was ruined. She had to go home and find something else. She looked down at her watch. It was four thirty. If she left now it would take at least an hour for her to get home and back with traffic. She could send Kyra to go get her something to wear, but that wouldn't work, either. Tamara stormed into her office to pull out the guest list to give to the people on the door, only to realize she'd left all three copies of it on her kitchen counter. Shit! Now she had no other choice but to leave. They had to have that list.

She grabbed Kyra. "Listen, I have to run back uptown, so I need you to take care of everything until I get back. Okay?"

She ran out of the club and got into a taxi. She gave the driver her address and began writing herself mental notes.

"Sir, do you think you can wait for me?" she asked when the cab was about to pull up in front of her brownstone.

"No, sorry. This is my last fare. I have to take my son to basketball."

Instead of wasting time arguing Tamara got her phone and dialed for another taxi. She was told the wait was less than ten minutes. That would give her enough time to go upstairs and change and come out. Tamara paid the driver and ran up to her door. Instantly it dawned on her that she had left her bag in the backseat of the taxi. She turned around to catch the driver, but he was already turning the corner.

She wanted to just sit down on the steps and cry. She had lost. She might as well give up. The club would be opening in less than three hours and not only didn't she have a guest list, but she had split pants and was locked out of her apartment. It was all over; she had failed. She was wrong, she was no match for New York City.

She thought about what she could do next. Her options were limited. She could call Kyra and tell her to act like she had a list or take a cab back downtown with split pants and no guest list. She could maybe stay at the door and send Kyra to get her pants from a boutique. Tamara called Mrs. Graham as her mind still rambled about.

"Hi, Mrs. Graham. I am so sorry to bother you but I have left my bag in the cab and don't have any keys to get into my apartment."

"Did you, now? Well, how did you do that? I guess it's none of my business how you managed to leave your handbag in a cab. None of my business at all. Okay, I can probably be there in about an hour."

"An hour? You live two buildings down!" Tamara looked to see if Mrs. Graham was hanging out the window, but the shades were pulled down shut.

"I'm not home, dear. My daughter taught me how to do that call-forwarding thing and I have my calls forwarded to my cell phone. I'm at the supermarket. But I should be finished in about an hour."

Tamara looked at her watch. It was almost five, and if she had to wait an hour for Margie it would be six, barely leaving her an hour to get back downtown in rush-hour traffic. There was no way she was going to be back by seven. She was fucked.

"Mrs. Graham—"

"Call me Margie, dear."

"Margie, listen, I'm having a really bad day. I just left my bag in a cab and I have to get back to work or I'm going to lose my job. Maybe I can pay you extra to come now. Please. I really have to get back to work."

"Come, now. Let me tell you something, money doesn't move me. It may move you young people, but I can care less about money," the woman said in a huffy voice.

"I'm not trying to buy you. I just need you to come now because, well, if you don't I'm really going to get fired."

"Well, I guess I can do my grocery shopping tomorrow, but I don't appreciate you trying to buy me off like that. I'll be there as soon as I can. But all this rushing isn't any good. That's probably why you left your handbag in the taxi. Not that it's any of my business. Not my business at all," Mrs. Graham said as she disconnected the call.

Tamara sat there for a moment trying to figure out what she could do to get out of this situation. She kept coming up with ridiculous ideas or nothing at all. She even thought of trying to climb up the window, but then she remembered the security gates that she had installed at the insistence of her mother, who was still having fits about her daughter moving to Harlem.

She called an emergency locksmith, but the soonest they could get there was two hours. Mrs. Graham would be there before then.

She wanted to cry but she just sucked the tears back up. As she sat she planned how she was going to tell her mother she was coming home and would have to move in with her for a few months until she was able to land another job. Just then, as if to add insult to injury, Jerome walked up to the stairs.

"What's wrong, sweetie? It's a little cold to be sitting on the steps."

Damn, she didn't have time or the patience to even deal with his stupidity. She looked up at him and just rolled her eyes and was about to say something smart when she suddenly heard "Jerome. What did I tell you about harassing my tenants?"

That shrill voice had never sounded more pleasant. She looked up to see Mrs. Graham coming up the street, cigarette in hand.

"Get off my property before I call the police and have you arrested for trespassing," the woman said, hitting Jerome on the back of his head as he scooted down the steps. "Got the nerve to be trying to talk to women and a grown-ass man like you still living with his mother. Move on outta here. You ought to be ashamed of yourself."

It was a miracle. Tamara's cranky old landlady had actually

come through for her! "Mrs. Graham, thank you so much. I really appreciate this."

"Hmph. Don't thank me too fast. It's going to cost you a hundred dollars. Don't want to charge you but I have to so you will make sure never to do this again."

"Okay, no problem. I just appreciate you coming. I can write you a check."

"No, I want cash."

"I'm sorry, I don't have cash, because I left my handbag in a cab. That's why I don't have any keys."

"Oh, honey, please. I'm just kidding you. I'm not charging you no money just to let you in your own place. If you ask me you're foolish to agree to pay for it. That's none of my business, of course. Not my business at all. But if I need something from the grocery store this weekend you'd better believe I'm going to come knocking," Mrs. Graham said as she opened her door. "You made me leave before I could even pay for my food. And I don't plan on going hungry this weekend. And I'm almost out of cigarettes."

Tamara shot past the woman into her apartment, then turned suddenly and kissed her on the cheek.

"Well, you ain't got to be doing all of that," Mrs. Graham said sheepishly. "I'm just glad I could help."

Tamara thanked her again and ran into her bedroom and pulled out a black dress, a big red belt, and silver accessories with red wedge shoes.

After she changed her clothes and grabbed the guest list she ran out the door. She would have to borrow some money from Kyra for her taxi ride. She exited her building and began to sprint toward Malcolm X Boulevard. She stepped off the curb to cross the street but was almost knocked down by a yellow cab.

"Miss! Miss! You left your bag," the cabdriver yelled out the window.

"Oh my gosh," she said to the man. "Thank you so very

much. And listen, are you sure you can't take me back downtown? I can give you—"

"Yeah, I can. Lucky for you my wife called and said she's gonna take the kid to his game. Hop in."

Okay, this is the second miracle this evening. I'm on a roll, Tamara thought as she got in the cab. She pulled out her telephone. "Kyra, I'm on my way. How is everything so far?"

"Okay, please hurry up and get here. Kendall keeps calling. Then Maurice calls right after him asking for updates."

"Just try to stall them. Is the deejay there yet?"

"No."

"What?"

"Yeah, and a few people are starting to arrive."

"Is everything set up?"

"Yes, and the photographers are here. But the black carpet looks a little purple."

"What?" Tamara couldn't believe her luck. This was just perfect, a purple carpet and a nightclub without a deejay, she thought, but there was nothing she could do.

Tamara dialed the deejay but his voice mail kept picking up. "Yo, you have reached Deejay Khali. I'm not available. Leave a message and I'll get back."

"Khali, this is Tamara. You better get your ass to Onyx Lounge. I gave you your money up front and you are very late. I'm not having this shit. You are not going to ruin me."

Right after she left a message for him, another call came through. It was Kyra.

"Tamara, Dalbert's publicist wants to now if we have a side entrance."

"No, tell them everybody must come through the front. We want every star to be seen."

"Okay."

Tamara hung up and clasped her hands together. "God, please throw just a couple more miracles my way."

A half hour later the cab pulled up in front of the club. Her heart racing, she stepped onto the sidewalk preparing herself for the worst. She looked around and almost wanted to cry, but this time for joy. The carpet was purple, but it didn't look bad. Photographers were lined on either side of the carpet snapping pictures. The food was set up, the place looked beautiful, the black and silver décor was sparkling, and Maurice's club owner friend was in front barking orders and greeting the beautifully attired guests who had arrived early.

Heaving a sigh of relief, Tamara handed him the guest list, then asked one of the bartenders to pour her a glass of champagne. She took it down with one big gulp. The cigar girls were walking around the club in black lace stockings and short white skirts and black shirts with white pearls. They were all wearing black cat's-eye masks. Shaunell looked awesome. She had on a black long dress with a train with diamonds coming up the side. She was a real diva.

The deejay was still setting up but nobody noticed because he was playing a mixed CD. Tamara was looking around. Everything was coming along, but she didn't feel relieved yet. It was time for another glass of champagne.

By eight the music was loud, and the club was over capacity. Both Maurice and Kendall were walking around like they were the most important men in the world. Everybody was trying to get their attention. When Kendall caught her eye he winked at her. When Maurice caught her eye he blew her a kiss. It had all come together, thank God. Tamara was happy, but she still couldn't wait until it was over.

Tamara spotted Aaron just before he grabbed her and planted a kiss on her cheek.

"See, I told you everything would turn out great."

"I know." She smiled up at him. "I was just worried."

He gave her a hug. "I'm sorry about the way I acted. It's just that when I want something I want it. And when I can't get it, then I sometimes act a little immature. I guess that's from being the only child."

"We all make mistakes." She shrugged. "I made a few myself."

"So, can I make it up to you tomorrow with a romantic Valentine's Day dinner for two? I'll cook whatever you want."

He smiled at her hopefully, and Tamara all of a sudden started remembering the good times they'd had before the stupid blowup. She would love to spend Valentine's Day with him. But no, she had to stay focused. She didn't want to get caught up again, and she sure didn't want him to make a promise she couldn't keep, so she said, "I'll let you know."

He raised his eyebrow. "You'll let me know? Right," he said as he walked away.

Tamara knew the next morning that she had arrived. She had come to New York and done what she was supposed to do, and that was make it happen. She poured a glass of orange juice and began to listen to her messages. The first message was from Maurice Harold.

"Good morning, Miss Murphy. I just wanted to tell you, you did an excellent job. I am so happy to have you on board. You have to get the *New York Post*. We are in there thanks to you, and on Page Six. What do you know about that? We're in the *Daily News*, too."

Tamara listened to all of her messages again. Yes, she decided, she was definitely a hit. *They love me, they really love me*, she said to herself. *And I love me*. And that was so important to her. She called Aaron and turned him down. She wanted to spend the day alone. Yes, it was Valentine's Day and yes, she was dateless, but by choice; and no, she was not going to sit back and watch Valentine-inspired television; she was going to go out and treat herself to the best spa treatment.

She took her time getting out of the house, then went and had a deep-tissue stone massage and a paraffin pedicure. She felt all the tension and stress she had encountered over the last month and a half drift away. She then went and took in the latest Will Smith movie. It was almost 8:00 p.m. when she strolled down 125th Street on her way home. She looked at a passing bus and saw an advertisement for MoBay's Uptown

Restaurant. She remembered the cabdriver telling her that they had great mojitos, and it was only two blocks away, just across Fifth Avenue. She decided to stop in and have a drink. As she went into the restaurant, she smelled the aroma of beef ribs and decided she would sit and have dinner, too!

She had taken a seat and grabbed a menu when she noticed her downstairs neighbor sitting alone looking miserable. Her straight black hair was covering her almond-shaped eyes, and she was looking down at the table while carelessly stirring her drink with her finger.

Now, there was someone who looked like they could use a friend. She got up and walked over. "Do you mind if I join you, or would you prefer to be alone?" she asked in a friendly tone.

"Actually, I don't prefer being alone, but I don't want to be with no man."

Tamara chuckled. "You're buzzed, aren't you?"

Dior raised her glass. "Why not? Care to join me?"

"With pleasure." Tamara took a seat. "By the way . . ."

"Happy Valentine's Day," both women said simultaneously.

CHLOE
JOHNSON

by Deja King

January 10, 2008

Chloe Johnson parked her 2008 candy-apple-red drop-top Benz in the circular driveway of her parents' estate. The moment her Manolos hit the pavement, Chloe was overcome by the ninety-eight-degree scorching heat, which was typical for a Houston summer. Not missing a step in her five-foot-four-inch strut as she reached the entrance of the three-story neoclassical gated estate beautifully situated on two acres at the fifth tee of River Oaks Country Club, Chloe turned the key in the lock, slowly opening the front door and entering the foyer. Once she was inside the comfort of air-conditioning, her heels tapped the herringbone floors as she passed the two-story mahogany library, making a beeline to the sunken living room. Upon her grand entrance, the first words out of Chloe's mouth were "I'm moving to New York."

The abrupt announcement lingered in the air as Mr. and Mrs. Johnson both remained silent for a few minutes wondering if they'd heard their only daughter correctly.

"My dear Chloe, you mean you're going to visit New York and do a little shopping on Fifth Avenue?" Mrs. Johnson, who bore a striking resemblance to movie star legend Dorothy Dandridge, asked with just a touch of southern twang in her voice as she sat on the plush silk taffeta chair in the huge living room.

"No, I'm moving there," Chloe stated firmly, eyeing her parents.

"You can't move to New York," Mr. Johnson said, calmly

taking the final sip of his cognac as he peered through the wall of glass overlooking the park-view setting. "You've been heading up our teen line for almost four years now. We need you here in Houston, helping to run the family business. The business that's been passed down to generation after generation and will someday be yours. You belong here in Houston, with your family," he continued. "So whatever idea you have about going to New York is out of the question."

Mr. Johnson walked over to the silky oak wood bar and poured himself another glass of Rémy Martin Louis XIII cognac and Mrs. Johnson continued to read her book as if the conversation were over.

Chloe marched forward and placed her Hermès Birken bag on the mahogany end table before sitting down on the cream mohair velvet couch. She lifted her chin up and primped her shoulder-length golden brown hair. Chloe then put a fingertip at the crease of her mouth to make sure her crème de la femme MAC lipstick was in place before speaking.

"Daddy, you know that I adore you, but I am moving to New York. It's about time that I make use of my journalism degree and pursue my goals. Of course I love cosmetics," she said with an undertone of sarcasm, "but my dream is to someday run my own magazine. That will never happen if I stay here in Texas. I'm sure you understand."

"No, I don't," he countered, jiggling the ice cubes in his glass. "What? You want me to give you my blessings and then place a few phone calls so you'll have the job of your dreams waiting for you in New York? Because I know you have no intention of starting at the bottom," Mr. Johnson said matter-of-factly.

"Actually, that's exactly what I plan to do. I don't want to use your connections. This is one accomplishment I will obtain all on my own," she said haughtily. When she saw his mouth harden around the edges she quickly changed tactics.

"Daddy, I've worked for the best, which is you," she said in a softer tone. "I'm more than capable to go to New York, excuse my French, and kick ass."

To her relief, Mr. Johnson let out a slight chuckle. She knew he always admired her fire—he always said it reminded him so much of himself.

"Chloe, I don't understand any of this. Why would you want to move to such a dreadful city when you have all this luxury right here in Texas?" Mrs. Johnson asked, placing her book down on the couch next to her.

"Mother, I wouldn't expect for you to understand," Chloe said dismissively before turning back to her father.

"Daddy, your country club friends and Texas are all you know. When I went away to Boston for college I realized there is so much more out there than debutante balls and bouffant hair." She ignored the grimace she was sure her mother flashed at that last statement and continued. "When I came home I was still afraid to be out in the world without the security of Daddy. But after working four years in the family business, it's time to cut the umbilical cord."

"My dear Chloe, I know a lot more than the country club and Texas. I've traveled the world and have been to every state and nothing compares to Texas. There is no other place for me. This is where I belong," he stated with confidence.

"Then let me have the opportunity to decide if your destiny is my destiny."

Mr. Johnson gave Chloe a puzzled look. "And how do you go about deciding that?"

"Going to New York and pursuing my dreams. If I fail, then I fail, but at least let me try to fly. Ever since I was a little girl you told me that cowards hide in the shadow of certainty and trailblazers step into the light of the unknown. I'm asking you to allow me to take the path of the unknown and see where it leads me."

"If you're serious about this, Chloe, then you have my support," Mr. Johnson said.

"Oh, Daddy, I knew you would understand." Chloe ran to her father and gave him a long hug. She took in the intoxicating smell of her father's cologne and felt safe in his strong arms.

She'd never be able to tell him, but that was the other reason Chloe desperately wanted to escape to New York—hoping to find the elusive Mr. Right. Of all the men Chloe dated, none of them could hold a candle to her father. Plus, the ones who did have it all, once they found out her dad was the legendary Leon Johnson, their focus was no longer on dating her but competing with him, and of course it was never a match.

Leon Johnson exuded the essence of power. He didn't have to talk about it or be about it, because he was *it*. Chloe had so much respect and admiration for her father, she thought no man would ever compare. But she decided the only way to break the cycle and free herself from her father's clutches was to go to a place where everybody didn't know her name.

"Of course I do. I was twenty-six before and I can identify with your need for independence," Mr. Johnson reminded her. "Just know, it won't be easy. You'll have to sacrifice a lot."

"I know—for one, the brand-new Benz you got me for my birthday. At least until I get settled I don't see the logic of taking the car with me. I understand most New Yorkers take taxis and subways. I'm looking forward to the experience. But I'll manage, you'll see, Daddy. When I come back home I'll have my dream job." *And my dream man*, she said under her breath before kissing her father, and then her mother, on the cheek.

"I'm sure going to miss seeing her face every day at the office," she heard her father say with a sigh as she closed the door behind her.

"Leon, don't worry, she won't be in New York for long. No Benz, and having to take taxis and subways . . . it took all my strength not to laugh. The girl was born with a Tiffany's spoon in her mouth for heaven's sakes. Struggling isn't even in her extended vocabulary. Trust me, Chloe will be back," Mrs. Johnson said with a chuckle.

She's wrong, Chloe said to herself as fire flared in her eyes. *After all, I am my father's daughter.*

* * *

Her first night in New York was spent just strolling down 42nd Street taking in the brash seductive signs of Roxy Delicatessen, Times Square Brewery, J.P. Morgan Chase, and Swatch. The top-notch visual styles combined with the lights and action made the streets sizzle with energy. She admired the New Victory Theater, New York's oldest active theater, originally named the "Theatre Republic." Built in 1900 by Oscar Hammerstein, the venue helped establish 42nd Street as the city's new theater district. Chloe then made her way to Restaurant Row on 46th Street between Broadway and Ninth Avenue. The three-block stretch had cuisine to enjoy from all around the world. Whether you were in the mood for Italian at the historic Barbetta, craving a French feast at Le Rivage, Russian cuisine at Firebird, Thai at Bangkok House, or steak from Broadway Joe, the choices were endless. Chloe couldn't remember if New York or Las Vegas was the city that never sleeps, but she figured they had to be running neck and neck. After relishing the nightlife of Times Square, Chloe decided to check out a club she read about in Page Six called One over in the Meatpacking District.

When Chloe arrived, the line was halfway down the block. The velvet rope separating entrance into the club and mere mortals desperate to enter was intimidating to her. In Houston Chloe's face was familiar on the social scene due to the numerous times she appeared in the business and lifestyle sections of the newspapers or local television interviews done on her and her family.

Chloe was a Johnson and in every city of Texas that was instant clout. Here in the big city of New York she felt like a faceless nobody. "There is no way I'm waiting in that long-ass line. I'm Chloe Johnson for heaven's sake. I've had intimate dinners with men who own their own country and I've never had to wait on them. Why should I have to wait to get into some silly nightclub?" she asked out loud, trying to hype herself up as she began to recall her pedigree.

Chloe stood at the side of the building and pulled out her mirror. She slid off the band that was holding her hair in a loose ponytail and it fell cascading around her shoulders. She then used her fingers to fluff it out before applying fresh lipstick to her full lips. Chloe scoped out her attire, and although she wasn't in her normal drop-dead flawless nighttime getup, her curve-defining True Religion jeans, formfitting blouse, and glam Italian Luciano Padovan stilettos would do fine. She unclipped three top buttons, giving just the right touch of cleavage. Chloe strutted toward the daunting doorman and stopped in front of him as if unfazed. "I'm Chloe Johnson and my people are waiting inside for me," she said with each word dripping of confidence. The burly gentleman stood impassive for a moment and Chloe could tell he was sizing her up. She raised her hand to her hip and tilted her head off to the side and looked up to the stars as if one herself, continuing with her performance.

"You can go right in," he said, letting her through the velvet rope. Once Chloe had passed the doorman and entered, she got an instant adrenaline rush and broke into a huge smile. But her smile quickly turned to fascination upon walking through the narrow hallway illuminated by a single red light leading into a scenic New York moment. It was simple but opulent with exposed brick and cinder block walls that rose above the rosewood floors and buttery brown leather booths to meet the vaulted twenty-foot-high ceilings and wide skylights. With the pulsating beat of Nas's latest track blaring from the speakers, the voodoo-inspired look was even more intoxicating.

"Would you like a drink?" the female server clad in a Versace microskirt uniform, which came dangerously close to revealing a bit too much, asked Chloe.

"Sure, I'll have a Bellini."

After the waitress walked off, Chloe took a seat at a small table beside her. She observed the predominately European

crowd that consisted of scantily dressed women who were gy-
rating their hips more seductively than any woman she'd seen
on a music video, unrecognizable men who presented the aura
of success, and of course sprinkles of famous actors, athletes,
and music entertainers whom you would only find lounging in
an exclusive New York City club.

"Here's your drink. But to sit at this table your tab has to
be a minimum of a thousand dollars," the waitress informed
Chloe.

"Excuse me?"

"You don't see the Reserved sign? It's there for a reason."

Chloe looked down on the table and in plain view was the
glossy card that said RESERVED.

"Well, I guess that means I'll be standing," Chloe said,
handing the waitress a twenty for her drink. She could easily
afford the thousand-dollar price tag but couldn't imagine
throwing her money away just to occupy a table. After downing another Bellini and observing the energetic crowd for twenty
more minutes, she was ready to call it a night. As Chloe made
her way to the exit she was startled by a pair of strong hands
clutching her waist.

"Leaving so soon?" a deep voice whispered in her ear.
Chloe turned around, furious that someone had the audacity
to put their hands on her.

"Who the hell are you and why do you have your hands
on . . ." Chloe's voice trailed off when her eyes locked with the
mystery man's. She had never seen such deep inviting eyes, and
they made her light on her feet.

"I apologize," he said, releasing Chloe from his grasp, but
her natural reflex pulled his hands back in. He smiled before
saying, "Does that mean you've changed your mind and have
decided to stay?"

Before Chloe could answer, the champagne bottle flying in
the air less than two feet away from them interrupted her
thoughts. The chaos exploded out of nowhere. Two sets of en-

tourages who were sitting in booths next to each other were now in a full-fledged brawl, fists swinging and bodies being thrown.

"We have to go," three imposing men said, whisking the mystery guy away. In the midst of all the action surrounding them, neither one had an opportunity to say a word; it all happened so quickly. In the blink of an eye he had vanished, and through the crowd of men fighting and spectators running for cover, Chloe had no way of seeing where he disappeared to.

Chloe headed home full of disappointment. For a brief moment in a club, a place she'd never expect it to happen, she felt a connection to a man unlike any other. Full of solemnity, she opened the door to her one-bedroom loft in Midtown. It was definitely not the caliber of her penthouse at the Villa D'Este, but it would do for now

For the duration of the weekend Chloe unpacked her clothes, had furniture delivered, and decorated the place, giving it a southern feminine touch. She fantasized about what might've happened if the fight never happened in the club and she had exchanged numbers with the mystery gentleman. "This is stupid, daydreaming about a man I'll never see again. I guess it just wasn't meant to be. I need to focus my energies on something I actually have control over," she reasoned, picking up the real estate section of the newspaper. Once settled in, Chloe planned on taking a look at some beautiful brownstones she'd heard about in Harlem. Harlem was supposed to be so hip and happening these days. Maybe she'd buy one. Or on second thought, rent one, since she'd heard how expensive those things were and she didn't want to have to run to Daddy for the down payment. Or maybe just rent an apartment in one.

But there were other things to concentrate on for the moment. Monday morning she had an interview with *Posh* magazine.

Out of all the publishing companies in New York City, *Posh* was the only place Chloe wanted to work. The magazine had debuted in 2000 and become the number-one lifestyle magazine virtually overnight.

The reasons for the success of *Posh* were that it blended high fashion with a bit of tabloid gossip, high-profile celebrities of every genre graced its front cover, and finally each page reflected nothing but superiority. If you weren't at the top of your game, then your name would not be found in the pages of *Posh*. In Chloe's mind, that was the only sort of magazine that was worthy of her presence.

Chloe woke up extra early to prepare for her interview. She was euphoric about taking a bubble bath until reality set in and she realized she was no longer living in the lap of luxury in Houston. There was no marble Jacuzzi tub awaiting her when she entered the bathroom, only a renovated shower. After taking a long, hot shower, she pulled her golden brown hair into a sleek ponytail. She opted to wear a tailored cream Gucci pantsuit with the pumps to match. After making sure her face was flawless, Chloe put on her emerald-cut diamond earrings, grabbed her purse, and headed out the door. When she got outside, the doorman hailed her a taxi and Chloe was off.

"Which way, lady?" the scruffy-looking taxi driver asked, not greeting Chloe in the manner she expected given her head-to-toe designer duds. It was obvious his only concern was her paying the fare and giving him a tip.

"Two seventy-six Lexington Avenue, please," Chloe said as she took a long glance at herself in the mirror, confirming that everything was on point. When the taxi reached her destination, Chloe read the meter and saw that she owed him eleven dollars. Before stepping out she gave him just that.

"Lady, where's my tip?" he demanded.

"Please," she said in an exaggerated southern drawl. "Tips are earned. You should've given me a compliment. Whether you meant it or not I would've given you a few dollars just for the thought."

He looked at her as if she were nuts, then hesitated and said, "I apologize, you're looking very lovely this morning—"

"Too late," Chloe said before slamming the door.

"Bitch," he screamed out the window before speeding off.

Chloe couldn't help but smile for shutting the taxi driver down. She knew everyone wouldn't have the southern hospitality she was used to, but if they wanted to get anything extra out of her pocket they would have to learn quickly. While Chloe was caught up in her thoughts she heard her cell ringing. Fumbling through her purse to retrieve her phone, she accidentally dropped both.

"Let me get that for you," a smooth bass voice offered. Chloe was already bending down and first caught a glimpse of the guy's pristine coconut-husk-colored Gucci loafers. Chloe loved a man wearing clean expensive shoes; she felt they spoke volumes about his grooming.

"Thank you so much," she said as they were both now on bended knee picking up her belongings. But once she was face-to-face with the gentleman and they locked eyes, Chloe immediately got butterflies in her stomach. He was one of the most handsome men she had ever laid eyes on. His unblemished milk chocolate complexion was decorated with full kissable lips and familiar profound deep brown eyes that seemed to know the answer to every question in the world.

"My pleasure," he said with what seemed the utmost sincerity.

"And they say chivalry is dead. They must've never met you," Chloe said flirtatiously as he helped her to her feet.

"Christopher, we really must be going. The driver is waiting and we can't be late," an attractive cinnamon-complexioned woman with French-roast-hued curls said.

Chloe assumed she was his girlfriend. *Damn, she's lucky to have him. Talk about love at first sight*, she said to herself.

"I have to go, but hang on to your purse. The next guy may not be so helpful," he added with an endearing smile.

Chloe watched as the couple got into the chauffer-driven

Maybach. Her heart dropped but she quickly picked it back up as she got her mind straight for her interview.

During her ride up the elevator, Chloe couldn't believe how nervous she was. Then it dawned on her that she never had to sell herself on a job, she was always handed whatever position she wanted. This was something brand-new for her and it was electrifying and nauseating at the same time.

When the doors opened on the twenty-fifth floor, Chloe took a deep breath and walked up to the receptionist desk. "Hi, I'm Chloe Johnson and I have a nine o'clock interview with Leslie Duncan."

"Yes, have a seat. Ms. Duncan will be with you shortly," the perky receptionist informed Chloe. Chloe sat down on one of the black leather couches in the waiting area. The entire floor seemed to belong to *Posh* and their fashionable décor didn't disappoint. The double glass doors had the company's name splashed across in ultramodern Bodoni font. There was an octagonal mirror on the wall that was followed by each platinum-framed *Posh* cover dating back to its 2000 debut, which Mary J. Blige graced.

"Hi, Chloe. I'm Leslie, and it's a pleasure to meet you," the tall, slender lady said as she extended her hand to shake Chloe's.

"Thank you, but the pleasure is all mine."

"Can I have Debbie get you anything?" Leslie offered as Debbie continued to flash all of her pearly whites.

"No, I'm fine."

"Wonderful. Then follow me to my office."

Chloe followed Leslie as she walked past all the offices aligning the walls. In the center were dozens of cubicles with eager-looking employees. Leslie had a corner office with a prime view of the city. "Have a seat, Chloe," she said, closing the door.

"You have a beautiful view."

"Thank you, it took me enough years to earn it." Both ladies just smiled. "Now back to you. I was going over your resume and I must say I was very impressed. I was also surprised that you're interested in an assistant position given your multiple skills and experience. You've recruited, hired, and trained twenty-five sales associates in less than a year, delivered a first year's gross profit fifteen percent above plan, negotiated a loyalty program with national vendors, resulting in eleven million in rebates to stores, and conceptualized a highly effective consumer advertising campaign that was featured in *Teen Vogue*, *Essence*, and *People*—and that was only the first two years. To say you're overqualified would be an understatement."

"Although I do have a degree in journalism, all of my skills and experience have been utilized in the cosmetic business. I figured since I'm branching off in a new profession, then starting off as an assistant and learning the business inside and out will enable me to take over the company one day," Chloe said with a huge grin. Both ladies laughed.

"Aren't you hilarious?" Leslie said, still smiling, but Chloe could tell the woman wondered if she was serious.

"Yes, I am."

"Honestly, Chloe, the job is yours. I mean, you were running a cosmetics line, and just looking how stylishly you're dressed yourself it's obvious to me that you can handle being the fashion editor's assistant."

"Wonderful! This is great news." Chloe was relieved the interview was over already.

"But I must ask you something," Leslie said, leaning forward in her chair.

Uh-oh, not out the woods yet. "Of course, what is it?"

"I couldn't help but notice that the company you worked for was Splendor Cosmetics. It's no secret that Leon Johnson owns that company. Your last name is Johnson—do you get where I'm going with this?" Leslie said, still grinning and being extra animated with her hands.

"As a matter of fact I do. Yes, Leon Johnson is my father." Leslie's mouth plunged as Chloe confirmed her suspicions.

"I knew it! I knew it," she repeated. "We run your family's ads in our magazine," she said as if revealing something Chloe wasn't well aware of. "Tell the truth, did you do something terribly naughty to get thrown out of your father's company?"

"Excuse me?" Chloe questioned with bewilderment written on her face.

"You can tell me. It would be our little secret," Leslie whispered as if Chloe was about to reveal a tawdry tale. "I mean, why else would you give up a great job with I'm sure a ton of perks, to come here and be somebody's slave? My goodness, please share, what did you do?"

Chloe paused for a moment and sized up Leslie Duncan. At that moment she came to the conclusion that if this woman could be the editor in chief of *Posh* magazine, then her dreams of someday running it would be easier than she thought. "Sorry, Leslie, I don't have any dirty little secrets to tell you. I just came to a point in my life where I wanted to put my journalism degree to good use. I know that might sound totally bland to someone like you, but that's my story and I'm sticking to it."

"Oh, Chloe, I understand. That's a great story and you should stick to it. But remember if you ever decide you want someone to confide in, I'm always available, except of course when I'm meeting with very important clients, which is pretty much all the time. Ha, ha, ha. I tickle myself. But seriously, I'm going to get you over to Human Resources and if you're ready we can get you started working today."

"Sounds like a plan to me, let's do this." Chloe grabbed her purse and the ladies headed out.

That evening Chloe didn't get home until eight o'clock. She was one of the last people to leave the office and that's exactly how she liked it. But she couldn't front; she was beyond exhausted. Her first thought was to run a bubble bath in her Jacuzzi, but once again had the pained remembrance that she wasn't in Houston anymore and soaking in her tiny tub would have to do. Chloe had begun undressing when her home phone began ringing. She knew it could only be a handful of people since very few had the number to her new apartment. "Hello."

"Hi, honey, how did your interview go?"

"Daddy! It's so good to hear your voice."

"I called you this morning on your cell, but you didn't pick up."

"Yeah, I accidentally dropped my phone on my way in the building." Recalling that episode made Chloe start thinking about the handsome man she'd met briefly. "I meant to call you back, but I got so caught up at work."

"Work? That means you got the job?"

"Yep, I sure did."

"Congratulations, my princess, I knew you would."

"I'm only an assistant, Daddy."

"Maybe on paper, but you'll be running that place before you know it. So, how do you like the person you're working for?"

"Her name is Kari Armstrong. She's the fashion editor. She seems pretty cool. Although I spent the majority of the day doing things like faxing and making copies. Can you imagine, who would ever have thought? It's all very humbling in a way, but since I have my eye on a much bigger prize I'm willing to suck it up."

"That's my girl. They'll never see you coming, and by the time they do it'll be too late."

"Exactly." Chloe could always count on her father to know precisely what she was thinking. "So, how's everything going in your world, any new projects brewing?"

"As a matter of fact there are."

"Really, like what?"

"I'm considering branching off into the music business."

"Daddy, I think we have a bad connection. Did you say the music business?"

Mr. Johnson let out a slight chuckle before answering. "Yes, I did. I'm going over the figures now, and if what my associates tell me is true, then this will be one investment I won't pass up."

"Wow, my father the music mogul. I like the sound of that."

"Business mogul will suffice as I have no plans to get heavily involved with the day-to-day operations. Hell, I may break the company up and sell it off piece by piece. You know I'm only emotionally involved in our family cosmetics company. Everything else is expendable."

"You always have your eye on the dollar. I guess that's why you're Leon Johnson and the rest of us are picking up your crumbs."

"Don't worry, my dear daughter, you won't be picking up my crumbs, because my legacy runs through your blood. You've had a long day so I won't keep you. Just in case I didn't tell you, I'm very proud of you, Chloe."

"I love you, Daddy."

"I love you, too, princess. Good night."

For the next few weeks Chloe worked day and night learning the ropes at *Posh* magazine. She studied her boss Kari's every move, taking in her strong points and weaknesses. On the outside Kari appeared to have the game all sewn up, but upon closer inspection that wasn't the case. She would purposely have Chloe and employees beneath her go to great lengths to accommodate her only to change her mind after they'd done so. Or she'd rarely give enough information or time to comply with her demands, yet routinely berate those who failed. And she felt no compunction about ordering Chloe to do things such as getting coffee or lunch anew if they had gotten too cold for her in the meantime. Chloe took these as signs of insecurity. She reasoned that Kari wanted everyone around her to seem incompetent so she would appear irreplaceable.

"Chloe, run this down to inventory. If they don't have it in, then I need them to stock each of these items. We have a photo shoot tomorrow and the last time I checked, the sizes they have are all wrong."

"No problem, but let me finish up this article Leslie asked me to edit for her and then I'll get right on it."

"Fine, but hurry up. And after you take care of that, please stop by the deli and get my lunch. You know the drill. I'll reimburse you when you get back." Kari shooed with her hand, dismissing Chloe.

"I swear she can be such a bitch sometimes," Chloe complained under her breath. After handling her business with inventory, Chloe made her way to the deli. Luckily she got there before the lunchtime traffic had the line going out the door. After ordering Kari's food, Chloe headed back to work. Right when she was entering the building, two women who were exiting without paying attention flung the door open, hitting Chloe.

The force of the door combined with the strong wind jolted her arms and sent the bag of food Chloe was carrying flying in the air. She turned just in time to witness a man catching the bag as if he played the position as a receiver on a professional football team.

"You again. I'm going to start charging you for my services," the familiar-looking gentleman said, handing Chloe the bag. She looked inside, making sure Kari's food was still intact, and to her relief it was.

"You're the same guy who helped me pick up my purse," she said as she straightened out her white silk belted blazer with matching patch shorts and hoped her makeup was as impeccable as it was when she had applied it that morning.

"That would be me. I'm starting to think you're accident-prone," he said jokingly.

"This was not my fault. Those women flew out the building, slamming the door into me as if I was invisible. I tell you, people in New York can certainly be rude," she said with a mock pout.

"I take it you're not from here?"

"No, I'm a southern belle. I'm a Houston, Texas, girl," Chloe admitted proudly.

"I thought I detected a tiny southern drawl, but you can only hear it on certain words when you get a little excited."

"Oh, you figured all that out in the two brief meetings we had?" Chloe said teasingly as she stepped forward and gently adjusted his tie.

"Let's just say I pay meticulous attention to every detail, especially when the person piques my interest."

Chloe could feel her eyes dancing at the idea of this mysterious, handsome man being interested in her. "So you find me interesting?"

"Very."

"How do you think your girlfriend would feel about that?" Chloe asked coyly.

"If I had one I would ask, but since I don't, there's no need."

"So, who was the attractive woman you were rushing off with when I met you the first time?"

"You must be talking about Dawn. She's my assistant."

Chloe hoped it wasn't obvious how thrilled she was to hear that Dawn wasn't his girlfriend and that he was single. "Well, I hope you treat your assistant better than my boss treats me."

"I take it that you work in here." He waved his neatly manicured hand at the building. "Who do you work for?"

"*Posh* magazine."

"Nice."

"And you?"

"I own Money Grip Records."

Chloe's eyebrows rose and she inwardly whistled her admiration. "Impressive. Your records dominate the charts."

It was his turn to raise his eyebrows. "You didn't strike me as the hip-hop music type."

"Why? Do I seem too uptight?"

"Not at all. Just very classy and sweet. But listen, we've been talking and I still didn't get your name."

"Chloe. Chloe Johnson."

"Nice to meet you, Chloe, my name is Christopher McNeil. Now that we've been formally introduced, will you accept an invitation to have dinner with me?"

"I would love to."

"Then dinner it is," he said, gently placing his right hand on her waist.

Chloe felt a familiar surge sprint through her body. "I know this might sound crazy, but a few weeks ago were you at a club and a horrific fight erupted?"

"Over in the Meatpacking District." Christopher nodded. "You're the stunning woman that slipped through my fingers. But then I guess you didn't."

Chloe swallowed hard. "The first time I ran into you again I knew you looked familiar, but I couldn't pinpoint from where. Wow, talk about meant to be," she said under her breath.

"I'm sorry, I didn't catch that last part," Christopher said.

"Oh, nothing, I can't believe what a coincidence it is that two total strangers would cross paths again in such a big city, that's all."

"I don't believe in coincidences. Some things are meant to be." Christopher pulled out a business card and wrote a number on the back. "Here, this is my office number and I wrote my cell number on the back. I hope you plan on giving me your number."

"Of course, but can you write it down? I don't have a pen on me."

Christopher pulled out another business card and jotted down Chloe's digits.

"I hate to exchange numbers and run, but I have to get back to work. I know my boss is wondering where the hell I am."

"I'm sorry, I didn't mean to keep you."

"Please, don't be sorry. Standing outside on a beautiful sunny day talking to you is a lot more enticing than going upstairs and being bossed around. But hey, you gotta do what you gotta do."

Christopher stood for a moment nodding his head. "Without a doubt I'll be calling you."

"I look forward to it." They both seemed frozen, unable to say good-bye. So instead of using the words they both turned and walked away.

Chloe couldn't believe her luck. She hadn't been in New York for even three weeks and had met a man who seemed like pure perfection.

For the rest of her day at work Chloe could not get Christopher off her mind. She daydreamed about the next time she would see him, hoping that finally she would be able to feel the softness of those full lips and the embrace of those muscular arms. At six foot two he towered over Chloe's petite frame, but that's how she liked her men—tall, strong, and with the presence of being a protector. Christopher exuded all these qualities and more.

"Chloe, don't forget to be here early tomorrow, so we can prepare for the photo shoot. I don't want any problems," Kari belted out, interrupting Chloe's daydreaming.

"Aren't I always early?"

"I suppose, but be here extra early," Kari snapped.

Chloe was starting to believe that Kari had a hard-on for her. No matter how many hours Chloe worked, it was never enough for her boss. She would always find some reason to nitpick at whatever Chloe did. Any suggestions Chloe made, even when beyond great, Kari would shut down. Chloe was trying to remain a team player, but feeling slighted by a woman she felt was somewhat beneath her was becoming more difficult to tolerate.

Chloe arrived at work at seven thirty, so early that she was the first one there. She didn't get much sleep anyway because she'd spent half the night tossing and turning, wondering why Christopher hadn't called her. Although it hadn't even been a day, Chloe felt their connection was so strong that he would've called last night. She had no time to dwell on it because she had work to do. After gathering all the necessary items for the photo shoot, she headed to the studio on the other side of the floor.

This was Chloe's first photo shoot and she was looking forward to it. The magazine was featuring the two hottest young female R&B artitsts on the scene right now, Taj and Melodic. Both would be gracing the cover—timed to hit the stands the month their debut duet CD would drop. It was all the buzz since both ladies had equal star power.

"Just getting here, Chloe?" was the greeting from Kari when she walked in at eight thirty.

"No, I've been here for an hour. I have all the clothes, shoes, and accessories lined up right over there," Chloe said, pointing to the corner area.

Kari rummaged through the stuff not acknowledging Chloe's hard work. "I need for you to go downstairs to inventory and bring up six more boxes of shoes."

"But I brought up all the shoes on the list you gave me last night."

"Well, we need more." Kari hurriedly added some items to the list as if they popped into her head at that second. "Here, take this, and bring these items up." She tossed the list at Chloe without even making eye contact.

Does this two-bit hussy know who the fuck I am? My father can buy this whole damn company twenty times over. I can make one phone call and have her trifling ass collecting an unemployment check, Chloe screamed to herself, though she was dying to say the words out loud. Her experience working at *Posh* magazine and for Kari was teaching her self-control if nothing else.

Chloe was rattled when she realized her cell was ringing. "Who could be calling me this early?" she wondered out loud. "Hello," she answered hesitantly.

"Hi, are you busy?" asked a cheerful voice.

"Who's this?"

"You forgot about me already?"

"Christopher, is that you?"

"Yeah, do you have a minute to talk?"

"Of course, I'm just surprised that you would be calling me so early."

"I know but I wanted to hear your voice. When I got home last night I couldn't find your number and when I came to work it was sitting right here on top of my desk, so I took a chance and called you. I hope you don't mind."

"Not at all." Chloe couldn't help but smile to herself. She knew there had to be a reason he didn't call the night before. "To be honest I was disappointed when I didn't hear from you. I was thinking maybe the feelings were one-sided, me being the one part."

"Please don't think that. I haven't been able to get you off my mind since running into you that very first time. If I had known you were working in the same building for all this time, I would've tracked you down. But then you might've thought I was a stalker."

"By all means, stalk me."

"I can feel you smiling through the phone," Christopher said after Chloe's comment.

"It's that obvious?"

"Yes, but damn, I love your energy. You have this glow about you that's so enthralling. I know I might sound crazy but it's hard to describe."

"You've explained yourself perfectly, because I feel the same way about you."

"Please have dinner with me tonight? Don't even go home. I'll pick you up right after work. I'm not taking no for an answer."

"Then yes, I will."

"Excellent, what time do you get off?"

"Around seven."

"I'll be out front waiting for you."

"Okay, I'll see you then." Chloe couldn't help but revel in

the tingly feeling you get when you first become totally smitten with someone. It's the sort of rush that keeps you on a natural high, and Chloe wanted to soak up every minute of it.

When Chloe got back upstairs with the additional items, Kari seemed to be in an even nastier mood. "It took you long enough. What? Did you walk to Bergdoff's and buy the shoes?" Kari snapped.

Chloe was in such a mellow mood after speaking to Christopher she simply brushed Kari's comment off her shoulder, which seemed to aggravate the woman even more. As Kari parted her lips about to drop another sarcastic line, Taj and Melodic arrived.

"Ladies, how are you?" Kari said as she ran over to the pair, honey dripping from her voice.

As Kari played kiss ass, Chloe was debating in her head what outfits would work best for each artist. Taj was about five foot seven with womanly curves and a chestnut complexion, so Chloe reasoned that the Roberto Cavalli numbers would accentuate her body perfectly.

Melodic was petite with a sun-kissed, dewy bronzed skin that would look amazing in the Zac Posen outfits. Yes, Chloe had it all figured out and was separating a pile for each young lady when Kari walked up.

"Chloe, what are you doing?"

"Selecting some outfit choices for Taj and Melodic."

"Did I ask you to do that?"

"No, but—"

"But nothing. You work for me. You do what I tell you to do and nothing more. Are we clear?"

Chloe's eyes and mouth hardened as she stared at Kari, but she managed to get out one word. "Crystal."

"Now go fetch some juices, the ladies are thirsty."

When Chloe left to go get drinks from the kitchen, Kari tossed the outfits Chloe suggested to the side and went with her own selections. Chloe took her time coming back since

Kari had basically relegated her to playing gofer. But by the time Chloe did return, all hell had broken loose.

"I'm not wearing this shit. It makes my ass look wide and flat," Taj screamed. "And besides my voice, this is my greatest asset," she shouted while slapping her ass to accentuate each word.

"What about me?" Melodic whined in her best spoiled little rich girl voice. "This outfit is drowning me. I know I'm slim but this crap has me looking like Nicole Richie. My fans will be demanding for someone to feed me a biscuit or two. I know that 'I'm hungry, feed me' look gets kudos in the fashion world, but from the streets I rep, no ass means no cash. So if this layout is supposed to help me sell some records, dig up another outfit . . . like now."

"Ladies, you look fabulous," Kari was saying over and over, causing Chloe to look at her as if she'd lost her mind. Taj's outfit had her flesh pulled in so tight that areas that should've been popping out were squished in, and parts that should be in were hanging out. It was a hot mess. Then poor Melodic was a replica of one of the Olsen twins before rehab.

"You must not be able to fucking see, because we look hideous. You better come up with something better than this or I'm out," Taj barked.

"Damn right, you not going to have me playing myself on the front cover of a magazine. You better step your game up and come correct or only thing you'll see is the back of me as I'm walking out the door," Melodic said.

The photographer, lighting crew, and everyone else zoomed in on Kari, waiting for her response to the dilemma, but the woman seemed bewildered, and did little more than sputter almost unintelligible words at one diva and then the other.

"What about this for you, Taj? And this for you, Melodic?" Chloe suggested, thrusting the outfits she had originally picked out at them.

"Chloe, how dare you? Didn't I tell you to mind your business?" Kari said, finally finding her voice as she tried to snatch back the clothes from the women. "Don't pay her any attention, she's only my assistant," she quickly told the singers. "And I don't know how much longer that will be."

"Nah, this is what's up," Taj said as she held the outfit against her body while looking in one of the studio's full-length mirrors. "I'm feeling this gear right here. This is what I'm talking about."

"Me too," Melodic piped up. "This right here is going to have me looking like my little ass is ready for the catwalk." She turned to Chloe. "You have excellent taste, what's your name?"

"Chloe. Chloe Johnson."

"You need to let her pick our clothes and you need to sit the fuck down," Taj said, pointing her finger at Kari.

The look on Kari's face was pure mortification and Chloe felt a surge of intense satisfaction run through her body, starting up from her toes and finally ending with an upward turn of her lips, that she couldn't hide. As embarrassed as Kari was, it was probably that smile that was the straw that finally broke the camel's back. After the singers went into their dressing rooms to suit up for their shoot, Kari stomped over to Chloe.

"The nerve of you, going over my head after I told you to stay out of it. You embarrassed me in front of everybody," Kari bawled.

"Although I would love to, I can't take credit for embarrassing you. You did that to yourself," Chloe said without missing a beat.

"You conniving bitch. You're trying to sabotage my career and I will crush you before I let you do it," Kari threatened with her finger pointing directly in front of Chloe's face.

"Get your bony finger out of my face before I break it. And, my dear, that isn't a threat, it's a promise," Chloe stated, not flinching. "I've only dealt with your bullshit for this long because I was focusing on doing my job. But between my editing articles, trying to assist Leslie, and taking your crap you're making it damn near impossible for me to function, so all bets are off."

"So, what's your point, you prima donna hillbilly?"

"The gloves are off. No more boxing, we're going to turn this into a good old-fashioned street brawl, so watch your back," Chloe said, brushing Kari aside and tapping on the dressing room door. "Taj, how do you like the shoes? Do you need me to bring in another pair?"

"No, honey, these here are perfect," Taj shouted through the door. "Melodic's right, you do have excellent taste."

Chloe smiled, and turned to find Kari shooting daggers at her with her eyes. *Well, it's on now. And damn if I'm not going to come out this the winner.*

The photo shoot was exhilarating, but the day was long, made longer by her anticipation of an evening with Christopher. Having to keep a change of clothes at work in case you needed to attend an unexpected event actually came in handy, she thought as she slipped on a classic red Diane Von Furstenberg wrap shirt dress, with a pair of animal-print Prada open-toe heels. She loosened her hair from its tight ponytail and let it cascade down onto her shoulders, then reapplied a coat of mascara and lipstick. She checked in the mirror again, and had to give herself a pat on the back. Sheer perfection.

As promised Christopher was standing outside waiting for her with a bouquet of orchids and pink roses.

"Thank you, these are beautiful," Chloe said, soaking in the scent of the flowers.

"And you look incredible," Christopher said, complimenting Chloe on her appearance.

"You look very handsome yourself. With your sleek pants and shirt you seem more equipped to be running a men's fashion house than a record label," Chloe said.

"I'm assuming that's a compliment, although I'm not sure that I like it."

"I wasn't trying to offend you. Call it ignorance on my

part, but I assumed all men in the music industry wore throw-back jerseys, sweatsuits, and jeans that fall below their waist. But seeing you in that suit changes my perception."

"I understand. And no, I'm not offended."

"Wonderful. Because seeing you tonight has been my only bright spot in a rather dim day."

"Why? What happened?" he asked with what seemed to be genuine concern.

"I don't want to talk about it. This evening is supposed to be about us, and I don't want anything to ruin it."

"That's fine with me, let's go." Christopher took Chloe's hand and escorted her to his car.

"Where to, Mr. McNeil?" the driver asked.

"Cipriani's, Two hundred Fifth Avenue."

"Wow, you got us a driver for the evening?"

"No, Pablo is my permanent driver. He takes me every-where."

"So? What? You don't have a license?"

"I have a license, it's just stressful driving in the city. Plus, parking is a pain," Christopher explained. "I like being able to come and go as I please, knowing that I have a car waiting."

"That does sound ideal. Plus, it must be nice being chauf-feured around in a Maybach all the time."

"I can't lie, it has its perks. But don't worry, I have a feeling your life will be filled with such benefits, too. Growing up in Bed-Stuy . . ." Christopher paused, seeing the confused look on Chloe's face. "Bedford-Stuyvesant, that's a somewhat unsa-vory neighborhood in Brooklyn—I never expected to be sitting here having dinner in establishments like this. Both my parents died of drug overdoses when I was eight years old. My grand-mother raised me the best she could but it was tough. In my household, being able to buy a new pair of jeans instead of rocking some hand-me-downs was considered a luxury. I'll never forget when I was fourteen and I came home from school ready to explode. I threw my backpack down on the floor, went into my room, and slammed the door. My grand-mother walked in as I was punching my pillow.

"She glared at me and said, 'Boy, why you come up in this house throwing your things and beating on the only good pil-low we have up in here?'

" 'I don't want to talk about it,' I told her.

"She said, 'Well, if you don't want me standing up in your face for the rest of the day you better start.'

" 'Today when we was at the gym, this guy named Danny Boy said I was wearing his old sneakers that his mom had given to the Salvation Army. Everybody in class started laugh-ing and teasing me, saying I don't have any parents and all I can afford is throwaway garbage that nobody wants. I feel like I'm not going to ever be nothing in this world,' I explained to her.

"And I'll never forget what she told me. 'You listen here, because if I leave this earth tomorrow, there is one thing I want you know. Nobody is ever going to give you anything in this world. Whatever you want you have to earn it. So don't whine about what you don't have. Use the brain that God gave you and figure out a way to get it.'

"From that day forward that's what I did," Christopher fin-ished.

"That's powerful. Your grandmother seems very wise."

"No doubt, when I need guidance I still turn to her for words of wisdom."

Chloe sat back absorbing every word as Christopher con-tinued to speak about his past. "You've told me about your childhood and your high school days but still haven't told me how you got into the music industry."

"Where do I begin? Believe it or not I first started off as a dancer. Then I branched off into being a rapper. I even came out with an album even though it didn't register on anybody's hit list."

"Seriously, you were a dancer and rapper? That would be interesting to see."

"If you say so," Christopher said, shrugging. "But then I branched out into music producing and had much better luck with that. I produced several hits for artists like Jay-Z, Mariah Carey, Usher, Mary J. Blige, Beyoncé, and then I started signing my own. Pretty soon I became so successful that it only made sense for me to open up my own label and get distribution from a major. With that I finally found my niche and it's been smooth sailing ever since."

"That sounds like a fairy tale."

"You're right. Every day I wake up counting my blessings. I worked hard and reaped all the rewards and then some. Life has been good to me."

"So, is the music industry as cutthroat as what you read about?"

"Even more."

"Really?" Chloe asked, giving Christopher a stunned look.

"You shouldn't be so surprised. Everybody thinks the music industry is so big, but it's actually very small, and because of that we're all trying to eat from the same plate. And everyone knows how greedy people are. So when you have that many hands scrambling just to get a bite, it's inevitable that the seven deadly sins will take a front seat."

"So, how do you survive it?"

"Love for the music. That has to be more important than the money and the fame. Because when you take away all the sprinkles, the music is all you have left. Enough about me, let's discuss you. Tell me about Chloe Johnson."

"My life is so boring compared to yours. We can get to me another time," Chloe said quickly. "But I would like for us to toast to a wonderful evening."

"I'll drink to that."

Chloe smiled to herself as she and Christopher clicked their champagne glasses.

After dessert and a few more glasses of bubbly, the two lovebirds left Cipriani with their arms wrapped around each other. Chloe had never felt so alive and didn't want the feeling to ever end.

"What's the next stop, Mr. McNeil?"

"We'll be taking Chloe home next, Pablo. Baby, what's your address?" Christopher inquired.

Chloe sat up in her seat and turned to Christopher. "I don't want to go home."

"Are you sure?"

"Positive."

Chloe felt as if she were on an exhilarating voyage that she never wanted to end. It seemed as if her normal cautious self that always followed the prim and proper dating rules had taken a backseat to a more adventurous Chloe. It was a complete no-no in her book to ever be intimate with a man on a first date, or better yet at least the first month. She would never even give in to a passionate kiss until after the third date, but Chloe's chemistry with Christopher was different. He was like a magnet pulling her in and Chloe welcomed it.

When the driver pulled up to the high-rise on the Upper East Side, Chloe knew this was her last chance to change her mind and go home. Once she stepped foot in Christopher's apartment, there would be no turning back. Her body would give in to their undeniable lust, but with the temptation of passion lingering in the air, combined with her champagne buzz, Chloe threw caution to the wind and followed her sexual desires. By the time they reached Christopher's top-floor penthouse, Chloe was practically out of her dress. Christopher's touch was more powerful than she had even imagined. He lifted Chloe up and carried her into his opulent master bedroom where the most inviting king-sized bed greeted them.

"Are you sure you want to do this?" Christopher asked between delectable kisses, each one more passionate than the other.

Chloe paused and stared deeply into Christopher's eyes. "I want you to make love to me unless that's not what you want."

Christopher didn't speak another word. He let his actions do all the talking. He unbuttoned his shirt, revealing the solid frame of well-defined muscles that Chloe had been craving to sink her nails into. When Christopher stepped out of his pants, divulging the sort of tool that every woman dreams of, Chloe thought she would have a mini orgasm without even being penetrated. Before she had the chance, Christopher gently removed Chloe's dress, exposing her lace black bra and panties. He ran his fingers through her hair, grasping it tightly as his tongue made love to her mouth. "Wait, I'll be right back," Christopher whispered as he stood up.

Chloe wanted to beg him to stay, not wanting to be out of his embrace for even a second. Chloe watched Christopher's rock-hard buttocks walking away from her and wondered where he was going until the hypnotic sound of Prince's 'Adore U' filled the room. Now the mood was right, and the scene was set up perfect for a night of making love.

"I want you to lie back and let me take care of you," Christopher said in a soft yet commanding voice.

That's exactly what Chloe let him do. She savored the endless peppering of kisses that led to his tongue stoking her clitoris and devouring her inner lips that pulsated with desire. Chloe gripped tightly to the silk sheets, not wanting to run away from the pleasure but becoming overwhelmed. Christopher held firmly on to Chloe's baby-soft skin, allowing his tongue to go deeper, bringing her to the ultimate climax. Chloe's moans of satisfaction seemed to arouse Christopher even more. As Chloe's body jerked, still calming itself from her powerful orgasm, Christopher sprinkled her stomach with more kisses as the tip of his fingers played with her nipples until the warmth of his mouth took in Chloe's succulent breasts.

"Baby, please let me feel you inside me."

Christopher reached over and opened the drawer in his nightstand, retrieving a condom. Once it was securely on, he looked up into Chloe's pleading eyes and gave her what she was begging for. Chloe let out a scream of undeniable ecstasy when all ten inches of thickness pressed through her tight walls. Chloe had had sex with only three other men in her past, but none of them came close to putting it on her the way Christopher was doing at the moment. She wrapped her legs around his waist, wanting to feel every thrust. They were both so engrossed in each other's euphoria that neither wanted to let go until finally reaching their orgasm simultaneously.

"You felt so incredible," Christopher said as he rolled over onto his back.

"So were you." Chloe snuggled up under Christopher and they fell into a deep sleep.

"Good morning, everybody," Chloe sang out as she made her way to her cubicle.

"You're late," Kari fumed.

"I know, but my yesterday evening and this morning were filled with such unexpected events I simply lost track of all time. Sorry."

"No, you're not," Kari shot back.

"You're right, I'm not," Chloe said with a toss of her head. "No sense in lying."

"Chloe, can I speak with you for a moment?" Kari and Chloe both turned to see Leslie Duncan.

"Ha, you're in trouble," Kari whispered.

"This isn't elementary school, Kari. Must you be so juvenile?" Chloe asked as she grabbed her purse.

"Chloe, please close the door behind you and have a seat," Leslie said sternly. Chloe began to wonder if being a half hour late was a first-degree crime in this office after all.

"Chloe, let me get right to it." The words *you're fired* rang in Chloe's head. "Would you be interested in the position of features editor?"

"Excuse me?"

"Yes, unfortunately Monica got a much more lucrative offer at another company and won't be staying with us, and so

I immediately thought of you. A final decision hasn't been made yet and won't be for at least a few more weeks. But before I added your name to the list of potentials I wanted to see if you even wanted the job."

"Yes, I want the job, but why me? I haven't even been working here for three months."

"Frankly, you've been getting rave reviews. Everybody tells me you're one of the hardest working people here. I've also been amazed at how you're able to juggle working for Kari—which I know isn't easy—and doing the magnificent job on a few of the articles you've edited for me. I especially loved the spin you put on the article covering the Hyatt sisters who claim to be fashion socialites but are more like social piranhas. Then after the wonderful feedback I got back about the photo shoot, I knew you should definitely be in the running. Do you know, both Taj and Melodic called me personally to say how magnificent you were yesterday?"

"Wow! I don't know what to say."

"Well, you're proving to be a force to be reckoned with in such a brief amount of time. But I'm not surprised. You're bringing tremendous work ethics from your prior job."

"So, who else is on the potential list?"

"From here, only you and Kari. We will also be interviewing potential candidates from the outside."

"Kari? But she's already the fashion editor. Why would she want to switch positions? Especially since she has access to fashion that hasn't even hit the runway yet?"

"Higher position equals much more money and perks, like traveling around the world. The features editor has a greater hand in deciding what articles dominate our pages. When you land that position you're entering the big leagues."

Chloe wanted to jump on top of Leslie's desk and break out into some ridiculous dance but used her better judgment. "I feel honored to be among the potential candidates. And thank you, Leslie, for considering me."

"You earned it. Now go out there and get some work done. We'll be chatting again soon."

Chloe walked out of Leslie's office thinking her day couldn't get any better until the most beautiful and biggest bouquet of flowers was sitting at her desk. She rushed to open the card.

To the woman who was created just for me. You're perfect and I can't wait to see you again.

Love,
Christopher

"What are you grinning so hard for? Your rich daddy send you some flowers?" Kari questioned sarcastically.

"As a matter of fact he did, but it's my other rich daddy. Are you comprehending? If not I'll explain. It's the daddy that gives you the best sex of your life. That sort of rich daddy, now choke on it."

"I see you're feeling yourself, but don't forget I don't care who your daddy is, you still work for me."

"Actually I'm feeling just fine, but obviously news travels around here pretty fast, because I don't recall telling you who my father is—especially since it's none of your business."

"Chloe, dear, I make it my business to know everything that goes on at *Posh*, including my assistant's background. Now excuse me, I have work to do."

Chloe sat down at her desk, rolling her eyes at Kari and continuing to make wardrobe revisions for a photo shoot scheduled at the end of the week with Halle Berry. The whole office was buzzing about having the classic beauty grace the cover and doing an eight-page layout with an interview included. This was one article Chloe would love to edit and kept her fingers crossed that Leslie would allow her to do so. She worked diligently for the rest of the day, not even taking a lunch break. To her surprise but gratification Kari remained mute and didn't bother her once. When Chloe finally came up for air she decided to try Christopher again and thank him for the flowers. She hoped he would answer, but the call went straight to voice mail. Chloe didn't mind hearing the sound of his voice before the phone beeped. "Hi, Christopher, it's me, Chloe. Thank you so much for the beautiful flowers, they're almost as perfect as you were last night. Call me when you get a chance, miss you." While replaying their lovemaking episode for the hundredth time, Chloe looked at her watch and realized it was six o'clock.

"Shit," she said out loud before turning off her computer, grabbing her purse, and rushing to the elevator. "I forgot I have an appointment to see that brownstone apartment. I hope I can still make it uptown by six-thirty."

Chloe's cell rang five minutes into her cab ride uptown, and Christopher's name popped up. "Hi, baby."

"Hi, where are you? I want to pick you up from work."

"I'm in a taxi going to Harlem."

"What are you going to Harlem for?"

"To look at a brownstone. I'm considering renting out one of the units."

"They have some beautiful spots that way. But instead of moving to Harlem I wish you would move in with me."

"Christopher, so cute."

"I'm not being cute. I'm being serious."

"We'll see how serious you are when I show up at your front door with all my luggage."

"Let me know when."

Chloe smiled, doubting Christopher was serious but glad his tone gave every indication that he was. "Did you get my message? I absolutely adored my flowers, they were perfect."

"I know. Just like you."

"Ms., we're here," the taxi driver informed Chloe as he pulled up to the three-story green-and-white brownstone in a clean tree-lined block. Even from the outside she could see that work had recently been done on the building. The windows were so clean they had to be new, and the steps looked as if they had recently been steam-cleaned. All of the brownstones on the block—and there had to be twenty on each side of the street—looked good, but this one was a standout. Chloe couldn't believe her luck.

"Wow, it's beautiful," she said out loud, forgetting for a moment she was still on the phone with Christopher.

"You love saying wow," he mocked.

"I can't help it. I have a word addiction."

"How long are you going to be there?"

"I shouldn't be any longer than an hour."

"I'm on my way, then, I'll pick you up."

"Cool." Chloe gave Christopher the address, paid the driver, and headed toward the building.

"What's your name, cutie?" a scrawny-looking brother sitting on the steps of the brownstone next door asked Chloe. She barely glanced at the man, who was wearing beat-up jeans and an army jacket, as she continued her stride. He then walked over and seized her arm. "Didn't you hear me talking to you?"

"Get your hands off of me," Chloe insisted, yanking her arm from his grasp.

"My fault, sexy lady. It wasn't my intention to offend you." The man put his hands up in mock surrender. "But you can at least acknowledge a brother? You know what I'm saying?"

"No, I don't. So excuse me," Chloe hissed.

"What the hell is going on out here?" a middle-aged woman with a blue wool coat, and a brown felt hat pulled down low over her graying dreadlocks, bellowed out as she approached them.

"It ain't nothing, Miss Margie. I was only introducing myself to this fine specimen."

"Jerome, didn't I tell you about harassing my people?"

"You said for me not to bother your tenants," the man said as he backed away. "I didn't know she was one of your tenants."

"Well, she might be if you leave her the hell alone. Now get your trifling ass off my stairs before I pull out my baseball bat and go upside your head."

"Oh, forget you. I'm outta here," he said with a sneer that revealed his yellow teeth.

The slimy dude pimp-walked his way down the block and Chloe was more than happy to see him go. He definitely gave her the creeps.

"Sorry about that, dear. Jerome is harmless but extremely nerve-racking."

"Don't worry about it." Chloe flashed a quick smile. "So, you must be Mrs. Graham?"

"Damn straight, but call me Margie. Everybody else does. I'm a little up in age but I'm not that old," she said, poking out her hip, showing she still had some curves to work with. She took a drag from a cigarette she held in her right hand. Her breath suggested it wasn't the first cigarette she'd smoke that day. "And you must be Chloe Johnson," she said as she continued up the stairs. "Well, come on and I'll show you around Margie's Diamond Palace. That's what I call my place." You're taking a look at unit two, correct?"

"Correct." Chloe waited patiently as Margie found the key for the lock and opened the door. The brownstone was nice, but no palace, but still if that's what the lady wanted to call it, it was fine with her.

"You got an accent. You not from here, are you?"

"No, ma'am. I'm from Houston."

The woman nodded. "Okay. Then let me explain. Unit two is on what you might call the third floor. Down there"—the woman pointed to a courtyard that was three steps below street level—"is what we call the garden apartment. I just rented that out at the beginning of the year to a girl from Canada. She looks half Chinese, if you ask me, but she says she's black. Not that it's none of my business. Not my business at all. And the first floor here," she said, pointing to the level they were entering, "is unit one. Girl from Atlanta moved in about five weeks ago. And the girl in unit three moved in last month. All y'all about the same age, I think. Maybe y'all can be friends. Not that it's none of my business. Not my business at all. Your unit is up here." She led Chloe up a flight of stairs.

"Take a look," Margie said, extending her arm to the open space. "This place has been completely renovated with every pipe, wire, outlet fixture, and appliance . . . Mama don't play," she boasted proudly. "I put a lot of money into fixing up this building."

"I see. This place is just . . . incredible." Chloe's eyes slowly took in the apartment as she moved from room to room. High ceilings with chandelier-like light fixtures, hardwood floors, a stainless steel kitchen, central a/c, and the living room and bedroom even had working fireplaces. "What's the square footage?"

"Between nine hundred and nine-fifty," Margie replied.

"Harlem, here I come." Chloe stood in the center of the apartment and made up her mind that this would be her new home. "I'll take it."

"That's what I like to hear. I'll get your paperwork pre- pared and hell, you can move right on in. That is if you have your first month's rent and security deposit. If your credit is bad, then I'll need three months' security."

"My credit is fine but is that legal, asking for all that extra money?"

"What, you work for the housing department?"

"No, I'm curious to know."

"Don't you worry your pretty little head. If your credit's straight and you have your money, then it's all good."

"Wow. Well, I definitely want the place and plan on moving in this time next week. Is that okay?"

"What's that, February seventh? You must need a place fast, huh? Not that's it none of my business. Not my business at all. You pay, you play. I don't care when you move in as long as you pay the rent. I live in the brownstone two doors down. I live in that place, and rent out this one. Just bring the money order over when you're ready."

Chloe did one last double take of the place and followed Margie out the door.

"Miss Margie, how are you?"

"Oh, hi, Dior." Margie turned to Chloe. "This is the girl I was telling you about who lives downstairs in the garden apartment. She's French. Dior, this is Chloe. She's moving into unit two next week."

Dior smiled and extended her hand toward Chloe. "It's good to meet you, and welcome to the building. I'm sure we'll be good friends."

Not likely, Chloe thought as she pasted a smile on her face. Having female friends had never been her strong suit. Most, like Kari, would start showing their jealousy after only a short while. "Good to meet you, too," she said in a polite but distant tone. She turned back to Margie. "So, are we finished here? I see my friend is here, and I don't want to keep him waiting."

Chloe climbed into Christopher's silver Range Rover waiting for her. "I hope you weren't waiting for me too long."

"Nope, I got here about five minutes ago. So, how did you like the place?"

"I loved it. It was more perfect than I'd imagined. In Texas they don't have homes like this."

"So I take it you're getting the place."

"Without a doubt. I'm coming back tomorrow to bring the landlady a money order."

"Do you need any help with the money you have to put down? I know how these owners be trying to rape you with these prices. With you just being an assistant and all, I know your funds are tight. I'll be more than happy to help you out."

"I appreciate that but I'll be fine. And I actually might be getting a promotion, which would mean more money."

"Is that right? So what's the new position?"

"Features editor. I would have a lot more responsibility and do a ton of traveling. If I can get this job, it could lead to so much more."

"More things like what?"

"Like everything. I mean, I hope to run *Posh* magazine one day."

"Chloe, I don't want to burst your bubble because I think you're incredibly bright, but to go from being an assistant to running a company would be practically impossible with your background. You don't have that type of experience. I mean, I admire your drive, I really do, but in reality what you're reaching for is basically impossible."

"That sounds strange coming from you. If anything I thought you would be my biggest supporter since you beat the odds and became a success story."

"That's why I'm giving it to you raw with no chaser," Christopher continued as he pulled onto the FDR going north. "Because I had to break my back to get where I am today."

"I'm willing to break my back, too, if that's what it takes."

"But you don't have to. Dealing with the snakes you'll have to encounter climbing that corporate ladder is no joke. They're vicious and more than willing to draw blood to ensure you never make it to the top. That type of bullshit will make you bitter and you're too sweet and beautiful for that. Chloe, I can take care of you. I know you've never had a man in your life who could provide for you, but I can. If you're with me you'll never have to struggle again. No more busting your ass at some job trying to make the rent. I got you."

Chloe didn't know whether to feel flattered or offended with Christopher's declaration. Originally she felt it wasn't of any concern to inform Christopher she was a daughter of a billionaire with a trust fund that guaranteed neither her nor any of her unborn children would ever have to work a day in their lives if they chose not to do so. But now with Christopher offering to take care of her as if she was a charity case, maybe the truth was warranted. "Christopher, there's something I need to tell you."

"Hold on, baby, I need to take this call." Christopher turned the volume completely down as his face grew intense by whatever the person on the other end of the phone was saying. "Yo, you sure? I mean, when I signed that label deal it was airtight, my lawyer made sure of that. I'm not about to sit back and let this bullshit go down. I'll be in my attorney's office first thing tomorrow morning to straighten this out."

"Is everything okay?" Chloe asked after Christopher finished his call.

"Remember those snakes I was just warning you about? Well, here they go."

"What happened?"

"Corporate bullshit, that's what. But before I get too vexed I'm going to have a conversation with my lawyer and if need be prepare myself for war."

"War? Who would want to go to war with you?" Chloe asked, getting out of the truck.

"I don't know, but I intend on finding out."

"Chloe, do you have the wardrobe revisions for the Halle Berry shoot on Friday?" Kari demanded hastily.

"Good morning to you, too," Chloe responded sweetly, handing Kari the finished list of revisions. "All the designers also agreed to include garments from next season that even store buyers haven't seen yet."

"What's the kicker? They better not try to stick us with any bullshit on the back end."

"Come on, Kari, this is Halle Berry. Plus, it's free publicity for them if we choose to use one of their designs."

"Don't try to school me on how this game works. You're just a cosmetics girl, remember. These designers pretend to be so helpful, but trust me, they always have an underlying motive and I hope you didn't agree to give them anything extra because it's your ass on the line."

"I didn't, so don't worry. Now, if that's all I need to get back to work." Chloe exhaled as Kari tossed her blond bob to the side and strutted her bony ass back to her office. Right when Chloe wanted to scream out in disgust, her phone started vibrating and Christopher's name popped up on the screen. "Hello."

"Hello to you. I was calling to see what you're doing tonight. I thought maybe we could have dinner."

"We can have dinner but only if I get you for dessert."

"That goes without saying. So I'll pick you up around six from work."

"Make that seven. I'm sure there'll be something my boss will want me to get done at the last minute."

"Then seven it is."

"I'll see you then."

"What has you smiling so hard?"

Chloe jumped, getting caught off guard by Kari's question. "Didn't you just go in your office? What? Are you like the floor patrol?"

"Funny. And no personal calls are allowed during working hours."

"What can I do for you, Kari?"

"I have an event to attend next week, so I need you to go to the 'closet' and pull a few dresses for me. You know my size."

"Yeah, less than zero," Chloe mumbled.

"I'm sorry, I didn't hear you."

"I said of course I know your size and taste. I'll get right on it."

"Good, and don't forget my lunch at noon. Grilled chicken sandwich—"

"On rye, hold the mayo," Chloe said, finishing her sentence. "I know, Kari, I've gotten you the same meal every day for weeks now."

Before going to the "closet" and selecting some dresses for Kari, Chloe made a detour and hopped in a cab headed to Harlem. She promised Margie she'd drop off her money order and didn't want to take the chance of anyone else getting her apartment.

"Pull over to the left in front of the green and white brownstone," Chloe directed the cabdriver. After handing him fifteen dollars, which included a five-dollar tip, Chloe shut the door and was greeted by the same knucklehead she had come across yesterday.

"Hey there, pretty lady. You miss Jerome already?"

Chloe couldn't decide what irritated her more, his grimy smirk or his uncombed hair. "Excuse me, you said your name was what? Jerome?"

"That's right. The one and only."

"Praise the Lord for that, but I need you to move out of my way, sweetie. I came back here today to see Margie, not to make small talk with you. So please go sniff after someone else, preferably on a whole other block, city, or state."

"Well, don't you have an attitude? You uppity broads with your designer clothes and slick corporate talk kill me. Don't no player like myself want to be bothered with that nonsense because women like you don't know how to treat a real man anyway. I already got me a woman. A professional woman with a good job. I hope some suave Casanova comes along and ruins your credit."

"Jerome, what I tell you about harassing my tenants? Get your trifling ass away from my property, you low-life no good-for-nothing. Don't make me call you out again, hear?" Margie yelled as she walked toward the brownstone.

Jerome turned his lip up and pimp-walked off in his beat-up Timberlands.

"Why me?" Chloe repeated, shaking her head. "Margie, hi, I was coming to drop off my money order. But if you have one moment can I ask you a quick question?"

"Go 'head, dear, but make it quick because I only got that *one* moment you said you needed."

"I didn't mean that literally, but okay." Chloe realized she needed to speed up her question when Margie started tapping on her watch. "Does Jerome not have a job or is harassing women on the block what he does for a living?"

"Child, Jerome is harmless. He's been trying to bother the other girls here, too, but just keep ignoring him and eventually he'll get the message. But if he keeps at you, I got a baseball bat that I keep right here in the hallway that you're more than welcome to use. Now I must be going, I got things to do."

Chloe was starting to have second thoughts about her decision to move to Harlem, but she had already given Margie her money and the apartment was drop-dead gorgeous. She paused as she watched a light-brown-skinned woman trot down the stairs. Another twenty-something female neighbor. *I hope she doesn't want to be friends, too.*

Still, things could be worse, Chloe reasoned before hopping in a cab and heading back to work.

"Where have you been?" Kari belted, walking up to Chloe's desk.

"Making sure I had everything you requested. Here is your lunch and in your office you have six beautiful dresses waiting for you."

"But I just came from downstairs and you weren't in the closet."

"Of course not, I was too busy arranging your dress choices in your office. I'm sure we had just missed each other."

"But you were missing for a very long time."

"The line was much longer than usual at the deli and when they finally did give me your order it was cold. So of course I had them make your sandwich all over again. I know how much you hate lukewarm food. So you better hurry before this one gets cold, too."

Kari gave Chloe a suspicious glare but said nothing more.

Chloe grabbed her purse and headed to the restroom to freshen up. When she got back to the office and saw how much time had passed, she was like the Energizer Bunny rushing to make up for lost time.

"Hi, Chloe," Leslie's assistant chirped when she entered the bathroom. The two rarely had time to chat but were always friendly when they would run into each other.

"Hi, how's it going?"

"Pretty good, you know, working hard. Leslie wouldn't expect any less."

"Yeah, I'm actually coming to take a quick break from my boss."

"From what I hear Kari won't be your boss for much longer."

"Really, who told you that?"

"Of course this stays between us, but Leslie is really pushing for you to get the job as features editor. She loves your work and feels you'll be perfect. Although Kari is a witch she does have her supporters, but Leslie carries a lot of clout, so your chances are excellent. But you didn't hear this from me."

"Thanks, Lily, you're the best."

"No problem. If I hear anything else I'll let you know. Now let me get back to work before the floor patrol comes looking for me."

Chloe wanted to break out into a celebratory dance at the idea of landing the coveted position but knew it was too soon. Having an endorsement from Leslie was priceless but not a guarantee. When Chloe got back to her desk the conversation she'd had with Lily motivated her to work even harder. She started working on articles Leslie gave her that weren't due for another two weeks. Chloe also completed another assignment Kari threw on her desk just so she didn't have to hear her mouth. By the time all her tasks were completed it was seven o'clock and she was ready for her date with Christopher.

She thought this evening was a perfect time to reveal who she really was to him. Not to say he didn't know her, but a lot of men were either intimidated, a Leon Johnson groupie, or felt they could never measure up to her father's reputation and no longer wanted to date her. But Chloe felt that she and Christopher spent enough time together that he had grown to care about her as a person and that her being the daughter of Leon Johnson wouldn't matter to him one way or the other.

Chloe's eyes started dancing when she stepped outside and saw Christopher standing in front of the car waiting for her.

"As always you look beautiful," he said before opening the door for her.

"I hope you'll always feel that way about me." Chloe got comfortable while Christopher walked around the other side and got in.

"Pablo, take us to Nobu 57 on 40 West 57th Street. Have you ever been there before?" he asked Chloe.

"No, I haven't."

"It's one of my favorites for Japanese food. I'm sorry, I should've asked . . . do you even like Japanese food? Because we can go somewhere else."

"Japanese is fine."

"Are you sure? Being a southern girl, you might not have had much exposure to different cultures."

"Don't worry, I've had my share."

There was no question in Chloe's mind she had to come clean with Christopher. She knew he didn't mean any harm, but his assumption that she was some clueless hick was misguided and she needed to set the record straight.

Upon their arrival the hostess greeted Christopher with a "we've been friends forever" smile, making it clear he was a regular. They bypassed the boisterous crowd at the first-floor bar and sat down in the sprawling dining room on the second-level balcony, which felt busy with rich woods, fabrics, and patterns. "Here's your regular table, Mr. McNeil, and enjoy your meal."

"I'm sure I will."

"I take it you sit here when you come," Chloe said as they sat down.

"From the first day the restaurant opened. I used to go to Nobu's downtown, but when they opened this one in Midtown it was much more convenient."

"Good evening, Mr. McNeil. Will you be having your usual?"

"Yes."

"And your guest?"

"Why don't you order for me since I'm sure you know what's good?" Chloe said demurely.

"My date will be having the black cod—if only for bragging rights you have to be able to tell everyone about your brush with this silky, brightly sweetened fish. It's mouthwatering."

"I can't wait."

"You can also bring me a bottle of wine."

"Of course, sir."

"I must admit I'm getting used to spending time with you and I'm enjoying it immensely," Christopher said, turning back to Chloe.

"I feel the exact same way. I only look forward to two things—moving into my new brownstone next week and spending time with you. The more I see you, the more I want to see you, if that makes any sense."

"It does."

"So, how was work today?" Chloe changed the subject to something less personal as the waiter came back to the table and opened their bottle of wine.

"Eventful. Remember the snake I told you about who is trying to buy out my record label from right under my nose?"

"Oh yeah, did you find out who it is?"

"Yes, this son of a bitch named Leon Johnson."

Chloe choked and spat out the glass of wine the waiter had just handed her when Christopher revealed the name.

"Chloe, are you okay?" Christopher stood up in concern. Everyone turned to see what was going on. The waiter gently patted Chloe's back, making sure she wasn't about to fall out in the middle of the restaurant.

"I'm fine. The wine went down my pipe the wrong way. No need to panic."

Christopher sat back down, looking relieved.

"Continue on about that snake you discovered."

"Are you sure? That can wait. Making sure you're okay is more important."

"I promise you I'm all better. Please continue, this is very interesting."

"I'm sure you've heard of Leon Johnson. If you haven't you must be living under a rock. He's our black Bill Gates and I'm still trying to figure out why in the world he wants to get into the music business. This man has more money than God but wants to fuck with mine."

"Are you sure?"

"Positive. I had my attorney look into it. Supposedly he wants to buy Atomic Records, which is my parent company. Then once he does that he plans on selling off all the boutique labels, which would include mine. I thought my contract was structured so that they couldn't sell off my label without my consent, but if a new owner takes over Atomic, it nullifies that part of the contract."

Chloe recalled the conversation she'd had with her father some weeks ago when he mentioned a deal he was considering that had to do with the music business. It was just her luck that the label would have to belong to the man she was head over heels for.

"So, what are your options?"

"My attorney is strategizing now, but this is a whole other ball game. I knew I would have to go to war with a big dog but not the king of the entire domain. I mean, he can bleed like anyone else. It's just a matter of me finding his weakness, because we all have one."

Chloe knew this was not the time to reveal she was the daughter of the snake he wanted to shred to pieces. She barely said two words throughout their meal. Even after devouring the chocolate cake with green tea ice cream she had no desire to say how delicious it was. Her mind was fixated on doing damage control.

"You were so quiet in the restaurant, are you feeling okay?" Christopher asked once they got in the car.

"Actually I am feeling a tad off."

"I hope it wasn't the food."

"No, the food was incredible. I'm just a little light-headed. I'll feel better once I lie down."

"Would you like me to come and take care of you?"

"Normally I would say yes. But I wouldn't be good company. Plus, I have nothing but boxes stacked everywhere from all the packing I've been doing." The driver pulled up in front of Chloe's apartment and got out to open the door for her. "I'm sorry I wasn't better company but I'll call you tomorrow."

Chloe leaned over and gave Christopher a kiss before getting out. When the car drove away she basically flew upstairs desperate to speak with her father. After locking the front door she grabbed her cordless, dialing her parents' number.

"Hello," Mrs. Johnson answered.

"Mother, I need to speak to Dad."

"Chloe, hello to you, too. It's very rude not to acknowledge me when you call our home."

"I apologize, Mother. How are you doing?"

"I was doing just fine until my only child called here and acted as if I was a stranger."

Chloe rolled her eyes, not in the mood for one of her mother's minilectures but still trying to be respectful. "Mother, I didn't mean to be rude. I have an emergency and I need to speak with Father."

"Your father went out of the country for business and won't be back until late next week. You can call back then."

"Did he leave a contact number I can reach him at?"

"I forget what hotel he's staying at. Call back next week.

I'm sure whatever is going on with you can wait until then. Now I must be going, Francine and Gail are coming over so we can discuss next month's social events. I'll talk to you later. Love you."

"The woman never seems to care about anything besides her overindulgent life," Chloe said, putting her head down when she hung up with her mother.

Chloe took a hot shower before burying herself deep in her comforter. She tossed and turned all night, wondering how she could make a bad situation right. She prayed that if she begged her father not to buy the record company he would comply. It wasn't as if he needed the money, but Chloe also understood at this stage in her father's life it wasn't about the money but the thrill of the hunt. But even if her father agreed, her biggest worry was how Christopher would react to the news that she was his daughter.

Chloe sat at her desk tossing paper clips in the plastic container unable to focus on her work; it had been like that ever since Christopher dropped the bomb on her. Since their dinner last week she had been avoiding his calls and when she did speak to him she would keep the calls as brief as possible, blaming her lack of time on work and unpacking her boxes now that she'd moved into her new place.

Today seemed especially hard because since they began dating this had been the longest time she'd gone without seeing Christopher. Chloe's energy was almost depleted, so luckily for her Kari was so preoccupied with getting pampered for the event she was attending tonight that she'd stopped in briefly to make some phone calls and hadn't been seen in the office since. Chloe looked somberly at the clock as her day came ticking to an end. Since she was unable to work, and Kari was nowhere in sight, Chloe grabbed her purse and left at exactly six. When Chloe opened the glass doors leading outside she was pleasantly surprised to see Christopher parked out front in his Range Rover.

"I was prepared to sit out here and wait for at least an hour, but you got off of work right on time," Christopher said after getting out of the car and walking up to Chloe.

"I know. Right? What are you doing here?"

"For one, I missed you. It seems like I haven't seen you in forever. I thought I'd surprise you and give you a ride."

"Surprised I am, but in a good way."

Seeing Christopher made Chloe realize just how much she missed him. The two hugged and Chloe took in the alluring scent of his cologne before they got in the truck.

"How was work?"

"Rather dead today. My boss has an event she's attending tonight, so she only came to the office for a brief moment."

"That's interesting because that's one of the reasons I picked you up."

"What do you mean?"

"I have an event to attend tonight and I wanted you to accompany me."

"I would love to but I need to go home and get a change of clothes."

"Don't worry about it. I have it all covered. The only stop we're making is to my place."

"I was wondering where we were going because this bridge isn't familiar at all," Chloe said, looking out the window.

"Yeah, this is the George Washington Bridge, we're headed to Jersey."

"But your place is in the city."

"Yes, I use that apartment primarily for business purposes, but where I'm taking you is my home."

When Christopher got off the bridge he took the Palisades Interstate Parkway. The highway was an endless stretch of wooded bliss. Fifteen minutes into the drive Christopher veered off right on the Alpine/Closter exit. After a series of turns he made a final left on Buckingham Drive, pulling up to a circular driveway with electronic gates. The brick manor center hall Colonial sat on beautifully landscaped private one-acre property.

"This is stunning," Chloe commented when the mahogany double doors opened up to a marble foyer with two iron rod and wood spiral stairwells.

"Let me give you a minitour," Christopher said as Chloe followed his lead. There were custom finishes and marble throughout the six-bedroom, five-bath mansion with high, domed ceilings. The lower level boasted a gym, recreational room, sauna, second fully equipped kitchen, barroom, and a gummite pool, waterfall, and spa out back. There were spectacular panoramic views of the Ramapo Hills to the west and a nature preserve to the north and east. Chloe did think Christopher's home was lovely, and the average girl would've felt as if she had died and gone to heaven, but this space was equivalent to one of her family's many vacation homes.

"You have truly done well for yourself. You should be proud."

"I'm an example that hard work and determination do pay off. Follow me upstairs," he said, taking Chloe's hand.

When they entered the bedroom, the first thing Chloe noticed was a pretty Asian girl dressed casually in a red terry cloth sweatsuit.

"What is she doing here?" Chloe said, totally confused.

"This is Audrina, she's a hair and makeup artist. She'll be making you even more beautiful tonight, if that's even possible."

Chloe felt herself blushing.

"Hi, Chloe, Christopher told me all about you and I'm excited about making you picture perfect. First, I want you to pick out which dress you would like to wear tonight."

Chloe let out a gasp, feeling overwhelmed by Christopher's kindness.

"They are all so beautiful," Chloe said, ogling the assortment of dresses. She couldn't decide among the champagne-colored embodied chiffon frock by Roberto Cavalli, the black vintage Herve Leger gown, a sparkly silver Michael Kors kimono dress, a Badgley Mischka platinum silk lamé gown, or the Gucci poppy-red organza voile ruffle-band minidress. "Christopher, I can't believe you did all this for me. What have I done to deserve to be treated this way?"

"Because you're you, and when I'm in your presence I feel alive. You don't need to do any more than that."

A single tear streamed down Chloe's face.

"Baby, I didn't mean to make you cry," Christopher said, wiping away the tear.

"I know, it's just that no one has ever done anything this special for me before. I'm speechless."

"If you let me I'll do special things for you all the time."

"Okay, lovebirds, it's time for me to work my magic on Chloe, so excuse us, Christopher," Audrina said, leading Christopher out the door. "So, have you decided which dress you're going to wear?"

"Yes I have."

"Then let's get to work."

When the stretch limo pulled up to Cipriani on 55 Wall Street, Chloe could feel her stomach bubbling. She had been to formal events twenty million times, but going as the date of a man she was falling in love with was exhilarating and scary.

"You are truly a vision," Christopher said as he helped Chloe out of the limo.

"I take it you like the selection I made?"

"Like is such a baby word. You have me so aroused right now that I'm tempted to skip this event and have the driver take us on a long detour of the city while we make love."

"I'm game."

Christopher smiled. "I bet you are and that's one of the reasons I find you so incredibly sexy. But the only problem is that this event is being held in my honor, and to miss it would be extremely rude."

"This event is being held in your honor? Thanks for telling me at the very last minute and also congratulations. What is the honor for?"

"Thank you, and I've been named the music industry's businessman of the year."

"Impressive."

"No, impressive is you in that dress."

Impressive was an understatement. Chloe chose a strapless white Emanuel Ungaro stunner that had embroidered stones highlighting her tiny waist. The flowing gown was accentuated with twenty-four-carat Lorraine Schwartz pink-diamond earrings and bracelet that Christopher got on loaner for the night. With Chloe's shoulder-length hair swept up with a few loose curls decorating her face, it brought even more attention to her bare shoulders. The finishing touch was the Jimmy Choo open-toe silk satin cross-over-strapped sandal that featured a Swarovski jeweled buckle. With Christopher draped in a tailor-made gray pin-striped Armani suit, the couple was timeless.

"Well, then let's go show me off," Chloe laughed as the pair walked hand in hand inside.

When they entered Cipriani, Chloe was blown away by the sixteen-thousand-square-foot venue. "This place is incredible," Chloe said out loud, soaking up the shindig. The place sparkled with luminaries like Denzel Washington, Jamie Foxx, Eva Longoria, Queen Latifah, Derek Jeter, Christina Aguilera, Ludacris, 50 Cent, Gabrielle Union—the list of heavyweights went on and on. It seemed that all of black Hollywood including entertainment giants graced the place.

"Thank you, I appreciate the love," Christopher said as celebrity after celebrity continued coming up and congratulating him on the honor. With all the grand balls Chloe had attended in her life, never had she experienced anything of this magnitude. Everywhere she turned, there were A-list stars laughing and drinking champagne, casually enjoying themselves, but Chloe fit right in. At first glance you would've easily mistaken her for a big-screen starlet. As Christopher continued to mingle, Chloe noticed the last person she wanted to see coming her way.

"Chloe, I had no idea you would be here tonight," Kari said, staring Chloe down. "Who are you here with?"

Before Chloe could dismiss her annoying boss, Christopher introduced himself.

"Hi, I'm Christopher McNeil. And you are?"

"Kari, I'm Chloe's boss at *Posh* magazine. It's a pleasure to meet you," Kari said, extending her hand toward Christopher's.

"It's a pleasure. You're very lucky to have such a competent woman working with you. She's something else."

"Yes, she is."

"Excuse me," Christopher said, turning his attention to an associate eager to speak with him.

"I had no idea this was the event you had me fetch your clothes for."

"And I had no idea my assistant would be here with the guest of honor. You've got yourself quite a catch there. What is he, some flavor of the month?"

Chloe could detect the sarcasm in Kari's voice. "No, he's actually my boyfriend."

"Really? I thought spoiled rich girls like you only had boy toys, not boyfriends."

"You thought wrong. But this isn't the time or place to have this discussion. I'm here to support Christopher, not to have a war of words with you. So if you would be so kind as to excuse yourself, I would greatly appreciate it."

"Cute. But there are so many more interesting people to chat with, so I'll let you be. But, Chloe, don't get caught up playing Cinderella tonight. I expect you to be at work on time tomorrow morning."

As Kari was walking away, Christopher caught Chloe rolling her eyes. "What was that about?"

"What?"

"I saw you giving her the look of death. I know she's your boss but she couldn't be that bad."

"Put it this way, if the devil ran with a crew she would be the leader of the pack."

"Ouch. That's pretty bad."

"And then some. But I don't want to think about Kari, I want to slow-dance with you. How about it?"

"Follow me."

Christopher and Chloe gazed deeply into each other's eyes as their bodies swayed to John Legend's live performance. The smoothness of his voice combined with the melodic sounds from the piano had Chloe feeling as if she were floating in the clouds. With the closeness of their bodies as Christopher's strong arms wrapped around her waist, Chloe knew that she had finally found the man she'd been dreaming of all her life. "I can't wait for us to go home so I can make love to you."

"You were reading my mind, because I was thinking the same thing."

"Mr. McNeil, I'm sorry to interrupt you but they are ready to present you with your award," one of the event planners informed him.

"Thanks. Let's go have a seat at our table," Christopher said, taking Chloe's hand.

The music came to a halt and everyone began taking their seats. Russell Simmons gave a praising speech before introducing the man of the hour. The entire room stood up and applauded as Christopher made his way to the podium. Chloe had flashbacks of the numerous occasions that her father had been honored and the countless adulations he received. Now here was Christopher, filling those shoes.

"That's my baby," Chloe cheered under her breath.

"Everybody please take your seats. I want to first thank you for coming out tonight to support me. I know that all of you could've been anywhere you wanted, but you chose to share this evening with me . . . and for that I'm eternally grateful."

The entire room seemed to listen intently as Christopher painted a colorful picture of his rise to success. The more he spoke, the more you couldn't help but to admire his fortitude of turning the negative in his life to a positive.

He finally closed out his speech by saying, "There is one final person I would like to thank. This remarkable individual has come into my life and in a short span has made me feel as if she's been with me forever. Chloe Johnson, you are an amazing woman and I'm so grateful we're able to share this special moment in my life together." Christopher held his plaque in Chloe's direction and all eyes turned to get a glimpse of the woman he acknowledged, but through all the stares one pair of eyes met Chloe's with disdain.

Please let me get that promotion so I can be done with you, Chloe thought to herself as she stared right back at Kari with the same contempt.

"You sure know how to make a woman feel extraordinary. Never did I see that coming," Chloe admitted as she laid her head on Christopher's shoulder on their limo ride home from the event.

"It wasn't my intention to put you on the spot, but I wanted to speak from my heart and I meant every word."

"I know you did and that's what makes it so wonderful."

Christopher lifted Chloe's chin and gently kissed her soft lips as their tongues began to meet. Christopher slid his hand up the side of Chloe's butter-soft skin as he caressed her inner thigh. Her seductive sighs of pleasure had Christopher's third leg in an upright position and he knew he couldn't make it home without feeling her warmth. With one touch of a switch Christopher had the hide-trimmed division blind raised so they were in complete seclusion. Before long Chloe was out of her dress, sprawled across the wide leather seats as they made love.

When Chloe awoke the next morning snuggled under Christopher's arm, she was about to close her eyes and go back to a blissful sleep until she noticed the time on the clock. It was eight thirty and she had to be at work by nine. "Oh, shit," Chloe belted out as she scurried from under Christopher's embrace.

The sudden abrupt movement awoke Christopher from his sleep. "Chloe, where are you going? Come back to bed."

"I can't. I'm going to be late for work. I have to go home and change. Kari is going to let me have it."

"Forget Kari. Call in sick. It's Valentine's Day. I want you to stay in bed with me all day."

"It's Valentine's Day. Oh, baby, I totally forgot. I would love to snuggle up under you for the rest of the day, but I'm up for this promotion and I have to be on my best behavior."

"You have to be the only woman I've ever met who doesn't have Valentine's Day cemented in their mind. So you'd rather rush off and not be late to some bullshit job than stay and be with a man who's trying to build a future with you?"

"Is that really even a question? Because there isn't a comparison. Of course I would rather be with you, but my job isn't bullshit, either. I've been working my butt off trying to solidify myself as a contender at *Posh* and I want to win."

"Is winning at *Posh* worth you losing with me?"

"Christopher, I can't believe that after the amazing time we had last night you would run this bullshit on me. What? I can't be with you if I want to have a career? Is that what you're saying?"

"Why would you want to? Do you know how many women are tired of working some job every day, putting in long hours, not able to have a life outside of their work? If they were able to find a man who loves them and wanted to take care of them so they wouldn't have to work another day in their life, they'd jump at it. But you seem to be willing to let it slip through your fingers."

"Are you saying that you love me?" Chloe questioned with her heart beating fast.

"Yes, I am."

Chloe walked back to the bed and sat beside Christopher. "And I was praying the feelings weren't one-sided," she admitted with a slight chuckle. "Christopher, I don't want to lose you and you are more important to me than a job. But I've never been a quitter and this job represents working through my own personal issues, so please give me the chance to do that. Love is about understanding."

"Point made. But know that you don't have to stay at *Posh* and be disrespected by Kari or anyone else. If it's so important for you to have a job you can always come work for me."

"You sound like my father," Chloe said, immediately regretting she had brought her dad up in the conversation.

"Your father? You never talk about your family. What business is he in?"

"A little this, a little that. We can talk about him later," Chloe said, giving Christopher a quick kiss on the lips. "But, baby, I have to get out of here. I'll call you later on when I get home. I'm finally finished with my unpacking, so I can actually take a breather."

"Excellent. Does that mean I should come over tonight and we celebrate Valentine's Day at your new apartment?"

"That sounds perfect. I'll see you tonight."

"Hold up, let me call my driver so he can give you a ride to your place. He should be right outside."

"That would be nice. I would look sorta crazy trying to fetch a cab dressed in my evening wear. Thank goodness we stayed at your place in the city, because if we were in Jersey I would have to throw the towel in and forget about work."

"Interesting, I'll have to remember that for the next time," he said, dialing his driver's number. "Pablo is out front. He'll take you home and then wait to drive you to work."

"I think I can get used to being with the music industry's man of the year. It comes with a lot of perks. Bye, baby."

"Bye."

Chloe hurried downstairs and Pablo was waiting in the silver Maybach to take her home. Once she got in the car, the first call Chloe made was to Kari. It was only a quarter to nine and Kari wasn't in yet, but Chloe wanted to leave a message because regardless she was going to be late to work.

"Hi, Kari, this is Chloe. I'll be about an hour late for work. Sorry for the delay." Chloe shut her cell phone and hated having to explain herself to Kari. She reflected on her conversation with Christopher and all the women who had no other options but to put up with crap from their bosses if they wanted to keep a paycheck. It was humiliating to say the least and Chloe knew she was blessed to have other options, because in this world that was the only thing that gave you some sort of power. The more options you had, the more power you garnered, and that was why people would always try to limit you from having any options.

After Pablo dropped Chloe off at work she went to the deli and had herself a breakfast croissant and then stopped at Starbucks for a caramel Frappuccino since she was late anyway. When she finally made it to the office, Chloe was surprised to walk in and see Christopher and Kari in what appeared to be a heated discussion. Kari stopped talking when she noticed Chloe coming near them.

"Christopher, what are you doing here?"

"I knew Pablo dropped you off a little while ago and I wanted to give you something you forgot at my place."

"Okay? But why are you talking to Kari?"

"We were discussing you, actually," Kari said with an evil smile. "Since you were late I decided to keep Mr. McNeil company while he waited for your arrival."

"Well, I'm here now, so you can go."

"Is your father Leon Johnson?" Christopher asked somberly. Chloe narrowed her eyes at Kari.

"I had no idea he didn't know you were 'the' Chloe Johnson, heir to Leon Johnson's fortune. I mean, why else would *Posh* hire a cosmetics girl if it wasn't for who your father is?"

"I bust my ass at this job and never was I hired because of who my father is. I work harder than anyone in here just because of that. And, Christopher," she said, turning to him, "I had every intention of telling you who my father was."

"When? After your father owned my company?"

"No, I was going to try and change his mind. It's just that he's out of town and I was waiting to speak with him before I told you."

"Why didn't you tell me from day one?"

"Because I didn't think it should matter. I didn't want you to look at me as Leon Johnson's daughter."

"But you are. You're what people would call a real life black American princess. I suppose a person like me is living in poverty by your standards."

"See, that mentality of thinking was exactly what I wanted to avoid. I'm proud of your success and you have accomplished a lot. That's my father's money, but everyone judges me based on it. I have dreams outside of being a Johnson and wanted to achieve them on my own merits, not my father's."

Kari clapped her hands, mocking Chloe. "Lovely speech, but the fact is you still lied, if not straight out, then by omission. Well, I would love to stay and listen to you try to squirm your way out of this, but I have a job to do and so do you unless you plan on losing both your job and boyfriend in the same day," Kari said as she walked off.

"Christopher, you have to believe it was never my intent to deceive you. I planned on telling you who my father was the night we went to Nobu's, but when you told me he was the one who was trying to buy your company I got scared. I didn't want you to think of me as the enemy."

"I hear everything that you're saying, but trust is essential for any relationship to work. I trusted you and let you in my world, sharing intimate details in my professional and personal life. But for your own reasons, no matter how valid you feel they are, you chose to shut me out because obviously you didn't trust me enough to let me in. I do love you, Chloe, but I can't be with someone I can't trust and who doesn't trust me."

"Christopher, please don't go, I love you."

"But not enough to tell me the truth."

Chloe watched with tears filling her eyes as Christopher walked out of her life.

"Chloe, are you okay?" Lily asked, noticing a visibly shaken Chloe on her way back to her desk.

"No, I think my boyfriend broke up with me."

"I'm sorry, what a bummer . . . especially with it being Valentine's Day and all."

"Everybody seems to have remembered that day but me. My day can't get any worse."

"Well, I was going to tell you later but since you're already in a bad mood, no sense in holding back."

"What? I'm not going to get the promotion?"

"It's not looking good, Chloe. As I told you, Leslie thinks you're perfect, but the higher-ups are afraid you may not have enough experience and are leaning toward Kari. I hate to be the one to bring you more bad news but I wanted you to be prepared."

"Thanks, Lily. I appreciate you letting me know."

"Of course and don't worry about your boyfriend. You're Chloe Johnson, for heaven's sake. Your father has more money than God." And those were Lily's departing words.

When Chloe got back to her desk, there was a box and an envelope that said *Happy Valentine's Day*. Chloe opened the card and read it out loud, "To our first and what I hope will be many more Valentines we will share together, because my heart officially belongs to you. Love, Christopher."

Chloe opened the box and the twenty-four-carat pink diamond earrings and bracelet she thought were loaners were inside. "I guess this was what Christopher was talking about when he said I forgot something at his place." Chloe closed the box and sat down.

"Oh, is the poor little rich girl upset?" Kari teased.

"Kari, please get out of my face. I'm not in the mood for this."

"What? You blame me for revealing your secret to your

boyfriend? Hell, you weren't going to be able to hide it much longer. A picture of the two of you from last night's event is in the *New York Post* Page Six section. Someone was bound to recognize you and inform Christopher who you are."

"That's not the point. You were being malicious and in turn you ruined a relationship with someone I care a great deal about."

"Get over yourself, Chloe. Don't blame me for your deceitful behavior. You try to pretend that you're so sweet and upstanding, but you're not. I'm glad your boyfriend dumped you. You got exactly what you deserved. And when I become the new features editor I'm going to make sure you get fired, too, because you don't belong here."

"I'll save you the trouble, Kari, I quit."

Kari's mouth dropped open as Chloe picked up her laptop and a few other belongings and left her standing there without saying another word.

"There's no place like home," Chloe said, staring out the window of her new apartment. She noticed the girl from the garden apartment getting in a taxi, and idly wondered where she was going. Probably to meet her Valentine's Day date. The thought depressed Chloe even more.

Chloe walked over and sat on her couch. "I have no man, no job, but I'm living in an incredible brownstone . . . one out of three isn't too bad."

Just then Chloe heard a knock at the door. She figured it was Margie.

"I'm sure I was the last person you expected to see," Christopher said.

"Yes, but you're also the only person I wanted to see. How did you get in?"

"As I was coming up the stairs a young lady was coming out and I caught the door before it closed. She gave me the screw face like she was a tad suspect, but I guess because I don't look like a serial killer she didn't make any noise."

Chloe let out a slight laugh. "That's funny. That must've been one of the other girls that moved into the building. I'm sorry, please come in."

"This place is outstanding. But then I'm surprised you didn't buy the whole brownstone instead of renting one apartment."

"Christopher, don't do that."

"Do what? Chloe, whether you want to deny or hide it, the fact remains you're Leon Johnson's daughter and it's something you should be proud of."

"Excuse me? I thought you hated my father."

"Hate him? I don't even know him. What I said to you was about business. I have a great deal of respect for your father. It's men like him who paved the way for up-and-coming businessmen like myself. If anything, your father is a blueprint to success. Am I furious that he wants to take over my parent company and put me out of business? No doubt. But I will deal with that on a professional level. But having a problem with your father doesn't change how I feel about you. What does concern me is that you don't trust me."

"Maybe it's not that I don't trust you but that I don't trust myself. It's so hard living your life being known as Leon Johnson's daughter."

"Yeah, and I'm sure it has a ton of advantages too. Chloe, you should stop fighting the fact that you were born into privilege. It's a blessing and in turn you should use that to bless others. Don't be ashamed or feel that you're not worthy, because you are."

"You think so?"

"If I didn't I wouldn't have come back for you. I can deal with you being the daughter of Leon Johnson, but what I can't take is you working at *Posh* magazine. You seem to turn into a different person working there. It's as if you're so determined to prove your worth that it eats up your self-esteem."

"You might be right. But it doesn't matter because I quit today anyway."

"What brought that on?"

"That vapid spirit of Kari's and constantly feeling I'll never measure up." Chloe heard her cell phone ringing and noticed it was a *Posh* number. "This is *Posh*, I wonder what they want. Hello."

"Hi, Chloe, it's me, Leslie."

"Hi, Leslie."

"Kari told me that you quit today. I hope that isn't true since I wanted to offer you the job as our new features editor."

Chloe let out a scream, unable to hold back her enthusiasm.

"I'll take that as a yes."

"Of course! Thank you so much, Leslie."

"No, thank you. And I'll see you tomorrow."

"Omigosh, Christopher, I got the job! I'm the new features editor at *Posh* magazine," Chloe said, jumping up and down. Chloe realized Christopher wasn't sharing in her excitement and calmed down. "Aren't you happy for me?"

"Less than a minute ago we both agreed that working at *Posh* was no good for you. But now you're jumping up and down acting like a five-year-old who's visiting Disney World for the first time."

"Excuse me for being happy about my job promotion."

"But you quit *Posh* today and for a good reason."

"That was before I knew I had gotten the job. I never would've quit if I had known."

"Nothing has changed, Chloe."

"Yes, it has. I will no longer be working for Kari and I'll have a position that requires a lot more from me."

"Yeah, like time. When you're working those long hours, when are you going to find time for us to be together?"

"I'll find the time. We'll make it work."

"No, you won't, because you're consumed with this job. I understand that now. Proving to your father and everyone else that you can establish a successful career without his help is more important than anything else, and that includes love. I wish you luck, Chloe, and I hope you find everything you're looking for."

"Christopher, wait! Are you ending things between us again?"

"No, because in all actuality it never really began. But we'll always have our dance."

Christopher kissed Chloe on the forehead and walked out the door, this time for good. Chloe stood paralyzed for a few minutes, not fully comprehending what had just happened. When it sank in that Christopher had left her she ran out of her apartment to beg him to come back. But when Chloe got outside she saw the back of his car as he drove off.

"Child, why are you running out here in this cold weather with no shoes on?"

Chloe looked up and saw Margie leaning out her window, cigarette in hand.

"Not that it's none of my business," the woman said as she flicked an ash. "Not my business at all."

"I had a falling-out with my boyfriend, and I was hoping to stop him from leaving."

"Listen here, you can't make nobody stay, especially not no man. If he wants to leave, let him fly like a bird, and if he comes back you know he's yours forever."

"Maybe you're right."

"I know I am. Shit, I been running these streets long enough to know how to handle my business and yours . . . trust. What you do is go back in your place, put on one of those freakum dresses like they say, have a couple of drinks, and have yourself a good time."

"I don't know, Margie. I'm not in the mood."

"That's why you need to make yourself do it. If not you'll get stuck up in that apartment feeling sorry for yourself and there ain't no happiness in that."

"You're right. Do you know of any place you'd recommend around here?"

"Damn sure do, MoBay Uptown. Right on 125th Street, near Fifth Avenue. Make sure you tell the bartender that Margie sent you and have him make you one of them Harlem mojitos."

"I will, and, Margie, thanks for the pep talk."

Chloe went back inside and slipped on her fiercest red Stella McCartney freakum dress and four-inch stiletto heels. She glistened her lips with lady vamp lipstick, wrapped herself up in a black Dolce & Gabbana shearling, and hit the pavement headed to MoBay.

It was only a little after eight, but the place was packed when Chloe walked in. She looked around, hoping to find a seat, but knowing she wouldn't.

"May I get a mojito?" she said after she squeezed in between some people at the bar and got the bartender's attention.

The bartender nodded. "One mojito, coming up."

"Wait," Chloe said, suddenly remembering Margie's instructions. "Make that a Harlem mojito."

The bartender smiled. "No problem."

Chloe looked around the club again after she paid for her drink. "Oh God," she said out loud to no one in particular. "That can't be Jerome over there, can it?" She wrinkled her nose and was turning back to the bar when she saw two more familiar faces. *Is everybody from 119th Street here tonight?* she wondered. The women were engrossed in conversation and didn't notice her, which was good. Being cordial to them in the building was one thing—after all, it was just being neighborly—but having to actually spend social time with them was another. Chloe never was good with female friends; they always seemed to get jealous after a while and she couldn't be bothered.

Out of the corner of her eye she noticed the one who lived on the first floor, Tamara, waving to her. She continued to sip her drink, pretending not to see. But then the Dior chick got in the act, practically climbing up on the table and waving both arms in the air.

"Hey! Hey! You live in our building. Come on over. We're saving you a seat!"

Chloe sighed and picked up her drink after giving the bartender a tip. *I'll just walk over, say hello, then go on my way*, she thought as she headed their way.

"Hey, neighbor! Happy Valentine's Day," Dior said when she reached them. "You've got to join us."

Dior's voice was slightly slurred, yet so cheerful and upbeat that she was actually funny. The girl picked up her almost empty glass. "Drinks are on the house!"

Tamara smiled and shook her head. "No, Dior. Drinks are on the house means the club is giving away free drinks, remember? What you mean to say is you're treating."

Dior turned to Tamara. "That's right!" She addressed Chloe again. "You're treating!" she said, pointing at the girl.

Chloe and Tamara burst out in laughter, and Dior joined them although it was pretty clear she had no idea what was so funny.

Chloe shook her head, pulled an empty chair from a nearby table, and sat down. "I guess I am at that. What's everyone having?"

Dior picked up a glass and raised it in the air. "We're drinking to Valentine's Day!"

"Excuse me, miss," Chloe said, trying to get the attention of a passing drink waitress. "Can you bring us three more Harlem mojitos? And I'm running a tab."

MONA LISA DUPREE

by T. Styles

"New York, behold, Mona Lisa Dupree is in the house!" she screamed out the car window.

Mona Lisa beeped the remote of her pearl-colored 2008 Escalade wearing a full-length black chinchilla fur coat, black Via Spiga boots, and a DKNY one-piece catsuit that hugged her curvaceous body. She looked up at the night sky wearing tinted Tom Ford glasses. Standing on the sidewalk, she took in the newly renovated million-dollar brownstone. Even under the purple haze of the night sky, the building was magnificent. When the time was right, perhaps she'd go ahead and purchase one herself, but for now renting the top floor of this valuable piece of real estate perfectly suited her needs. The green and white paint on the large stones was so vibrant the building looked unreal. She also noticed window flower beds filled with flowers in bold shades of green, bronze, and deep yellow.

Washington, D.C., might have been where she was born and raised, but she was ecstatic about moving her movie agency business, the Dupree Project, there because New York was known for its new talent. When she saw the two U-Haul trucks she'd rented to follow her to New York from D.C. pull up in front of the building, partially blocking the small street, she quickly approached the brownstone's door. She had a lot of things and had to be quick to avoid causing traffic delays. The moment she climbed up the cold concrete stairs and put her hand on the door, a man rushed past her, ran up the stairs, and took control of the handle.

Somebody's in a hurry, she thought.

"Well, hello there," he said. He had a toothpick in the corner of his mouth and was dressed inappropriately for the January weather. Wearing only a white Sean Jean T-shirt, he tucked his left hand inside his oversized blue jeans, still holding the door with the other. Mona could tell he was desperately trying to remain warm, while hanging on to the little hip-hop he had left, by sporting designer clothing.

"I'm Jerome, and you are?" he asked, revealing a set of yellow teeth.

When she saw the moving men briskly walking in her direction hauling some of her extra-large boxes, she said to the man, "Do you live here?"

He shook his head no.

"Well, get out of my way because I'm busy and not interested." Mona brushed him aside and unlocked the door. "Take everything to the third floor please. My place is up two flights," she continued, directing her attention to the men. She smiled when she saw Jerome being pressed behind the door due to its being open so wide. The moment he could, he ran back down the stairs.

"Damn . . . what I do to you?" he asked, wiping his running nose with his sleeve.

"You didn't do one single thing to me." She could tell he was the pesty bugaboo type. "Because I didn't let you. Now . . . have a good night."

"Whatever," he said, waving her off. "Ya'll are too uppity in this damn building."

She was halfway in the building when she heard, "Aye, Jerome!" The voice was serious and loud. "Why you been dodging me!"

Mona Lisa squinted her eyes to get a good look at whoever was calling the pest by name. Even without seeing his face she took notice of his voice. It was mesmerizing and sounded similar to DMX's raspy, sexy voice. As she waited for the stranger to come into view, her phone began to ring and vibrate inside her pocket. She removed the BlackBerry from her coat, saw it was Cindy Williams, her assistant, and pressed Ignore.

Eventually she saw the face belonging to the voice that held her attention. His dark chocolate complexion was flawless and he was neat and stylish in his black wool pea coat with blue jeans. Most importantly, he was wearing size-*twelve* brown Kenneth Cole shoes.

Ummmm, Mona thought to herself. *I think I see a boy toy.*

Out of breath, the tall handsome man stood in front of Jerome, clearly frustrated with him. Mona was sure he'd warranted his rough disposition. Now she was interested and, more importantly, she suddenly found the time to stick around. Besides, this *was* her neighborhood and as far as she was concerned, she had the right to know what was going on in and around it. Letting the door close behind her, she stood on the steps and boldly listened to their conversation.

"What up, man?" Jerome asked with a slight attitude. Horns beeped in the background.

"What's up? I was gonna ask you the same thing. A lot of work went into repairing the electricity at your mother's house. So why haven't I gotten the rest of my money?"

"I was gonna give it to you," Jerome responded.

"When? Your moms said she gave you the money to give me already, and just so you know I'm not trying to hear that wait-for-my-tax-returns bullshit."

Jerome looked embarrassed when he saw Mona still standing there, ear hustling. "I thought you were busy." He frowned, looking up at Mona.

"I have a few minutes to spare." She smiled, looking at him and then the stranger. "Besides, they haven't moved all of my things in yet." She took one step down the stairs.

"I guess you weren't too busy after all," Jerome said.

"Nope," she said, walking all the way down. "Just too busy for you."

"Well, what you coming back down here for, then?" Jerome said, his voice dripping with sarcasm.

"I overheard your friend here is an electrician. And since you never know if you'll need one, I'd like to keep in contact." She stood right in front of Mr. Chocolate and licked her glossy lips.

The stranger grinned.

Mona flashed him a smile as bright and vibrant as Janet Jackson's. The diamond earrings she was wearing brought more attention to her beautiful face and luscious naturally pink lips. She was now disappointed that she chose to wear the full-length fur coat instead of the cute pink short one. Then he'd be able to see that she had a derriere as fat and round as Beyoncé's. Still her mocha-colored skin was perfect. And the winter frost had given her a nature makeover by turning her cheeks a rosy red.

"I'd like to keep in contact, too." He paused, looking her up and down and running his hand over his five o'clock shadow. "But I have to admit, I hope you won't have any problems here."

"Why is that?"

"Because I installed the electricity for this building. So if something's wrong, it'll look like I'm not doing my job."

"Oh . . . I don't foresee there'll be any problems, then," she stated. "Well, give me your number anyway because if something does go wrong, I'd feel better contacting the man responsible."

Handymen were another one of her weaknesses. He reached into his pocket, retrieved a gold card case, and handed her his business card. She didn't bother to look at his name. It was as unimportant as his dating status. Besides, Mona almost never called a man by the name his mama gave him. His finger brushed over hers when Mona reached for the card and she tucked it inside her coat pocket.

Jerome sucked his teeth. "Ain't this a bitch? You ain't have five seconds for me but you give him twenty."

"What are you talking about?" Mona asked, hoping he

wouldn't bother to answer the question because she couldn't care less. "This is strictly business." She winked.

"Yeah, right!" Jerome shot back, walking away a little.

She was just preparing to blow the handsome stranger a good-bye kiss when her phone began to vibrate.

What does Cindy want?

"Excuse me," she said, walking slightly away from the handsome electrician and the asshole Jerome. "What's up, Cindy? I'm kind of busy."

"I'm sorry. It's just that I was trying to reach you before you meet Dayshawn tomorrow afternoon."

Dayshawn Knight was one of her new clients. If things went as planned, he would be the answer TVEA Productions was seeking for their new picture, *Melted Velvet*. The executives were specific when they sought Mona's assistance. They needed a fresh face for the role of Tyler Densburg. The picture was about an ex-porno star who married a white female mayoral candidate. The moment she saw his audition tape in her truck, she knew he was perfect. He had the almond-colored complexion, coal-black wavy hair, and muscular physique necessary to be seductive in this movie. And most importantly, he had the charisma and masculinity to make any movie fan swoon, so Mona wasted no time sending the following message from her BlackBerry a little over an hour ago after seeing the tape.

Cindy, he's perfect. Set up a meeting with him for me tomorrow. I'll meet him at my house here in Harlem. Let me know when he confirms.

Immediately she replied with:

I hope you arrive safe in New York and I'm happy you like Dayshawn! He is awesome. I called him and he can be at your place by 1:00 p.m. tomorrow. He lives in the New Jersey area, but before you meet him please call

*me. Preferably tonight. I have something very important
to tell you about him.*

Mona's neglect to respond was probably the reason Cindy
was calling her hysterically.

"Don't worry about anything, Cindy," Mona said as she
watched the movers carry the last of her things inside. "I've
seen everything I need to. He's perfect for the part! Now, did
you get a hold of Melonie Crew?"

"Yes, but I have to tell you something about Day—"

"Like I said . . ." she interrupted as she noticed the electrician fidgeting in the cold air. "The only thing I want you to do
now is get me Melonie Crew. I got a lead that another agency
is trying to cast her for another movie. We have to move fast,
so whatever you have to tell me about Dayshawn can wait."

"All right . . ." Cindy said in a defeated tone. "I'll get right
on top of it."

"That's my girl," she said, placing her phone in her pocket
after abruptly ending the call.

Walking back over toward the electrician who was in a
heated conversation with Jerome, she decided to diffuse matters with her presence.

Tapping him on the shoulder, she said, "Now, what do I
call you? The maintenance man?"

"You can call me whatever you'd like." He smiled, facing
her. "Just as long as you call me."

His line was a little weak, but for the sake of meeting a potential new conquest she'd let one corny line slide. Just as she
was preparing to put her flirt game into full mode, the mover
she'd flirted with earlier came walking down the steps. Sure,
she'd given him the impression that she was interested, but
that was how she treated all attractive men upon first contact.
Those who held her attention the longest won the prize, but
this poor soul didn't realize it.

"Everything's inside," he said, eyeing the maintenance man
before looking back at Mona. "We're unpacking your boxes

now." He held his clipboard with a pen in hand. "Can I get you to sign here?"

"Sure!" she responded. She signed the agreement, confirming the completion. "Now, they *did* place the boxes in the rooms according to the labels?"

"Yes. But can I talk to you for a second in private?"

"Sure," Mona said lightly. "Well, Maintenance Man, it was nice meeting you." She extended her hand. He accepted. She noticed it was soft and knew it would feel soothing over her body. "*Trust*, I will be in contact." She held his hand two seconds longer.

"I'm looking forward to it," he replied before looking at the tall mover once more. The mover was staring at him like Mona was his woman and he was in violation.

Walking over toward the U-Haul truck, she said, "What's up? It's kind of cold out here and I want to get inside."

"I just wanted to tell you that it was nice talking to you earlier," he said, placing one hand on her shoulder. It was there all of ten seconds before she gave him a look that said, *Don't touch me unless I give you permission to.* He removed his hand and said, "I was thinking that maybe I could come down here and spend some time with you in the future. I mean . . . New York isn't really that far from D.C. and it wouldn't be a problem."

"I'm sorry . . . uh . . . um . . ." It was then that she realized she didn't remember his name.

"John," he said, saving her from the embarrassment of asking.

"Thanks, John." She smiled. "But I'm not the dating type."

"I thought we connected earlier. Did I do something wrong between now and then?"

"No!" she said, placing her French-manicured hands out in front of her. "You're a really nice person and a hell of a mover. It's just that . . . *well*, I love the single life." The wind had blown her long hair in her face and she brushed it away.

His eyes narrowed. "You know people could read you the wrong way, right?"

"Yes, I do." She smiled again. "And it's my job to set them straight."

"Are you a man?" he said, shaking his head. " 'Cause you sure act like one."

She giggled, took two steps in front of him, kissed him on his lips, and said, "I don't carry things like a man. I just put them in their place like one. Good night, John."

With that she walked off. When she did she noticed a short middle-aged woman with locks, smoking on the steps of the brownstone next to hers. She had on a blue wool coat, and a brown felt hat was pulled down low over her graying dread-locks.

It wasn't the first time she'd met the woman, but she felt just as uncomfortable as she did that first time. It was as if the woman could see right through her.

"How are you, Mrs. Graham?" Mona Lisa said politely to her new landlady.

"Didn't I tell you to call me Margie? Everybody calls me Margie. No need for you to be any different. I see you're finally moving in. Welcome to the neighborhood. Welcome to Margie's Diamond Palace," she said between puffs on her cigarette. "I heard you talking to Jerome. I was going to jump in and tell him to leave you the hell alone, but I seen you was handling yourself. Did better than I coulda, to tell you the truth."

Mona smiled.

"Yeah. Did him right up. I don't think he'll be bothering you no more. I had to chase him away from that pretty Chinese-looking girl that moved into the garden apartment, and from that cute girl who moved into the first-floor apartment, but I can see that you ain't gonna have no trouble with him. You from D.C., right?"

"Born and raised."

Margie nodded. "I always heard them D.C. girls can handle themselves. Not that it's none of my business. None of my business at all. Well, I'll let you get back to your moving in. Remember, I'm just two buildings down, so if you need anything just ring the bell." The woman stood up, smashed the butt of the cigarette on the ground with her slippers.

"I will," Mona replied.

"And don't try so hard to fit in," the woman said over her shoulders. "Let things occur naturally."

Mona turned to look at her. "I'll be fine."

"Good to see a woman who can handle herself," the woman said loud enough for Mona to hear, though not turning around.

At that moment something told Mona that the move to her new neighborhood would be far from boring.

The smells of the freshly painted walls were strong inside Mona's third-floor apartment. Mostly everything was unpacked and in its appropriate place. It took her three hours to get things semiorganized, and she still had lots to do. She was tucked under her burgundy goose down comforter in her king-size bed. The window was slightly open to provide her with the chilly atmosphere necessary for her to remain asleep. But like clockwork, at three o'clock in the morning, Mona arose and nestled her feet inside the blue furry slippers next to her bed. Like she always did when she woke up in the middle of the night, her mother came to mind. Even now, she resented the way she abandoned her. If it weren't for her father, Devin Dupree, Mona would've felt lost.

Devin had raised Mona Lisa alone since she was seven years old. Although it might sound wonderful, with a father caring for his daughter full-time, it didn't begin that way. In fact, life with her father was how she got her views on men.

Her mother, Lyla Clark, died of a broken heart after chasing behind Devin for ten years, only to realize he didn't love her in return. On a rainy night in August, she called her daughter at three o'clock in the morning after leaving work as a waitress, drove to the Woodrow Wilson Bridge, parked her car, and jumped off. Mona was so traumatized that even now she couldn't sleep through the night.

After her death, Devin was forced to step up and care for her full-time. Instead of shielding her young eyes from his male chauvinistic ways, he allowed her to see firsthand how he used and threw women away like trash bags. When he was done, he made it his business to embed into a young and impressionable Mona's mind that the *only* thing men wanted was sex. And no matter what they said, she shouldn't believe anything differently.

As a teenager, and then a woman, she shielded her heart to prevent suffering her mother's fate. From her first intimate encounter to the next, she dogged every man she slept with the *moment* it was over. The result? A twenty-nine-year-old self-proclaimed nymphomaniac.

Walking over to the window, she fanned the blue chiffon curtains out of her face, which were being controlled by the breeze. Her nipples peeked from under her silk pink La Perla nightgown. She grabbed her arms and rubbed them rapidly to stay warm. She watched a few people walking up and down the street. She realized it was true what they said: New York was the city that never sleeps.

She closed the window slightly. Realizing she wouldn't go back to bed for at least an hour, she grabbed her blue velour robe and walked into her office. The cherry-wood desk was dressed professionally with a bronze *Casting Agent of the Year* paperweight and a gold matching pen holder. The files of Melonie Crew and Dayshawn Knight lay neatly in front of her. The brown walls were adorned with the degree she'd earned from Howard University. Certificates from *Women in Film and Television* and the *Alliance of Cinema, Television and Radio Artists* also were dressed in gold frames on the walls.

She pulled the string on her desk lamp for light, and located her laptop computer. Once it was on, its glare momentarily irritated her eyes. Because the light was bright enough to provide sight, she cut the lamp off. When her Sony Vaio laptop loaded, she opened her e-mails. The first one she saw came from Harry Turnstile of TVEA Productions. The subject line was blank.

Mona Lisa,
I trust you arrived safe in your new home. I was happy to hear that you have some great prospects for the new picture! We're anticipating offering deals in the next month or so. With that said, we're counting on you. The entire production team is sitting on the edge of their seats. Rather than wait for the casting call, we'd like to meet them this Saturday. We're having a huge party for the opening of Xtreme Measure. It is a black-tie affair. I look forward to seeing you there.
P.S. Are you bringing a date this time?
Harry

If there was one thing Mona couldn't stand, it was people bothering her about being single. She'd never been in love or a committed relationship in her entire twenty-nine-year-old life. This had nothing to do with her healthy appetite for sex, which unlike some women, she made no apologies for. It was by choice. The only man who came close to making her change her mind was Nat Singeltary. Just the thought of him made her body shiver with nostalgic delight.

They had met at Howard University after her roommate eloped with an athlete who was drafted into the NBA and she was forced to admit that her meager income would not support her healthy appetite for Prada shoes, MAC makeup, and oh yes . . . regular living expenses, despite her father's help.

When she mentioned around campus that she had a room available in an apartment she rented five miles from the college, Nat was the first to contact her. Originally she refused. In fact, she told him to get out of her face. Living with a man in college was unheard of. Eventually she changed her mind after interviewing two women, one of whom licked the snot off of her lip as she spoke, the second who swore she was on the verge of suicide if she didn't pass her chemistry class.

To her surprise, they quickly became the best of friends/roommates *without* intimacy. That all changed when they shared a bottle of champagne on Valentine's Day 2000. With both of them drunk and horny, it was no surprise to either of them when after the last glass was poured, they shared each other.

Believing they could *now* be friends/roommates *with* benefits, they decided to continue to sleep together, with no strings attached. But when her best friend Ray pointed out that the two were closer than they realized, Mona Lisa became afraid and returned to her old ways of using and abusing men for sex, starting with bringing a stranger into their apartment for a red light special.

This upset Nat and forced him to confess how he truly felt about her. So on graduation day, he prepared an elaborate meal and asked Mona to do something she never did in her twenty-two-year-old life, "commit." The next morning, frightened, and unwilling to face love, she left him without an answer along with the apartment they shared. She never saw him again.

Picking up the phone, Mona Lisa decided to call the one person she knew would still be awake at three o'clock in the morning, her father, Devin Dupree. He worked the midnight shift as a computer engineer for Loyola College.

"Hey, Daddy," she said after eyeing the pictures of Melonie and Dayshawn.

"Hey, sweetheart," he said after letting out a hard cough. "How's the city life?"

"It's okay," Mona sighed as she grabbed a bottle of water she kept under her desk.

"Just okay?" he asked before letting out two excessively hard coughs. "I'd figure you'd be enjoying yourself by now."

"I just got here, Daddy," she laughed, placing the bottle back on her desk. "But it's a little different being away from home."

"You're not getting lonely, are you?"

"No, Daddy!"

"You sure? I don't want you getting soft on me."

"I'm not, Daddy. You know I've always been a loner. I'm tough. Anyway, how are you? You don't sound so good."

"I'm fine."

"Now, is that you talking or did you get a doctor's opinion?"

"I'm gonna see the doctor tomorrow."

"Daddy! You promised to see him last week! Something isn't right. You've lost too much weight and you're weak all the time. I'm starting to worry."

"Don't," he said quickly, sounding as if he was trying to conceal his cough. "Let me worry about me. I'm more interested in you and your business. Did you get the actor and the actress you wanted for the new movie?"

"I think so," she responded, trying desperately to respect his wishes by not dwelling on his health condition. "I'll know if they're what I'm looking for after the auditions. I'm meeting with Dayshawn tomorrow."

"That's my girl! Always showin' 'em how it's done," he boasted.

"Thanks, Daddy. So how's the job?" she asked

"The same as always . . . boring."

She laughed. He chuckled.

"So, have you met any new interesting women?"

"Naw. I've retired my player's jacket."

Mona doubted she was hearing her father correctly. "Come again?"

"I don't have time for women nowadays. You're the only woman for me."

"And you're the only man for me, too, Daddy." She smiled. "Well . . ." She yawned. "I have a long day tomorrow. I'm going to try to get some sleep."

"If you can't, call me back."

"I will, and call me when you hear something from the doctor."

"Don't worry about me. Knock 'em dead in New York!" He let out a cough so hard it rocked Mona's eardrum. "Sorry," he mumbled apologetically.

"Don't be sorry, Daddy," she said softly. "Just get better."

"I will . . . good night, Mona . . . and remember, stay a playa!"

When she hung up she was preparing to go to her room and was scared shitless when she heard someone buzzing her intercom. The main door leading to the brownstone was locked, but someone was trying to get her attention. What bothered her was that no one outside of her father, Cindy, and Ray knew her address. Rather than playing the guessing game she crept to the window to see who obviously had the wrong apartment. But when she saw who it was she was shocked.

"I can't believe he did that shit! Who in the hell comes over to somebody's house at three o'clock in the morning unannounced! What did you say?"

"What do you think I said? I told him if he even thinks about disrespecting my house again it would be on!" Mona responded as she slipped into her black Jean Paul Gaultier bishop-style long-sleeve one-piece dress. Afterwards she struggled getting on her gray snakeskin Louis Vuitton knee boots. The phone dropped on the hardwood floor, causing a cracking sound in Ray's ear.

"What are you doing?" she yelled in her squeaky high voice.

"Getting dressed! You know Dayshawn's on his way. After seeing his audition tape I'm excited to meet him!"

"That's right! You are hooking up today! But don't try to skip the subject. Main man coming over to your house unannounced sounds odd. You sure you didn't give him an invitation?"

"Okay," she started after putting on her boots. Walking toward her large vanity mirror, she put on her two-carat diamond earrings and diamond tennis bracelet. "I want to tell you how I met him, but I don't want to hear your mouth, either."

"Go ahead," Ray said.

"I'm serious!"

"I'm listening." Her tone was sarcastic.

"I met him when I moved in yesterday. He looked like somebody I could have fun with. You know, to pass the time with in Harlem. Maybe he took my kindness the wrong way."

"You're such a freak."

"Am I really?" Mona said in a condescending tone. "I mean . . . what have I always preached?"

"What are you talking about, girl?"

"You know what I'm talking about. Tell me what I've preached from day one?"

Ray cleared her throat and reluctantly quoted Mona's motto in life, "Never sleep with size-ten feet or smaller, never sleep with anyone you work with, and work hard and play harder."

"What's the last one?" Mona asked, pleased at hearing her friend recite her life's lesson.

"Oh . . . never, *ever*, fall in love."

"You got it!" she giggled. "*Anyway*, what's up with you and Sony?"

Sony was a whole different story because even though Ray had a doctorate in psychology, she knew nothing about life. It wasn't like she wasn't successful. Ray was five foot four inches and sported a short style. Her complexion gave off the illusion that she was part Hawaiian, even though she wasn't.

"I don't know." Her mood changed. "He called me today and said he had to talk about something. I think he wants to end us."

"Well, if he does can you handle it?" Mona asked. Now fully dressed, she was spreading the fresh flowers she purchased from the florist in her beautiful multicolored vase on her dining room table. Afterward, she turned the music on on her iPod stereo system, and let Maxwell flow from the speakers.

"I'm not sure."

Mona stopped what she was doing and exhaled. "Listen, Ray, I know it's tough, but you should probably prepare for the worst. Don't get me wrong, I want you to be happy, even if it means being with Sony, but I'm afraid that's not what he wants."

"I think he loves me."

Although she'd gone to Yale to get an education in psychology, Ray was irresponsible when it came to love. She was still convinced that if you loved somebody hard enough, you could make them love you in return.

"Trying to discover what men want is impossible. Some things simply aren't meant to be. You're a beautiful girl and most men would kill to take a doctor home to their mother! Let him come to you for once."

"I know," Ray said after taking several deep breaths. "But I was really hoping—"

"Hoping is for fools," Mona interrupted. "You're much too smart for that. Now listen . . . I have to go. But just so you know, I really *do* want things to work out for you."

"Thanks, Monee-D. Call me when you meet your new client."

"I will. And don't forget to check on Daddy for me."

"You got it . . . but you know he stay gettin' fresh with me when you're not around?" Ray laughed.

"That's just his way. He's harmless."

"Yeah, but I don't know if I am." Ray giggled. "You know I'm vulnerable right now."

They laughed.

"Girl, you better stay away from my daddy!" Mona joked as she fluffed her couch pillows.

"I can't make any promises." She smiled. "But I *will* look after him for you while you make that paper. Love you, girl!"

"Love you back."

Just when she ended the call, she heard music booming from loudspeakers outside. She pushed her red velvet drapes aside and saw a brown-skinned girl with spiral curly hair entering the brownstone, only after shaking her head in disgust at the driver of a white BMW.

Please don't be Dayshawn, Mona thought. She hated thinking that someone coming to visit her was already irritating her neighbors. When she saw the owner of the car park directly in front of her building, she was sure it was him. But when she saw a man holding a brown paper bag, wearing a pink fur coat, pink-tinted glasses, blue jeans, and, if her eyes saw correctly, pink boots, she doubted herself again.

Buzz. Buzz. It was official. She could see him from her living room window pressing the intercom button for her apartment. "Shit!" Mona yelled as she put her face in her hands and then dropped them by her sides. She pressed the intercom button praying the apparently flamboyant gay man had reached the wrong floor.

"Is this the infamous Miss Dupree?" the voice rang from the speakers.

"I think so," Mona responded carefully.

"Well, it's meeeee, sweetheart!" he sang in a loud, high-pitched voice. "Your new leading man!"

Mona's heart dropped. How would she convince TVEA he was the strapping strong man who was needed for the role? She leaned back against the wall and focused on her recessed lighting. She needed an answer quickly. She stood up straight, brushed herself off, and buzzed him in.

He knocked three times before she opened the door. Immediately he stepped in, holding a greasy brown paper bag that smelled of fried chicken. Without even asking, he hugged her as if she were his long-lost cousin. The bag made a rattling sound as their bodies pressed against it.

"Heeeeey!" He smiled, rocking her slightly. The fur from his coat stuck to her lip gloss.

"Hello." She smiled, upon her release. "It's nice to meet you," she continued halfheartedly. "Please . . . come in."

It was too late. He was already inside. Mona was stuck. She still couldn't believe it was him. But then she saw *them*. Those alluring eyes. Even through the tinted shades he wore, his eyes captivated her, the same way they did on the audition DVD.

"Make yourself comfortable," Mona said, hoping she sounded polite. Finally able to move, she closed and locked the door behind her. Afterward she plucked the few loose fur hairs from her lips. "I just have to make a quick call." She smiled again.

"Oh, don't worry about me, darlin'," he responded as he removed two takeout containers from the bag, placing them on her new dining room table. "I'll get us set up!"

"*Okay*," she responded. She wasn't sure what get *us* set up meant, but she did know she wasn't eating anything from that greasy bag.

Walking over to her living room, she quickly picked up the receiver of her antique black and gold phone. She waited impatiently for Cindy to answer. She could still see Dayshawn moving about in the kitchen. The phone rang all of two seconds before Cindy picked up. "He must be there."

"Yes, he is, and why didn't you tell me he was gay?" Mona whispered into the telephone as she continued to watch him. Now he was in the dining room with two of her best white china plates.

"I tried but you wouldn't listen," Cindy said defensively.

"You should have tried harder! How on earth am I going to convince TVEA that he can do this part?"

"Are you kidding me? You're Mona Lisa Dupree! You can convince anybody of anything!"

"Not this time." Mona took another peek into the living room. "It won't fly."

"How many careers have you launched?"

Silence.

"Your clients get the major roles! I would never have scouted him if I wasn't sure you could mold him for this part. He *is* what they're looking for!"

"I don't know about this, Cindy."

She was listening to her assistant while glancing at Dayshawn at the same time. He went from taking the containers out of the bag to dishing out helpings of food on the plates. She had to admit, at first she wasn't thinking about eating whatever he brought with him. But the longer she smelled it, the more she was considering changing her mind.

"I'll let you know what happens," she continued, eyeing large helpings of macaroni and cheese.

"Okay . . . and remember, Mona . . . you *are* the Dupree Project. Not the other way around."

When she hung up she called Ray.

"So how does he look? Details . . . details and don't hold back!" She was talking nonstop and Mona couldn't get a word in edgewise. "Is he everything you hoped for?"

"Not really."

"Wh . . . why not?" Ray hesitated.

"He's gay," Mona replied.

"He's *what*!"

"Flaming," Mona said firmly.

Just as she said it, he screamed, "Dinner's served!"

"Was that him? Oh my Gawd, he is gay!"

"I told you! I'm worried they won't go for it. Don't get me wrong, Hollywood has tons of gay and lesbian actors and actresses. But . . . he's so out there! Too in your face."

"I don't think you should sign him."

"Why not?"

"It's just too early," Ray replied. "Especially after the thing with Iesha."

"Fuck Iesha," Mona Lisa retaliated. "I made her ass! It's because of my agency that her career has taken off."

"I know . . . and how did she thank you?"

"She thanked me by trying to ruin me," she responded while listening to Dayshawn sing along to the music in the air.

"Don't you wish your boyfriend was hot like me?" he sang.

"Exactly!" Ray said. "She stopped coming to rehearsals, missed tapings and everything else. They were threatening not to deal with you or your clients after that mess. If that hadn't happened so recently, I would say go for it. But the bottom line is, it did."

Silence.

"Don't do it, girl! It's not worth it!"

Mona wasn't sure if she was necessarily agreeing with Ray, because no matter what, she was known for making her own decisions and going against the grain.

"All right . . . I'll talk to you later."

When she hung up she stared at him like he was a science project. *Can I mold you? Are you worth the chance?*

And as if he read her mind with his fur coat still on, he walked over to her, spun around like he was modeling, raised his hands in the air, dropped them by his sides, and struck a pose.

"Get a good look, honey, because this is me," he advised, pointing to himself. "I'm gonna be gay today and I'm gonna probably be even gayer tomorrow, but I *can* nail that part. I read that script from front to back and I know I can do this! Trust me!"

"It's just that . . . uh . . . I don't know about this," she said as the smell of the food in the background caused her stomach to growl.

"I'll prove it," he said, removing his coat and tinted glasses, placing them on the leather sofa. "I read somewhere that in college you dabbled around with acting a little."

"I did a little somethin' . . . somethin'," she teased. She was impressed with his research skills.

"Well, act with me. Give me a scene from your favorite romantic movie."

"What?!"

"I said give me a scene from your favorite romantic movie. Come on . . . I know you have one."

Mona thought long and hard and said, "I'm not gonna lie, I'm not big on the romance thing."

"Are you kidding me?" he laughed. "You're a casting director."

"I know. It's not something I'm not proud of. In fact the only love scene that did it for me was the one I saw you in recently."

"Well, thank you!" He winked, placing his hands on his hips, striking yet another pose. "And trust me, my love interest in that movie was a bitch!"

"You two were awesome together," Mona laughed. If nothing else, she was discovering that she liked him. She could feel his genuine spirit.

"There has to be some other scene somewhere in the world that moved you."

She pondered again before remembering that she loved the scene when Dwayne busted in on Whitley's wedding on the TV show *A Different World*.

"I love it!" he exclaimed after she told him. "I know that scene from front to back." Suddenly he dropped to the floor and did twenty push-ups.

What in the world is he doing? she thought. When he arose, he became the man on the audition DVD. He lowered his eye lids a little, opened his chest, and looked at Mona as if she were the love of his life. His demeanor had become stern and he was giving off sex appeal similar to what the singer Tyrese did for her. If it wasn't for the pink shirt he was wearing, she'd be fanning herself right now. He was now *totally* into character.

"Whitley, I love you . . . and if you'll have me, I want you to be my wife," he said, reciting Dwayne's lines. With that he took two steps toward Mona Lisa and gently took her hand.

Mona remained silent.

"Will you have me, Dwayne, as your lawfully wedded husband, from this day forth, to have and to hold, in richer or poorer? Baby, please! Please!"

She was mesmerized. Wrapping one arm around her waist, he placed a passionate kiss on her lips. Their lips remained connected for five seconds before he released her and walked back to the table to sip the wine he'd helped himself to earlier.

She was stuck. Motionless yet convinced. He *was* Tyler Densburg, lead actor in the movie. Her eyes were still closed when he said, "Open wide?"

When she did, he shoved a forkful of homemade macaroni and cheese into her mouth, courtesy of Sylvia's in Harlem. One noodle missed her lips and dropped to the floor. And after savoring the good cooking, she felt cheated. She also noticed that Dayshawn was now himself again.

"Ummmm," she said, appreciating a piece of the best Harlem had to offer.

"Just a little something, something to welcome you to the Big Apple." He winked before picking up the noodle that had fallen on the floor, and throwing it in trash. "So, can we eat now?" he questioned, taking a seat at the table. "I don't know about you but I'm hungry! We can talk about all this business mumbo jumbo later."

"Sure . . ." She smiled, impressed with his confidence. *Besides*, after taking a sample of food she wanted more. "I hope your schedule is cleared for Saturday," she continued in between forkfuls.

"I don't have too much planned." He chewed. "Why?" Dayshawn was now deep into his corn bread.

"Because you'll be meeting the execs from TVEA. I want them to meet their new leading man."

"Yeah!" he yelled, jumping up from the table and squeezing her tightly.

Mona Lisa had a big day ahead of her and she was anxious. After all, in less than six hours she'd be attending the premier party for *Xtreme Measure* and introducing TVEA to Dayshawn and Melonie. Even after seeing how wonderfully he read the lines for the role, she still wasn't convinced they'd buy in. The only comfort she had was her choice for supporting actress.

To ease her mind, she decided to go to the corner market to drop off her dry cleaning and see a little of the city. She stepped out of the brownstone, and the cold air almost knocked her over. Luckily she chose to wear her insulated black velvet jogging suit by Baby Phat, with her leather jacket over it. The hood hung stylishly over the back of the jacket and revealed the pink satin lining. Her hair was pulled into a fun ponytail with a few loose ends hanging on the sides. She was also rocking a Dior Christal soft pink diamond watch along with her three-carat earrings.

The first thing she noticed was a handsome Puerto Rican man staring her way, while holding a woman's hand. Being the flirt that she was, she winked and surprisingly he winked back. She giggled when she saw the woman smack him in the face.

A few blocks later, she noticed everyone moved quickly. *Why the rush?* she thought. Still, she quickened her pace for fear of looking out of place. She was officially a New Yorker. The moment she put a little pep in her step, a tall, slender woman bumped her shoulder, forcing her to take two steps back. She gripped her shoulder and eyed the woman with disgust.

"Next time say excuse me!" she yelled. But it was too late; she had disappeared into the crowd.

Rubbing her arm again, she shook her head while continuing to look in the woman's direction. When she turned around, she was bumped again.

"What is wrong with you people!" she screamed. This time she walked briskly.

When she finally made it to the cleaner's, she was relieved. Dropping off her clothes, she proceeded to the corner store on the next block. She grabbed a basket and placed fresh flowers inside it, along with a few tomatoes, onions, and other items to prepare her famous homemade salsa. When she was finished shopping, she grabbed an *Essence* and *Posh* magazine. Walking up to the counter, she smiled at the Arabian clerk, who said, "Anything else?"

"No, thank you. Unless you can make the city move slower," she laughed. Mona was doing her best to make small talk. It didn't go over too well. He ignored her.

"*Okay . . .*" she said, realizing he was just as rude as some of the pedestrians she'd come in contact with. "Just trying to be friendly."

"You can't be too nice around here," a familiar voice said.

She knew right away who the voice belonged to. She'd heard it before she saw his face. She turned around and saw the maintenance man. Once again he looked handsome wearing a brown leather jacket, Evisu blue jeans, and a brown wool hat.

"You sure can't," she responded as she turned back around to face the clerk, handing him the money for her purchase. "And present company included."

"Don't be that way." He smiled. "We got off to a bad start."

"Is that what you call it?" she asked, grabbing her bag and change. "Because the last time I was nice to you, you made a surprise visit to my house at three o'clock in the morning."

"I'm sorry. I wasn't thinking." He placed the water bottle on the counter, reached into his pocket, and gave the clerk two dollars. Snatching the bottle, he ran out behind her, leaving his change.

"I'm sorry," he said, running next to her. "I thought we connected and I took it too far."

"Yes, you did," she replied as she allowed him to grab the large brown paper bag out of her hands. She hated when men assumed they were going to have sex with her, because she controlled her body.

"Let me make it up to you," he said.

"And how do you intend on doing that, Maintenance Man?"

"Let me buy you dinner."

"Not interested. I can buy my own dinner," she teased. She was giving him a hard time because he deserved it.

"Okay, you tell me. What can I do to make it up to you?"

She gave him the once-over and knew exactly what she wanted. After all, it had been four days since her last sexual conquest and she was due for a refill. She had to admit, his light brown skin, New York accent, and strong physique did things to her.

"Well, what are you doing now?" she asked, arriving at the steps of her brownstone.

"Hanging with you." He smiled. "That is . . . if you let me," he added, remembering where wishful thinking had gotten him last time.

"I think I can go for a little company," she teased.

When they reached the front of her brownstone, the maintenance man accidentally tilted the bag and two tomatoes dropped to the pavement and rolled in front of a girl with Asian eyes, light skin, and long black hair. The girl bent down to pick them up and handed them to Mona Lisa.

"Hello," she said, revealing a light French accent. "I'm Dior. And you are?"

"Mona Lisa," she said flatly, not sure if she liked the girl. She placed the tomatoes back in the bag.

"I saw you moving in yesterday, but I was rushing out and didn't have time to say anything. Welcome to the building."

"Thanks," Mona Lisa said as she observed the girl giving the maintenance man an up-and-down look before turning back to her with questioning eyes. Mona gave her a stare that said, *And?* The girl took the hint.

"Enjoy," Dior said, as she walked off down the street.

"I will," Mona Lisa said in a matched tone.

The girl walked out of the building and Mona Lisa shook her head.

"Never met your neighbors, huh?" he asked.

"Not really," Mona Lisa said, brushing the entire situation off. She had one best friend and as far as she was concerned, she was plenty. "I'm a loner."

Once inside her apartment, he placed the bag on the counter and looked around. He complimented her on how her home looked like an ad straight from the pages of an Ethan Allen catalog.

He was still observing her furnishing style when she approached him with a glass of water on ice. He gulped it down and handed her back the glass. She placed it on the breakfast nook.

"So, what can I do to make it up to you?" he reminded her after licking his lips. "You never did say."

"First, you can answer a few questions."

"Shoot!" he replied, standing as straight as a soldier in line.

"Are you looking for a commitment?" she asked, frowning at his stance.

"Uh . . . well . . . maybe if I—"

She quickly cut him off. She knew if she was going to keep him as a plaything he had to pass the test. With one hand pointed at him and the other on her waist she said, "Let me tell you something, if you're going to lie, the door's that way."

"Okay," he said, sensing he could mess up a good thing if he fronted. "To be honest, I'm loving the single life."

"Okay . . ." She smiled. She was pleased with his first response because she wasn't looking for a relationship in any shape or form. She discovered that although some men claimed to want no strings attached, after one night with her, they always changed their minds.

"Second, are you gonna get all lovey-dovey on me?"

"Naw," he laughed. "You'll be straight."

She was satisfied with his answers and removed the barrette holding her hair to let it hang free. Not saying another word, she softly covered his lips with her own. His breath was minty fresh, which gave him two additional points. He lifted her up off her feet and moved toward her bedroom.

"What," she said in between soft kisses, "you don't have an imagination?"

He smiled. She winked and he made a detour. Truth was, she didn't want to soil her sheets. Sensing she didn't want to have sex in the bedroom, he carried her over to the kitchen counter and sat her on it. Their tongues danced in and out of each other's mouths the entire time. Without leaving her lips, he aggressively pulled her pants off and she quickly removed her shirt, exposing her perky large breasts. Reaching into her sock, she grabbed a magnum condom and handed it to him. When he tore open the packaging unfazed by it being for the extra-large type, she hoped for the best. When he eased inside her wetness, she was happy he was worthy of its gold label. Her head lightly banged up against the kitchen cabinet, never stopping their flow.

"Ummm . . . I knew when I met you, you'd feel this good," he praised.

He gripped her round, firm butt and she could feel him pulsating inside her. If she pushed into him, she was sure it would be over. But because she wasn't close enough to an orgasm, she decided to make it last.

Damn. He got it going on, she thought. She expected him to be well endowed after peeping his shoe size, but this was ridiculous.

"Shit! Why do you feel so good?" he said, breathing heavily into her mouth.

"Just keep doing what you're doing, honey," she responded, still in control. "I'm almost where I need to be."

After the next eight strokes, she was there. Shortly after, he followed.

"Mmmmmm!" she moaned. "I knew I'd have fun with you."

"Oh, you did, did you?" he said, coming down off their sexual roller coaster after slowly pulling out of her. "I'm happy I didn't disappoint you." He disposed of the condom in her trash and she frowned at him.

"I am, too." She smirked, hopping down off the counter.

After slipping back into her clothes, she reached under the sink, grabbed the disinfectant, and did her best to wipe their indiscretions off the counter. The smell of bleach was strong and filled the room.

"So, what's your story?" he asked. His eyes searched hers for some kind of emotion, but they were vacant. Mona Lisa was excellent at concealing her feelings in front of others.

"What do you mean?" she questioned, plopping on the

couch next to him, as she playfully rubbed her hand over his hair. Normally he'd be gone by now, but she'd give him five more minutes to entertain her. After all, he had installed her recessed lighting.

"I never met a woman who didn't have a story." He placed his hand on her thigh and rubbed it vigorously.

"Behold . . . now you have." She smiled. "But why would you say that?"

"It's just that most women I deal with want a commitment. So the fact that you don't is different."

She sat Indian style on the couch. "Well, I'm not like other women. I *am* different."

"I see," he said, placing his arm on the back of the couch so that it was directly behind her. "Different how?"

"You love your freedom, I love mine, too."

"There has to be somebody out there you're feeling." He smiled as he grabbed one of her legs and massaged her foot.

"Nope."

"Everybody has met that *one* person who has changed their world."

Immediately Nat came to mind. She got up, grabbed a bottle of wine off her minibar, and poured herself a drink.

Downing every bit, she said, "All right, Maintenance Man. I'm gonna have to get up with you later. I have a big function to attend tonight. But thanks for the ride."

"I see," he said as he stood up, walked toward her, and placed a kiss on her cheek. "Now you're kicking me out."

"Not kicking you out . . . just sending you home."

"*Well* . . . he's a lucky man. It's not often you find a woman who's cool with letting a brother live," he continued, planting a soft wet kiss on her forehead. "Call me later. Maybe I'll give you a little something before you leave."

She remained cool despite wanting to throw her glass at him. To her he was a characteristic example of a man saying one thing too many. It would be a long time before she saw him again.

* * *

Opening night brought out the heavy hitters in the movie industry. Colorful designer evening gowns and custom-tailored suits graced the ballroom inside the Waldorf Astoria. People were engaged in conversations about their current and future projects. Elaborate gold and cream settings adorned each table. In the middle of it all sat Mona Lisa looking graceful in her red designer gown by Ella Moss with her matching strapped sandals by Louis Vuitton.

"Wow!" Melonie said, observing all of the stars her young career hadn't allowed her to see before now. "I can't believe I'm hobnobbing with the stars." She couldn't keep still due to being so excited.

"Believe it," Mona Lisa said as she sipped her merlot. "After hearing you recite your lines, I know this part's for you. If things work out," she continued, wiping the corner of her mouth with the white cloth napkin before placing it back in her lap, "the people you see today will be your peers. Just nail the casting call tomorrow."

"I will!" she said excitingly. "I won't let you down."

Mona Lisa searched Melonie's eyes, hoping what she was saying was true. What worried her about Melonie was the fact that she was too much in awe of the *lifestyle* instead of chasing her own dream. Even now Melonie sat at the edge of her seat so that she could pivot around to see everyone. She had already received twenty autographs so far.

Still, Melonie had the look TVEA was going for. Long brown hair, hazel eyes, and quiet sex appeal. Her light brown skin and wafer-thin body were also necessary to seal the part of Desiree Holmes, the *other* woman in the movie. She favored Meagan Goode.

Glancing over, Mona smiled at Dayshawn because he had respected her wishes by wearing a respectful black tuxedo. She let his choice of the baby-blue tie slide so he'd be able to hold on to one ounce of who he really was . . . a man who adored color.

"This is great, Mona! I can't believe I'm so close to Quentin Tarantino!" he said excitedly while chewing a piece of dinner bread.

Mona smiled. "They're just people."

"We are people and *these* are legends," he responded.

She smiled at his boyish innocence and wished Turnstile would hurry up so she could overcome his objections. She looked around the crowd and saw him nowhere. She had a speech prepared to give him the moment he commented about Dayshawn's flamboyancy.

"Mona . . . introduce me to your clients," Drake Craven, a TVEA executive, said, approaching Mona's table. He seemed to have come from nowhere, but then again, most snakes do. Mona could see in his eyes that the only person he wanted to meet was Melonie. He looked handsome wearing his black suit, white crisp shirt, and black silver-accented tie. His dark chocolate complexion and large white smile made him irresistible to *most* women.

"Sure . . . but where's your wife?" Mona responded as she grinned at him. "I don't remember seeing her here tonight." She looked around the party, pretending to be searching for her. But Mona knew he always left his wife home on party nights. He'd cheated on her at least eight times, that *she* was aware of.

"At home with the kids," he replied nonchalantly. He seemed to know full well what she was doing, trying to prevent him from reaching his prey . . . Melonie.

"In that case, this is Melonie," Mona said, pointing to the starstruck actress. She was already staring at him with schoolgirl eyes. Remaining in her seat, she reached up and extended her hand. He kissed it softly and gazed into her eyes. *"Uh . . . mm!"* Mona yelled, clearing her throat and breaking him out of the hypnosis he was attempting to put her under. "And this is Dayshawn." He shook his hand and Dayshawn held it a moment longer. Drake snatched it away and wiped it on his pants leg. Mona smiled. "And now since you've met everybody, I trust you'll have a nice night."

"I got it . . . I got it," he said. "Mona . . . it's nice to see you again," he continued as he grinned at her. "And you, too," he said, quickly turning to Dayshawn. "Good luck, guys. You're working with the best."

Whatever! Mona thought, raising her glass in the air. *Get your punk ass away from my table.*

"Melonie, stay away from him. He's bad news," Mona advised.

Melonie removed the smile from her face, looked down at her plate, and then back at Mona. "I will."

"I'm serious."

"I know."

Once again she looked for Turnstile. Instead she spotted the *woman* she hated more than failure strut through the doors wearing a pearl-colored dress by Nina Ricci. Her hair was in a classy bun and she completed the look with her six-carat diamond set. Mona developed an immediate headache the moment she reached the table.

"Well, looky here! If it's not Mona Lisa Dupree, the soon-to-be washed-up casting director."

"And if it isn't Iesha Champagne Carter," Mona retaliated in a coy tone. "The has-been actress nobody in Hollywood wants to work with."

"Now . . . now, Mona," she sang, sitting next to her, uninvited. "You of all people should know my name is Shawna Carter. Despite me not having anything to do with your *so-over-it's-not-even-funny* agency."

Mona smiled. "As I recall, I'm the one who rejected you. And is that a new nose you're wearing?" Every time she saw her she had another plastic surgery operation to take away the past.

Shawna blanched. "I hear you live here in New York now. How many quick fucks have you run through thus far?"

Dayshawn and Melonie gasped.

"One." Mona grinned, raising one brow. She was making it clear that she was far from being ashamed about her love for sex. "But I have my eye on a few more. And how many oodles and noodles have you sucked down today?"

"Haven't had to, sweety," she said. "I know you've read the papers."

While Mona and Shawna took turns poking holes into each other's reputation, Dayshawn and Melonie sat quietly observing the two. Dayshawn was giving the look of *I can't stand this bitch* while Melonie was hoping to be like her. She'd followed her career and mirrored herself after her every move.

Mona Lisa hated her guts. They'd been college-mates at Howard. Mona Lisa remembered how she'd beg her for some of her Cup of Noodles soup because she was too broke to afford her own. Iesha was looked upon as being weird back in their college days, and if it hadn't been for "fly girl" Mona, she would have remained the laughingstock on campus.

To better her reputation, Mona convinced her to take part in school movie productions and plays. Surprisingly enough she was good. Iesha quickly found her niche . . . acting. When Mona won her first account years later, and needed an actress for the right part and thought only of Iesha, she nailed it and Mona was able to cast her in slightly larger roles.

Eventually Mona came to her about a part in a movie she was casting titled *Slighted* alongside Angelina Jolie. They loved her, so much so that her career skyrocketed. She was now big time. When MGM requested Iesha again in a smaller role, she agreed, provided MGM would make sure she had fresh pink roses in her dressing room every day, a limousine ride to and from every taping, and last but not least, a massage therapist on call. What pissed Mona off was not her unreasonable demands, but the request that everyone including Mona call her by her new name . . . Shawna Carter. Even upon granting her impositions, she still was unprofessional.

Somehow they were able to complete the movie, but Mona

made it her business to never deal with Shawna again. So it was funny to Mona when DreamWorks sought her assistance to find new talent for a movie with Denzel Washington. Shawna immediately contacted Mona Lisa after hearing she had the inside track. Mona responded by ignoring her and the two had been enemies since.

Now bored with Mona, Shawna directed her attention to Melonie, who was staring at her. "So . . . you must be one of Mona's new clients."

"Uh . . . yes . . . I am. And I'm also a fan of yours." They shook hands. "Do you mind signing my napkin?"

"Sure," Shawna responded, adding her name to the many already present on the list.

"I've watched every movie you've ever been in."

Mona was disgusted with how Melonie was acting considering she had told her to remain calm and not come across as a groupie.

"Well, isn't that something?" Shawna said, glancing over at Mona Lisa. The look on her face said, *Now I got you, bitch*. "Well, if you ever want to talk to me about anything, you should know that I'm available to you."

Mona Lisa stood up, abruptly pushed her chair back, and said, "Shawna, walk with me."

"Sure . . ." She smiled. She stood on her feet, handed Melonie her card, and followed Mona Lisa to a corner.

"So, what's up?" Shawna asked with her hands on her hips. She seemed amused at how upset Mona was until she felt the *smack*.

With that Mona quickly grabbed Shawna's forearm and pulled her toward her. "Play it off," Mona whispered. "People are watching." She pointed. Shawna rubbed her face since all the blood had rushed to it.

They both saw all eyes on them. Seeing the two archrivals together was bound to be news, so they both had to remain cool. Shawna feared the press even more than she feared Mona Lisa.

"Good girl," Mona encouraged.

Smiling and regaining her composure, Shawna snatched her arm away from her and said, "You're gonna regret putting your hands on me, bitch." After that she smiled at a few people who raised their glasses in their direction, still shocked to see them together.

Shawna and Mona waved.

"And you're gonna regret it even more if you don't leave my clients alone."

Shawna stared at her inquisitively and replied, "Are you threatening me?"

"No! I'm making a promise. Stay out of my life," she said, pointing at herself. "And I'll leave you to yours."

She walked off and left Shawna standing alone. She had almost reached the table when she saw Turnstile there. "Shit!" she said to herself.

She had wanted to prepare him for Dayshawn *before* he met him, and now it was too late. If she hadn't been fooling with Shawna she could've done that. Now he was speaking to Dayshawn, who was swaying with every word he made.

"Oh, I see," was what Mona heard Turnstile say when she approached the table. His face was beet red.

"Well, I see you've met my clients," she said, breaking him from the trance he was in.

"Uh . . . yes . . . I did," he said, wiping the sweat off his head with the white engraved handkerchief. "But if you'll excuse me." He looked at Dayshawn and then Melonie. "I'd like to talk to Mona alone."

Neither of them objected. And when they were alone, Mona said, "Before you say anything, hear me out. Dayshawn *is* what you're looking for in this movie. I've heard him read his lines and I'm asking you to accept my professional decision and let him audition."

"But he's all wrong!" Turnstile's cheeks jiggled as the words exited his mouth, and light sprinkles of his spit hit her face.

"*Please?*" Mona started turning on her sex appeal. Although she didn't sleep around for a break, she reserved the right to use her charms when necessary. She intertwined her arm with his and continued. "Trust me . . . you won't be disappointed."

"But . . . but—"

"Have I steered you wrong yet?" she interrupted.

Fixing his eyes on her breasts, he said, "No. You haven't."

"Well, why would I start now?"

"But—"

"Trust me, Turnstile," she interjected. "I pick *only* the best."

"That's what you said about Shawna."

She didn't let him know the low blow he just dealt hurt. "Everybody makes mistakes . . . and she was mine."

"All right . . ." he said reluctantly. "I'll let him audition."

"Thanks . . ." She smiled. "We won't let you down."

She was proud of her skills of persuasion until her Black-Berry began to move in her purse. When she grabbed it, she saw a number she didn't recognize. Figuring it was one of her past sex interests calling from a different number, she gently pressed IGNORE. But the unknown caller was persistent and called back again. Deciding it must be important, she excused herself from Turnstile to answer the call.

"Hello," she said as she held the phone with her right hand and used her finger to press her ear with the left, to mute the background noise. "Who is this!" she yelled.

"Is this Mona?" an unfamiliar male voice asked.

"Yes. Who is this?"

"Nat. You have a minute?"

Mona Lisa stood silent, in the middle of the floor.

Mona Lisa was getting prepared to feed her sexual needs by a man she'd met in the bank the week before. She was trying to focus on his touch, but Nat, and the conversation they'd had, threw her off.

She thought about him all day and was hoping the handsome stranger would change things for her. Nat was given her number by Vincent, a mutual friend. He had run into Mona the day before she moved to Harlem. Had she known he still kept in contact with Nat, she would've advised him against giving out her number.

The conversation was short because Mona made it that way. He wanted to know how she was and what she was doing. She kept her responses to the point, trying to give him the hint she didn't want to talk. Eventually she used the party as an excuse to end the call despite leaving shortly after anyway. As soon as she hung up she was sorry she'd done so. It was good hearing his voice after all their time apart. But still, she thought, it was for the best. *I don't have the time or inclination to get caught up with some guy looking for a relationship.*

"You feel so good."

Mona focused on her latest conquest. There was something about Grande Stewart's smoky gray eyes, muscular body, and size 12 shoes, which had caught her immediate attention.

"How does this feel?" he asked as he stood at the foot of the bed and massaged Mona's left foot as she lay flat on the bed. He was wearing nothing but white Hanes boxers.

"Ummmmm," she moaned. "Nice."

"I'm just getting started," he said, licking his full lips.

She'd closed her eyes to savor all of the attention she was getting by this perfect stranger when the phone rang. At first it startled her because lately she'd been receiving an excessive number of prank calls. And normally her phone would be off whenever she participated in her favorite pastime . . . having sex. But with her father ill, she had to be available at all times.

"Excuse me." She winked as she extended her arm to grab the BlackBerry off the nightstand in her room. "Hello?"

"Mona . . . it's me," Ray said in between sniffles.

"This better be good," she said as the stranger playfully pulled her legs and placed all five of her toes in his mouth at one time. "Scratch that, this had better be damn good!"

"He doesn't want me," she cried.

"Whooo . . . doesn't . . . want . . . you?" she asked. It was difficult for her to show compassion in between getting her toes sucked.

"Sony! He told me his wife found out about us and he doesn't want me anymore."

"Okay . . . calm down," Mona said, trying to regain her composure even though he had now placed her second set of toes in his mouth. "Maybe it's for the best."

"Don't say that, Mona!"

"I'm serious! He's nothing but trouble," she explained as the stranger began to run his tongue up her inner thigh. "Shit!"

"What's wrong?"

"Can I call you right back?"

"Why? What are you doing?"

"Nothing. Besides, you wouldn't want to know," Mona continued. When he moved his tongue over the tip of her clit, it was a wrap. She could no longer contain herself. "Ahhh . . . my . . . goodness," Mona cried out.

"I know you're not having sex while I'm on the phone. That's so gross!"

"In that case I'll call you later."

She didn't even give Ray a chance to respond before she hit the red button and tossed her phone on the table. But five seconds later, the phone rang again. Against her better judgment she answered. "What, Ray!"

"This is Turnstile! Have you heard the news?"

"No . . . why . . . what's going on?" she asked, pushing the stranger off her with her feet. She sat on the edge of the bed and he fell to the floor.

"Melonie was locked up for placing a Molotov cocktail in Drake Craven's car!"

"What!" she asked, standing up straight. "I don't understand!" She began pacing the floor.

Why would she do something so careless? But then she remembered. He was the same man who was so eager to meet her at the party. It all made sense now. A young and impressionable Melonie had fallen victim to one of his high-profile games.

"You don't have to understand, just do something! And when you're done, come to my office . . . or I'll start going elsewhere with my business!" He abruptly ended the call and Mona ended her party.

Mona was tired and weary when she reached home. Her night had just ended at eleven o'clock. Upon getting the news about Melonie, she had to bail her out of jail and subject herself to Turnstile's verbal abuse. He threatened to have her blacklisted if his production didn't go down as planned because of Melonie's tirade. And with the weight he carried in the industry, she knew he could.

When she reached the front of the building she heard Jerome yell, "Hey, beautiful lady. You got a minute? I need to talk to you about something."

"I don't even have a second," Mona grumbled.

"Really? What if I say it was important?" Jerome said, flashing his yellow teeth.

"Not now, Jerome," she said, cutting him off and entering her building. There was no way she'd waste her precious time on him.

"Whatever," he said, waving her off.

When he was out of sight, she placed her key in the door and was pushed inside by someone.

Turning around, she looked into the face of a man she hadn't seen since she first moved to Harlem. He must have silently run up the building steps behind her. Which meant he must have been sitting in his car waiting for her to show up. But why?

"John?" she said as if she didn't know.

"I came by to talk to you. Got a minute?" he asked, standing in front of her in the narrow hallway of her brownstone.

"Uh . . . actually," she hesitated. "I was getting ready to—"

"It'll only take a minute," he interjected, backing her against the wall.

He smelled as if he'd been drinking all day, and the gray overalls he wore smelled of sweat and funk.

"Okay," she said, trying to find a way to get out of this. "What do you want?"

"I wanna know why you played me like you did."

"John, I don't know what you mean."

"You know what the fuck I mean," he said, growing increasingly upset. "So stop playin' games!"

Her body fell limp up against the wall.

"John, whatever I've done to you, it wasn't intentional," she managed. "Now if you'll excuse me." She stood up straight, preparing to walk around him. "I have a few calls to make."

But when she tried to push past him, he grabbed her by the arm and attempted to pull her out of the building's door until her neighbor stepped into the hallway. Her golden brown hair was swept up into a neat ponytail. She was gripping a thick black bathrobe and it appeared as if she'd just woken up.

"Excuse me," she said, looking at John and back at Mona. "I'm not trying to interrupt anything, but I heard you out here and figured I'd let you know the mailman delivered some of your mail to my box. If you want to step inside, I can give it to you."

"Oh . . . yeah . . . I'll get it now," Mona responded, staring at John. She could tell he was angry at the very timely intrusion. He glared at Mona, and then the neighbor, and left the building.

Silence stood between them for a few seconds as Mona got herself together. "Thank you." She smiled.

"No problem," she replied flatly. "Good night."

Mona walked to her apartment and thanked God for preventing what could've happened.

Mona Lisa walked into the hospital room as quietly as possible. She could hear the low hum of the machinery her father was connected to. She was doing her best to prevent disturb-ing him. She couldn't believe he'd been in the hospital for a week before she was notified. But that was just like her father. Always trying to take care of things on his own, and not worry her.

"Ms. Dupree?" a thin black middle-aged man said the mo-ment she entered. He was wearing blue hospital scrubs and a gold name tag that read Dr. David Scribner.

"Yes." Mona shook his hand and noticed it was ice cold. Her eyes moved from the doctor to the closed eyelids of her fa-ther. She felt he was preparing to tell her the worst. Placing her blue Hermès Birken bag down on a chair, she did her best to remain calm. "How is he doing?"

"Please have a seat, Ms. Dupree," the doctor requested.

"I'd like to stand."

He paused. "All right. Let's walk over here." With that he placed his hand on her back and guided her to the other side of the room. When he was sure he was out of earshot from Devin he said, "Your father has been diagnosed with prostate cancer."

Mona placed her hand over her opened mouth and imme-diately felt the tears streaming down her face. "Wha . . . what do you mean?"

"Apparently he's been experiencing problems for quite some time now and since he didn't seek attention, his condi-tion has progressed."

"Oh my God. Is there something you can do?" Mona said in near hysterics.

"We've scheduled surgery for tomorrow. After that he'll be put on chemotherapy. As I said, the condition has progressed, but we're still holding out hope."

"What am I gonna do?" She was crying so heavily that her stomach began to ache.

"The very best you can do is to just be strong for him." The doctor put his hand on her shoulder. "I understand you live in New York. Will you be staying here in the area for the surgery?"

Mona jerked her head back. "Of course I will."

"Good. I'll leave you two alone," he said, handing her a napkin he had in his pocket.

"Thank you," she said, wiping the tears from her face before facing her father, who had awakened.

"Hey, you!" she said, trying to appear as if things couldn't be better. "If you wanted attention, all you had to do was ask."

He laughed and when the pain was unbearable, gripped the sheets.

"Don't do too much, Daddy," she said as she adjusted his pillows to make him comfortable. She then placed her hand over his and felt his IV. She was frightened. She already lost her mother and couldn't bear to lose him, too.

"I'm fine, honey." He smiled. His almond-colored complexion was now dark and dry. "At least I know what's going on." Pausing for a moment, he continued. "I'm glad you're here, sweetheart."

"Where else would I be? I'm mad at you, though, that you didn't have the hospital contact me sooner."

"You're just getting settled there in New York, and I didn't want to be a bother." He smiled weakly. "Besides, I'm not going to let a little thing like cancer get me down."

"You'd better not," Mona said, while trying to blink back her tears. "I'm going to stay here in D.C. for a few weeks until you're out of here and back on your feet."

"No!" He tried to sit up, but then fell back in the bed.

"Daddy, please don't strain yourself."

"Mona, I don't want you putting your career on hold just to stay here with me. I'll be fine. You go on back to New York."

Mona shook her head. "I'm going to be here when they bring you into surgery, and I'm going to be here when you get out. You might as well not even argue about it."

Her father looked at her, his love apparent in his eyes. "Okay, how about this? You stay until after the surgery, and then you hightail it back to New York and take care of your business."

"But, Daddy—"

"No. That's my final say. And to throw your words back at you, you might as well as not argue about it."

Mona sighed. "We'll see." She lifted his head slightly to give him a drink of the water next to his bed.

"Now, tell me. Have you met any wonderful young men in New York yet?"

Mona flashed a wicked smile. "A few."

Her father shook his head weakly. "Listen to you. Okay, but don't pass up the right one just so you can sample the rest."

Mona couldn't hide the shocked look on her face. Was this her father, the biggest playa in the world talking? The man who always encouraged her to have her fun but never get serious since it would only lead to hurt?

She looked at him as he dozed off again. Cancer had really changed him, she thought.

The surgery was successful, the doctor told her the next day. They managed to get all of the cancer out, and there was every reason to believe that her father would make a full recovery.

"Can I see him now?" she asked anxiously.

The doctor shook his head. "He's in recovery, and he's so heavily medicated he'll probably be knocked out for the rest of the day. Why don't you go back home and get some rest? You look like you can use it."

Bright and early the next morning, Mona was back. Her father was weak, but he was conscious, and seemed eager to see her.

"There's something I want to talk to you about," he said after she'd been there only ten minutes.

"Okay . . ." she said slowly. Whatever it was, it sounded serious, she thought.

"Baby . . . I've had a lot of time on my hands since I've been here. And I've been thinking about how I raised you. I was a terrible father."

"No, you weren't, Daddy!" Mona said, holding his hand again.

"Yes, I was."

"That's a lie. You didn't leave me like Ma did."

"Don't say that. Your mother's death was partially my fault."

Silence.

"Had I treated her nicer, and with more respect, maybe she never would've felt the need to take her life."

"I don't believe it's—"

"Let me finish, baby," he interrupted. "I'm very serious about this. I should've spoken to you a long time ago. I *was* a terrible father. And I want to do as much as I can to make things right . . . before it's too late. You never should've seen half of the things I showed you, or told you half the things I told you."

"Because of you, I'm a better person. I got my own things and don't rely on men to validate me. Love complicates things."

"Do you love your father?" he asked with doe eyes.

"That's different."

"How is it, Mona? Look at me. I'm in the hospital alone. I hurt so many people and now karma has returned to punish me. I don't want you to suffer the same fate I did, sweetheart. I want you to have a full life, with a family of your own."

"What if I don't want a family?"

"We all do."

"Well, I don't, Daddy," she responded as she got up and began to pace the room. "I love my freedom. I don't believe in love stories and that's why I appreciate that you taught me what the world is really about."

"Sweetheart, whatever happened to that young man you dated in college?"

She knew exactly who he was talking about.

"I forget his name but I know you remember him," he continued.

Silence.

"I never saw you happier than when you were with him. And one minute he was there and the next he was gone. Was it because of me? Because of all the things I told you about not committing yourself?"

"No. We were just roommates, Daddy."

"Are you sure? You used to talk about him all the time. Have you ever wondered what it would be like if you two made it?"

"It wasn't like that," she repeated.

"Maybe not . . . but everybody around you saw differently . . . even me." He yawned. "This medicine is starting to take hold of me again. Hey, sweetheart," he said, patting her hand. "I don't want you fussing over me. Go back to New York and handle your business. Besides, you know Ray will be checking on me."

Mona kissed her father on his cheek. "Okay . . . I'll leave, but I'll be back tomorrow before heading home. I love you, Daddy."

"I love you, too," he said, his eyes getting heavier. "Now let me get some rest."

She took care of a few details with the doctor before leaving the hospital. The moment she got in her truck, she thought about everything her father had said. *Finally* she was unconsciously admitting to herself that she did feel *something* for Nat, even if she didn't know what the *something* was.

She retrieved her BlackBerry from her purse and scrolled through the address book. *I'll just call him to see if he's okay,* she thought, tapping on her steering wheel with her French-manicured nails. She didn't have his number, but she knew Vincent Wright would since he gave Nat hers. *Where's his number!* When she found it she shook nervously as she gave her index finger the permission to dial.

The phone rang one time before she hung up. *What am I*

doing? This is so fucking stupid. When she thought about how desperate she had almost appeared, she thanked herself for coming back to her senses. She was pulling out of the parking lot of the hospital and on her way to the hotel at the Embassy Suites in D.C. when her phone rang. The name on the display read *Vincent.* He was calling her back.

I can't believe I'm really doing this! Vincent had not only contacted Nat, he also arranged a meeting on the same day. Her legs shook as she sat in the front seat of her car and watched the crowd of people passing by a busy office building in downtown D.C. There were people walking up and down the sidewalk in business suits and dresses. Her palms sweated and she constantly wiped them on the crumbled tissue paper in her lap. She wondered what he looked like . . . what he smelled like . . . and most importantly, if he thought about her as much as she'd thought about him over the years.

"Okay . . . breathe, you can do this. He's not God . . . he's just a man," she said out loud. The moment she laid eyes on him she said, "Oh my Gawd!"

He was wearing a black tailored suit by Theory. He completed his look with a black shirt with burgundy pinstripes. His hair was neatly cut and her heart melted when she saw the dimples that had won her over every time he smiled back in college. He looked taller but she was sure it was only because he was standing straight and not slumped over like back in the day. He favored Jenson Atwood so much that it was uncanny. Nat walked directly to the truck and jumped in. She'd told Vincent what she'd be driving earlier. As he closed the door behind him, she inhaled the cologne called Fresh he was wearing. His eyes were bright and his teeth were so perfect they looked unreal.

"Mona Lisa Dupree . . . where in the world have you been?" he joked.

His eyes were mesmerizing, and his lips were as hot as L.L. Cool J's.

"I've been around," she said, still not believing he was sitting in her car.

"I'm not going to lie, when Vincent told me you wanted to see me I didn't believe him," he stated, placing the seat belt over his crisp suit.

"Why?" she asked, turning the ignition on.

"Because when I reached out, you blew me off."

"Nat, I'm so sorry about—"

"There's no need to explain," he interrupted. "All that matters is that we've reconnected. Besides, I want to talk about the present, not the past."

"Me too . . . but I do want you to know that I realize I could've handled things differently," she responded, focusing on the red car that had pulled out of the parking space in front of her. "I hope we can move past this."

"I can if you can." He winked. "Now, I don't know about you, but I'd love to get some food and play catch-up. So will you have lunch with an old friend?"

His lips. Oh my Gawd! They look even better than I remembered, she thought.

"Mona," he said, waking her out of the horny state she was in. "Do you want to have lunch with me?" he repeated, thinking she hadn't heard him.

"Yes." She smiled even though there were a few things she'd like to do, none of which concerned food. "So, where are we going?"

When they reached the Capital Grille on Pennsylvania Avenue in D.C., Mona Lisa was eager to be seated to order her meal. She figured the quicker the food reached the table, the more she'd appear in control, because as it stood, the only thing she thought about was jumping on top of the man candy in front of her. When the caviar arrived, she grabbed cracker after cracker and swallowed them down. Afterward, they ordered their meals. Mona chose Kona-crusted aged sirloin with caramelized shallot butter and Nat ordered the sliced filet mignon with cippolini onions and wild mushrooms.

Nat attempted to engage in small talk, but a nervous Mona busied herself with her meal. Truth was, she didn't know what to say to him. She looked everywhere in the restaurant except at the man who had captivated her heart for so long

"When are you gonna stop avoiding me?" he asked after putting the last of his meal in his mouth. Placing his fork on his empty plate, it made a clinking sound. "I've never known you to eat this much or to be so quiet."

"I'm not avoiding you," she laughed as she fiddled around in her purse for nothing. "Why would you say that?" When she realized she was probably making herself look ridiculous, she grabbed her water glass and gulped it down. But when she attempted to place the glass on the table, it fell on her dress instead.

"Oh no!" she yelled, looking over the table for something to wipe it up. The cool Mona had been replaced with Cindy from *Three's Company*.

Nat ran to her side with a clean cloth napkin and begin to soak the liquid from her lap. Although it was a kind gesture, seeing him work so diligently between her legs aroused her. His face was inches away from her lips. She contemplated kissing him. She imagined if she did, he would return the favor, and they'd embrace and everyone in the restaurant would cheer because she'd finally realized love. She moved in, but so did he. Back to his seat.

"It's a good thing it's only water," he said as he scooted his seat closer to the table.

"I guess," she said as she removed the last few drops from her lap.

"I think I got it all . . . so, what's up, love?"

"Huh?" He'd thrown her off by his tender use of words.

"I want to know what's going on in your life."

"Nothing outside of working hard and playing harder." She ran her fingers over the edge of her wineglass.

"Well, you look great!" he complimented.

"Whatever, Nat," she said, waving him off.

"I'm serious. You're still beautiful."

She smiled.

He winked. "Now . . . stop keeping me in suspense. What have you been doing with yourself?"

"*Well*, I finally got into showbiz."

"Stop playing!" he said, sitting up straight in his chair. "You're an actress now?"

"No, boy! Acting is not for me! I decided to stay behind the scenes."

"Doing what?"

"I'm a casting agent. Production companies hire me to get the right people for the right parts." She picked up her wine-glass and took two sips. When she saw the waiter she ordered another glass. "It's hard work, but I'm enjoying it."

"That's great, Mona! I always imagined you'd be doing something big."

"Thanks." She blushed. "Now what about you? I can tell by the suit you're wearing that life is good."

"I'm doing okay. I'm an entertainment lawyer."

"You call being a lawyer okay?"

"Well, it's nowhere near as exciting as what you do. I deal primarily with club and bar owners in D.C."

"Wow . . . I never knew you were interested in entertainment," she continued as she devoured another glass of wine before getting the waiter's attention for another.

"Me either. It just came to me after Danny asked me to help with the paperwork for this spot in N.E. It wasn't until then that I discovered I was pretty good at it."

"What's the name of the club?"

"Grown and Sexy."

"Cute name," she laughed.

"I know. I chose it when I became part owner."

"So you're a lawyer and a club owner, too?"

"Yes," he said, moving to the next topic. "So, where do you live now?"

Suddenly she felt herself becoming a little dizzy. She could usually handle a glass of wine or two but never a full bottle. What was worse was that whenever she drank any liquor, her sexual drive was heightened. And for Mona that was a recipe for disaster.

"Mona . . . are you okay?" he asked as he looked at her with concern.

"Oh . . . sure . . . I'm fine." She smiled. Her speech was slurred.

"So, do you want to fuck?"

"What?" Mona didn't know if she heard him correctly. She was positive she was hearing things as usual when she had too much wine.

"I said . . . where do you live?" he repeated, confused.

"Oh . . . where do I live?" she laughed after hearing his *real question.* "In Harlem."

"You moved to New York?"

"Yes. And I love it."

"So, what brings you back to D.C.? Visiting?"

"I wish. My father's been diagnosed with cancer. He had surgery yesterday."

"Sorry to hear that. Are you okay?"

"I'm dealing . . . it would be easier if I didn't have to do this alone," she blurted out. Had she not been under the influence of alcohol, she never would've shown her vulnerability.

"Well, I'm here if you need me. What do you say we hook up for lunch tomorrow?"

"I can't. I have to head back tomorrow morning."

"So you better be easy on the wine, then." He pointed at the glass in her hand.

"I'm fine," she lied.

"You sure?"

Suddenly she felt like an unseen weight was being pressed

on her head. Mona hadn't realized that she hadn't slept a wink upon hearing the news about her father. Mixing sleep deprivation, the excitement of seeing Nat, and an entire bottle of wine was deadly. She needed to sprinkle some water on her face in the restroom. But when she stood up, she could not hold her balance. She was on her way to the floor before Nat caught her.

"Hey, you."

Mona opened her eyes fully and saw Nat lying next to her in the hotel room bed. The top of his shirt was unbuttoned and his tie had been loosened.

"Hey," she said as she tried to lift her head before letting it fall back to the pillow. "How long have I been out?" She rubbed her forehead.

"A few hours," he responded as he continued to place a cold washcloth on her face. "I had to look in your purse to find out what room you were in. You don't remember talking to me the entire way here?"

"No," Mona said, shaking her head.

She was beyond embarrassed. She was sure he'd never want to see her again after this. Only amateurs couldn't handle their liquor. Not Ms. Casting Director of the Year. But at the same time it wasn't just the drinks; it was the lack of sleep and all the worrying about her father.

"I ran you a bath. You think you can make it to the tub?"

"I think I'll be fine." The fact that he cared warmed her heart.

"Okay, but before you move, sip on this," he said as he gently lifted the back of her head forward and placed a cup of straight coffee to her lips.

"Yuck! No sugar?" she laughed, moving her lips.

"Naw . . . you need this straight up. Now get some of this up in you." When he felt she had enough, he placed the cup on the nightstand. "I hope you know you scared me to death," he joked.

Placing her head back up against the pillow, she said, "I'm so sorry, Nat. This isn't usually like me. I hope you let me make this up to you."

"Oh, you will." He smiled, placing one finger on her nose.

"I wish I didn't have to head back home. We could've had lunch tomorrow."

"Don't worry about that, there'll be plenty of time for us to get together."

She couldn't get over how considerate he was. She'd thought by now that things would be different. The only thing that changed was that he got sexier and went from wearing jeans and T-shirts to suits and ties.

"Now let me help you to the bathroom."

As drunk as she was, she had plans to make him love her again. When she looked in his eyes she was sure it would be easy. Besides, very few got over Mona Lisa. After all, she had ended their thing, not the other way around. And although she realized it was too early to be considering a relationship after so many years, if she had to pick a man, he would be it. He was the reason she couldn't see anybody else, and together they were complete.

"Now . . . put your arm around my neck," he ordered as he stood by her bed.

When she did, he lifted her up. She placed her head against his chest and inhaled his cologne for the thirtieth time that night. Mona got excited at the idea of him bathing her. Sure, she could do it herself. But why when he could do it for her? She laid everything out in her mind. The moment the towel hit the floor she'd be sexing him in the bathroom. Her plans went down the drain when instead of bathing her, he sat her on the edge of the tub. Her feet were touching the cold porcelain floor.

"I think you can handle it from here." He smiled.

"Actually, I'm still a little light-headed," she said, rubbing her forehead. So what if she looked desperate? It was all or nothing and if he shot her down, she could blame it on the liquor. "It's not as if you hadn't seen my body before."

"You're right . . . I have . . . but I'd never take advantage of you. Now relax. I'll be waiting in the room."

Still a little drunk, she was sure he'd want her after bathing. The night wasn't a bust after all. The only thing that changed was that she'd be fresh when he took her. This was even better.

Soaking in the warm water, she placed the wet washcloth over her face and let it remain. The heat from it was soothing. She imagined how her life would change with him back in it. Finally she'd have somebody in her corner . . . someone to depend on, despite everything and everybody else.

After she had finished bathing, she dried her body off with the large white towel and put on the white velour bathrobe. When she reentered her room, all of the lights were completely out with the exception of a lamp next to her bed. Nat was sitting in a chair with his head tilted to the side . . . asleep. The glow from the lamp allowed her to see how handsome he really was without him knowing she was looking. She wanted to kiss and hold him.

Sliding into bed, she watched him for a second, until he opened his eyes.

"Hey there," he said, sitting up straight. "How long have *I* been out?" He wiped his mouth with his hand before clearing his throat.

"Well, I've been in the tub for about twenty minutes."

"It seems like I just dosed off. How do you feel?" he asked as he sat straight up and adjusted the sheets so that she'd be comfortable.

"I'm fine." She stared. "Just fine."

"Good." He winked.

"I'll be better if you stay, though." She had to say it.

"I'm not going anywhere. I'm going to watch you sleep."

She exhaled. Knowing she'd have him for a few more hours comforted her. With him she could be vulnerable . . . not someone with all the answers. "I'm sorry about how I treated you in the past, Nat. I was young . . . but I'm a woman now."

"Stop talking like that. You didn't do anything to me I didn't allow."

That hurt.

"Now get some sleep," he advised.

She had no intention of sleeping. She was going to enjoy all the time they shared. She didn't want to let one minute pass without spending it with him. But somewhere along the way, she had drifted off to sleep. And when she opened her eyes, the sun was shining through her window, and he was gone. All that was left was a note next to the bed on hotel memo paper.

Mona,

I'm sorry I didn't get a chance to say good-bye. I put my number in your BlackBerry. Message me when you can. Don't worry about me. I caught a cab back to my car. Stay in contact.

Always,
Nat

"Melonie, what was going on in your head! Do you realize what you've done?" Mona asked as they sat in Augie's Restaurant off Broadway. She was finally able to get a hold of her. Melonie had been avoiding her calls since Mona bailed her out, but had finally decided to show up on her doorstep earlier that day.

"I don't know, it just happened, Ms. Dupree," she cried as she wiped her nose with the same napkin she used to wipe her eyes. "I'm not trying to mess stuff up for you or me, but he played me!"

"Do you hear yourself? This isn't some bullshit-ass job! You had the possibility to become everything you've ever dreamed of." And then you go and have an affair with Drake? And then you drop a Molotov cocktail in his car—in his $400,000 Maybach—because he drops you?"

Melonie put her head on the table, knocking her fork to the floor. The waiter came by and picked it up, leaving the two alone again.

"I can't believe I did that," she continued, crying harder. "I thought he liked me!"

"Melonie . . . men lie to get what they want. I learned that early in life," she said as she rubbed her hair.

"He told me I was different and that he never cheated on his wife before me. He said she doesn't appreciate him and that I was the kind of woman he needed in his life. Then right after I go to bed with him he tells me it's over and that he's staying with his wife!"

Mona was enraged and made mental notes to get back at Drake for what he'd done to an innocent twenty-two-year-old girl. "Melonie, I wish you would've talked to me about this, sweetheart."

"I knew you didn't want me going there, you warned me about him, remember? But he was so nice to me. He told me he'd help my career."

"Look where it's gotten you. A possible felony conviction and you very well may have lost this major role. I hate to come down on you but I want you to remember this!"

Sitting up straight, she pounded her fists on the table. Wearing two pigtails, she looked even more like a child. "Can you help me, Mona?"

"I'm not sure."

"I shoulda never listened to her! I'm so stupid." Melonie wiped her tears some more, this time smearing mascara all over her face.

"Listened to who?"

"Shawna."

Mona jumped up. "Come again?" she asked calmly.

"Shawna. She called me after the party and said he was interested in me. When I told her I didn't think it would be good to mess with him, she said he could possibly further my career, and that he was in the process of leaving his wife."

Mona sat quietly in shock.

"So I went out with him, and he was everything I dreamed of. Everything. And just like that, he changed. He didn't want me anymore. He agreed to meet me one last time at the Drake Hotel, and told me it was over. The first person I thought about was Shawna. I didn't have anywhere else to turn. She seemed so understanding I thought she was my friend. We met at Emily's Restaurant the same night."

Mona couldn't believe what she was hearing. She was trying to remain calm but knew her face was beet red. Thoughts of the many ways she'd ring Shawna's neck ran through her head.

"She said it was wrong how he treated me," Melonie continued. "And suggested I should pay him back. It was her idea to throw a Molotov cocktail through his car window."

Now it all made sense. Shawna had done something similar in college when her boyfriend, a quarterback, dumped her. She didn't waste any time throwing a Molotov cocktail through his car window. Mona was thinking about how to handle her when suddenly the conversation she'd had with Ray last week came to mind.

"Mona, you have to hear this shit. Do you remember Jai?"

"Not really," Mona said as she sat in a salon chair with her feet soaked in warm water. She was preparing to get a pedicure. "Who is he?"

"Oh my Gawd! I can't believe you forgot about him. He was the one you shared a cab with after the Prince concert last year. Remember . . . you fucked him and brought him back to my place because you knew I was having that card party."

Mona remembered who he was now. He was a beautiful man of Indian descent who Mona thought was the most gorgeous man she'd ever seen, next to Nat. "Oh . . . I remember now. You ran into him?"

"Not really, but he's dating one of my clients."

"Hold up, ain't this some sort of conflict of interest?"

Mona asked as the Chinese woman removed the polish off her big toe.

"Yeah, but I can trust you," Ray giggled. "Anywho, turns out old girl is Shawna's cousin."

"And?"

"And it turns out that Shawna is not the person you think she is."

"What do you mean?"

"Girl." Ray lowered her voice as if to make sure no one else would hear.

Mona was struck as Ray ran off the details. She was right; it turned out Shawna was not the person she'd thought.

"Melonie, listen to me," Mona said, softly touching her hand. "I'm not going to lie, I don't know how much of this I can fix. But . . . give me a few days and I'll let you know."

"Thank you—"

"I'm not done," Mona advised. "Stay away from Drake and Shawna. Because if I get your ass off the hook, it belongs to me! The only reason I'm doing this is because she used you to get to me, but you know right from wrong."

"I'm sorry."

"Don't be sorry . . . just be careful and remember everything I said."

"Okay."

"Now go home . . . I have a lot of work to do."

After hearing about Melonie, Mona realized she had to be around friends, so she called Nat and Ray and to her surprise, without hesitation, they made the five-hour drive to New York that same night. She had been up all night before thinking about her next step.

"Are you okay?" Nat asked as he sat next to her on the couch in her living room. She had just run down everything that occurred with Shawna and Melonie.

When she told them about the incident with John a few

days before, they both grew concerned. Ray looked as if she were about to admonish Mona, but then shook her head and said nothing.

Nat put his hand on Mona's thigh. "Can I get you anything?"

"No . . . I'm okay," she said softly.

"Maybe you should eat something," Ray said, handing the cup to Mona before taking her place by her side.

"Not hungry," she said. "I have to think about my next move with Shawna."

"Are you sure you're not hungry? I can go pick up something real quick," Nat said, rubbing his hand on her back.

"I'm fine," she replied.

"Well . . . we can either mope around here," Nat continued, looking at her and then Ray, "or we can get out and have some fun."

"I don't know," Mona said, not in the mood to leave the house. "I kinda want to relax."

"Let's relax when we're dead," Ray laughed. "I'm with Nat. It's a beautiful city, so we might as well enjoy it."

Mona knew there was no use fighting with them. Besides, if they came all the way to see her at the last minute, the least she could do was show them a good time. "Well . . . let me get dressed!"

Mona decided to take them to the Cherry Café. She heard about it from Dayshawn and figured it'd be a chance to impress them. She knew the moment they saw the cherry-wood paneling and the warm use of lights they'd be mesmerized. The club was crowded, but they were still able to move around it comfortably. The deejay was playing "Go Getter" by Young Jeezy and R Kelly, one of her favorite songs.

When they got in they checked their coats. Mona wore a pair of tight-fitting Baby Phat blue jeans, a black low-cut top, and her black Via Spiga boots. She chose the jeans because Nat and Ray were dressed a little casual, not realizing they'd be going out tonight. Still, Nat looked handsome in his blue jeans, chocolate button-down shirt, and chocolate shoe boots. Ray looked good, too, with her blue jeans, red button-down top, and red Emilio Pucci shoes.

"This spot is nice," Nat yelled to Mona and Ray over the music.

Mona couldn't take much credit because this was the first time she'd seen it herself. She was pleased Dayshawn didn't let her down.

"I'm happy you like it." She smiled, staring him up and down. His eyes caught her stares and she looked away.

"I saw you checkin' me out," he teased, whispering in her ear.

"Whatever," she said, waving him off.

"I see somethin' I like already," Ray said.

"What about Sony?"

"What about him?" she questioned, pretending she didn't care. "Now if you'll excuse me, I'm on my way to offer him a little of Chocolate City's finest."

Mona laughed and was relieved to be alone with Nat.

"Can I get you something to drink?" he asked as he led her over to an available table with large plush brown seats. His hand rested on the small of her back and made her feel secure.

"I'll take whiskey straight up."

"Damn! Whatever happened to wine?"

Mona laughed. "I need a strong kick right about now."

He winked. "You got it."

Mona used the time to go over in her mind how she was going to gain control over the situation. She didn't want to risk another night ending like it did the last time they hung out. She couldn't wait to down her drink so she'd ease up a little. Between what happened with John and being so close to Nat again, she was an emotional wreck.

She smiled when she saw him walking back toward her with two drinks in hand, until he was intercepted by a sexy black woman with more curves than the letter S. A wave of jealousy overcame her. She tried to play it off by focusing on people dancing on the floor, but her eyes always found their way back to Nat.

She played things out in her head. *If I approach him, I'll look desperate. But if I don't say anything, I'll look like a punk.* She was trying to remain the same cool, calm, and collected person she was when she had walked through the door. It angered her that he was still holding a conversation with another woman with her drink in his hand, and then an idea popped into her mind. *I don't want my drink all watered down and shit. So if he wants to talk to her, that's cool with me, but he won't have my drink in his hand.*

Standing up from the chair, she sashayed in his direction. The girl was saying something in his ear and he apparently found her amusing. He was having such a good time that he didn't see Mona standing in front of him.

She tapped him on his shoulder and said, "My drink please." She was so jealous that she didn't realize her hands were on her hips and her neck was rolling, until she saw the surprise in his eyes. She dropped her hands, stood up straight, and tried to appear as if she didn't just trip on him.

When the woman looked directly at her, she saw she was much more beautiful than she'd realized.

"Are you Mona?" she asked loudly to be heard over the music. She extended her hand.

"Yes, I am," Mona said as she gripped her fingertips lightly instead of her full hand.

"Nat was just talking about you."

"He was, was he?" Mona stated sarcastically, looking at him.

"Yes . . . he was telling me he came all this way tonight to meet you. You're a lucky woman. I'll leave you two alone. Nice meeting you, Nat." She walked away.

Mona took the drink Nat was handing her and they walked

back to the table. She was grateful the music was loud so that she didn't have to find the words to say why she'd reacted the way she just did. Hell, she didn't even know.

"She seemed nice," Mona said finally, sipping her drink before placing it down on the table.

"She seemed cool enough, but I want to talk about you."

"And what do you want to talk about now?" she said, crossing her legs.

Before he could answer, the deejay played "Lost Without You," by Robin Thicke.

Nat stood up from his chair and extended his hand. "How about we talk about this on the dance floor?"

She raised her brow and tried to not seem so anxious to rub her body against his after so long. "Sure."

While dancing she let her head fall into his chest and he wrapped his arms tightly around her waist.

Why does he feel so damn good? she thought. Being with Nat wasn't just sexual, it was deeper, and being in Harlem only added to the vibe.

"So, how are you feeling about Harlem now?" he asked as he ran his hand up and down her back like strings on a guitar.

"I still like it," she said as she saw Ray swaying on the dance floor a few feet over. "I won't let what happened earlier stop me, if that's what you mean. I called the moving company and told them what happened and they fired him."

"Okay, but I just want you to be careful out here," he said as he looked down into her eyes. "And slow down a little."

"Slow down?"

"Yes . . . if you're anything like how you were in college, you could get hurt, Mona. I just want you to be easy, that's all."

"Are you calling me a freak?"

"No," he said as he touched her face. "I would never say anything like that about you. I just want you to remember that the times have changed. You can't be so friendly. I care about you. Always have."

She blushed. "I *am* careful but you don't have to worry about me. I'm grown," she said as she allowed her head to fall into his chest again. Even with the music booming, she could hear his heartbeat. "Let's talk about you now. How's the club?"

"It's going very well. As long as Danny's happy, I can't complain. I'm not going to lie, I'm worried about taking the next step."

"You can do anything you put your mind to, no matter what it is."

"You have a lot of faith in me."

"It's true!"

"You know, this is tight."

"What?"

He smiled. "Being able to talk to you about my life."

"It is," Mona said softly. "And, Nat?"

"Yes."

"I'm hoping we can keep this together. I don't want to lose contact with you."

"Losing contact with me is not even up for discussion," he said, giving her his trademark wink.

"Good." She winked back. "And I hope you know you guys are staying at my place tonight."

"I don't see why not."

"Good . . . because we have a lot of catching up to do," she said, kissing him on his cheek. "But first," she added, searching the club, "let's find Ray."

"I know but I don't understand why she would stoop so low," Mona told Nat on the phone the next day. "That girl is innocent."

"I know, love . . . some people are like that. Iesha let stardom get to her. But karma's a mothafucka. She'll get hers."

"I want to see her get it. I mean, she hasn't shown the least bit of remorse after almost ruining Melonie's career before it really got started."

"Is that what you want? Just for her to show some remorse?"

Mona thought about it for a moment. "Well, that would be nice."

"Personally, I don't think she's the type, but who knows? But whatever you do, don't stoop to her level."

Mona knew by his response that she couldn't share her plans with him. "I won't."

"All right, Mona Lisa, hit me up after you meet with Iesha."

"I will."

Mona threw her BlackBerry in her pink Prada purse. Sitting in her car, she was wearing blue jeans, a black leather Blue Couture jacket with oversized shades by Tom Ford. She spiral-curled her hair and looked more like a model than somebody preparing to jump in Shawna's shit.

She got word from a mutual friend that Shawna was still in town, and having lunch at Calcutta Café, with a friend. From her truck she could clearly see them dining through the restaurant's large window. All she needed was for him to leave for five seconds. Her wish was granted five minutes later. Mona walked quickly across the street like a model on a runway.

"Hello, bitch," Mona said as she sat in the stranger's seat. "Nice shoes. What are they . . . Payless?"

"Hello, Dupree. I've been expecting you," she responded as she sipped on her red wine. "How's your little protégée?" She smirked. She was wearing a beautiful white fur jacket, and a matching white pantsuit.

Mona didn't want to admit it, but she was killing her outfit. "How do you think she is?"

"I don't know," she responded, taking a deep breath. "If I played my cards right, she should be either locked up or crying her eyes out."

"Do you realize who you're fucking with?" Mona laughed. "I thought I made myself clear when I said stay away from my clients."

"Made yourself clear?" The woman giggled.

"Or maybe I should smack the taste out of your mouth again."

"Try it," Shawna retaliated. "And after all, I didn't make her doing anything, I just suggested it."

"You think this is funny, don't you?"

"Hilarious," Shawna said as she dipped her bread into some seasoned olive oil that sat on the table. "You know . . . you should really do a better job of controlling your clients. If not, they'll ruin your career."

"You could have ruined her career, too, you know. And that girl never did anything to you."

Silence.

"You're going to regret this," Mona said finally.

"Am I?" Shawna asked sarcastically. "Please get out of my face. My date is on his way back."

Mona turned around and confirmed that he was returning to the table. "Are you sure you don't want to make this right? To at least apologize?"

"Puleeze." Shawna rolled her eyes.

"Your time will come."

"I'm sure," she laughed.

Mona had gotten halfway across the street when she turned around and walked back over to the restaurant.

When she reached the table she said, "Nice coat," then knocked the glass of red wine all over it.

"You bitch!" Shawna screamed as she jumped up. The wine had now run from her coat to her white pants.

Mona laughed all the way back to her truck.

It didn't work. She wasn't remorseful, so I'm handling matters differently. Also . . . I wanted you to know that I was thinking about you. It feels good having someone to talk to. Hit me when you can. Mona.

When she hit the button on her BlackBerry to send her message, she waited eagerly for his response. Like clockwork, he responded seconds later.

Don't worry about her love. You tried to handle things civilized. She's burned her bridges and she'll get what's coming to her. P.S. I was just thinking about you too.

Mona placed the call she needed to and waited for the black Mercedes-Benz to appear. Still sitting in her car, she tried to talk herself out of seeking the type of revenge she wanted. A part of her felt Shawna deserved what was coming her way, and another part of her felt guilty for stooping to her level. The moment she changed her mind about ruining her life, Scarlett's 2007 Mercedes-Benz SL class pulled up and parked next to hers on a street in Harlem.

The first thing Mona saw was Scarlett's wild fire red curly 'fro. Her light brown skin that was kissed all over with freckles. She was wearing an orange Loomstate shirt, jeans, and a black leather coat. When she got out she waved at Mona wearing black leather gloves. She had the energy only fitting of a nationally syndicated gossip reporter.

"Mona! It's sooo good to see you," she said, jumping in her truck and hugging her. "I see business is good," she continued, looking around her truck.

"I could say the same thing about you," she responded, pointing to her ride.

"Well, you know me . . . where there's gossip there's money."
They laughed.

"So . . ." Scarlett paused. "Are you sure about this?"

"Yes."

"You don't look like it." Her voice sounded concerned.

"I know . . . it's just that . . . I tried reasoning with her, but she didn't care about what she did to that girl."

"I heard."

"You did?" Mona was surprised.

"Of course," Scarlett said, pushing her arm. "I'm the press!" They laughed again.

"I just want to make sure you're okay with this, because as much as I want the story, I don't want to pressure you."

"The fact that you even asked makes me sure I want to give it to *you*. Any other magazine reporter would've snatched this out of my hand faster than I could turn it over."

Mona had liked Scarlett the moment she met her years earlier. Although she worked for the media she still had honor. She wanted the story, but not at the expense of those she cared about. Mona met her the moment the story broke that Iesha had become too big for Hollywood. Instead of printing things that weren't true, Scarlett contacted Mona to be sure the facts were right. Since then, Scarlett was the only person she respected in the cheesy tabloid industry.

"So what do you have for me?"

"Everything you need is right here," she responded, handing her an overstuffed sealed manila envelope. Scarlett reached for it but Mona didn't turn it over. "I have one request. Before you run the story, call me first."

"Of course."

Mona took a deep breath and released the envelope.

"Don't worry, I'll be sure to call you before I make a move."

"I know." Mona paused. "So, what are you getting into tonight?"

"I'm taking my jet out to visit my baby in Florida," Scarlett said as she stuffed the package in her oversized red Coach bag.

"You actually bought it?"

"Sure did, girl. I've had it for a year now."

"I'm in the wrong line of business," Mona joked. "I got to dig up some dirt."

They laughed.

"Do you fly yourself?"

"No. I hire a pilot."

"You're doing big things," Mona said, nudging her arm.

"Well, anytime you want to borrow it . . . let me know."

"I'm gonna hold you to it!"

"You can. So, what are your plans for the *big* day?"

"What *big* day?"

"Valentine's Day. I know you're doing something."

Mona was silent. She hadn't given any thought to the day, let alone spending it with anyone. In the past she'd go out to celebrate the single life. But since Nat had resurfaced, she wondered if she was crazy for wanting to spend it with him.

"Give me a second, Scarlett," she said, reaching into her purse when she felt her phone vibrate. It was a message. *Smile. Someone cares. Nat.*

"Who has you grinning from ear to ear?" Scarlett teased.

"Oh," she said, clearing her throat while trying to remove the smile from her face. "A friend just sent me a message."

"A friend, huh?"

"Yep."

"Must be a hell of a friend to make you smile like that."

"He is."

"You sound so much better, Daddy." Mona was speaking to her father on the phone while watching Dayshawn cooking in the kitchen.

"I am better. But how are you, sweetheart?"

"Things were a little hectic at first but it looks like everything will work its way out."

"That's my girl."

"You know it."

"So, I hear you and Nat have reconnected."

"Where's your seasonings, honey?" Dayshawn sang out, interrupting the call. He was preparing shrimp fettucini with alfredo sauce for them.

"In the cabinet next to the plasma TV."

"Who's that?" her father asked.

"Dayshawn Knight."

"Oh, your new client. I see you two have gotten close."

"He's a wonderful person. He comes over from time to time to go over his lines."

"I see. So, what's up with Nat?"

"Nothing, Daddy, we're strictly friends."

"So, is he dating anyone?" he continued.

"No, he spends a lot of time at the club with his best friend, Danny."

"Well, I'm still rooting for you two."

Mona didn't respond although she couldn't help but blush. She'd feel strange if she admitted that she was rooting for them, too.

"Anyway, Daddy, have you spoken to Ray? I haven't been able to reach her."

"Nope. I haven't seen that sexy thang since last week."

"That's about the last time I heard from her."

"Are you two okay?"

"I hope so. Maybe she's busy with Sony."

"Yeah, I told her to leave that cat alone a long time ago."

"Me too. Maybe she'll get it sooner or later. Well, Daddy . . . I have company so I have to go. You take care and call me tomorrow."

"I will. Bye, sweetheart."

The moment she placed the receiver down, Dayshawn walked up to her holding a fork filled with noodles and one large shrimp.

"Open up. Well . . . what do you think?" he said with one hand on his hip while he waited for her response.

"Ummmm."

"Say no more." He grinned.

She was still savoring the bite when her cell phone rang.

"Make me a plateful of that, Day," she said, walking toward it.

"You know it! I got to make the salad first, though," he said as he busied himself with preparing it.

"Hello," Mona asked in between chewing.

"Mona, it's me. Scarlett. I have the article written and ready to go. So can I go ahead with it?"

Silence.

"You there?" Scarlett asked.

"Yes," Mona responded, swallowing the last bits of food. "Congratulations."

"Thanks. But I'm calling to make sure it's okay with you before I turn it in."

"Thanks for remembering."

"No problem," Scarlett said softly.

"Can I call you back first?"

"Sure . . . hit me when you can."

When she ended the call Dayshawn yelled, "Dinner's served!" Mona was instantly revived from the stupor she was in. She walked over to the table as she burdened herself with whether or not she should be responsible for ruining Shawna's career. After all, they used to be close.

When she walked to the table Dayshawn continued, "Now, yours is over there. You have more than me since I have to watch my girlish figure for this movie." He laughed heavily although Mona didn't. "Are you okay, boss lady?"

"Yeah . . . I am."

"You don't look like it," he said, disappearing into the kitchen and returning with ice water. "Here . . . drink this."

She did.

"Thanks, Day," she said, placing a quick kiss on his cheek before tapping his leg. "Let me handle something real quick and then we'll have dinner."

"Sounds good."

She walked to the phone and scrolled through her address book. She didn't know why she even had Shawna's number in her phone. But she pressed the Send button the moment she found it. The phone rang four times before she received her voice mail. Mona hung up. Seconds later her phone rang and she saw it was Shawna.

"So, you're screening your calls now?" Mona asked.

"You owe me money for my suit. I figured that's why you're calling me," she said sharply.

"I could've done worse than that. I'm calling to give you one last chance to make things right with Melonie."

"What do you want me to do? Say I blew up his car?" She paused. "Well, forget about it."

Mona hated to admit it but she was right. She didn't blow up the car, Melonie did. But all Mona wanted from Shawna was to hear some form of regret.

"Hello!" Shawna said angrily.

"I'm here, Iesha."

"Listen . . . I don't have time for games. I told you the moment you placed your hands on me that you would pay, so you fix your own problems and leave me out of it."

"Remember this conversation, Iesha."

"You remember it!"

Click.

Mona was done. It was obvious she didn't care, so neither would she.

"Hey, Scarlett," Mona said after speaking with Shawna.

"Yep."

"Run your story."

"Thanks, girl."

Mona was lying by the fire on top of her raspberry-colored comforter watching Jerry Springer. The bitter taste of the merlot she was drinking excited her because she knew a buzz would follow shortly. Sifting through her mail, she came upon a letter from Scarlett Deveau. She quickly opened it.

Dear Mona Lisa,
Enclosed you'll find the article that will be printed in the next week's Enquirer. *I wanted you to be the first to read it.*

Scarlett

Setting the first page aside, she began to read the next.

Imitation of Life
By Scarlett Deveau
Shawna Carter dazzled America on the big screen with her stunning beauty and charm. It's no secret that she gets the major parts and the money to go with it. So the question remains, who is Shawna Carter? It just so happens that she's actually a he. Shawna was born as Isaac Carter, from Washington, D.C. This should come as a shock for those who have idolized her and followed her career. And although she has had a complete sex change operation, this news is bound to change the roles she receives.

Mona continued to read the story until it was over. Scarlett didn't miss a thing. She covered all of the information she'd given to her in the packet, and then some. She even included a picture of Shawna before her sex operation. You could clearly see that Shawna and Isaac were one and the same.

After an hour and two more drinks, she couldn't care less about Shawna's fate. After all, she chose it. And despite Shawna's attempt to ruin her career, she was still able to convince Drake that it would be better for all parties if he let the "blown up" Maybach situation go. When he balked, she reminded him of his wife and that she might have known about his car, but she didn't know about Melonie. The issue was dropped. She was even able to work her magic on Turnstile by convincing him that Melonie could still do the part. It took some persuasion and an accidental tittie sighting to get her message across, but it worked nonetheless.

With her career repaired and her father doing better, she realized things were going her way except for two things. First, she hadn't spoken to Ray and was worried something had happened to her. Second, she didn't know if she should fall again for the only man she ever loved.

Picking up her phone she sent Nat a message.

Thinking of you. What are you doing?

Seconds later:

Thinking of you too. I'm playing with Cara. Danny was sick today so I'm watching her.

Her response:

Sorry to hear about Danny. I hope things work out. You're a wonderful person for looking after Cara.

His response:

Nonsense. It's my duty.

Mona smiled. She thought it was cute that Nat was looking after Danny's daughter. She admired their friendship. She also noticed he was great with children.
Her response:

You're too cute. When can you make it back to New York? I want to show you around. Besides, I'm in need of some meaningful conversation.

One minute passed. Two minutes passed. Three minutes passed and still no response. Mona even turned her phone off and back on, thinking the network was running slow. Still . . . no response from Nat.
With nothing else to do she tried to contact Ray again. The phone rang four times like it had in the past before going to voice mail. Seconds later she received a message from Nat.

I'll make it out there next month sometime. We'll arrange something soon. I'll hit you later.

Mona didn't know where their relationship was leading, but she *did* know she wasn't waiting until March to find out. She was thinking about what to do next when she smelled a foul odor coming from her kitchen.

Shit! I forgot to take out the trash.

She had crabs yesterday and was too lazy to throw them out earlier. Now they were stinking up the place.

She slipped on her black North Face coat and Timberland boots. The first person she saw when she opened the building's door made her frown.

"Get out of my way," Mona moved quickly to place her garbage in the trash can.

"See how you are? That's why you didn't know that guy had been sitting in his car waiting on you for an hour."

Mona whirled around to face him. "What guy? What are you talking about?"

"That guy who moved you in. I saw him in the car drinking wine out of a bottle and looking pissed, and I figured he was waiting on you. I tried to tell you when you was going up the steps, but you ain't had no time to talk, remember?" Jerome leered at her.

Mona placed her hand on his hand and gave him an icy stare. "You could have figured out a way to say something, you know, Jerome. That could have turned out to be a danger-ous situation."

"Like I said, I tried. It's not my fault you don't never have time to speak to a brother."

Mona considered his words. He was an asshole, but he was also a neighbor. And had she given him even the slightest time of day the whole situation with John might have been avoided.

"I'm sorry for acting that way . . . let's start all over," she said, extending her hand.

They shook.

"So, now can I get your number?" he spat out as he tried to pull her closer to him.

"Get the fuck off of me," Mona said, snatching her hand away.

"Jerome, what did I tell you about harassing my tenants?" Margie said as she walked up on them.

"Aw, not that shit again," Jerome grumbled. He looked at Margie, then spat on the sidewalk.

Margie's eyes widened. "Boy," she shouted. "I know you didn't just—"

Before she could get her next words out, Mona stepped forward and slapped Jerome upside the head with an open hand.

Margie started laughing. "I couldn't have said it better myself," she managed to get out.

"Y'all's a bunch of crazy-ass women in this building," Jerome said angrily as he backed away. "I ain't got no time for none of you broads." He glared at Mona. "Especially you!"

"Bye, Jerome!" Mona chanted at his departing back.

"I've got to say, you D.C. girls do know how to handle your business," Margie chuckled after he left. "Say, you don't look so good. Not that it's any of my business. None of my business at all."

"No, just a long night," Mona said, still trying to determine if she wanted to have a conversation with the obviously nosy woman.

"You look out of sorts. You want to talk about it?" Margie said as she pulled out a cigarette. "I don't proclaim to be a miracle worker, but I've seen a lot of things in my fifty-somethin' years here in Harlem."

"No, I'm good," Mona said as she started to turn around and climb back up the steps. She suddenly stopped in her tracks. "You know, I could use some advice. Would you take a chance at rekindling a romance with someone after six years? Even though you were never really together to begin with?"

"Child, I'm probably the last person to be asking about romance stuff." Margie lit her cigarette. "I thought you were going to ask me something easy. But still, I guess I'd say that life's too short not to live it to its fullest . . . so while you're here . . . make it worth your while. But remember, I'm no expert."

Mona smiled. "You'll do in a pinch."

It was settled. She would pursue Nat and give herself a chance at love. She knew just where to start, by planning a dream date on Valentine's Day he'd never forget.

Everything was set. Mona planned a *sextacular* evening that would start with a drive from New York to D.C., in a red stretch Hummer limousine. Once she scooped up Nat, they'd be whisked to a landing strip in D.C. where Scarlett's jet and a hired pilot would be waiting to take them to New York. While in the jet, they'd sip on Cristal and enjoy each other by indulging in a little foreplay. Once in New York, she'd take him to a suite in the Waldorf Astoria where they would be surrounded by relaxing music and catered food with a chef.

With everything in order, a day before Valentine's Day, she realized she hadn't heard from Nat in almost three days. The last message she sent him earlier read:

Nat,

I'm hoping you will join me tomorrow. I want to do something I've never done with you . . . be honest. Will you trust me again and join me for Valentine's Day?

When she hadn't heard anything, she decided to call him again and each time she couldn't reach him. She was so busy planning that she hadn't realized she didn't confirm if her guest of honor would be present.

When her phone rang, she jumped up thinking it was Nat. She was disappointed when she saw it was the maintenance man and pressed IGNORE. When it rang again she saw it was Ray and quickly answered it. "Where in the hell have you been?"

"It's a long story," she said.

Mona couldn't help but detect her sadness.

"I have something to tell you about Sony. Can we meet to-morrow? I was thinking about driving down there."

Mona wanted to talk to her friend, but the next day was out of the question. She had plans for Nat and Nat alone. "To-morrow . . . might . . . not . . . be good."

"You have plans?"

"Yes."

"On Valentine's Day, huh? I'm glad somebody has a date," she breathed heavily. "Especially you 'cause I know you don't usually go in for doing anything on Valentine's. What about next week?"

"That'll be perfect," Mona said, relieved she gave her an out.

"Okay . . . I'll call you then. Good luck on your date, and tell Nat I said hello."

"I will." Mona blushed because she didn't have to tell her it was with him. "And don't worry . . . things will work out."

"Bye, Mona."

When she ended the call she tried to call Nat again, and once again nothing. She decided if she didn't hear from him today, she'd take a ride to D.C.

She was hungry, and deciding she didn't feel like cooking anything, she threw on her jacket and headed out the door to get some takeout from Amy Ruth's, yet another eatery that Dayshawn had turned her on to.

"Sorry," she said when she almost bumped into a woman who was coming into the building as she was coming out.

She couldn't believe it when the girl, who she had to admit was dressed almost as good as she, had the nerve to give her an up-and-down look as if appraising her. *Who the hell is she to be appraising me?*

"I said I'm sorry," Mona repeated, giving the girl a look that said *And I'm expecting you to say the same.*

"No problem," the woman said in a lilting southern accent. "I guess you live in the building."

"Yes. I'm Mona Lisa Dupree. I'm up on the third floor."

"That's nice. It was good meeting you," the woman said as she stood there without bothering to return the introduction.

"Yeah, well. If you say so," Mona said before walking off.

Mona was riding in a red stretch Hummer limousine on the way to steal Nat away. She looked sexy and radiant in her one-piece red minidress by Ella Moss with her Via Spiga heels. She was playing Beyoncé's "Upgrade You." Her glass was full with champagne and she was anxious when she saw the street leading to his house. She'd gotten his address from the Web.

When she pulled up to his block in Upper Marlboro, she smiled at the beautiful brick home he lived in. Her heartbeat raced and her stomach was knotted. She contemplated telling the driver to pull off, but the thought of losing out on love again made her continue with her journey. When she saw his white Mercedes next to a Cadillac SUV in a driveway, she knew she was in the right place.

"This is good," Mona said to the female chauffeur. She was a beautiful white woman with blond hair. "I'll be right back."

"No problem, ma'am."

Mona exited the limo only after ensuring that her makeup was on properly. She knocked on the door and took several deep breaths. When he came to the door, and she saw how handsome he looked wearing brown slacks and a black cashmere sweater, she smiled. He didn't.

"Mona?" he said as if it was a question. "What are you doing here?"

"I'm here for you." She opened her long black fur coat to reveal her dress.

He looked behind him, stepped out, and closed the door slightly. "I'm confused."

"I know, Nat . . ." She paused. Having to be true to herself frightened her. "Let me explain. My life couldn't be grander. I have everything I ever wanted." She continued tugging on her coat and pointing to the candy-apple-red limo waiting for them. "But out of all of my accomplishments, and all of my accolades, I was stupid enough to let the one thing that meant the most to me go. You."

"Mona, don't—"

"Please, Nat." Her eyes were brimming with tears. Placing her hand on her chest, she continued. "I let you go and I'm sorry. I'm sorry for running from us. But if you'll allow me to, I'll make it up to you. From this day to the last. For the first time in my life, I can admit that I am in love. With you," she said, touching his chest. "And I'm asking you . . . to love me in return."

Before he could answer she heard a female voice say, "Honey, who's at the door?"

Mona was struck. *Who is this woman and why is she calling him honey?* As if to answer the unspoken question, the woman appeared wearing black slacks and a beautiful royal-blue sweater. Her hair was pinned up in a bun with a few loose curls falling down the sides. She was extremely attractive and favored Gabrielle Union.

"Oh . . . uh . . . honey, this is Mona Lisa, my friend I was telling you about from college," he responded, placing his hands in his pockets.

"Hello, Mona," she said, extending her hand. "It's a pleasure to finally meet you."

Mona quickly blinked back the thankfully unshed tears and unconsciously extended her hand to her. The woman looked at Nat when she saw the shock and pain on Mona's face, waiting for him to provide some clarification.

"Mona, this is Danny, my fiancée."

Mona almost stumbled and Nat reached out to grab her. She couldn't believe what she'd just heard. When she got her balance, she held on to the guardrail for support and Nat released her.

"*This* is Danny?" Mona said, trying to be sure she heard him correctly.

"Yes," Nat said slowly.

"Will she be joining us for dinner?" Danny asked, eyeing the limo in front of their home.

"No," Mona said quickly. "I won't."

"Okay . . . well, let me go get Cara. It was a pleasure meeting you, Mona."

Mona just nodded. She was at a loss for words. When Danny disappeared into their home together, she found the words to say, "I thought Danny was your friend."

"She is. She's also my life."

That hurt. "Why didn't you tell me?"

"I thought you knew. We even talked about me taking the next step at your house."

"I'm confused!" she said, rubbing her hands over her forehead, her diamond rings shining like flashlights. "I thought you loved me."

"I do . . . but as a friend."

She was devastated. "So, is . . . Cara . . . yours, too?"

"Yes, she's my daughter."

Mona had heard enough. He was a liar just like every other man she came in contact with. She felt stupid for ever believing men were any different. She should not have listened to the old lady, her father, or anybody else who told her she should follow her heart. There was nothing else to say. He had deceived her and it would be for the last time.

She ran back to her limousine. The sounds of her high heels clicked loudly against the concrete pavement and rang throughout the neighborhood. She felt Nat running for her, but she wanted nothing more to do with him. And fortunately, he wasn't quick enough to catch her, because just like that, she was gone.

The tears stopped flowing when she was about fifteen minutes from her house. She was done with men and she was done playing games. She decided to go back to her old ways. Besides, there was nothing wrong with her to begin with, and if people had a problem with her, they could kiss her ass.

The moment she pulled up on the block, she saw the maintenance man walking to his car.

"Hey, Jasmine," Mona called from the backseat. "Pull up next to him."

"Sure thing ma'am."

When she did, she rolled down her window and said, "So . . . you feel like hanging with me for a minute or two?"

He smiled, walked over to the limo, and got in. "I thought you were dodging me."

She smelled his cologne and instantly got aroused. "I'm sorry handsome." She smiled. "Let's kiss and make up."

"Are you okay?" he asked. "You look like you've been crying."

"I couldn't be better. Now, are we gonna talk or get busy?"

He respected her wishes and removed his pants, leaving his shirt on. He moved over to her, his cold hands on her warm legs as he removed her panties. Still on the backseat, she turned around so he could see what he was getting ready to get into. She wanted it doggy style.

He moved toward her and she stopped him short. "Put this on," she said, handing him a condom.

He did. And when it was on, he grabbed hold of her waist and slid inside her.

Ummm. This is how it should be. This is all they're good for.

After he brought her to an orgasm she said, "Happy Valentine's Day. Have a good night."

"What?" he said, putting his pants back on.

"I said have a good night."

"You throwing me out?"

"No . . . I'm sending you home."

"You know you can't keep treating people like shit, Mona! One day you're gonna get what you deserve."

As she watched him exit the limo she thought to herself, *I already have.*

When he was gone she fixed herself up and yelled to the driver, "Jasmine . . . where can I go to get a drink around here?"

"There's a really nice place called MoBay. My man, Julian Meyers, is playing sax tonight."

"Take me there!"

Mona walked slowly into the club. Already she liked the atmosphere. It was crowded, but the crowd was mature, and all well dressed. And the music was soothing. She looked at the saxophone player, a light-skinned man who looked to be in his late twenties, with dreads that hung down his back. *Damn, now, he looks sexy as hell*, she thought. *I might have to add another notch to my belt tonight. Hell, it is Valentine's Day.*

As she scanned the spot for a place to sit, she noticed the three women in her building sharing a table and looking as if they were having a good time. She was contemplating going over to them before her phone vibrated. Looking down at it, she saw she had a message.

> *Mona. I feel terrible about all of this. I hope you know I would never do anything to mislead you. I hated seeing you that way. Please . . . please call me. There's something going on between us that we have to talk about. Nat.*

Mona wasn't dealing with him. He'd already taken everything from her, including six thousand dollars for planning the evening. But what was done was done. She decided to turn her phone off. Looking up at the women, she saw they appeared to be enjoying each other's company.

The light-skinned girl with the French accent seemed pretty tipsy, the one with the big butt who lived on the first floor was waving the waiter down, probably for another round of drinks, and the one who lived on the second floor—the cool, calm, collected southern woman who always acted as if she were better than everyone else—was sitting there almost pie-faced, and just running off with the mouth. Mona Lisa figured, *What the hell.* After all, the least she could do was buy the big-butt girl, Tamara, a drink for saving her a couple of weeks back.

"Hello, ladies," she said when she reached their table. "Do you have room for one more?"

The light-skinned girl with the French accent looked up. "Sure, but let me buy, okay?"

"Dior, I think she meant do we have room for one more person at the table," Tamara said with a giggle. "And anyway, I'm getting the next round." She looked at Mona. "Do you like mojitos?"

"No, no, no!" the southern belle said. "Not just mojitos. Harlem mojitos!"

"Sorry, Chloe." Tamara turned back to Mona. "Do you like Harlem mojitos?"

"Look," Mona said as she pulled a chair from another table and sat down next to her neighbors, "whatever it is you ladies are drinking, I'm drinking. Because damn, if you all don't look like I want to be feeling. In fact, order me three drinks, I have a lot of catching up to do! And, oh, by the way, Happy Valentine's Day."

MoBay Uptown

February 14, 2008—Valentine's Day

"Is that man fine, or what?" Mona Lisa said, pointing to the man making his rounds serenading the tables in the club with his saxophone. "I wonder what size shoes he wears." She stood up to take a look, but couldn't see because her view was blocked.

"Why do you care about his shoe size? What? You're planning on buying him some footwear?" Chloe asked.

Mona chuckled. "No. I'm just wondering if his horn is as big as his sax."

"Ooh, you are so bad," Chloe said, slapping her on the back. "You really are."

Mona turned to her. "Girl, how many drinks have you had?"

Chloe shrugged. "I don't know. Hey. Want to hear a joke? What is a southern belle's mating call?"

"I don't know. What?" Tamara asked.

"I'm so drunk!" Chloe said with a grin.

Tamara, Chloe, and Mona all burst out laughing.

"Really? You don't seem drunk to me!" Dior said with a puzzled look on her face.

Mona looked at Dior, then turned to Tamara. "Is she for real?"

Tamara nodded. "She's just feeling good. Dior, that was the punch line to the joke, honey."

The puzzled look stayed on Dior's face another few seconds before she, too, started laughing. "Oh, that's so funny! Southern belles say they're drunk so people will know they're horny." She started pounding the table. "That is *so* funny!"

"Dior, stop. You're going to spill the drinks," Tamara said, moving hers out of Dior's way.

"You're right." Mona started laughing. "She is feeling *very* good. In fact, I'd say she's half drunk."

"Uh, uh, uh!" Dior held up a finger. "A lady gets inebriated, never drunk."

"Okay, you're inebriated," Mona said with a smile and a shrug.

"Half inebriated," Dior corrected her. She turned to Chloe. "I *knew* you were from the South. I could tell by your accent. You are, too, Tamara?"

Tamara nodded.

"I guess we all are," Mona added.

"Really? Where are you all from?" Chloe asked.

"D.C.," Mona said. "Not real South, but a little."

"I'm from Atlanta," Tamara said.

"Well, I have you all beat. I'm from Texas."

Mona raised an eyebrow. "I didn't realize we were in a competition," she said, taking a sip of her drink.

"No, of course not," Chloe said quickly. "I was just saying, we Texans are real southerners."

"And people from Atlanta, Georgia, aren't?" Mona said coolly.

"Well, yes, but . . ." Chloe paused. "Aw, what the hell? I guess I'm just competitive by nature. Of course, we're all southerners."

"Not me," Dior piped in. "I'm a northerner. A real northerner. In fact"—she stood up and surveyed the club—"I bet I'm the most northern person here."

"Girl, will you set your ass down?" Tamara grabbed her arm and pulled her back in her chair.

"Dior, you are something else." Mona shook her head. "But I gotta admit you're a lot of fun."

Dior leaned across the table. "So, you like me, then, huh?"

Mona looked at her in surprise. "I never said I didn't."

"Hah!" Dior took another gulp of her drink. "You weren't the most friendly person when I first met you. In fact, none of you were. I thought all of you were kind of mean."

"Me?" Chloe's hand flew to her chest in a show of astonishment. "Me? Mean? I can't believe you would believe that of me."

Mona chuckled. "Oh, I can."

"What do you mean?"

"Please. You were downright snooty when I first met you. I introduced myself to you and you never even told me your name."

"Oh, I'm so sorry! My name is Chloe. Chloe Johnson."

Tamara laughed. "Well, yeah, we all know that now since we've been sitting here throwing back mojitos."

"Harlem mojitos," Dior corrected her.

Chloe shrugged. "Well, I've never been good at making friends with women."

"Why? You think all women are jealous of you?" Mona asked with a sly smile.

"Well, no. But, well, yeah. Kind of. I'm just saying . . . well, all of you are good-looking women, too, so you know what I mean. Don't you find other women get jealous because you're beautiful and you dress so well?"

"Oh my God," Tamara gasped. "You are such a damn snob!"

"No, I'm not! I'm—" Chloe stopped. "Hell, maybe I am." She giggled and took a sip of her drink. "But, well, what about you?" She challenged Tamara. "I've not noticed you going out of your way to be extra friendly. Oh, you've always been polite and everything, but always so businesslike. I've never even seen you smile until tonight."

"What do you mean?"

"She has a point," Dior said.

Mona nodded her head in agreement. "Even when you helped me out the other night, you did what you had to do and then it was almost like you were dismissing me. I didn't mind, of course, but then I didn't care enough about you to mind."

Tamara grimaced. "I'm sorry. I've just been so caught up in my job that I haven't been really personal with anyone. I don't mean anything by it."

"Well, if I'm a snob, and Tamara's a snow queen, what are you, Mona?" Chloe asked.

"Ooh, ooh, I know!" Dior raised her hand as if she were in school. "Mona is the sexually liberated woman of the new millennium who—"

"Dior, are you calling me a ho?"

Dior jerked her head back. "What?" The look on her face made all the women burst out in laughter, and even Dior joined in after a minute.

"No," she said when she finally caught her breath. "You just seem to be the kind of woman who knows what she wants and isn't afraid to go after it."

"Ahem," Tamara said, looking around the table. "But you do seem to have a lot of traffic coming in and out."

"Girl, please! I live right under her," Chloe said with grin. "You should hear the way them box springs be working."

"I can't believe it. All of you are calling me a ho!"

The women all started laughing again.

"Actually, I'm quite proud of my sexuality. I don't see any reason why I can't have as many bed partners as a single man. And when one's not available, I have no problem bringing out one of my little toys."

"Ooh, you are so nasty!" Dior hooted.

"What? You're going to tell us you don't have any sex toys?"

"Well, yeah," Dior admitted. "But I don't go around telling people I do."

"Well, you just did," Chloe pointed out.

"That's because you guys are a bad influence," Dior said with a pout. Again, the women started laughing.

An hour and three more rounds of drinks later, Chloe sat back in her chair and said, "I guess you all have been wondering why I'm dateless on Valentine's Day night."

"Um, no. I wasn't wondering at all. You don't have to have a date to have a good time, you know," Mona said. "I'm sitting here having a ball myself."

"Same here," Tamara concurred.

Dior said nothing.

"Well, make believe you're wondering," Chloe said haughtily. "So since you're wondering"—she ignored the face Mona made at her—"I was supposed to be having a romantic dinner with my boyfriend."

She paused as if waiting for someone to press her for details. When no one spoke she continued. "But then he had the nerve to dump me. On Valentine's Day! He said I had to choose between him and my job. And I just got this great promotion!"

Mona reached over and patted her hand. "Yeah, that is tough. You okay?"

Chloe nodded. "I'll get over it. But I really thought this guy was going to be the one, you know? I actually imagined him and me might spend the rest of our lives together."

"Yeah, I know what you mean." Mona sighed. "Actually, I had big plans for Valentine's Day night also. I made all of these elaborate plans with a guy that I really thought was worth it, and then it turned out that he's living with a woman and has a kid. I found out when I showed up at his door in a limousine."

"Oh God. That sounds awful," Tamara said.

"It was. Serves me right, though. I should have known better than to let my guard down." Mona turned to Tamara. "What about you? What's your sob story?"

Tamara let out a sigh. "I realized I've been making some really bad choices when it comes to men lately. I almost slept with my employer, who has both a wife and a girlfriend—"

"Wow!" Chloe exclaimed.

"And at the same time I was messing with this guy who acted like he wanted to get married after only knowing me for a few weeks. Like I said, bad men choices. So I just needed to get my head together before trying to figure where someone else's head was at."

Mona nodded. "That makes sense."

Chloe looked over at Dior. "Why are you so quiet, all of a sudden?"

"Because I've got you all beat, but I'm too ashamed to tell you about it."

Mona sat up straight in her chair. "Come on, we laid out our embarrassing tales to you!"

Dior took a deep breath. "Okay, but I don't want any of you to think differently of me when I tell you."

"Just tell the story," Chloe urged.

"Well—" Dior let her head fall on the table in dramatic fashion. "Oh God, I can't tell you!"

"Girl, it can't be all that bad," Tamara said with a puzzled tone.

"No?" Dior raised her head and looked at her new friends. "I met a guy over the Internet and arranged to meet him for a blind date."

"On Valentine's Day?" Mona whistled. "That's pretty gutsy. So what happened? Did he stand you up?"

Dior shook her head. "No. Actually he's here."

"What? Where?" Tamara, Chloe, and Mona started craning their necks, looking around the club.

"He's right there, sitting at the end of the bar looking out the window," Dior said dismally.

"Who?" Mona stood up to get a better view. She gasped.

"Oh my God! Say it ain't so!" she said, sinking back into her seat.

"What? Who is it?" Chloe asked. She and Tamara jumped up to get a look.

"Jerome?" they asked simultaneously.

Chloe started laughing so loud that Mona had to put her hand over her mouth.

"Are you serious? What the hell were you thinking?" Tamara asked in an incredulous tone.

"Oh God, I'm so embarrassed." Dior covered her face with her hands.

"But why would you go out on a date with Jerome?" Mona asked. "You can't be that hard up."

Dior took a deep breath and then told them the whole story.

"I can't believe he lied like that!" Chloe said.

"Hmph!" Tamara said. "I can. Just like Miss Margie says, that's one trifling individual."

Mona looked around the table. "Well, we can't let him get away with playin' our girl like that, can we?"

"Hell no," Chloe said.

"What do you have in mind?" Tamara asked.

Dior waved her hand in disgust. "Forget it. He's not worth the trouble."

"Quiet, Dior!" Mona commanded. "Okay, girls, how about this?"

"No, I'm serious," Dior said firmly. She drained her glass and waved to the drink waitress for another round. "I acted stupid, so I got played for stupid. The last thing that I want, though, is for Jerome to even suspect that it was me whom he played, so let's just leave it alone."

Mona sucked her teeth. "If you insist."

"I do." Dior looked around the table. "Besides, if he hadn't pulled that little stunt, I would never have wandered into MoBay and gotten to know all of you here! Think about that?"

"You know, you're right." Tamara nodded. "Which means we could have continued to live in the same building for years only nodding to each other on our way in or on the way out, and giving each other the evil eye when we thought another one of us was looking at one of our male guests a little too hard."

"Aha!" Dior pointed a finger at her. "I knew you were giving me the evil eye a couple of weeks ago."

"Shut up!" Tamara started laughing.

"But it is true," Chloe broke in. "And look what we would have missed out on. Like I said, normally I can't stand hanging out with a bunch of women, but I can't remember when I've had such a good time. I guess we should be grateful to Jerome in a way, huh?"

"Aw, hell no!" Mona said with a snarl.

"Yeah, I wouldn't go so far as to say we should be grateful to that asshole," Dior added.

"For real," Tamara added. "I mean, yeah, he may have been the reason we all met up this evening, but I don't know . . . somehow I think it was bound to happen. Look at us, four young women—"

"Four beautiful young women," Chloe interjected.

"Four beautiful, successful young women," Dior added.

"Four sexy, beautiful, successful young women," Mona said.

"Okay," Tamara said diplomatically. "Here we are, four sexy, beautiful, successful young women, living in one of the most exciting cities in the world, and ready, willing, and able to claim it as our own. Hell yeah, we would have wound up friends."

Dior grinned. "How the hell could we not?" She raised her glass for a toast, which everyone joined. "To us!"

"May our friendship stay tight, even after our tits and asses start to sag!" Mona added.